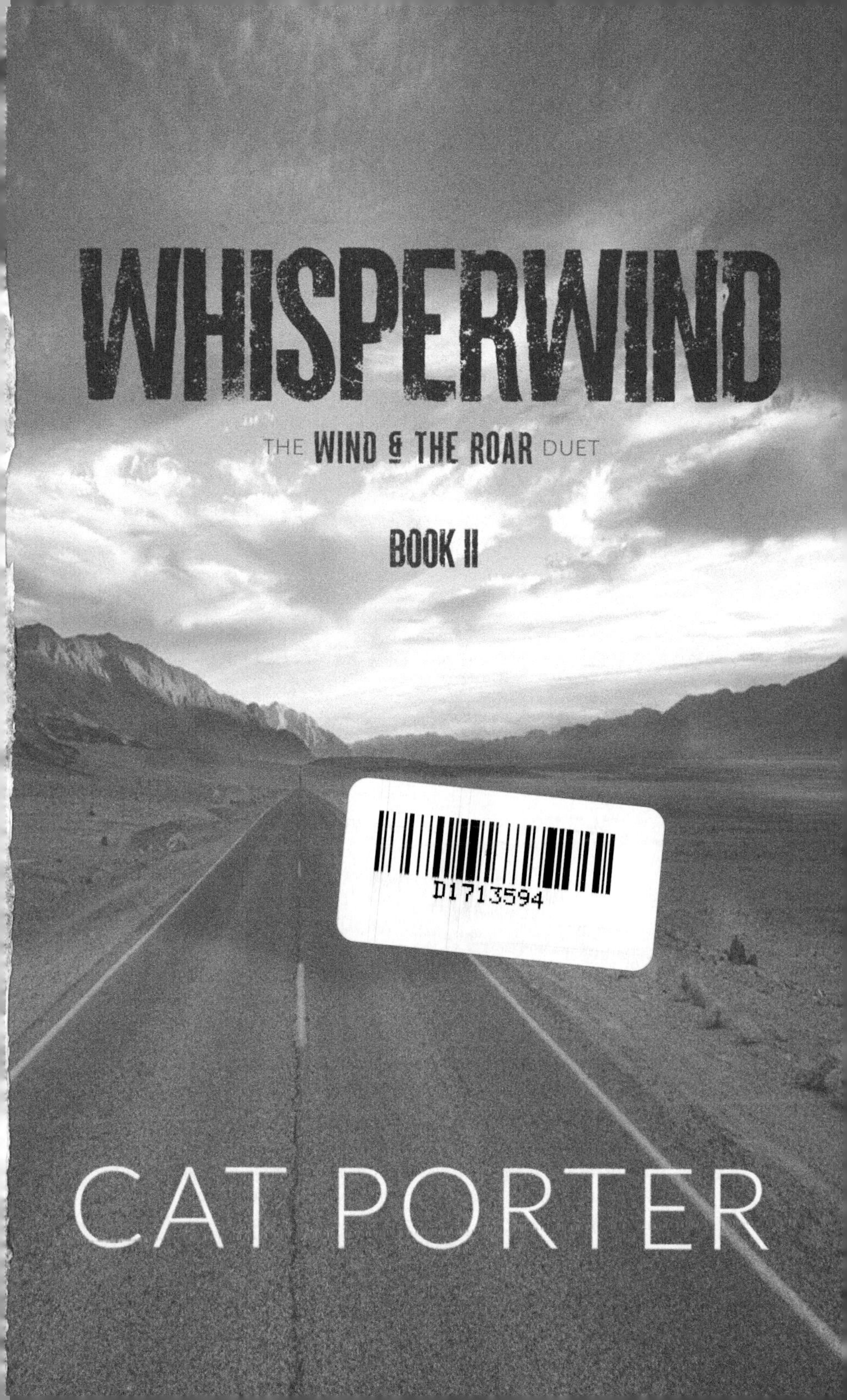
WHISPERWIND
THE WIND & THE ROAR DUET
BOOK II
CAT PORTER

Whisperwind
Book 2 of The Wind & the Roar Duet
Cat Porter ©2021
Wildflower Ink, LLC

Editor
Jennifer Roberts-Hall

Content Editor
Christina Trevaskis

Cover Designer
Najla Qamber
Qamber Designs & Media

Proofreader
Jezzie Hughes

Special thanks to Willow Aster

Visit my website at www.catporter.eu

ISBN: 978-1-954633-05-6

ALSO BY CAT PORTER

- Lock & Key MC Romance Series -

Lock & Key

Random & Rare

Iron & Bone

Blood & Rust

Fury

Lock & Key Christmas

The Dust and the Roar

The Fire and the Roar

The Year of Everything

Lock & Key - The Series Boxed Set

Boxed Set of books 1-4

- The Wind & the Roar Duet -

Friends-to-Lovers Rockstar Romance

Whirlwind

Whisperwind

Dagger in the Sea

Mediterranean Romantic Suspense Adventure

- Unraveled Destiny Series -

Steamy Arranged Marriage Historical Romance

Wolfsgate

Ironvine

CHAPTER ONE

@JUSTJANA

NOW CONFIRMED: Beck Lanier is engaged!

Spotted at New York's JFK airport after their flight from Athens, rock guitarist Beck Lanier and his new lady love, photographer Violet Hildebrand, were spotted hugging and kissing goodbye. The sexy couple took a moment to pose with fans, and Beck confirmed they are ENGAGED! It's official! Congrats to the beautiful couple!

Young Freefall fan Penny Cole spotted the loved up duo on her way through JFK and took these pics <click HERE for gallery> Cole writes that, when asked, Beck confirmed his engagement, and he and his fiancée were happy to pose for pics with her and her friends.

"It was so exciting! They're both so nice. He's the coolest guy ever! And the hottest! I'm so happy for him. For both of them!" remarked Cole about her experience.

**See pics <HERE> of Beck and Violet's romantic hugs and intimate kisses goodbye at JFK*

**See a closeup <HERE> of the gorgeous ring that Beck gave his lady love in Athens*

**See pics <HERE> of their engagement party with friends at a café in Athens*

Unfortunately, the newly engaged couple's time together was

abruptly cut short when Beck had to rush home to L.A. to be with close friend, Freefall bass guitarist, Jude Decker, who has been hospitalized for exhaustion as the band's manager, Ford MacGregor, stated in a press release early this morning. Our thoughts and prayers are with Jude, his family, and the band.

How will this affect the band working on their upcoming album? That remains to be seen.

In the meantime, we're thrilled that the brooding bad boy of rock has found his mate! Will there be wedding plans soon? We hope so!

Be sure to Like, Comment, and Follow, and hit that notifications bell to stay in the know, and don't forget to check our Stories for up to the minute updates #BeckLanier #EngagementNews #celebnews #allthenews #allthesexxy #sexxytimes #ViBeck #couplenews #justjana

CHAPTER TWO

BECK

JUDE STUDIED me as I sat down at the edge of his hospital bed. I'd gotten in too late last night to make visiting hours, so I woke up early this morning and got myself here first thing. His face was paler than usual, the blue veins on his skin visible, and the black smudges under his eyes giving him an even starker appearance. I took his cold tattooed hand in mine.

He squeezed my hand. "You're getting mushy on me, Becks."

"Deep inside, I've always been mushy," I murmured. "And you know that."

A small grin perked his lips. "You look different."

"I met up with Tag in Greece for a week. Got lots of sun and fresh air."

"Hmm, and that's not all, I'll bet." His grin grew wider. "That's why you look like you swallowed the world. How is that asshole?"

"Same asshole we've always known." I laughed. "He's doing real good. Still ambitious, still doesn't let the crazy get to him. He surfs the waves of it all."

"He was always good at that."

"Right?"

"You must have had a blast. Endless women, huh?"

"One."

His eyes widened. "One? Only one? No way."

"Yes way. So glad you left me that box of goodies in my bag."

"Oh right—I did, didn't I?" He shifted in the stiff bedding. "Is she Greek? Did she come to L.A. with you?"

"Would you believe, I've known Violet for years? She's from my mom's town in South Dakota. After the tour, when I went to Meager for a week to hole up, our paths crossed one night."

"Cool. You really like her, don't you? I think I'm seeing more than sun and surf on you, here." He laughed softly.

"I like her a lot."

"Shit, did my drama interrupt your trip?"

"No, We'd just landed in New York when my dad called and told me."

"Eric's been great. I'm glad my mom wasn't on her own here last night." He swallowed. "I didn't do this on purpose. That's what everybody's thinking, but it's not true. We were just partying, hanging out with Sig and his band, having a good time. I overdid it, obviously."

Overdid or overdosed? "Yeah, Jude, I get it."

"You're too nice to yell at me, to cuss me out."

I only sniffed in air, my hand tightening over his.

"I'm sorry…" his voice broke.

"Stop. You don't owe me any apologies. I love you, Jude. We've been friends since we were young and stupid boys. I worry about you, that's all."

"I don't want you to worry about me."

"I always have." My voice came out sharp and I didn't mean it to.

He sank back onto his pillow. "Can you open the blinds for me? I really hate not being able to see outside"

"Sure." I darted up from the bed and raised the blinds. A grim urban landscape filled the window. "Better, huh?"

"Yeah. Sometimes I just want to make everything stop, you know? I'm so tired."

"I know, Jude. This was one fucking exhausting tour. We're all tired. But somehow we've got to make better choices for ourselves and stick to them. And at the end of each choice is our love of the music, of our band. The thing we always dreamed of, the thing we're doing now. Choose that, Jude. You need to be on that road, we all do. That's where the good times are, the significant ones that last."

"I fucked up the schedule now. We're due in the studio real soon, right? I don't even know what fucking day it is. Now how are we gonna…"

"It's okay. We'll figure it out, all of it. Don't worry. We will work it out. We're big boys."

"Professionals." He cracked a tight grin.

That word had never felt so charged, so heavy like it did right now. "We have a deadline, and we'll keep to it. Myles, Zack, and me will get started, get some melodies down, some lyrics, and we'll keep you in the loop, of course. And when you're ready to come to the studio, we'll all be ready to make it fly."

"Okay. Sounds good."

"Tell me what you're thinking, Jude. I want to know. I need to hear it from you. I need to know where I can help."

"It used to be fun." His voice was above a whisper. "Maybe it can't be fun anymore, now that we've hit it this big. Now that there are all these things we have to keep doing to keep the rat wheel turning and turning fast. It feels like everything changed and I didn't realize. Can I even catch up?

"Don't get me wrong, Beck. I'm grateful for everything we've achieved, everything we've got—the solid album, the sold out tour, the fans, the money—first time in my life I'm not worried about rent or food. But the last month just felt like I was grinding myself into a pulp. And with you and Myles fighting—"

"We weren't always fighting."

"No, you weren't. But that tension was always between you, spoken or unspoken. The fuck of it all is that the two of you jam so well together when we play. When you let go of all that crap and fly. There was so much noise all of a sudden. Getting to the fly part became hard work, and that sucked. The last month felt like I had to make myself show up at some job."

"I get that. I do."

He let out a breath. "Then suddenly the tour was over and I realized how tired I really was, physically and mentally, on top of feeling cut off from what had become our every day normal. I felt cut off from you guys, the crew. I didn't know what to do with myself, especially knowing that in a few weeks we had to get back up on that horse again. Part of me wanted to scream and run away. I got…scared." He swallowed. "If this is what it's always going to be like, I don't know if I can…" His voice was breaking, his gaze glued outside the window. He was trying to make sense of his feelings, he was pleading, and it broke my heart.

Jude was always the one leading the charge, clearing the air of bullshit. If any of us felt pushed around, stomped on by too much advice, by reviews, by it not happening for us the way we'd wanted, Jude was the one who had faith and insisted we just had to keep on keeping on.

Keep performing no matter where, keep practicing, no matter how tired we were or not in the mood, keep going to clubs, parties, shows to meet people, jump on any opportunity. Jude and I had been L.A. club kids. He knew DJ's, owners, bouncers, promoters and they loved him. He also knew the drug dealers and the junkies.

From when we'd first decided to create our own band back in high school, Jude and I had been tremendously focused as we partied and hung out, and we'd found good people with the same ideas for music that we had. We'd met Zack and Myles, hooked up with Ford, and felt that everything had clicked into place at last, and it had. Freefall had created hit songs, performed all over the world, at clubs, huge arenas, top festivals.

Jude was the one who'd been high on the whole damn experience with a grin on his face no matter the lows that we sank in along the way. I tended to worry about our ultimate direction, about over exposure, and I often navigated our course. That's where Myles would get pissy with my insistence, but then he'd put all that emotion and frustration into his powerful performances. And Zack, the steady soldier, was the even voice of practicality, who stepped in when he had to, and always stepped up, giving all of himself to his drums.

Jude's glazed eyes snagged on mine. "But seriously—playing bass for Freefall *is my job*—how cool is that? I love that, man. I'm so grateful." His cold fingers curled into my shirt. "I really am."

"I know what you mean."

"I want to find it again, Beck. I want to go back to that thrill … I got to…"

"I know, Jude. We will. It was one long fucking tour. It was exhausting. We don't have to do that again. Not like that. We're going to take our time and find our groove together again. A new album is like a new beginning. Things will be different this time. And I promise I won't let you down."

"You never let me down, Becks. Never. But what's Ford gonna say? I already fucked up in Copenhagen. He already gave me the do-we-have-a-serious-problem-here talk."

After our show in Copenhagen, Jude had disappeared at a party. He'd taken off with a crew of people to go to another club without telling us. We'd finally found him incoherent in the corner of a nightclub at a table with twenty other people laughing and drinking. Zack and I had gotten him out of there through the kitchen to a waiting cab back to the hotel.

"What if Ford sends me away to some detox center and then…and then what? I don't want to get sent away. My mom…"

"Slow down. Slow down. Ford believes in you, man. He believes in all of us, and he wants the best for us. Dude, that's his job description. We will figure this out together."

Together, yes. That's what we'd do. Figure this out and do it together. As far as new songs went, we would work out the basics, and when Jude was ready, he could dive right in and the whole thing would take off, spin, like it always did.

Only, now I knew that "like it always did" no longer applied to anything in my life anymore, did it?

"We got this, Jude."

OUTSIDE IN THE HALLWAY, Dad and Jude's mom, Clarice, were speaking with a doctor.

"His brain function is shot," the doctor said. "They've been touring for over two years back to back, correct?"

I joined them. "Yes, we have."

"And you are…?" the doctor asked.

"Jude's bandmate."

"This is my son." Dad put a hand at my back.

"We're all family here," said Clarice.

The doctor tilted his head at Clarice. "This is what happens sometimes for certain individuals who are consistently overstimulated, like musicians who are on tour over a long period of time. After a while your basic normal endorphin function no longer performs, and you constantly live in that hyper state. Then the lows are dismal and you search for new sources of stimulation. So you keep trying new things to find some kind of stimulation and to self soothe. We see that Jude had been diagnosed as bipolar and had been put on lithium—"

"Which he stopped taking a while back," I said.

Clarice shot me a pained look.

"Good for him. We took a brain scan," the doctor said. "There's no sign of bipolarism."

"What?" she said.

"We're now testing for a wider range of possibilities that fit the profile of his symptoms. I really feel that something else is at play here. In the meantime, with proper nutrition and self care, he can improve quickly, but of course—" The doctor glanced at me. " —he needs to stop the opioids and any artificial stimulants. There really wasn't a whole lot in his system, but his level of exhaustion and malnutrition definitely contributed to his collapse. Now is a good time for him to switch gears. I'll let you know the results once I get them."

"Thank you," Clarice murmured and the doctor left us.

"Clarice, I have an idea," Dad said.

"Glad to hear it, Eric, because I'm at a loss right now," She took in a deep breath, fighting tears. "It's better news than I expected to hear, but..."

I put my arm around her. "What is it, Dad?"

"When Jude gets released, he could come stay with me."

"What do you mean?" Clarice wiped at her eyes.

"Pam and Poppy are out of town for a while, and I'm on my own with this one—" He pointed at me. "Jude needs a clean environment, a positive refresh. He can live with us. I have a good friend, Ed, who's a life coach, he does great work one on one, has a lot of experience with artists. I think that would really help him declutter and get focused. Being in a non-clinical environment, a home he's familiar with would be terrific. And if Ed thinks Jude has more intensive issues that need deeper help, we'll go that next level."

"Eric, you've done so much for my son over the years, so much. I can't impose on you."

"Jude's been like a son to me, and you know that. I want to help him find his way. I need to." Dad's brow furrowed.

"You and Beck were there for him when his father and I didn't know how to be."

"I could've done better, obviously," Dad muttered. "We know more about all this stuff now than we did back in our day. If we can get him the right help right now, it would be a major turning point. He has his whole life ahead of him and he's so talented, so bright. Our boys aren't kids anymore. They're hard working adults but the world they're rolling in is a crazy fucking playground, and I know it all too well."

"That you do," she said.

Dad shifted his weight. "I just finished a project and don't have anything else lined up right now, so I'll be home with him every day, every night. I'll have Ed, the life coach, come to the house to work with him, and my trainer, too. I'll bring in a nutritionist. Shit, I could use a mindset and body refresh myself. No comments from the peanut gallery—" He tilted his head at me.

"None at all," I said.

"Thank you, Eric." Clarice and Dad hugged, and she went in to see Jude again.

"Dad, are you sure about this?"

"Totally sure. I tried helping Dave, but he wouldn't let me. He fought me, he fought the doctors, his therapist, because he knew better. Now worms are eating him in the ground, and his kid is out there on her own. I love Jude—the two of you grew up together. It's great news that the doc thinks it's a medical issue, but Jude still needs to deal with a lot of shit. And if I can help him, I will."

"Dad." I hugged him, and he thumped my back.

Clarice came out of Jude's room. "He's sleeping now. His color is coming back." She smiled.

"Why don't I take you out for a quick lunch," Dad said. "You need a break."

Clarice began to protest, but I jumped in. "Go ahead. I'm going to stay here. I'll call if anything happens."

Her hand touched my arm. "Thank you, honey."

"Of course."

"All right then. That would be very nice," she said to Dad.

"Good. Let's go. We got a lot of catching up to do." He and Clarice took off down the hallway, and I sank onto a small sofa in the seating area opposite Jude's room. I checked my phone—Nine fifteen. That meant it was ten fifteen in South Dakota. I licked at my lips. Maybe she was still asleep, still in bed...*fuck yeah.*

I sat up and texted Violet.

"Good morning, fiancée."

I waited.

Those three dots that danced came up onscreen, and my stomach tightened.

"Is it official on social media???"

"IT IS."

"How's Jude doing?"

"I just saw him. He's okay. Exhausted. The docs are doing lots of tests which is good - there might be something else going on, it's not so much the drugs.
And when he gets out of here, he's going to go stay with us at our house to chill and get on track."

"WOW! Wonderful!
And how are you doing?"

"I miss you. Are you still in bed?"

"Yes."

I pictured her naked, stretching out, her gorgeous body twisting next to me in our bed in Mykonos, like she did every morning when she woke up. Then I'd stroke her, lick her strategically, we'd fuck.

I typed:

"A bed without you SUCKS and I don't like it."

"Don't use that word with me now!"

"SUCKS
SUCKSSSSSS
slurp
lick"

"YOU ARE EVIL 😜 EVIL, DIRTY BOY"

My dick twitched in my jeans as I typed:

"I'm YOUR dirty boy. You neeeeeed me, baby?"

"Yesssss."

FUCK YEAH. I typed, my pulse pounding, fingertips flying over the tiny keyboard:

"My tongue is swirling around your ankle, trailing up your silky thigh, my teeth are nibbling on that soft damp skin as my fingers dip between those gorgeous legs."

"Go on, go on, go on, DIP IN, yessss…."

"Touch yourself."

"I AM."

"Hmm I can smell you…. I'm gripping your thighs tightly and now my tongue is diving into your wet pussy, sliding, swirling…so juicyyyyy."

"YESSSS I'm so wet!"

"I'm teasing your tits with silk scarves. Now I'm tying your wrists to the bed with them—you're at my mercy - I lick you…oh fuck you taste so good. I'm sucking on your clit, slowly, slowly sucking on your pussy, going in deeper… I'm eating you and you're thrashing on the bed, screaming my name. Scream my name."

"BECKKKKKKKKK"

"I cut you loose and…"

"AND???"

"Now you're riding my face."

"YES YES"

"I'm holding your sweet ass tight and you're grinding down on me. You're moaning, you need me bad, and I'm dripping with you, I'm drinking you in. I'm pinching those nipples that are hard for me. Pinch them, Violet."

My flesh heated, my pulse drummed as I shifted my legs. I wanted her so bad I could taste her, I could feel her under me, on me.

"Come on me, Violet."

No text back. I waited, my jaw grinding.
Finally the three dots hopped on the screen…

"Motherfuck that was amazing…. I've never been tied up before"

"Noted. Did you get loud for me?"

"I couldn't—Gigi & Jessa are home! I buried my face in my pillow"

"I want to bite your ass right now. Lift it up for me, baby."

"You're back." A familiar male voice stunned me out of my Violet sex reverie, and my overheated body jolted upright on the sofa. Ford and Myles stood over me.

"Hey." Myles's eyes narrowed. "Are we interrupting?"

CHAPTER THREE

VIOLET

I GROANED into my pillow as I lifted my naked ass in the air, my fingers sliding up and down my wet. Fuck, I was going to come again.

Heaving for air, I stared at my phone screen for Beck's direction as I tugged on a sore nipple with my free hand.

Nothing. Damn.

My bedroom door shoved open a few inches, scraping on the floor. Luckily it was warped with age and humidity and you had to shove twice to open it. I quickly twisted back on the bed, covering myself with the sheet.

My sister stood in the doorway of my bedroom at Gigi's, two steaming mugs in her hands and what looked like a newspaper under an arm.

Squeezing my legs together, I wiped my damp hair back from my face. "Hey."

"Hey, Sleeping Beauty, it's after ten already. Get up." She put down the coffees on the bedside table.

"My body is still in another time zone, or two, or in between the two."

"Were you having a bad dream? You look flushed and…"

I sat up, smoothing my top down my torso. "No bad dreams here!" My voice rocketed to chipper.

She handed me a mug. "Drink some coffee and that will snap you right back to our time zone."

I sipped, the sunlight stinging my sore eyes. "Yum." I took another swallow. "Good to see you again, Jessa."

"Good to be home." We hugged. "Although we're not at home. Please tell me what the heck happened with Mom and Dad. I came home after more than two months away and …" She blew out a huff of air, her blonde hair falling in her face. It had gotten lighter in the sun of Europe. It suited her. She swiped it back.

"Dad had an affair, and Mom overheard them on the phone having a post game discussion."

"Ugh. I can't believe…Anna Jeffries?"

"I know. Dad said they were at a dinner party together and they got flirty, etc, etc."

"How could he do that to Mom?" Her voice was small. "How?"

"I don't know. He did tell me he was sorry it happened, that it was a mistake. But from what Ladd tells me, his mom is all aflutter about Dad. She thinks they're having a hot affair."

"Oh brother."

"Enough about all that." I sat up in bed. "So tell me all about your trip."

"I loved it. I got a lot out of the seminar, which was great. And then I took off and saw all the things I'd been studying and wanted to see—the museums, monuments, buildings. And I managed to eat at a few of the right places too. A friend from the seminar traveled with me to a couple of cities, but then I did the south of France and Barcelona on my own."

"Good for you."

She drank again, crossing her legs, averting her gaze.

Something was up. "What is it?"

"Nothing." She pressed her lips together.

"Did you meet someone?"

Her cheeks turned beet red.

It never failed, her blushing. Unlike me, my sister had always been shy about boys. And after the fire, she didn't trust them very much. She'd go out with guys on a couple of dates at the most, and then stop taking their calls. Jessa was a virgin.

While I sought out men for temporary entertainment, Jessa kept her distance, but at the end of the day, we both did the same thing: We never got involved.

Is Gigi here?" I asked.

"No, she's at the supermarket."

"Spill. Jess, come on. I told you my adventure when you messaged me in Europe. Now you tell me yours. Between us, promise. As always."

She took in a breath. "I met someone in Monte Carlo. I only spent one night there."

"Did you—"

"No. We met, had a good time together on the town, and then I went on to Barcelona, and … there he was."

"He followed you?"

"He wanted to see me again."

"He's Italian, right? Or French?"

"No. American."

"Oh, that's too bad."

She laughed. "Why?"

"Because you were in Europe."

"Well, he was American." Her teeth scraped her lip. "I didn't give him my real name."

"Of course you didn't."

"I said my name was Violet."

"Oh geez."

"I decided I wanted to be brave. Take a risk. Be more like my sister."

My heart swelled as I squeezed her leg. "Oh, Jess…"

"He was really sweet. Funny, charming. And polite."

"And good looking?"

She blushed again. "Very, very good looking. He's some kind of fitness professional."

"Oh. So he's not a skinny, pale, history professor with glasses who barely ever sees the light of day?"

She let out a soft laugh, shaking her head.

"And?"

"And?"

"Jessa!"

"I slept with him."

I gasped and coffee spilled from my mug. "You did?" I set the mug on the night table.

"Yes, we had sex."

"This was your first time, right?"

"First time." Her fingers picked at a seam on the quilt. "We enjoyed a few days together, and that was that. I'll never see him again."

"Oh, that's a shame."

"Is it?"

"Did you sleep with him because you liked him and really wanted him or only to get your first time over with, to do it?"

"I liked him. A lot. So I figured it was a good opportunity."

A good opportunity. Oh, Jessa.

"Good for you. I'm glad you chose well and when you felt the time was right for you. That's important."

"Thanks. Me too."

"So..."

"So?"

"Jess, did you like it? Was he good to you?"

She took in a deep breath, a small smile spreading on her face like she was taking in a table laid with all her favorite foods. "It was very...he was very ... good. Not that I have anything to compare it to, but I was not disappointed. Not at all." Her lips swept up in a smile. "I was impressed."

"Wow! I'm glad, I'm really happy for you. Wonderful. I've always wanted that for you."

"I know. Your first time wasn't so…"

"Let's not go there." I drank my coffee.

"Once, we spent the whole day in bed in his hotel room" —Jess's face went a deeper shade of scarlet— "just talking and kissing, talking and touching, talking and…fooling around. The whole day. Then we went out for a really late dinner, which is very European, and walked around the city hand in hand. It was kind of magical."

"Here's to you, Violet." I raised my mug at her, teasing her at the use of my name with her hot dude. "So tell me, did Violet come a lot? I do love a good, hard, prolonged orgasm. And multiple orgasms back to back are out of this world. Did I see stars? Was I loud? I usually am rather loud—"

"Oh my gosh, stop." She reddened even more.

I loved teasing my sister. Jessa had definitely gotten all the sweet good girl genes from our family DNA.

"Did you get his phone number? His email? His facebook? His Insta? Are you staying in touch?"

"No, no, no, no, and heck no."

"What? Why not, you weirdo? You just said it was a wonderful experience and that he was so nice and everything was magical. Sounds like the beginnings of a steamy love affair." Jessa only twisted her lips and rolled her eyes at me. I continued to prod. "Does he live in Europe, is that it? How old is he?"

Her face tightened. "Violet—"

"Is he older? He's older! Oh, Jessssssaaaa…"

"Enough about me. Why don't you tell me about your engagement to a rockstar? What the heck, Violet? You said you and Beck were just—"

"Engagement?"

"It's all over social media with pics of the two of you kissing at a restaurant in Athens when he gave you the ring. Then posing with these girls at JFK, who posted about meeting the two of you, and Beck confirming your engagement. Insta and Twitter are on fire, the two of you are trending."

"Oh fuck."

"Let me see that ring."

I stretched out my hand with Beck's ring.

"Oh, so pretty!"

"It is."

Jessa bit her lip. "There's just one little bitty issue."

"What's that?"

"This." Jessa put the newspaper on my lap. Our local from Rapid. My fingers suddenly cold, I picked it up. It was folded to the social page. "Right here." Jess pointed to a prominent box in the Engagements section.

"Ladd Jeffries and Violet Hildebrand are engaged to be married. Mr. Jeffries and Ms. Hildebrand first met…."

My stomach churned.

"Ms. Hildebrand is the daughter of Meager's famed Hildebrand ranching and commercial land development family and Mr. Jeffries is the only son of…."

Sour filled the back of my throat. My breath grew choppy.

"A wedding date is being decided upon. Congratulations to the beautiful couple and their proud families."

"Fuck no!" I fisted the paper. "What the hell did Ladd do? No, no, no."

"I'm afraid yes, yes, yes. And the other news is—"

"There's more?"

"Just Jana on Instagram found out, and she released a "what the hell is going on here?" post, because, you know, you're engaged to Beck Lanier and she lurves Freefall."

I fell back on the bed on a loud groan, my arms flinging over my face.

"This is truly next level, Violet. Is this what a throuple is?"

"Oh my God, Jess! No."

"Okay, so please tell me what's going on."

I told her how the engagement to Beck happened.

"Wow, he's something else. Fantastic."

"It's fantastic that Beck and I are fake engaged and all the world thinks it's for real?"

"He doesn't want to lose you. And you like him. A lot." She grinned, her face lit up. "This is a whole other kind of romantic. So exciting."

"I'm glad you're excited. Do Mom, Gigi, or Dad know?"

"I don't think so. It all blew up pretty late last night after you got in, and I didn't mention it to them. I wanted to talk to you first. But they'll probably be hearing all about it today." She let out a stiff laugh. "About both your fiancés."

"Crap."

"So the question is, will Mom and Dad hear about you and Beck first? Or you and Ladd? And which will Lenore hear first? And then when Lenore finds out about you and Ladd, what will she think? EEK. She might send Finger after you." Jessa let out a laugh.

"Shut up!"

"All right, all right. So now tell me about what happened with Ladd."

Heavy banging on the door reverberated through the house, and my body jerked.

Jessa lunged from the bed. "What's going on? Who the—"

"Violet! Violet open this damned door now!"

Speak of the devil.

CHAPTER FOUR

@JUSTJANA

CRAZY NEWS CONCERNING rock guitarist Beck Lanier's new fiancée—*Or is she?*

Less than a day after Beck confirmed his engagement to South Dakota photographer Violet Hildebrand, a newspaper in Rapid City, SD published an announcement that Ms. Hildebrand had just gotten engaged to mining scion and local millionaire Ladd Jeffries, who, local sources tell us, has had a relationship with Ms. Hildebrand for months.

<Click HERE for pics of handsome Mr. Jeffries>

I'm confused, are you?

We certainly hope poor Beck is not up for more heartbreak!

What's going on, Violet?

Was she engaged to Ladd Jeffries, but then lightning struck with Beck?

Who's the real fiancé? And who's the fling?

Follow, Like, and don't miss our Stories for up to the minute updates!

#AllTheNews #allthesexxy #JustJana #becklanier #couple-news #BeckAndViolet #ViBeck #coupledrama

CHAPTER FIVE

VIOLET

I OPENED the front door and there stood Ladd, lips twisted, hands on his waist over a dark-green Polo shirt and perfectly pleated khaki pants.

I winced. The visual of him after Greece was a shock to my system. "Stop ranting and get inside. This is a good neighborhood."

Scoffing, he pushed past me into Gigi's living room and stopped short at the sight of my sister, arms crossed. "Oh. Hi Jessa." She only scowled at him. He turned to me once more. "You lying, cheating whore."

"Don't talk to Violet like that," said Jessa.

"A compliment from you first thing in the morning?" I said. "Wow, I feel special."

"You want to explain this?" He whipped out his phone and shoved it in my face. There was that picture of me and Beck naked on Tag's account.

"Since when do you have Instagram?"

His face streaked with red, a sharp grunt escaping his throat. He took back the phone and tapped and swiped, and shoved it in my face once again. "And this?"

A picture of me and Beck arm in arm surrounded by the

fangirls at JFK with a title banner "IT'S OFFICIAL - BECK IS ENGAGED!" on a gossip website.

"Oh, that photo turned out nice."

"You went to Greece with him?"

"I did."

"I told you—"

"Did you and Sissy enjoy Mexico?"

His eyes flared as he raised up and away from me.

"Did you have to pay her to go with you, or did she actually want to fuck you for a whole week?"

He inhaled deeply, closing his eyes for a moment. Points to Ladd for trying to control his anger. "I'm going to ask you one more time." His voice was brittle, dry wood in the hot sun. "What the fuck is going on with you? We had an agreement."

"I never agreed to anything, Ladd. You kept going on and on about what you wanted and your brilliant strategy. Why did you go and put an announcement in the paper? Who the hell does that without actually getting engaged first?"

"I was getting the ball rolling on a solid idea, and now you and Kurt Cobain over there shot that to shit."

Laughter ripped from my chest.

"Seriously, what is it with you two? Did his cock hypnotize you?"

And his mind, and his soul, and his heart. I crossed my arms. "You have no idea."

"Goddammit." Ladd rubbed his neck. "My mother is very upset. This is social humiliation on an insane level."

"What about my family? My friends? You had no right to put that announcement in the paper. You were trying to twist my arm, you asshole!"

He charged at me, his face snarled in rage. My chest constricted, adrenaline raced through my veins, and I didn't move a muscle. Jessa darted forward, clasping my arm as Ladd's finger stabbed the air in front of me. "You did this on purpose, you fucking cu—"

"Stop it!" Jessa's strong voice rang out, and Ladd froze, towering over us both. My chin lifted, my heart swelled. Jessa never yelled, never wildly contradicted or confronted. With great difficulty she stood up for herself, let alone someone else. "Get out of our house. Now." She marched to the front door and opened it, gripping the knob, her green eyes lasering Ladd, her chin wobbling. "Get. Out."

"I swear, you are going to regret this!" He charged down the front steps to his car which was parked at a sloppy angle in the road.

Jessa shut the door firmly and locked it. Her hands pressed against the paneled wood. He was gone, for now.

Jessa swiveled around. "Let's get out of here. Come with me to the house?"

"Sure. Let me take a shower and get dressed." I headed upstairs.

The house. The house.

I froze, my hand clutching the banister.

Dammit. What about Whisperwind now?

CHAPTER SIX

BECK

"WHEN'S THE WEDDING?" Ford asked.

I typed out a quick *sorry babe - got to go xx* and tucked my phone back into my pocket. "Aren't you informed?"

"Of course I am."

"It's all over social media, man." Myles sat down next to me on the sofa in the hospital hallway.

"Between us, she's not really my fiancée."

"Not *really?*" Ford chuckled leaning against the wall. "Oooo tell me more."

"I got ahead of myself on that, but—"

"But?"

"But we're together."

"Whatever it is, I'm happy for you." Ford squeezed my shoulder. "You look good. Violet and time away certainly agreed with you."

"How's Jude doing today?" asked Myles. "We were here last night with his mom and your dad."

I filled them in on Jude's status and Dad's idea.

"Sounds good. That's a start," said Ford.

"Jude's anxious about your reaction to all this."

Moving his suit jacket out of the way, he planted his hands on his waist. "I care about him, and I want to see him healthy and stable. Jude's a good person and a brilliant musician, and I want to see him take care of himself."

"He wants to do better," I said.

"I'm going to visit with him." Ford's eyes flared at me and Myles as he turned. "Behave yourselves." He went into Jude's room.

Myles leaned forward and cleared his throat, and a prickle raced over my flesh. We had to have this conversation. We hadn't seen each other or spoken since he punched me at the restaurant.

"Speaking of doing better…" Myles clasped his hands together tightly. "I want to apologize for assaulting you at the restaurant. I really regret that."

"Because you found out she was lying?"

He tilted his head. "No, because it was wrong. I saw that photo, assumed the worst."

"You mean you assumed the worst of me."

"Of everything and everybody. But I took it all out on you. I shouldn't have come after you like that and in public. I lost it. I'm sorry."

I held his gaze. "Okay."

He brushed a hand down his mouth, letting out a heavy breath. Myles had toppled from his mountaintop of crisp righteous indignation and had sunk into the dry weeds of humiliation and humility, and he was a little dazed, in shock.

Know the feeling.

His smile faded. "The thing that shakes me up is I brought Lisa into our lives, our family, on our tour, and had no idea what was going on in her head. Was she faking it the whole time and having a good laugh at me? At both of us?

"You'll never know."

"You're right. What I do know is that all of it fed right into my frustrations about a lot of other shit."

"It was a long, long tour, and we all blew a lot of shit out of proportion."

"I also want to apologize for being an asshole when Mae dumped you the way she did. You were hurting and I was being a dick. When I saw Lisa's photo and read her post, I didn't know what to feel first."

"I felt like I'd gotten pushed off a ship into black water and suddenly I didn't know how to swim."

"There was that, yeah." He crossed his arms at his chest. "Then the rage kicked in."

"Have you talked to her, seen her?"

"No. I've tried, but she's nowhere to be found. Hasn't returned my calls, nothing. She hiding under a rock somewhere where she belongs. "

"Stay away from her, Myles. And her friends, too. Hell knows what else she can dream up and spin you in."

"That's what Mack said."

"You talked to our lawyer?"

"Hell yeah. I remember what you went through with those stalkers."

"Good for you."

"Was that Violet in those photos of you in Nashville?

"That was Violet. She leaked the photos."

"Good woman."

"She is."

Two nurses walked by, their gazes lingering on us. They recognized us.

Myles leaned closer to me. "This whole thing with Jude is a real wake-up call. Him getting better is what matters. Us making a new album together matters."

"Totally agree. I saw Ford's email about our studio time next week."

"Yeah. It's going to be weird without Jude. He's always been our WD-40."

I let out a laugh. "That's true. Our flow will definitely be different, but I figure we can work out basics and develop a good number of pieces, some solid ideas for him to play with when he's ready to join us."

"That's a good plan. I've got a lot of material I'd like to show you guys."

I met his gaze. "Great. Look forward to hearing it."

"Yeah?"

"Yeah. Absolutely."

"Cool." His shoulders eased. Had he been anxious about bringing that up with me? "You must have a ton of stuff ready to go."

"No, I don't, Myles. Not this time."

A nurse with a cart of medications stopped by Jude's room. She checked her chart, picked up a cup with pills and went into his room.

Zack ambled down the hallway toward us. "Hey, you two."

"Hey, Zack" I got up and gave him a hug.

"All good?" His eyes darted from me to Myles.

"All good." Myles stood up and they slapped hands.

"Awesome." Zack grinned.

The nurse came out of Jude's room, leaving the door open, and Ford gestured us inside. Jude turned, a grin lighting up his face at the sight of us.

Zack let out a laugh. "Let's go see our boy."

CHAPTER SEVEN

VIOLET

I PULLED up to our house, and my stomach pitched at the sight of Dad's truck towering in the driveway. "Great."

Jessa undid her seatbelt. "He's not the devil, you know."

Dad and Jessa had always been very close. She was the baby in the family, and she'd been Daddy's girl from the very first. Five had been the Crown Prince, and me? Classic middle child, straddling all the lines, depended on by everyone, always self-sufficient, and everyone always assumed I was.

"I'm not in the mood for anymore confrontations today, that's all." I snapped off my seatbelt. "But I do need to talk to him about Ladd."

The front door was unlocked and we entered the house. "Dad?" He came out from his office, a room to the right of the entrance.

"Violet?" Behind me, Jessa walked through the front door and his face lit up. "Jessa, you're back?"

They hugged. "Hi, Daddy."

"I loved all the pictures you sent me."

"I'm glad. It was the best trip."

His gaze darted to me, his lips pressing together. "And did you enjoy your little vacation?"

"I certainly did." Had he seen the photo of me and Beck?

Had he heard the engagement news? *For Pete's sake, which engagement news?* My gaze darted to his desk. The newspaper lay there, still rolled up in plastic.

His eyes narrowed. "I didn't know you went to Greece."

Jess moved away from us toward the hallway. "I'm going to head to my room, and—"

"Are you moving out too?" His sharp tone stopped her in her tracks.

She shifted her weight, her cheeks blooming with pink. "I-I don't want to be in your way…"

"I am not having an affair with Anna Jeffries!"

We all averted our gazes. I broke the loud silence. "Speaking of whom, Ladd found out about you and his mommy, and he is very upset and very angry."

"Dammit, she told him?"

"He found some gift that she'd ordered for you."

"Oh Jesus. The Tiffany cufflinks?"

"That's it. Guess you made quite an impression in the coat room."

He let out a groan, brushing a hand down his face. "She only did that because I lost one of my cufflinks that night and—"

I held up a hand. "Do us a favor—TMI."

"What the hell does that mean?"

"Too much information!" Jessa wiped the hair back from her flushed face.

He let out a groan. "Sorry."

"Did you accept her dazzling gift?" I asked.

"No, of course not. I told her I didn't want any gifts from her, just my own damn cufflink back."

"She found your cufflink?"

"Yes, she found it, and she still has it."

"Cute," I said. "She's trying to lure you with flashier ones while holding yours hostage so you can come'n git it."

"Oh geez," Jessa groaned.

"Keeping it real."

Dad glared at me. "Those cufflinks were my grandfather's, and I want it back."

"Priorities, huh? But what you did to Mom, what she's going through now doesn't quite rank up there with those cufflinks, does it?"

"Violet—"

"I don't want to hear it, and I'm not the one who needs to hear it." I let out a breath.

"You're right."

I cleared my throat. "You should know, Ladd thinks that you seduced Anna to have a direct line to her bank account and to marginalize him."

"Are you kidding me?"

"No, I am not kidding you. Do you think I want to be having this conversation with you right now? I assured him—and I hope I'm right—that this was just a one-time incident and not an ongoing thing. He's concerned about a public scandal in general and because of Anna's boyfriend."

"Yes, Armand Castillo who I know."

"Awkward."

"It's not a big deal, they have an open relationship."

"Is that what she told you?"

"That's what he told me a couple of months ago on the phone. He was calling from his estate in Aruba where he was vacationing with two young women on a long weekend."

I blinked. "I just can't keep up with you kids any more."

"I'm going to make some coffee." Jessa headed to the kitchen.

"Yes, please, I wish you would," Dad said. "I haven't had a good cup of coffee in forever."

"What are you doing home this time of day anyway?" We followed Jessa into the kitchen.

"I woke up tired, worn out, so I decided to take it easy and work from home." He threw himself onto a stool at the island, letting out a heavy sigh. "What else did Ladd say?"

"He's concerned a scandal would screw up Powder Ridge. He wanted me to dissuade you from seeing her again."

"I'm not seeing her."

"If you say so."

Jessa hit the coffee grinder, her jaw tense, shoulders tight.

Dad's phone rang in his office. "I better get that." He left the kitchen.

"Dad having an affair, Mom not here—it's all flipping me out." Jessa poured the ground coffee into the filter of the electric coffee maker. She hit the buttons. "What is this Keurig doing here?" She gestured at the new coffee capsule appliance on the counter.

I chuckled. "Dad must have bought it now that he's living alone without me or Mom to make his daily brew."

My phone buzzed. Gigi. "Hey, Gig."

"Hi, honey. Where are you?"

"Jess and I are at Dad's house. Are you back from the supermarket?"

"Listen, I need to tell you something. Sue Anne just called me." Gigi's voice was serious.

Sue Anne was Gigi's childhood friend. She lived down the street from Whisperwind. "What is it? Is she okay?"

"Whisperwind has been sold."

The air knocked out of my chest, and I sunk onto the bar stool. *Ladd actually did it. No hot air, no empty threats. He fucking did it.*

Gigi continued, "The day before, the Putnams left for San Diego to visit their kids like they often do. But then yesterday, professional movers showed up in a huge truck and Sue Anne went over there and asked them what was going on, and they said the house had been sold. By nighttime they were done and gone, and the house empty. I'm sorry, honey. They didn't say a word to anybody, no sign of any realtor, or strangers visiting. You know Sue Anne, she would've noticed. She was shocked, she had no idea. None of us did."

I did. "Oh."

"Are you okay?"

"I don't know."

"Honey—I'm so sorry."

"Thank you for telling me." I tapped End Call.

"What did Gigi say?"

I stared at the grain of the granite countertop.

"Violet?"

Dad returned to the kitchen. "What's going on?"

"The Putnams sold Whisperwind," I breathed. "It's gone."

Jessa gasped. "Oh no!"

"Gigi just called. Sue Anne told her. The Putnams just took off. Didn't say a word to anybody, they sold it on their own it seems. A mover came for their things."

"I can't believe this," Dad muttered. "With everything going on, I didn't realize that the Putnams were even interested in selling right now. Last time we'd talked…ah shit."

My head buzzed and wobbled on my neck. I clasped my hands together, squeezing, but they were numb. I should never have gone to Greece. What was I thinking? I wasn't thinking, I was feeling. Being impulsive and wild. Self-indulgent. *Stupid, stupid girl.* If I had been here, I could have…I don't know what I could've…but something. Something.

I didn't know anything anymore.

"I'm sorry, Violet." The press of Dad's hand on my shoulder interrupted my self-flagellation. "I know how much you wanted that house. I'm sorry I couldn't get it for you."

"I know. Everything's tied up in Powder Ridge now. Anyway, it was just a dream."

"It was a dream project, preserving that house, bringing it back." Jessa put a full coffee mug in front of me. "And I wanted to help you do it."

I stared at the steam. So like smoke. "Well, Jess, maybe Ladd will hire you to design the townhouse development he wants to build there."

"Why do you say that?" Dad's voice was sharp. "What makes you think Ladd bought it?"

Dammit. My hands wrapped around the smooth, hot mug. Blistering hot.

"Violet. Tell me."

"He was irked that I'd broken up with him, and then about me and Beck."

"Beck?" His eyes narrowed. "Lenore's son? The musician?"

"Dad…" Jessa implored.

I sat up straight. "Ladd told me he'd spoken to the Putnams and made them an offer, and they were considering it. They obviously accepted."

"Why would he do all that?"

"He thought us getting engaged would solidify his position at Powder Ridge. Like I said, now with you and his mother hooking up he's paranoid that you're cutting him out of the project."

"That's ridiculous."

"That's Ladd. That's the way he thinks," I snapped. "He said he'd buy Whisperwind and hang onto it to guarantee my cooperation because he knew I was spending time with Beck."

"Why didn't you tell me all this sooner? I would've—" His phone beeped and he scanned his screen, his forehead furrowing. "Is this why Cliff at the bank is congratulating me on your engagement? You agreed to this bullshit?"

Jessa bit her lower lip, eyes wide. *WHICH FIANCE?* was stamped all over her face.

"Ladd and I are not engaged. I did not agree to anything. But he was so sure of himself, he went and published an announcement in the paper."

"While you were out of the country? He's a piece of work." His jaw tensed. "By the way, is this Beck the one you were with in Nashville? Or was that someone else? Were you with him in Greece too? For God's sake, Violet—"

"Slither back down from your moral high ground, Marshall. Yes, I was with Beck in Nashville and Greece."

"That's something. You must like him a hell of a lot."

I met his gaze. "I do."

"Dad, the auction is coming up," said Jessa. "What are we going to do if Anna and Ladd pull out because of all this?"

"That won't happen. Business is business. We all have a lot riding on this, and it's too good an opportunity to throw away because of … bullshit." Dad's phone buzzed. "I need to take this." With his mug in hand, he left the kitchen. "Great coffee, honey!" his voice rang out from the hallway.

It was bullshit to my father, but it wasn't to Ladd.

Now he had Whisperwind in his holster.

My lungs pressed together, the walls pressed together. I gasped for air.

"Violet?"

I ran out of the house.

CHAPTER EIGHT

VIOLET

I STARTED MY CAR, the roar of the engine reverberating through my seat, my veins and muscles. Hollow veins, weak muscles barely hanging on. I made my way into town, shot down Clay, then took the turn.

My phone rang. I had no curiosity to see who it was. To talk. My phone rang. Rang. Rang. My windows were wide open, the hot air buffeting my face, my hair flying in a tangled mess. I hit the gas harder, swerving on the curve of the road.

I was a tangled mess. I leaned my head back and sucked in a breath as I drove.

The weedy and narrow asphalt road. The old birdhouse mailbox. My foot jammed on the brake, and a sob stuck in my throat.

Holy fuck. No.

My heartbeat screeched to a burning halt at the sight of the huge fence that now surrounded the property.

Whisperwind stood behind a gleaming new and very tall metal fence.

A border, a barricade. A block.

I pushed open the heavy door of the Cougar and stumbled toward the fence.

"Private Property" declared a big, bold sign.

A warning. Keep away, step off. Not yours. No Entrance. Stay away, stay back.

My fingers slid into the cold metal webbing of the fence, tightening around the coils. Something rumbled through me, a shudder, cold and icy.

I clamped my eyes shut against the image before me. This was fucking real. It was happening.

Hiccupy breaths sputtered from me, sour churning in my insides. Everything I knew was different now, gone. I was the lone runner on the track, and everyone else had already reached the end. Not me. I kept running but somehow…

All the little girl hopes and one day dreams had popped like the fragile childhood balloons they were. *Silly Violet.*

My head sank against the goddamn fence. Now I was the outsider looking in. Looking at. No touching. No entering.

Step away.

I was the outsider to Whisperwind. Me.

My vision blurred, tears streaming down my face, stinging my cheeks, that sour tide bucking up my insides. The faded blue shingles of the house blurred into a watery grey blue, and I squeezed my eyes shut.

"Violet, sweetheart?"

Twisting, I wiped at my face with my arm. "Gigi? How did you…"

"Jessa called me. I thought I'd find you here. Oh honey, I know this is hard."

"I w-wanted…I…I…"

She took me in her arms. "I know. But now you need to let it go."

A cry ripped from me as I sank into my grandmother's embrace. She held me tight, kissing the side of my face, stroking my hair. "I know what you're feeling. I know. I tried to keep it after Isi, her brother, and my uncle died, but it was impossible. And that hurt.

"I felt so guilty that I had to give it up. But Whisperwind needed so much that I couldn't give. If I had tried, I wouldn't have been responsible to my own family or to Whisperwind."

I snuffled into her shoulder. "I was so sure I could do it." I hiccuped a sob.

"You wanted to buy it back and make it glorious again."

"Make it a glorious home."

"I knew my parents, my grandparents, even Jeremiah Dillon himself wouldn't have wanted any of us to be burdened like that. When Wreck gave me Leo's stash of money that he'd found at the go-kart factory, it wasn't a huge amount, but it was a lot. I knew I had a choice to make after I paid off the debts: save Whisperwind or save the General Store building, but I couldn't do both.

"I thought it was smarter to save the store building, to hold onto that. Right on the main street of town, it had the most potential for the future. I was afraid this house would be a never-ending money pit, like it was for Isi and her father. None of us were going to live here.

"My brother had his home, I had mine, and anyhow neither of us needed all this space or could pay the damned taxes. And the real estate market was awful back then. What if we poured the money into renovating and maintaining it and then still couldn't afford to hang onto it or even sell it for a good price if need be? It would've been a devastating loss. So I chose to hang onto the General Store building."

"You chose well, Gigi."

She turned me in her arms and we faced the house together. "It was hard for me, but I told myself it was a home that had been well-loved and well-lived in. And that's the truth, isn't it? Many generations of Dillons have passed through it, dreamed, created, cooked, gathered, celebrated, argued, sang within those walls. The Putnams certainly had a time of it here. Five children now all grown."

"I never got to hear that whisperwind."

"Oh, that old story?"

"It's true, isn't it? You said you and Uncle Ryan and Isi and her brothers had heard it when you were little."

"All of us had been playing up in the turret room, it was storming that afternoon, and suddenly a rush of sound whooshed around us—delicate and powerful all at once. It was odd. But we had wild imaginations. We all huddled together. Ryan and James were sure it was Jeremiah's ghost. Leo heard that and started to cry, and me and Isi held onto him. But we were scared too.

"The story goes that Jeremiah's children had first heard it, that whisper of the wind, they called it. The turret room had been their nursery. They all figured something had been off with the construction in the room. Was it the windows? A crack in the molding or the wood paneling? The seal on the roof? They never figured it out, and it remained a wonderful, magical mystery that only happened once in a great, great while."

"When the house wants it to happen."

"Probably so."

"I think some things should always remain magical mysteries."

"Me too. That's when Jeremiah named the house. When he had his own family, when he was truly happy and settled with the woman he loved."

I leaned my head against the fence. "I'm sure he thought it would always stay in the family, and now it's lost. I'm so t-tired of l-losing things, Gigi."

She clutched at my arms. "Honey, is this about the fire? Is it?"

I pulled away from her, my body stiffening.

"Violet, you can't save everything. And you don't have to make up for that fire, for Five. He—"

"Don't. Please." My teeth gnashed together. "We all lost a part of ourselves that night. I thought if I could do this, hang onto this piece of family history, make it beautiful again, preserve it, it would make up for…" My shoulders dropped, a low moan escaping my lips. "Dad was going to help me. I just had to wait until Powder Ridge got off the ground."

"The Dillons have never been good at holding onto things. Not like the Hildebrands."

I let out a sigh. "True."

"Brigands and firebrands, they used to call us back in the day. But our legacy can't be boiled down to only objects, property. Our legacy endures in other, significant ways. My grandfather's go-kart factory that was once a big Meager success story, then died a slow death, became the clubhouse of the One-Eyed Jacks Motorcycle Club, thanks to Isi. Your mother turned her father's wilting diner into a modern coffee house, which brought the tourists back to Meager and set off a renaissance for our little has been town. The Dillon General Store building is now three brand new stores, which have refreshed Meager and made it a destination in the Black Hills. That's powerful to me, that vision, those choices, those opportunities dared and taken."

I wiped at my eyes. "Yes."

She squeezed me into her side. "Listen to me, Violet Isadora, you have not failed. You have not lost. You've barely gotten started. Whisperwind was built from Jeremiah Dillon's hard work, his persistence, his gumption and defiance, the very same virtues that are in you.

"Jeremiah's family had come to the Dakota Territory on a homestead, grew wheat like so many others, but that didn't last. The earth here was fickle for wheat farming. Disastrous for so many. He ended up leaving the farm to his brother and sold his share of seeds and started trading and bartering until he finally set up the store. As the town grew, he set up a gambling den on the second floor of the store."

I wiped at my nose. "And then he invested in a brothel, right?"

"That's right. He knew that to grease palms politically and in business with the railroad czars who ran everything, you had to be in the game to make the deals, to make things happen. And that game was booze, cards, and women."

"And that's how he met his Clara."

"Yes. Him falling in love with a young prostitute caused a huge scandal, but he didn't give a damn. He married her and built this glorious house and they had lots of babies and grew old together here.

"The townspeople thought he was arrogant to build such a fancy house back then when most in these parts had next to nothing—and for a prostitute, no less. How gaudy, how shameless."

"But he didn't give a damn."

"Not one. He was proud of his accomplishments, of his wife, and basically said fuck you to everyone by building this house and living here. Now is your time to build your success your way.

"Violet, take all these feelings you're feeling right now and let them move you forward, not hold you back, honey. Forward. Don't let anything or anyone hold you back. Get your Jeremiah Dillon on."

I want to be the roar, I'd declared to Beck years ago. He hadn't forgotten that, and by taking me to Greece, he'd given me the opportunity to spark my movement forward toward that roar.

"I know it's been a difficult time for you with everything that's going on with your parents, with Ladd, with Beck, and of course, the anniversary of the fire. It's a hell of a lot. I think you should let Jeremiah's success fuel you, not make you sad. Let it inspire you." Gigi hugged me. "Young lady, you have a lot to live up to, as a Dillon *and* a Hildebrand."

My lips wobbled into a small grin.

"Keep the spirit of Whisperwind in your heart, baby. I have. Let it feed your roots as you grow." She gestured at the house on a sigh. "Anything's possible. Even a big yet delicate St. Anne's style mansion in the wilds of the Dakota territory." She let out a soft laugh.

Swiping the damp hair back from my hot face, I took in the house through the mesh of the fence.

You're on, Jeremiah.

CHAPTER NINE

VIOLET

I OPENED my eyes and the bottle of ouzo Beck had gotten for Lenore stared at me from my dresser top.

Dang! I need to give that to her!

It was eight in the morning. As I turned on the shower, I texted Lenore asking her if I could stop by on my way to work and bring her the bottle.

She texted back:

"I'm in Rapid - have appointments all day. But Finger's home - he'll be leaving around 9 for Nebraska. Or you could come over tonight and we could drink a glass together?"

Hmm…I wasn't sure what made me more anxious? A one on one with Lenore peppering me with questions about my relationship with her son, and why we were fake engaged, and why the newspaper said I was engaged to Ladd? Or a one-on-one with the legendary biker outlaw president?

Finger it is!

I got ready in record time and flew out the door.

In their driveway, two massive, majestic Harley-Davidsons stood guard. Huge, hulking chrome. Seasoned. Powerful. Intimidating—kind of like the bearded biker wearing mirrored sunglasses standing next to them, who raised his glasses and eyed me as I slammed the door of the Cougar and strode up the front walk.

"Morning!"

"Good morning, pretty lady—can I help you?" He had messy, long black hair streaked with gray, and a toothpick sticking out his mouth that I was sure had taken up residence there back in the eighties.

"I'm dropping something off for Lenore. That okay with you?"

"She's not here."

"I know, I just talked to her." I stopped. "And…who are you?"

He tilted his head, a smirk growing on his thick lips, fang-like teeth gleaming in the morning sun. He was amused. On his worn out leather vest hung the patch of the Flames of Hell, Finger's motorcycle club. Was he their security guy? He shifted his body, and I spotted a patch on his jacket: Vice-President. Oh, he was a big, big gun.

The front door flew open and filling the entrance was Finger in all his rough and rugged magnificence. "It's cool, Drac. Hey, Violet, how you doing?"

"Hi. Um, I hope I'm not interrupting anything or—"

"You're not. Come on in. Lenore told me you might stop by."

I grinned, but my feet had frozen in place.

"Go on. Don't worry, he won't bite." Drac laughed loudly.

Finger opened the door wide, gesturing me inside. "Ignore him."

I raised the bottle of ouzo as I made my way through the door. "This is for you and Lenore. A little taste of Greece from Beck."

He took the bottle. "Ah. Nice." He placed it on the bench in the foyer. *Oh, that bench.* "I look forward to trying it. Never tried it before."

"Make sure you have lots of appetizers with it. That's ouzo at its best."

"Good to know." He pulled on his leather jacket. So many creases, so many patches on it. A life on the road.

"I'm glad I caught you before you left. I'll get going then. It was good to see you."

"Hang on there—" His scratchy, low voice boomed and I stopped in my tracks. "I got something for you."

"For me?"

"My VP, Drac, outside, just brought it to me, and I was going to swing by the Grand and leave it for you. But here you are."

"Here I am…" The heels of my high-tops ground into the floor. What could Finger possibly have for me?

"Beck told us that you're related to Isi."

"Yes, I am. She was my grandmother's first cousin."

"Heard her sing a few times back in the day. Met her once."

"Really?"

"I was a young pup and had just transferred to our charter in Nebraska. In the summer, our regional club out here would sponsor a charity run to a campground and have these massive blowout weekend parties with live shows. She sang at a couple of those with different bands."

"I've heard stories."

"At the time, Drac had just hooked up with his old lady, Krystal, and she was always taking lots of pics especially at these events. I asked her to go through 'em, and she found these." He took an envelope out of his jacket and gave it to me. "They're just seven photos, but it's something, and I thought you'd like to see them."

My pulse skipped as I tore open the seam of the envelope. Old square photos of faded Kodachrome slid into my hand. My breath caught at the sight of a young woman, younger than me, commanding a high platform stage—one hand raised high while she powered into the microphone in her grip at a downward angle. Below her, a long line of bikers in leather and heavy beards pushed at the wild audience, keeping them back. Just like pictures I'd seen of Woodstock and Altamont.

"I thought you'd like to have the originals."

"I-I can keep these?"

"Yeah, they're for you."

My lower lip trembled as I leafed through the shots of another world, another age, and there, there was my cousin Isi, her hair flying, a bandana wrapped around a jean clad thigh, long earrings, a cutoff T-shirt ripped at the neck, and boots, singing alongside the sweaty lead guitarist as he jammed down on his chords. Powerful, provocative, and all in.

All in.

All in.

Everything slowed down around me, inside me. Finger's voice cut through my haze, and I blinked up at him. My body swayed.

"Violet, you okay?" With a firm grip on my arm, he led me to the bench. I sat, gulping in air and all the images again and again. "Hang on…"

A cold glass of water was placed in my hand, and I drank. "Thank you."

He placed another envelope on the bench next to me. "I asked Krystal if she had the negatives, and she did, so those are in this envelope. I figured you'd like to have them, being a photographer."

I pressed the photos to my chest. "Finger, thank you. This is so thoughtful of you. Thank you so much."

"You bet."

Sniffing in air, I held up a photo which showed Isi and the band from behind, an enormous crowd spread out before them. "Krystal must have been onstage here."

"Yeah. She was a crazy chick. Still is."

"Hey, that's my old lady you're talking about." Drac let loose a rolling laugh from the open doorway, a lit cigarette in his hand.

"Drac, thank you for these. Please tell Krystal for me. Actually, I'd love to talk to her if I could."

"Sure, I'll give you her number." He lifted his chin.

My attention went back to the picture in my hand. "This crowd is ginormous."

"Our parties were famous back in the day." A slight smile twitched Finger's lips beneath his beard.

My gaze went back to the shot. An ecstatic crowd, and Isi performing for them, holding the stage, holding them in her thrall, her voice rocking them, and they loved it.

I cleared my throat. "My grandmother had gone to a few concerts—not these club ones, I don't think—and she has some pics, but none so close up, and none of Isi around this time. This is early days. She'd told me that Isi used to vagabond with different groups, join in for a few songs or sing backup for them here and there, whenever she could. This is … I have no words."

A hot shaking sensation simmered in the pit of my stomach, spreading its volatile heat all through me, bursting in my chest.

"A couple years after these shows I met Isi," Finger said. "She was with a band then, and they were on the road. That night they'd played not too far from our clubhouse in Nebraska."

I picked up the envelope with the negatives. "I think Beck's dad was in that band too, just starting out then."

"Oh yeah? Huh." He rested his hands on his hips. "That night after their show, a couple of my brothers had gone to their motel to party with them, and a fight broke out. I showed up with more of my brothers just as shit was about to fly. And Isi was trying to get control of the situation all by herself."

"Then her man showed up," Drac said on a chuckle.

"Yes, he did." Finger dragged a hand through his beard. "But Isi didn't wait for no man. She dove right in, head first on her own."

FINGER AND DRAC left for Nebraska, roaring off down the street on their bikes, but I remained on the front porch of the house. I took in the morning air. A dog barked down the street. A child's bicycle bell rang out. The photographs in my hand were no longer blurry, and I wanted to share them with Beck.

I took pictures of the photos and messaged them to him.

"Look what Finger found for me!"

I leaned back on the slanted wooden Adirondack chair going through the prints once again. Isi was all in. No fear. No doubts, no regrets. All in, in the high, driving it home, keeping it together, keeping on, going big.

My chest expanded. She was here, showing me her passion, how it affected her, how it affected all those she performed for.

At this young age she was sneaking out of the house and talking her way in to singing with bands at wild biker extravaganzas, at bars and nightclubs. She took risks, she made connections, she was out there doing, doing, doing. Creating. Living.

Because if she didn't, she'd suffocate.

I know, Isi, I know what that feels like. I know.

I'd been steadily working on my craft since I'd gone and done that first summer workshop. I'd taken more seminars, more classes, put myself out there and I loved working, learning, growing.

But since Powder Ridge had jetted into full gear, I'd jammed my passion into a corner and put it on hold. Then Beck had crossed my life once more and everything exploded for me. Everything.

Isi was showing me my way. First through Beck's dad, now his step-father. These weren't coincidences. I knew they weren't. They couldn't be. No. They were beautiful divine links of fate.

Links of creative energy, desire, of love.

And at the very core of each was Beck.

My phone beeped, and my heart jumped. It was him.

"AMAZING! I LOVE this! Will show my dad.
I have a question for you—
Why is my fiancée engaged to Ladd Jeffries???"

I laughed as I typed, a ripple of warmth swirling inside me.

"Lies!
She's NOT engaged to him and she never, ever will be."

CHAPTER TEN

VIOLET

"SIGN HERE, PLEASE."

I signed the Federal Express device, and the delivery man handed me a small box. "Have a good one."

"Thanks, Tim. You, too." I charged over to my desk at Hildebrand & Hildebrand, grabbed my scissors, and cut at the tape sealing the box.

Inside lay a blue gift box. Ribbons of baby blue and gold sprang and coiled in my fingers. A thrill raced through me. *This boy*. He loved giving me gifts and I was enjoying them.

I FaceTimed Beck. He was still in bed. "Good morning, sleepy."

"Hmm." A warm groan rolled in his throat and made my heartbeat skip a beat. "Hey, baby." An electric grin sparked over Beck's face. "Open it."

"Is this some kind of high tech vibrator gizmo that you're going to control from L.A.?"

"Damn, that's a great idea. I'll have to look into that. But no."

I propped my phone against my desktop and ripped off the ribbons and opened the box. A little replica of a Mykonos windmill lay nestled inside. "Beck!" I took it out and flicked at the sails, and the little wheel spun.

He laughed. A soft laugh, lazy, sensual. He was pleased.

"Crazy boy sends me a sweet island souvenir."

"You like it?" He lifted up from his pillow, resting his head on his hand, his bare torso visible.

"I love it."

"I meant to give it to you before we left Greece, but suddenly, a hell of a lot was going on and it ended up in my suitcase instead of my carry-on. I didn't want you to forget the amazing time we had together on the island."

"I'll never forget it. Any of it." My voice was a rough whisper. *No matter what happened between us, I would never forget.*

"And I didn't want you to forget that to me you're the wind. Strong and powerful and dynamic."

I melted inside. "Violent, I think you said."

"I did." He laughed. "So, I showed my dad those pics Finger gave you. He loved them."

"Finger said he met Isi too."

"No kidding."

"Those images and the emotions they're stirring have been inspiring a lot of ideas for me."

"Good! Go with it."

"I am. Beck, thank you. If it wasn't for you, Finger wouldn't have known, and I would never have seen these photos, let alone have them in my collection. He got me the damn negatives, would you believe?"

"I do believe. That's Finger. I'm glad."

"How's Jude doing?"

"Better. The doctor is looking at Lyme's disease. It seems to fit the pattern of his exhaustion."

"Wow."

"Myles, Zack, and I are going to see each other at the studio today. Everyone wants to meet my fiancée."

My fiancée.

My pulse skipped a beat. I liked the sound of that when Beck said it. In that velvety voice, a curl of heat around the word "my." All delicately wrapped in a cheeky tone. He was teasing me. Teasing, not pushing me to be his real fiancée and set a wedding date.

Unlike every other man I'd ever gotten involved with, he wasn't spitting out annoyance and irritation, dishing out demands and ultimatums because I wasn't toeing his line. And I had no urge to retort with distracting sass. None at all.

Down deep, I knew that Beck meant what he said. It was his truth and I could trust that, rely on it.

Something curled inside me. Sweet heat. "Beck?"

"Yeah?" He stretched out on his bed.

"I miss you."

"Baby." Those blue green eyes gleamed at me, and that heat curled deep, deep inside.

CHAPTER ELEVEN

VIOLET

"WHY ARE WE DOING THIS?"

Dad charged ahead of me toward the Meager Grand. We'd gotten back to Meager from a small farm in the next town over that Dad would be listing for sale. I'd taken photos to upload on the company website.

But first, lunch. And Dad had decided that today we would eat at the Meager Grand.

His hand smoothed down his shirtfront. "Because I want to see my wife. I miss her."

"Do you now?"

"I do. And I thought it would be nice to have lunch with my daughter at the best restaurant in town."

"It's not a restaurant. It's a coffee house that has a brunch and dessert menu."

He stopped and pivoted toward me. "And I would very much like to enjoy that *brunch*. May I, Violet?"

I held the door of the Grand open for him. "Right this way, Mr. Hildebrand."

Dad headed for the counter where Mom was speaking with a customer. I headed for a table with two comfy easy chairs with a full view of Clay Street from the big bay window.

My phone rang. "Uncle Mad?"

"Hey, Violet. I was trying to call your dad, but his line's been busy, and I didn't want to leave a voicemail, so I thought I'd give you a try."

"Glad you did. We were in Pine Needle on business, and now we're at the Grand for a bite. What's up?"

"I just got back from the upper pasture, and I spotted Ladd out on the Frick."

My back shot up straight. "You did?"

"Yeah. He was with this older man who was in a suit and tie. Dark hair with lots of gray and a goatee. He was obviously showing him the land, pointing, gesturing, the two of them discussing."

"You're sure it was Ladd?"

"I'm sure, honey. I looked through my rifle lens. It was Ladd. Struck me as odd. I don't know why, just did."

"Thanks for letting me know, Uncle Mad. I'll tell Dad."

"Sure, hon."

Dad came to the table, placed his briefcase on the floor by his chair and took his seat.

"How did it go, Romeo?"

"I ordered for you."

"Oh goodie."

He shot me a sour look.

"Uncle Maddox just called me. He spotted Ladd this morning surveying the Frick with some mystery man in a goatee and suit."

Dad's brow furrowed. "Ladd hasn't come to the office, nor has he been taking my calls since all this engagement bullshit—"

"And the you and Anna screwing bullshit."

Dad's attention was on his cell phone.

"Here are your coffees." Shelby placed our iced coffees on the table.

"Thanks, Shelby."

"You bet, Mr. Hildebrand. Your food will be right out." Shelby shot me a strained smile, tilting her head toward the kitchen as she swept away from our table. No doubt, she wanted the tea on my engagement(s).

I leaned back in my cushioned seat and took in the view of Clay Street from the long bank of windows. A black Cadillac Escalade came to a rolling halt. The front passenger door opened, and a young man in a navy suit jumped out and briskly entered the coffee house. He was on a mission.

The Escalade was massive and very shiny, except for the sides and tires of the car, which betrayed a recent drive through mud and dirt.

A prickle raced over the back of my neck. "Dad." He met my gaze, and I tilted my head toward the front sidewalk where the SUV idled. "Rather fancy and a tad dirty. Recently dirty."

The side of his cheek ticked. "Colorado plates." He got up from the table, and tracked out the door of the Grand.

"Dad!"

What the—

I followed him to the Escalade, my pulse hammering in my neck. Dad tapped on the glass of the back passenger door, and the window slid down silently. In the back seat, Ladd sat with a very handsome older man with a grey speckled goatee. Armand Castillo, Anna Jeffries's silver fox billionaire boyfriend.

"Marshall," said Ladd. "You know Armand."

Dad ignored Ladd. "Armand, good to see you."

"Hello, Marshall. We stopped to try the coffee. I hear your wife owns this place and it's very good."

"She does, yes, and it is very good."

Ladd tossed me an emotionless glance from his Cadillac throne.

"We've missed you at the office," Dad said to Ladd.

"I've been busy with Armand."

"I stopped by to pick up Anna on my way to Chicago," said Armand. "Ladd is showing me the Black Hills. Very picturesque."

"Excuse me a moment." Ladd got out of the car, brushed past Dad, adjusting his jacket, and made a beeline for me.

"Taking Mr. Castillo on a tour?" I asked.

A smile erupted on his face, his dimples in full glory. "I thought you'd be with your boy toy fiancée. The public humiliation I've been enduring—first that slutty sex pic on social media, and now this engagement cock-up—"

"That's your cock-up. And, to confirm, you and I as a couple are over."

"Thank fuck," he said. So brightly, so smoothly, as if we were talking about the weather.

I slanted my head toward Armand. "I assume your mother has finally accepted that she and my dad were a momentary cock-up?"

"I'll admit, she did have a schoolgirl crush on Marshall, but I fixed that." He dug into his jacket's inside pocket and presented me with a gold cufflink, the letters MH engraved on it. I grit my teeth. Dad's cufflink.

I shoved it in my jean's pocket. "You fixed that, huh?"

"I did. I invited Armand to come out for a visit, and he and Mom had a very, very warm reunion."

"Sounds spicy."

His lips twisted. "She's going with him tonight to Chicago for a few weeks. You women always need steady dick or you wither."

I let out a dry laugh and clamped my jaw shut. Now was not the time to engage, and he was certainly pushing all my buttons, and the shithead knew it.

"I have a question for you, Ladd. Suddenly, I'm curious. Were you and I only about Powder Ridge? Was it only business between us for you?"

"Wasn't it?" His lips twitched, and he leaned in closer on a chuckle. "I did like you for a while there. We had our laughs. You were a good fuck. It was fun."

This was Ladd's definition of our "relationship." Probably

any relationship. Convenient, suited his purposes. A transaction for his benefit. Entertaining for a spell. How had I ever—

Be honest, Violet.

This had been my usual fare for years now by choice. Ever since Five's death. *Target, have fun, get what you can, get out. Next.*

Ladd's assessment of us was the goddamn truth. I took a step back from the sharp smell of it. Everything felt different now. Smelled different. I was different.

My pulse quickened as my gaze went to my cowboy boots. The colors, the textures of Ladd's words, his tone, his stance, all of it so very unattractive, distasteful. I'd been ruined, and in the best possible way.

"The auction is in two weeks." A tight grin shifted over Ladd's face.

"I'm looking forward to it. New beginnings for all of us."

"Yes, exactly."

I shifted my weight at the zest in his tone. "And what about Whisperwind?"

Ladd shot me a smirk. "What about it?"

Armand's assistant brushed past me, juggling a bag of food and four extra large coffees in a cardboard holder. Ladd darted to the vehicle, opening the door for him. He said goodbye to Dad, gave me a cool nod, and climbed into the luxe SUV. The heavy door slammed shut. Final. Ominous.

A shadow settled over me as the vehicle took off down Clay and disappeared around the curve. I didn't like this.

I handed Dad his errant cufflink, and his fingers curled over the gold, forming a fist.

CHAPTER TWELVE

BECK

"HEY MAN," I greeted Myles in the lobby of The Shed, a top recording studio in Los Angeles. He'd texted me last night to meet up early in the lobby.

He shifted his sunglasses over his head. "I have something for you." He handed me a shopping bag.

"What's this?" I opened the bag. My brown leather boots that Lisa had stolen. "Are you kidding me?"

"No."

"You didn't have to—"

"Oh yes, I did." His grin deepened into something dark. "And I had a good time doin' it."

"I won't ask."

"Don't ask."

"I appreciate this."

"I want to wipe the slate clean."

"Me too."

We tagged hands.

"We here to create greatness, gentlemen?" Greg, our sound engineer, brushed past through security.

"You bet." Zack flung himself at me and Myles, throwing his arms around us.

Going through security, we all followed Greg inside and down a dark corridor to the studio.

Memories of the last time we were here, which was the first time, came rushing back to me with the smell of the freshly polished glossy floors of the hallways.

That day we'd been impressed with our surroundings, impressed with ourselves, nervous, excited, ready to take on the music world. Now, all of us were sort of jaded. One of us was in the hospital, one on cruise control, and the other two licking their wounds.

We set up.

Myles played us one of his new melodies. I listened, blew out a few chords. Zack's drums beat out underneath, veered off. We stopped, we talked, we started. I tried a new fragment.

We got frustrated.

Without Jude's bass interrupting, offering a new direction. An offbeat, subversive we-hadn't-considered-that direction. Without his positive energy which fueled us like high battery power. It all felt rough. Patchy.

But we had to do this. For Jude if nothing else. To give him something to look forward to, hold onto. Who was I kidding? We all needed that.

Enough "without." Time to focus on what the three of us had.

We started again, me on my acoustic guitar taking the melody somewhere different, Myles listening, diving in with his lyrics, changing them up to fit the chords, adding an unexpected kink in a lyric that needed a different tempo. He took notes on his changes. And again, and again, until something more specific flickered in our darkness. Something of interest. Something that intrigued all of us. We could hear it.

Breaking for food, we headed outside for fresh air. One of the assistant sound engineers and Zack shared a lighter over cigarettes outside. Zack shook his head at him, took a few steps back and walked away from him.

"What was that about?" I asked.

His jaw jutted out. "Dude asked me if I needed any blow or X. Fuck, remember how impressed we were with that convenient access the first time we were here?"

"Yeah, I remember. That accounted for Jude wanting to keep playing well past our bedtime."

"And look at us now." Zack ambled off back into our studio.

"Hey, Beck, how's things? Great to see you guys back in again." The sound engineer leaned back against the brick wall, sucking on his cigarette.

"Great to be back." I followed Zack back inside.

Was it? Was it really?

CHAPTER THIRTEEN

BECK

THE LIMO PULLED up at the crowded bar, and I let out a deep breath, my sweaty palms brushing down my black trousers. It did nothing to ease my rattled insides. Myles and Zack grunted as the chauffeur came to a sharp stop behind another limo at the curb.

Behind the velvet ropes, a mass of photographers leaned over to get the best shot, shouting out to the celebrities in front of us exiting their vehicle to enter the party. The entrance to Verity, a new restaurant and bar which was holding a party for the release of the band Hard Up's new album was packed with PR people and security. Hard Up was part of the same record company as we were.

"Remember"—Ford's gaze went to each of us—"you don't have to stay long. You only need to make an appearance. A positive one."

"Jesus, man, we really don't need a babysitter, you know?" Myles snapped as he took in the crowd through the darkened windows.

He was nervous, and I got it.

"No, you don't need a babysitter. I wanted us to do this together. I like hanging out with you guys. And here comes the pep talk: This is an opportunity for you to show unity, harmony, and how psyched you are to work on the new album—if that subject comes up, and it probably will. As will the subject of Jude. When we get of the car, don't answer any questions they lob at you. Just grin, stand together, let them get their pics, and we go inside."

Our door was opened and a sudden roar of noise invaded the limo. "Let's do this." Zack exited the vehicle to a thousand flashing lights, and we followed, waving, grins on our faces, standing together.

Inside, we wandered around the dark, high ceilinged restaurant filled with people and loud music. Ford got involved in a conversation with several record company execs, and we kept to ourselves.

"Beck, hi!" Astra stood in front of me wearing a dazzling gold dress with a long black gossamer cape over it.

"Hey, Astra, good to see you."

"With clothes on, right?" She giggled.

I let out a laugh. "That was a little awkward at first."

She moved in closer to me. "I hope there's no—"

The music blared up around us and we both winced. I leaned into her. "No worries on my end. I have no issues with you and my dad doing whatever…that's up to him and you."

"I don't want it to ruin our friendship."

"Me either. I'm cool with it. Seriously. How's the album going?"

"Final touches are happening now and I'm so excited. How about you?"

"We got back into the studio yesterday."

"Terrific! And so it begins. All the best with it." She squeezed my arm. "I mean it."

"Thanks. Good to see you."

"Good to see you too." She disappeared into the crowd.

I spotted Zack and Myles with Naomi and two of her assistants at a table, and I joined them. A couple of girls we knew from our video shoot production teams passed by and we caught up.

The artistically laid out finger food was plentiful as were the colorful cocktails that were brought to our table. Hard Up made a quick speech, thanking us for coming, and their latest single flared over the speakers again. Zack got up and danced with one of Naomi's assistants. Myles had some girl I didn't recognize in his lap, and they were laughing.

"Need another drink?"

I stiffened at the sound of that voice. Mae.

She placed a cocktail in front of me and slid on to the leather sofa next to me. Her perfume, that once familiar smoky-sweet scent slammed into me and my back straightened. "I got you a seven and seven." She moved the glass closer to me.

"I don't drink those anymore."

"Okay. Don't drink it." A smirk overtook her glittery purple lips. "How are you?"

"Are we really doing this now?"

"Why not?"

"Is this your way of handling the negative press you got for what you did? Are you going to say something funny, so maybe I'll crack a smile, and someone will take a pic of that, and it'll get posted, proving to the world that all's good and we're pals now?"

"Bitter."

"What did you expect?"

"I am sorry that I didn't talk to you first. But I was in a situation and—"

"You were fucking Petra behind my back."

"Behind your back? We had an agreement."

"We had an agreement that you would communicate what you were doing. Communicate to me, not your fans."

"This was a clusterfuck." Her tongue swiped her upper lip. She was carefully forming her words. "It got out and I wanted to be the one who released that news, be up front about it. Me, not some gossip site, so I had to do it fast. I tried calling you that night, but your phone was off."

"I was prepping to go onstage, last concert of the tour. Remember that? I saw the post on someone's phone just before going out on stage. Just after the whole world did."

"Oh."

"Oh. It was fantastic."

"Wow, you're upset?"

"I was upset by the way you handled it. That sucked, and I deserved better from you. I thought you were all about honesty?"

"I am. The timing was really bad. I was going to tell you that week, when you got off the tour, because—"

"'Cause you already had plans to go to Europe with her?"

Her cat eyes held mine as she drank. "I hear you've got yourself a new woman."

I didn't say anything.

She inched in closer to me. "It doesn't have to stop, you and me. You know how I roll. We can still… Does your girl know? Would she—"

"Mae—*I'm* not into it. I'm in a committed relationship now, and you know what? I love it. I guess I have your clusterfuck to thank for that, because it made me realize that your scene doesn't do it for me."

Her gaze flitted down my open shirt to where Violet's wind charm hung from the leather cord. "A *monogamous* committed relationship?"

"Monogamous. I'm in love with her."

"Oh. Okay." That surreptitious smile of hers curled her lips. In that moment, me and Mae charged through my memory. From that first time we'd met at her house and she'd kissed me in her walk-in-closet and took off her clothes and mine before I realized what was happening, through all the booty calls, the playing guitar together, working on songs together, talking music, going to parties and clubs together.

That mutual understanding we'd shared had been freeing to me, a liberty when I'd felt boxed in under the glare of the spotlight—my own spotlight in addition to the son-of-Cruel-Fate's-Eric-Lanier spotlight.

Mae was in my world and understood everything I was going through—the emotional highs and the lows, the frustrations and the wins, the insane schedule—without me having to explain or make excuses.

There had been no pressure of expectations and no defining what we were. We were two consenting adults enjoying our time together. The public had turned us into #CoupleGoals and we'd went with it, hadn't we?

The public didn't know that Mae was into polyamory and had two other relationships going on at the same time as ours. As long as we used condoms, I hadn't given much of a crap either way. It's what worked for her, and I thought it was cool. Why did we all have to adhere to society's "principles" in our personal relationships? We weren't all made the same way, were we?

Petra had been my stylist and we'd known each other for a while. I'd introduced her to Mae. But from the second I'd read Mae's Instagram post about the two of them, seen the photos, something had snapped. Snapped like a cable that held an astronaut secure to his spaceship. Now, I was spinning in an unknown galaxy.

Knowing that Petra was one of Mae's partners had shifted everything from a delightful haze, suddenly everything was in sharp focus. A gritty black and white. Suddenly, I didn't like being one of many when convenient. Suddenly it was all a game, a pretense. And I was reeling.

I didn't know who her two other partners were, and I'd never cared to know. I never gave it much thought, and we didn't discuss them. At the time, I only went with what felt good, and it was cool and easy. Plus, I'd felt like I'd won the jackpot, and everyone told me I had—the guys, the public, the fans, Dad. I'd kicked my legs up and eased back in my La-Z-Boy.

Sitting with Mae now, smelling that odd tobacco and rose perfume of hers again, I realized I'd never gotten to know her, know her to her bones, nor had I let her know me. Not like the way it was with me and Violet.

With Violet it was an immediate intense rush on all levels that I was open to. Violet didn't fill gaps. She embraced me whole and hugged hard. She held on.

And so did I.

That's what I needed.

That's what I wanted.

Violet had burst inside me and taken root, whipped through me, pushing new air into my lungs, new sap in my veins. And now everything was different, and I wanted different things. Real things.

Mae clinked her glass with the one she'd set before me and I blinked, meeting her amused gaze. "Congratulations on your engagement. Is Violet here tonight?" She put a hand on my arm. "Do you want me to leave? I don't want to make things awkward."

I shifted my gaze away from her smirk. That smirk that I used to like. Girl next door quirky, hints of playful dirty. "No, she's not here, but I'd like you to leave anyhow."

She let out a hissing noise and sat up straighter. "Wow. Alrighty then." Was she waiting for me to say I was joking? To stay? She was. No one ever said no to Mae Sullivan, did they?

I pushed the drink away from me, and grabbed the beer bottle I'd been nursing. She got up from the table, glass in hand, waited a moment, and strut back into the crowd.

Myles sent his girl off. He leaned into me. "You okay, man?"

"Better than okay." I drained my beer.

He thumped me on the back. Ford brought over a journalist from a European online music magazine just as Zack returned to our table. We had a breezy and quick q and a session and said our goodbyes.

"Can we leave now? I need a fucking cigarette." Zack slapped his chest pocket where his pack was tucked.

Myles gestured to the girl he'd had in his lap earlier, and she trotted back over to him with a huge grin on her face. He slung his arm around her, and her face lit up. "Let's get the fuck out of here."

I pushed back from the table and got up. "Let's get the fuck far, far away."

CHAPTER FOURTEEN

@JUST JANA

COUPLE NEWS!

Reuniting and it feels so good?

At a recent party given by Panic Records for rock band Heavy Duty's latest release, former couple Beck Lanier and Mae Sullivan were reunited.

Partygoers were pleased and surprised to see this former hot couple of rock and roll having an intense *tête-à-tête* at a table to themselves.

<See the Gallery of photos of this hot duo HERE>

They had lots of catching up to do. Did absence make their hearts grow fonder … and hotter?

Judging from these pics, sparks were definitely flying.

At the party, there was no sign of Freefall guitarist Lanier's alleged fiancée, photographer Violet Hildebrand. Is there trouble in paradise? Or was that just a vacation fling that ran its course?

Nothing has been confirmed as of this time.

Beck was also spotted all cozy with R&B artist Astra Picket. Don't these two talented hot young musicians look amazing together? We think so! *<Click to see the photos of Beck and Astra flirting at the party HERE>*

Follow our stories for updates on this story and many, many more.

#Follow #Like #LinkInBio #JustJana #becklanier #MaeBeck #maesullivan #hotcouples #reunion #ViBeck #allthesexxxy #allthenews #couplenews #AstraPicket

CHAPTER FIFTEEN

VIOLET

"WE'RE all set for the auction." I closed my folder and slid it onto Jessa's desk at H&H.

She leaned back in her chair and leafed through her large sketchbook of ideas for Powder Ridge. "My first real project is about to begin. These sketches are so different from the final ones we decided on with the architect. Funny, huh?"

My gaze went to her computer screen, where she'd brought up a draft of the architect's designs for the golf course lodge. "That's how it usually goes. You have a first idea, but the more you get in there, the more you learn about your subject, get your feels on…everything changes like malleable clay. You change it, and I think a piece of you changes too."

Jessa smiled at me. "What about you?"

"What do you mean?"

"Are you looking for work?"

"Damn, Jess, you just got back and you're trying to get rid of me already?" I hopped down from her desk.

She shut her sketchbook and sat up in her chair. "That's not what I meant, and you know it. I meant your photography. Now things here are on track, and I can't thank you enough for picking up my slack while I was in Europe."

"I'm glad you went, and I was glad to do it. I needed to. I'm proud of the work Dad and I accomplished together. I want this for him."

Her lips pressed together. "Me too."

"Anyhow, Europe was good for you." I waggled my eyebrows.

"Will you ever stop?"

"Hmm…no."

"Says the girl with two fiances?"

"Ooooo. Checkmate and draw, girl. However, that was just for one day." I shrugged, laughing.

"I thought the plan was that after the auction you would be devoting yourself full-time to your photography?"

"That was the plan."

"You got to do all that new and exciting work in Greece, which is amazing, so you're in an even better position now than ever, right?"

I nodded, putting the files I'd been organizing back in their pile on my desk. She took hold of my arm, turning me to face her. "Violet, you don't have to stay here. You don't."

"Mom and Dad are a mess right now, I—"

"That's their mess." She held my gaze with her luminous green eyes. "It's been ten years. Ten. Years."

That tightness grabbed my throat like it always did. "Stop."

"No, not on this. You need to—" Jessa's phone rang, her eyes went to her screen and narrowed.

"Who is it?"

"Unknown caller. I don't answer those calls."

"Could it be your lover boy tracked you down?"

"There's no way."

"Go on, answer it. Be adventurous. It could be destiny calling."

She rolled her eyes at me and hit the button on her screen. "Hello…yes? I'm Jessa Hildebrand … That's right." Her serious gaze flicked up at me. "Yes … Right ... I am, that's correct …

Really? Oh. That certainly would be quite a job. And the budget?" Her eyes went round and big.

"I see. Yes, yes, it is. It's quite an old house, there may be structural issues, electrical, plumbing … Oh. Okay. Yes, I do know a very good architect." Her eyes flared once again. She'd heard astounding news.

Jessa cleared her throat, a hand gripping the edge of her desk. "I certainly appreciate the offer. I work from the offices of Hildebrand & Hildebrand in Meager. 103 Clay Street, 2nd floor. Yes, that's it. Okay then. I look forward to receiving the paperwork. Thank you, Mr. Daniels. Yes, I'll call you soon. Goodbye." She clicked off her phone, squeezing it between her hands, her jaw tight, staring at me.

"What is it?"

"You are a witch."

"Me?"

"Destiny called. It was the lawyer representing the new owner of Whisperwind. He wants to hire me to spearhead the renovation of the house and design the interior."

"Really?"

"Really."

Stunned, the two of us.

"I'm sorry, Violet. I should have asked about Ladd, but I was so surprised. I'll call him back and tell him no. This must be some sick joke of his, right? He's twisting the knife some more?"

"No, no, wait. This means he's not going to rip it down, right?"

"Right."

"That's good news. Maybe he wants to fix it and flip it, make a buck."

"I suppose."

"You have to do it. You, a Dillon, will be the one bringing it back to life in today's world, making it beautiful again and in a new way. We always said you'd do it. There. Dream came true."

Her head dipped. "But…we were going to do it together."

My jaw trembled, a slight thing, but it was there. I took in a breath. "You have to do it, Jessa. Plus, you need something fun other than Powder Ridge and Dad and Ladd hanging over you. It'll be your own project, and a perfect opportunity to build your business, your brand, doing what you love the most."

"You're sure?"

"I'm positive."

"He'll probably sell it at twice the price."

"Give it your best, top of the line all the way."

A small smile fluttered along her lips.

My breath burned in my chest.

"He said he wants to start immediately."

"Get sketching, woman."

My phone beeped with a text. Sara. I could definitely use a girl's night out. A mid-morning cocktail would be even better. I clicked.

"V- I don't believe this shit at all. But you should be aware. Love U"

Now what?

I tapped on the link to a Just Jana post on Instagram.

Mae and Beck breathing on each other's faces overwhelmed my screen.

My pulse skidded, my mouth dropped open, oxygen suddenly a rare commodity. Mae and Beck cozy with drinks at a party. Her tongue lashing her lower lip as she gazed at him like one of Dracula's thirsty vampire maidens.

Mae and Beck together again. Rock's hot couple.

The floor wobbled underneath me, and I ground my boots into the wood grain. He had one of his dark, broody unreadable looks on his face. His generous lips in a firm line, unsmiling.

Lips that I knew very well.

Lips that my body knew very well.

Lips that were once mine.

Mine.

No.

I read the stupid post. *Did absence make their hearts grow fonder? Reuniting and it feels so good?* The snarky, cutesy tone stung like a poisoned arrow. Not one. A hundred poisoned arrows rained over me, a dark cloud of them descended and pierced my flesh as I swiped through the fucking photo gallery of their intimate *tête-à-fucking-tête* at a Hollywood restaurant.

The fucking hashtags hit their mark but with different arrows.

#AllTheSexxy

#HotCouples

#HotNights

#PartyTime

#Celebs

#Reunion

#MaeBeck

MaeBeck...that had been their moniker when they were all the couple goals once upon a time. Sour rose up my throat.

"What the heck is it? What's wrong?" Jess came up alongside me. "O-oh."

"A whole gallery of photos of their intimate time together at a music industry party."

"Violet, don't."

"Mr. I-can't-lose-you. Mr. I-want-you-in-my-life-we-can-make-this-work-long-distance-is-nothing ..." I swiped and swiped and swiped.

"How many photos are there, for crap's sake?" Jessa shifted her weight.

"Twenty-seven, it says." I swiped to the end. Endless shots of them tilting their heads at each other. Beck dressed in black, his shirt open, revealing his perfect chest adorned with his beaded necklaces AND MY WIND CHARM.

My heart stuttered in my chest. He still wore it, and he wore it that night. The last shot was of Mae laughing at something he said, only he wasn't laughing.

"And if we needed reminding, here's a gallery of photos chronicling Beck and Mae's entire relationship, so we can put it all into proper context."

"Is that Astra Picket?"

"Yes, it is. Yes, Jana, they do look good together." My chest hurt. My eyes, my stomach. I tossed my phone on Dad's desk.

"These gossip sites print whatever they want to attract viewers. They make suggestive assumptions all the time. That's what it's all about, grabbing people's attention as they scroll through."

"Twenty-seven pictures don't lie, Jessa."

"Oh come on, some paparazzi just shot a ton and posted them all. They just broke up, so it still sells. They saw each other at a party and talked. Violet, I don't even know Beck, but it doesn't look to me like he's enjoying himself."

"It was bound to happen, wasn't it?"

"Bumping into each other at an industry party? Yeah, of course. So what?"

"What do you mean so what? I'd told him long distance wouldn't work, but he kept insisting."

"Did he? That's terrific." A grin lit up her face.

"Long distance with a guy who half the world wants to jump. With a guy who could have any girl he wants with just a glance, a snap of his fingers. Who's always on the road."

"Slow down. Don't spin this into a drama in your head just yet. That's too easy to do. Talk to him about this. I'll bet he's not thrilled."

"He can do what he wants. He obviously is." The desks, the chairs, the laptops, the desktops, my framed photographs of buffalo on the prairie, the wild mustangs galloping over a valley all moved closer to me. Closer. Closer. I couldn't breathe.

I grabbed my phone. My bag.

"Where are you going? You're upset—Violet! Wait! Let me come with you."

"No, no, you have a job to do, and you need to get started. You don't want to disappoint your new client. I have to get the hell out of here."

CHAPTER SIXTEEN

BECK

I STRODE into the house and went straight to the fridge, grabbed the bottle of coconut water, and gulped. All of it.

"What's wrong?" Dad's voice had me turning around toward the living room. He lounged on the huge sectional sofa with earphones around his neck. "Something happen at the studio?"

"It's that shitty beginning time where things are rough, where you can't feel it or hear it yet. We're all a little uptight without Jude. It's just not flowing, it's ... not good." I tossed the empty container into the recycling bin.

"Don't label it yet. Don't do that. It's a process, you know it is. It's never the same experience each time. Did you think it'd be easier this time around since you're all such hot shit?"

"Maybe." I crossed my arms around my chest, my gaze going to the backyard where Jude was practicing meditation with Dad's life coach, Ed. "How's that going?"

"Good. Jude's all up in it so far. Tell me more about your sessions."

"We've had a few good ideas. A lot of fragments. But there's no...connection yet."

"How many days have you been at it?"

"Three."

"And without Jude. Ease up."

"And then today, we were actually onto something and suddenly Myles says "dudes, I got to leave in an hour and a half, I have this dinner thing I have to go to."

"Uh-huh. Like you all had to go to that party last night?"

"Exactly. So he says that and we try to get back into the zone we were in, but it was impossible, because suddenly the clock was ticking over us, and basically Myles had checked out, and it became a struggle, and then…fuck it. We lost it. Tomorrow Zack has some photo shoot Naomi set up for him. So it's gonna be another suck ass session."

"Come here." Dad took off his headphones and went to the tape deck. "I want you to listen to this."

"Dad, really, I'm not in the mood right now for Astra—"

"It's not Astra. It's a blast from the past. Listen." He hit a button and a woman's dark, smoky laughter filled the room. A lopsided grin cut across his face. His eyes lit up.

"Eric! I liked that. Ooooh, that was good."

"You did?"

"Yes, yes! Play it again. This time, try it slower, okay?"

Guitar chords burst forth, and Dad bobbed his head in time with his past self.

"Again," the woman said.

"I can be strong
Won't be long"

Her singing flared over his chords, and my spine stiffened to attention. My blood backed up in my veins, flooding me in a hot rush. Earthy, sexy, confident. Dad's vocals joined hers in a beautiful harmony.

Her lyrics about missing her lover, yet hanging on stung. My eyes shut. The sting of leaving Violet at JFK seeped through me.

I made my way deeper into the living room and we listened side by side. Dad winked at me, lifting his chin. "It's me and Isi."

Isi, the singer for Dad's band in their early days in South Dakota. Isi, Violet's second cousin, who'd had an untimely end.

Dad put a hand on my shoulder as we listened to the two of them discussing and singing together, playing chords for one another, working out beats. Laughing. She sang, trying different lyrics as Dad played on. They backtracked, they kept pushing forward. He stopped the tape, and I blinked.

"After you and I'd talked about her, I hunted around for this." He pointed to the cassette tape in the deck. She'd given it to me to work out a few riffs. And then she was gone. I hung onto it. Maybe I should've given it to her family, but I wanted to hold onto a piece of her." His index finger knocked at the desk. "Of this."

"I like this song."

"Me too. She'd come up with these lyrics and was desperate to put a melody to it right away. She wanted it for her boyfriend. He'd come for a visit—it was freaking Valentine's Day, and we were on the road. That was one crazy night among many.

"We'd done a show that went south—where were we? In the boonies somewhere. Oh yeah, Nebraska. We partied at the motel, some chicks showed up, then a bunch of local bikers showed up. It was a scene and quickly became a mess. Of course, she decided to get us out of the mess. Then her old man who was from another motorcycle club showed up…"

"A total scene."

"Next day, she was on fire to put this in shape. I haven't thought of all that in a long, long time. And I have you and your Violet to thank."

"Good times, huh?"

"They were, Beck. They were."

"Was the melody yours or hers?"

"Mostly mine, but the lyrics are all her. I may have adjusted a couple. You know how it is when you write with someone else."

"Sure."

"You don't sound too sure." He drank from a bottle of Fiji water.

"Working without Jude is different."

"Different is good, for all of you. That's how you grow, get better." He let out a heavy sigh, a hand scrubbing down his face. "I'd promised Isi I'd help her finish the song. She'd been so excited about this one, and I was too. But we didn't get the chance to finish it 'cause she got killed.

"We'd been on our way over to Michigan for some festival. An important one, we were really psyched. Record company execs would be there—we'd developed a minor reputation by that time. It was all good, all of it. Even when we scraped together money for gas or beers or had a shitty audience like that night in Nebraska, it was still good. We were hanging on. And then fucking boom. It was all over."

"Could I work on this song?"

"You like it that much?"

"I do."

A grin swept his features. "Me and Isi get billing."

"Of course."

He popped the tape out of the deck, tucked it in it's box and handed it to me. Smudged blue ink writing lay on the sticker on the cassette. My pulse thudded in my neck. The plastic box was light, but the weight of the world was in my hand.

"I'm all nostalgic now. I'm going to call Longhat, see how's he doing." Dad's drummer from his band, Stewart Longhat. "That day, Isi had taken off without telling us to go find her brother who was on the run from the law and a bunch of drug dealers. It was a mess. She was frantic about him. Anyhow, she'd left her stuff behind, and after, Stewart was the one who'd packed it all up and brought it back to her family in Meager—her clothes, her guitar. They were close. That was a rough time for him."

My eyes filled with water, my throat burned. A low noise escaped my throat. So much loss.

"Beck? Hey, what's going on?" Dad's voice was gentle, his hands on me.

"You lost Isi…You lost Dave…"

"Son—" His hands dug into the sides of my face, and he raised my head, his intense gaze boring into mine. "You're worried about losing Jude?"

Losing Jude, losing Violet…

Sucking in a breath, my gaze darted outside at Jude cross legged on a mat inner listening. "Today at The Shed, all those same assholes were there, humming in the background. They offered me and Myles coke to get over our late afternoon slump. Myles and I both knew better than to make a big deal out of it, but we were both thinking the same thing: how's Jude going to come back to this? How? Yeah, sure, I know there are plenty of musicians who would kill to have studio time at The Shed. I know how lucky we are, to get in there, to afford it—"

"Shed or no Shed, if it's not working for you psychologically, emotionally, it's not good for you. And what you described before, Myles having a dinner thing to get to? This is L.A., one of you will always have "a thing" to go to. Something glittery yanking on you, that you need to do to keep the glitter up. This town caters to your demons with a smile, and when you're trying to get the deep work done…"

"I guess I got to suck it up."

"Maybe you all could do with a serving of rough and raw."

"Rough and raw?"

"Somewhere out of your usual habitat. I don't know if the guys will be up for it."

"You have something in mind?"

"Stewart's place in South Dakota. He has a ranch with a studio. He works with people off and on when he's in the mood and when he needs to make some cash."

"Hadn't he quit the band at one point?"

"Isi dying wiped him out. He couldn't function, let alone play. Then his Dad got sick and he went back to the reservation to help him out and he started drinking too much. But less than a year later, our replacement drummer, Teddy, quit 'cause his girlfriend got pregnant with twins, and I got Stewart back."

"And the rest is Cruel Fate history."

"That's right. Stewart was smart. He got sober, saved his money, and bought his own property in the Black Hills, a small ranch. He built a recording studio there, and a lot of different artists have gone out there to work with him—some country cross over types, instrumentalists, solo artists, folk artists. It's nothing fancy like you're used to, but he gets the job done, and he's got an amazing ear. He teaches music to kids from the reservation and brings kids out to ride at his place, too. He's a quirky motherfucker, you either like him or you don't. And he either likes you or he doesn't."

"Do you know where the ranch is, exactly?"

"Is it close to Violet, you mean? It's outside of Sturgis somewhere. So, yeah, it's close to Meager. Or was it your mommy you wanted to—"

"Dad." We laughed.

"I think this is a solid idea. If you guys were to go there to work, you'd all be away from your usual distractions and temptations. No getting in your fancy ass cars and taking off for sushi and club hopping, or some party you got to be seen at, or to score women."

I let out a short breath. "That sounds like a huge relief right now. And it would be perfect for Jude when he's ready to join us."

Dad gestured at Ed and Jude outside. "You could hire Ed to come out too."

"Hell, I think we all need to be somewhere totally different... nature, fresh air, no fame noise, no bullshit distractions." I rubbed my hands over my scalp.

Dad's brow furrowed. Ed had taught me this rubbing my head coping mechanism to self-soothe when stress had hit me on our first tour. It had hit again today.

"Look at it this way—you could go to Stewart's to focus on getting material into shape, come up with a song list. Then you come back to The Shed for all the bells and whistles, and record the final version. See how it goes."

"Call him, Dad."

He smiled. "I will. He may be free now, maybe not. However"—he fingered Isi's cassette—"we have something that I'm positive Stewart would love to work on with you."

"Shit, that'd be awesome."

"It would be. You got my permission to use it. I guess you'll need Violet's or whoever…"

"I'll talk to her grandmother, Georgia, who was Isi's first cousin." I let out a heavy breath.

"What is it?"

"That party we had to go to the other night? Mae was there, she came over to chat—"

"Uh-huh."

"We talked for maybe forty-five seconds and a thousand photos were taken of this monumental moment and transmitted around the world."

"Astra mentioned it. Have you talked to Violet?"

"She's not answering my calls. A lot's going on for her now and she's in suspicious mode. Then again, I think I like that she's upset, ticked off. It means that I matter to her. That's how I'm choosing to look at this."

"You're serious about her."

"I am."

"I'm going to call Stewart right now. You need to get to South Dakota pronto, and in more ways than one."

CHAPTER SEVENTEEN

VIOLET

I CLICKED save on my composite and brought up another photo.

Beck deep in his guitar riffs early one morning by the pool at our hotel in Mykonos. His head bent, his fingers furiously darting over the frets, an other worldly look on his face. He was in his zone. Playing, creating, listening. How he listened, deeply, with everything, body and soul.

I removed a few spots in the foreground, played with the ambient lighting, refined the shadows over his hair, the line of his jaw, his guitar.

My breathing deepened. I missed him. A lot. I'd captured these perfect moments of him and us back in Greece when time had stopped for us.

Now it all had crumpled.

My phone beeped. A text message from Tag with three links. The videos were ready? I brought up his text on my laptop and clicked on the first. Tag's YouTube channel. The video titled "My Summer Vibes" played.

Tag careening through the air, the girls laughing, dancing around the pool in slow motion. All the water sports. My shots of Tag on the water board with Irina, the drone shots of everyone diving off Alessio's yacht. I laughed at the closeups of Gabrielle's perfect little peach of an ass.

The skydiving outside of Athens. Tag tumbling in the air like it was the most natural thing in the world. It was for him. He was in a state of bliss.

I hit the next link. Kaspar's channel on YouTube. His new music video was in premiere mode.

Sweeping shots of the sea, the rocky coastline. My shots of Kaspar and Tag in the pool, Irina and Tag kissing and swimming in the pool, the close ups of the orange soda which sponsored the video. Interspersed were shots of Tag, Kaspar, and Beck posing in those suits on the yacht. They jumped in the water, and it came off amusing and unexpected.

It all blended to Tag onstage at the concert on the island in front of the huge crowd, the lights sparkling in the island night, smoke and lights. Tag and Kaspar high-fiving each other, and Tag dancing onstage and leaping off into the crowd like a rockstar.

My shots of Beck playing with Andoni. His simple drum beat was primal wildfire all over again. Beck, oh Beck, folded over his guitar as he jammed on his chords, his head knocking back, his face illuminated in the spotlight, alive with the music they were creating, his body moving to the sound.

Kaspar hopped up and down at his boards, the wild boy and the wild crowd chanting, singing, throbbing. A grin spread from my lips to my insides.

I clicked the last link into another tab on a website for the jewelry line - *Savage Senses Jewelry - Tag x Alessio collaboration.*

Goosebumps flared over my skin as my shots in slow-mo of Irina and Gabriella swimming underwater in their tiny bikinis, the jewelry glimmering at their waists, necks, wrists. One caught up with Tag and they both circled each other and embraced. Lars had really brought up the light effects in editing. There was a gentle, erotic, otherworldly quality to it all.

My pieces of the girls on deck in their long see-through

gauzy tunics whipped by. Their airy sensuality was delicate yet vibrant all at once. Irina's angelic face was perfection—the innocent angel teasing and playful. She let loose a mischievous smile and then turned her head up to the sun. Holy shit, she was good.

The music was surprisingly haunting but simple, and the way Lars and Tag had edited all these pieces made for an evocative whole, a feeling, *that* feeling—the Tag vibe but here, it was elegant, sophisticated, not just quick and tumble in your face daring fun.

I eased back in my chair.

I could smell that salty sea air, feel that cool water on my skin. Be free, live wild, swim with Irina in that blue, blue water…*I'd done all of that, hadn't I? Me and Beck together.*

Tag wasn't selling bullshit. It had all been real. It was the treasure of possibilities and it was so real to me I could taste it all over again. A living, breathing, emotional postcard.

My teeth dragged over my lips as I scrolled down to the credits on each video. My name was included in the list of photographers, and I took in a deep breath.

I texted Tag:

They're SO GOOD. SO good. You and Lars are amazing.
THANK YOU!

The likes and views soared into the thousands on YouTube as Tag texted me back.

Namaste, Violet - Thank you ! 😀😀

Adrenaline surged through me. I'd done this. Me. And it was out in the world in a huge, crazy way. I'd been a part of a team that was focused on bringing a specific brand to the table and we'd done it. And now thousands of people were watching and enjoying it.

This is what it was all about, wasn't it? This is what it felt like. Abundance. I closed my eyes and breathed deep. And Beck had made it happen for me.

My phone rang. Beck. I bit my lip. I'd not answered his phone calls for long enough. "Beck?"

"Violet, finally. I've been trying to call you—"

"What's up?"

"You're mad at me."

I had been mad at him. Annoyed and jealous. But seeing all the footage from Greece, and seeing it all edited and beautifully packaged with music and....

Tag had given me one of his shoves and he didn't even know it. What timing that boy had.

I let out a breath. "I'm not mad. I was irritated, but not anymore."

"You weren't jealous?"

"Beck Lanier, watch what you say."

A warm laugh rolled over the line. "I miss you, Violet."

"Did you miss me when you were chatting with Mae?"

"I did. Very much. She came over and sat down, started talking like nothing major had happened. We had it out. She left.

"You don't owe me any explanations. We're fake engaged after all."

"Babe, she congratulated me on our engagement."

"So sweet." I smashed my lips together as I assessed the color saturation of the Aegean Sea on my photo on my screen. "Did you tell her it's fake?"

"Violet."

"You and Mae looked very attractive together. High life glam and all. It made an impression."

"So did you and Montana Guy when I first spotted you together. Super hot duo. All the couple goals."

My head knocked back and I roared with laughter. "Are you serious?"

"But you didn't want to be with him, did you, baby? Didn't even want to lick him."

"You got me there, lover boy."

A low, growly sound escaped him and a buzz shot through me. "See how powerful a good image can be, Ms. Hildebrand? A photographer once told me, it can make imagination reality."

"So true. And by the way, what's the deal with Ms. Astra Picket?

"Astra's sleeping with my dad."

"Oh my gosh, she's the one you saw him with?"

"Yep."

"Holy crap, what a visual…oh my, that's hot."

"Down girl. That's my dad." We both laughed.

My phone beeped a message. Flint, the guitarist from the Lunatics.

"Nice pic on IG, babe!
Did U see my comment??
R U still in Europe?
You only hanging with the big boys now?
Come out to Oregon!
We need you baddddd, beautiful!"

"Violet? Am I distracting you from a text message?" Beck's voice broke through.

"Oh, sorry. I just got a job offer from one of the bands I've shot here. They're in Oregon on a small tour and want me to come out and shoot."

"Oh. Nice. Their manager texted you?"

"They don't have a manager. I know the lead guitarist."

"You do, huh?"

"I learned early on that sleeping with the talent can get messy and stupid, and there are infinitely more important things to deal with on a shoot than getting off with the hot musician who flirted with me that night just to flirt. Top of that list of important things to deal with on a job is my reputation as a professional."

"Amen."

"They'd asked me to join them on tour a while ago, but I'd turned them down because I was committed to working with my dad until the auction. But now that Jessa is back and things are all set, I could do it."

"Is that what you want?"

My gaze settled on the paused video on my screen. Alessio on his yacht with his ultra sexy, dark and moody Roman features, his generous lips snarling, a silver necklace hanging from his mouth. Magnetizing, alluring, and my image.

"I want to work full-time as a photographer. That week in Greece opened that mental door wide open for me. I can't forget how it felt, how it tasted, and I don't think I ever will. Isn't that what you've been telling me to do, go for it all the way?

"Yes."

"Well, I've never been on a tour with a band before, and I've always wanted to. What interests me is getting the full-on experience of a band working it on the road. It's about time, isn't it?"

"But it would be a mistake for you to keep being free-for-hire-Violet. You're beyond that now, you shouldn't go back because—"

"Is that the issue? The money? Or is it that now the tables would be turned, and you don't like it? I'd be doing the long distance, the on the road rockstar life—"

"Yeah, maybe. But you know what I really don't like? Being fake engaged to you. Because what we have is not fake. It's very real and very beautiful. Fuck engagements and labels. Everyone wants a label to make it easier to skewer us all over their own map and pick at us, and I gave it them. As far as I'm concerned, we are together with a capital fucking T."

Determined words, a challenge that punched through the drum of my chest and fisted in my heart. "Them's fightin' words, Lanier."

"Oh no, no, no, baby. I'm not a fighter, I'm a lover. Your lover. Although, I will fight for you if I'm pushed."

Heat shuddered over my flesh, and an animal-like sound escaped my lips before I could bite it back. "Beck…"

"I'm yours, baby. Only yours. All yours."

My eyes closed as his simmering voice smoldered through me.

"Is going on that tour what you really want right now? 'Cause if it is, you should do it, but for some kind of money, because you're worth it."

"Honestly, it really isn't what I want right now. I've started working on a new idea, and I want to stay in Meager to focus on it rather than go on some long ass no frills road trip for pennies."

"I look forward to hearing about your new idea when you're ready to share."

My chest expanded. He knew. How I loved that he knew and appreciated and respected the process of creating. "I look forward to sharing it with you when I'm ready to share."

"Violet?"

"Yeah?"

"Come on, baby. Say it. Let me hear it. I need to hear it. Why do you keep fighting it, sweetheart? Why? We're together." His voice ached into the line, into my ear, my veins. "We're together."

I glanced at my screen. At Tag and Beck flying through the air over the water. Tag's voice came back to me: *"Stop wondering, start feeling."*

"We're together," I repeated.

"That's it, lover girl. Together—capital fucking T."

CHAPTER EIGHTEEN

BECK

"WELCOME TO SOUTH DAKOTA. AGAIN."

Clear-eyed and intelligent. That's what I saw in Georgia Drake's eyes, her stance, in the way she firmly shook our hands. Just like her granddaughter.

"I remember you, Eric. I do." She grinned at my dad. "You were the quiet, polite one."

Dad chuckled low in his throat. "I grew out of that."

"Have a seat." She gestured at her kitchen table. "Could I offer you both coffee or—"

"No, thank you, Mrs. Drake. We're good. Thanks for meeting us today." Dad and I sat down.

"Please, call me Georgia." She took a seat. "Violet didn't mention you were coming."

"I didn't tell her," I said. "I wanted to surprise her, but we wanted to talk to you first."

"She's here. She's still sleeping upstairs."

"She is? I assumed she'd be at the Grand already."

"She took the day off."

"We have something for you," I said, lowering my voice. "But I didn't want Violet to know about it just yet."

Dad took the mini cassette player from his leather backpack

and pushed the button, placing it on the kitchen table in front of Georgia. Isi's laughter rose from the player, and she stiffened.

"Play it again, Eric, this time, slower, okay?"

Georgia's gasp was muffled by Dad's chords and Isi's strong voice. Her hand went to her chest as her lips parted, her breaths quickened.

"Georgia—"

She raised a hand, shushing me. I slid back against the wooden chair and listened to the past with her. Dad's fingers tapped out the rhythm of the song on the table, his gaze elsewhere.

"I liked that. Oh wow, I liked that a lot, huh?" Isi's voice was warmer, quicker. *"Okay, let's—"*

Georgia hit the stop button. "Where did you get this? What's going on?" She brought the player closer and studied the handwritten label, her eyes narrowing.

"When I told Dad that I ran into Violet here in Meager and that she'd told me about Isi, Dad flipped out. He told me how he'd been on that last tour with her and the Silver Tongues, helping them out."

Dad folded his hands on the table. "We'd gotten to be friends, and I helped her with her songwriting. That's us working on some ideas that she'd come up with at the time."

Her eyes glimmered in the morning light coming through her cafe curtains.

"Mostly I was lugging their crap around, driving the van," said Dad.

"Yes, that ugly green van."

"So ugly." Dad chuckled. "I'd sing backup for her, and sometimes the guys would let me pitch in onstage with my guitar. One night she wanted a sounding board and we got some good work done. After that we started working out melodies and lyrics together pretty regularly. This was the last time we'd worked on material together.

"I'd hung onto the tape this one night so I could keep

working out a few things she'd asked me to the next morning. But a few days later she'd taken off to look for her brother."

Georgia only nodded.

Dad sat up straighter. "I got to meet Wreck one night too. Wreck had shown up at our motel after a show in Nebraska. It was Valentine's Day."

She pointed a finger at Dad. "Yes. He'd given her a beautiful big red ring that night as a gift."

"That's right." Dad grinned, his knuckles knocking on the wood. "I remember that ring. She loved it. It looked great on her."

"I buried her with that ring on her finger." She took a long sip of water. "She'd told me she was mad at herself because she didn't have a gift for him for Valentine's Day. And after he'd left, she'd worked on writing a new song as a gift for him, and she'd mentioned you were helping her."

"I believe this is that song."

"Really? Do you think so? You worked on lots of songs together, she told me."

"I remember these lyrics," said Dad. "Whatever happened to Wreck? I'll never forget him and his brothers at her funeral. He was… He still in town with the club?"

Georgia cleared her throat. "Wreck was killed a few years later. Some bar fight in Texas."

"Oh, no. I'm sorry to hear that."

"Yes, it was a terrible tragedy. His little brother, Lock, is with the club, has a wonderful wife, Grace, and they have a little boy they named after him. They fixed up Wreck and Isi's cabin here in town and made it their home." She took the tape out of the player and rubbed it, a faint smile perking her lips. "This is remarkable, to hear her sing like this. To hear that powerful, beautiful voice again. I never thought I'd hear it again. Gave me chills every time, and it still does." She swallowed hard. "Thank you for this."

I leaned toward her. "I have a favor to ask you, Georgia. More like your permission."

"Go on."

"Isi never got a chance to finish that song with my Dad. I'd like to work on it with my band, and perform it."

"You would?"

"I like it very much. Her lyrics, her voice, are very special, all of it hit a nerve for me, and I can't stop thinking about it. And if you agree, I'd prefer if you didn't tell Violet about this, because I'd like to surprise her with it."

She touched the side of my face, her hand warm against my skin. "You are a very special young man."

"Your granddaughter is very special to me."

Her fingers curled around the cassette as her other hand clamped over mine. "You have my permission."

"Isi will be given authorship along with my dad and my band, and once it gets completed and released, I was thinking I'd like the royalties to go to a charity. If there's a cause Isi felt strongly about, please let me know."

"What a wonderful idea. Isi had a thing for the wild horses out here." She opened her hand with the cassette. "You'll need this, right?"

"That's yours to keep. I already made a digital copy," said Dad.

"Everything's digital now." She shook her head as her fingers stroked Isi's handwritten label on the tape. Dad gave her the scratched-up plastic cover.

She put the tape in the cover. "Now I have a question for you, Beck."

"Of course."

"There's all this talk about you and Violet being engaged."

"Yes."

"She won't discuss it."

"Has she denied it?"

"No. So, is it only a rumor?"

"To be frank, when pictures of us came out of me giving her a ring our last night in Athens, people made assumptions, and I chose to go along with them. It was as if the universe had given me that moment on a silver platter, and I took it."

"You ran with it," Georgia said.

"Jesus, Beck," Dad muttered, folding his hands on the table.

"Maybe it was wrong of me, manipulative, but that Ladd guy was hovering over her and it pissed me off, and I really felt he was up to no good. It was impulsive and not something I would have done ordinarily. But how I feel about her isn't ordinary, and I had to take the risk. I had to. I don't want to lose her, Georgia."

Her lips tipped up as her fingertips brushed my hand. "Finish Isi's song, Beck."

The air in the room had changed. "I will."

Dad's hand went to my back and burned there. He gripped my shoulder as he let out a long, tremulous exhale. "Thank you, Georgia." His voice was hoarse, low.

"Thank you for saving this," she said. "A true treasure."

My heart thrummed in my chest. "Would you mind if I go wake Violet up?"

"Oh, Beck, I wish you would." She laughed, a rich laugh that followed me all the way up the stairs.

CHAPTER NINETEEN

VIOLET

THE HEAT PRICKS *at my skin.*

Higher and higher the flames rise around me, licking at me, imprisoning me in the center of our living room. I recognize the old striped sofa, our family photo in that thick, brass frame. Panic tightens its grip on my throat. I want to flee, scream, but I can't. I can't.

That crackling gets louder, louder. The hiss, snap, pop louder. My eyes travel up to the ceiling where the wood beams are on fire. Every single one.

The kitchen is visible through an opening in the flames, but Five isn't there. He isn't laying lifeless on the floor.

Five! My scream is a croak sticking in my throat. My breath cuts in the smoke.

"Violet." A sharp whisper in my ear, that low voice. His. I turn.

"F-Fi—Five!"

"Save me, Violet." His long arm reaches for me, and my heart pounds. I urge my feet to move, to run, they don't, they can't. I can't move. I can't…

Five gets closer. The heat from the fire blazes around us hotter, smoke thicker, flames brighter, hissing louder.

It doesn't stop him. It never stops him.

"Save me." His voice is so loud, my ears hurt. His fingers reach toward me, and I try to reach out to him, but I can't. I can't move. His

long fingers are on fire as they clamp around my throat burning my skin, throttling my scream. Flames shoot up his arm to his chest, his neck. His eyes flare with red gold.

His voice a dagger in my ear, sharp, cutting. "Save me." I can't see anymore. I'm only burning, burning.

Burning with Five.

Behind me, his angry growl. "Violet." All around me heat. All around me Five. Taunting. "Violet. Violet. Violet." I'm being held. I can't move. Can't move.

No.

No.

No.

Low moans fill my ears. Is that me?

"Violet, baby—"

My body jerked, but it was held fast by a firm wall. A familiar scent filled my senses.

Not smoke.

My eyes shot open—I'd been flung in a catapult and landed. The familiar brocaded drapes were closed. The guest room. Gigi's house.

My fingers gripped damped cotton as ropy muscles tensed around my waist. "Baby, it's okay. It was a nightmare. You're okay," a soft whisper eased through me. "I'm here. I got you."

"Beck?"

"Babe."

I turned in my bed. "Beck? Beck, you're here? How can you be here?"

Lips pressed against mine and a luxurious warmth seeped through my flesh. "I'm here." Taking me fully in his arms, he pressed me closer against his body in the shadowy dimness.

I curled up against him, snuggling into his body, the perfect pillow. His scent of freshly washed cotton and leather filled my dazed senses.

"You were having a nightmare. You okay?"

"Hmm." I nestled into the beautiful and familiar lines of his chest as his hand stroked through my hair. His jean clad leg went over my hip, securing me against him, keeping me close.

"Hmm. Wait—why are you here?"

"Two reasons, the most important being, I had to see you." He stroked my lower back. "I saw Tag's videos. They're awesome. Congratulations. I missed you so bad watching them."

"He and Lars did a great job editing all that footage. It's so crazy seeing my name as part of the team on all their posts."

"You made your dream come true, baby."

"Thanks to you." My glance caught the time on the bedside alarm clock. "Holy crap, it's ten thirty? I can't believe I slept this late." I pushed myself up, and my head ached, my stomach queasy. "Ugh."

"Have a rough night, sailor?"

"I went out with my friend Sara to celebrate the videos' release, and things got a little crazy."

"Oh? How crazy?"

"It was ladies' night at Dead Ringers, this Saloon between Rapid and Meager."

"Saloon? Did you pick up a cowboy or a biker? Or both?" His fingers dug into my flesh.

"No, no, lover boy. It was all about the shots. Too many shots. I can still taste that Malibu on my tongue."

"Gimme—" Holding my chin firmly, he took my mouth. A deep, tongue-fucking kiss that sparked everything that had been put on mute since we last saw each other. My every nerve ending was a live wire coursing with high definition technicolor. A vibrant ease, an alert relaxation, the sexiest of highs that only came to me when I was with Beck now seeped through me.

"Hmm, coconut sweetness." He licked at my lips, his eyes glimmered with heat. "I brought you a little something." He leaned over to the floor and grabbed an orange gift bag. My pulse skipped a beat. An *Hermès* gift bag. One of the most exclusive luxury brands on the planet.

"What did you do?"

"A gift for my wild girl."

Four thin, rectangular, orange boxes were in the bag, each wrapped with the company ribbon. I took out the first and pulled on the brown ribbon, opening the box. A silk scarf with a purple and inky blue colored pattern, its soft smoothness seducing the skin of my hand. "Holy crap, it's gorgeous."

"There are three more in there."

"Four scarves?"

"You said you'd never been tied up before. Only the best for my woman's insane body."

"Beck…"

He kissed me again. A deep, take no prisoners kiss.

"I haven't even brushed my teeth yet…"

He only laughed. "I know how you taste every which way and everywhere." His fingers stroked down my hips, making lazy promises to the heated pulse between my legs. "I missed you so much." He lifted my chin and his lips took mine. Our tongues found one another, and something inside me glowed and heated like molten rock. A first kiss. That's what this felt like. A heady, all the feels, first kiss that opened up a brand new world of sensual delights.

That attraction between us was still there, still bright, still strong. I pushed the gift bag away and brought a leg up over his hips and nestled myself deeper into his body.

He grunted at the friction, and his hand slid to my ass and held me between his legs, against his hardening cock as I ground slowly against him. My clit pulsed, sending need shooting through me.

His hot hands slid past the waistband of my pajama shorts and cupped my bare ass, a groan escaping his lips. "Oh yeah…"

My fingers dug into the soft waves of his hair. "There was a cover band playing last night. They played a Freefall song and …"

"You got horny for me?"

"Hmm. I missed you so much." My hands went to his belt

and I unfastened it, his top button, zipper. "I cheered for them extra loud."

"What are you doing?"

"What do you think I'm doing? Holy crap, this is like my fantasy of Edward come to life—"

"Who the hell is Edward?"

"The vampire in "Twilight"? He comes to Bella's room at night to watch her sleep, to keep her safe. Then one night she wakes up and sees him, they kiss—their first passionate kiss and he almost loses control, and he stops himself. But you're not a vampire and we can go all the way." I wriggled out of my shorts, peeled off my tank top. "You keep your clothes on, I like that—"

"We can't."

"Why not, Edward?"

"Your grandmother is downstairs, Bella."

I flicked my tongue in between his lips. "Such a good boy."

"I really am, goddammit. But we both know how wild my cock makes you, baby, and you get loud," he chuckled.

I shoved at his chest and humped his leg, rubbing my tits against his soft T-shirt, his hard torso. "I can be very quiet if I need to be…"

Laughing, he grabbed my hands and pinned me down on the mattress. "We can't. They're waiting for us."

I hitched both my legs around his hips and wriggled against him. "They? Who's waiting for us?"

"That's my other reason for coming here. My dad's here too."

I froze. "What?" I released my hold on Beck and we both sat up. "He wanted to see Georgia and talk old times. Last night we went to his drummer, Stewart Longhat's house. He lives outside of Sturgis. Dad and I hung out with him and his wife yesterday and we spent the night there. We talked music, played together in his studio. It was so great to play with my dad, with both of them."

"That must have been amazing."

"I have news. Zack, Myles, and Jude are coming out to stay at Stewart's ranch so we can work on material for the new album."

"You mean, Freefall? Freefall is coming here?"

He let out a soft laugh. "Yep, that's my band."

"Are you kidding?"

"Not kidding. We need to get out of L.A. and focus. We've been working on getting a few things down, we need to be somewhere distraction free, somewhere different, with different people, especially with Jude coming back. I really believe it will be good for all of us and this new record."

"How's the studio at Stewart's?"

"Very no frills set up, but that's fine. We've got our laptops if we want to access other sounds, layers. We'll see what we come up with, and if we want to get fancier, we can record other tracks in L.A, polish them up. But Stewart knows what he's doing. He's a real cool dude. I haven't seen him since my parents broke up—that was twenty some years ago."

"Freefall is coming to South Dakota."

His finger tapped my lips. "Shh. In secret to work on their new material and record."

"Oooo." My tongue flicked at his finger.

"Dad and I are going back to L.A. later today, and in a week I'll be back with Zack and Myles. Jude will come a few days after that." His index finger traced lazy circles around a nipple. "Are you going to be here or are you going to Oregon on that tour?"

I stroked the side of his face. "I'll be here."

"How about you come to the ranch and shoot us while we work on the new album?"

I got up and slid my T-shirt back on. "You don't have to create jobs for me, Beck."

"Hear me out. We're going to be in this totally new for us environment. You'll be documenting us at our worst, our best, experiencing us putting together our new songs. That's great essay material for you, and possible album or promo material for us. Something totally new and fresh."

"This is you talking off your ass to get me a job and to get me in your bed again."

"You like my ass, Violet."

"I do." I clutched at his gorgeous hard, tight butt. "But I don't want to be handed opportunities like this because you hand them to me or pull the levers."

"Baby, this is how the art world works. You create, you put it out there to be seen, because it must be seen. And people connect it to it, and because of your work, these people connect with you. But first they have to see it or read it or hear it.

"You want a job working with a band at work? Here you go. Honestly, what does it matter how you get a job, especially a job you really want? Would taking a job shooting a high school graduation be more worthy or of some kind of greater value to you because you put an ad in the local paper and they happened to call you? Is that how you define doing it on your own or a true success?"

"No, I wouldn't. For years I've created the jobs I really want —all by myself."

"I know you have, and I love that. And I love the work you did for Tag and Kaspar and so did they. Now millions of people are enjoying it too. You delivered, and that's what counts. I threw you in that frying pan, but it was up to you to function on that hot skillet and come up with the goods. And you did."

"Janus Tisch shot the photos for your last album. He's next level and the hottest—"

"He is. And? He did all our promo from the beginning, even two of our music videos, and it was fantastic. But now we'll need a new vibe to match our new album. And I'd like to see what you come up with, Ms. Hildebrand. Then me and the guys will consider showing it to our team."

"Ah."

"Every artist's goal is to be different, not better than the other guy. You love to create, and everyone will be able to smell that right away. They'll smell your honesty."

My teeth scraped over my lips. "But don't you have to convince the guys, your manager, the record company first? Why don't I just do it, keep it between us, and see what happens?"

"You need to get hired and paid for it. Tag already posted his video, and Kaspar's is out too. Alessio's. That's gold right there. You update your online portfolio, your website, Instagram, all of it, and be ready. When our manager, Ford, calls you, you raise your rate times five at least."

"If he calls."

"He'll call. This is an opportunity for you to produce the unique product your client didn't know he needed."

I tucked my legs underneath me. "That's always the bottom line, isn't it?"

"Yeah, baby, it is." He licked a trail up my thigh.

"Beck?" I breathed, my fingers stroking though his thick, silky hair.

"Hmm?"

"I love how you understand on that level, encourage me, push me. You're a working artist. I've never had that before. You get it."

"I get it." He raised up, brushing my mouth with his. "So does Edward the vampire have a Harley?" His lips twitched.

I grinned, my fingers brushing over his stubble. "No, he has a couple of Volvos."

He rolled his eyes on a scoff. "Oh, come on…"

I tugged on a lock of his hair. "Hey, one is a pretty cool black SUV."

That dark smirk slashed his sexy lips and a coil of warmth went off inside me. "I'll come get you with my Harley, lover girl. Does that do it for you?" His low laugh shuddered through me, and he smoothed his palm over my hard nipple and I let out a gasp. "That's what I thought." Liquid heat rolled through me, and I squirmed, my breath deepening as he kneaded my breast. "They're so many dirty things I want to do to you right now, baby."

"Do them. Do them all, and use the scarves, I beg of you."

"Ah fuck..." He pushed up my shirt and licked my nipple, once, lashed it twice, and moved down my naked torso as my hands nestled in his silky hair. My heartbeat kicked up as I spread my legs for him.

His teeth bit the inside of my thigh, and I gasped at the sting. "Tsk, tsk. He's a vampire, isn't he?" He suckled the throbbing flesh.

My leg twisted around him. "You are so good to me."

He laughed softly, his tongue flicking at my center, and with each gentle yet intense lash, a rush of memories hit me: beach, wine, laughter, cold sea, hot sun, soaring in the sky. Clinging to him and coming, coming, coming.

His lips found my clit, and my hips rose to meet his mouth. His low moans hummed against my sensitive skin, filling me with a new kind of ache. I clenched my jaw, desperate to control the noises rising in my throat, desperate for more friction, for more, for everything from Beck.

I lost his warmth over my naked body, and I blinked. He had risen up over me, his tongue licking his now glossy bottom lip. "That's all for now."

"What? No...wait...I can be quiet, I promise, come on."

"You want me, woman, you got to come to Stewart's."

I raised up on my elbows. "To be your in-house groupie? To suck your cock on demand in between sessions when tensions are high? Do I get a collar and leash so I'll always be on call and ready to serve?"

"Fuck, there's an image..." He put a wet finger across my lips, and I grabbed his hand in mine and took that finger that tasted of me in my mouth and sucked up and down. Up and down, my tongue swirling, lips locking around his long thick finger. "Goddamn, Violet." His jaw tensed, his cock bulging under his jeans against my middle. My insides throbbed. I wanted that beautiful hard cock inside me NOW.

"I can't believe this—oh my God—Eric Lanier!" my mother's voice boomed through the house.

Jerking back, Beck's finger slid from my mouth with a wet pop. "That's my mom."

Beck jumped off the bed, the mattress dipping under the sudden shift of his weight. "Get dressed, and let's get downstairs." He adjusted himself in his jeans. "Ah, shit."

I scrambled out of the bed and ran to the closet. "Think of The Muppets or something. The Teletubbies. Barney?" He let out a groan as I tugged on panties, jeans, a bra, a T-shirt. I hit the adjoining bathroom and returned quickly.

The bedroom was now flooded with sunlight and Beck stood at the window, the sun highlighting his beautiful messy hair, his ringed fingers on the drapes which he'd pulled to the edge of the window.

Beck, my harbinger of light.

From the very first, he had swept away my shadows with his own rare luminous light, hadn't he? With him there were no shadows, no more smoke. I swallowed down the emotion that had gathered in my throat, and smoothed back my hair. "How's that cock doing?"

He turned around and shot me a grin that I felt down to my toes and then zinged back up through my center again. He put a finger to his lips. "Shh. He'll hear you and start losing control again."

"Yum." I managed to find my mascara in the mess I'd left last night on top of the dresser, and swiftly applied it. Beck's reflection came up behind me in the mirror, his finger tracing a line down my back. "That nightmare you were having seemed real intense."

"I'm good." I focused my attention on the tube of mascara, twisting the cap tightly. "Nothing but an ugly monster in the shadows," I lied to Beck.

I lied because every moment of every day I lied to myself about the monster in my shadows.

CHAPTER TWENTY

BECK

"SO THIS IS OUR MONTSERRAT?" Myles quipped, referring to the renown recording studio on the Caribbean island where many famous musicians, like The Police, had recorded.

I ushered the guys into Stewart's studio. Music stands, microphones, a recording booth, and a panel that looked like maybe Fleetwood Mac had been there back in the day.

"Without the palm trees, the blue sea, and the babes in bikinis." Zack checked out the drum set in a corner of the room. "Oh, man, this is his kit…"

"Oh well. It's our magic little studio on the prairie," said Myles.

"You're only going to find your magic if you put in the work." Stewart, a tall burly Native American man with long black hair peppered with salty gray, filled the door frame. His face was expressionless except for one thick black eyebrow shooting into a sharp angle. "You all moved in?"

"Yes. We really appreciate you letting us stay here at your house," I said.

"There's plenty of room, might as well use it. You came out here to work, so no sense in going to some hotel which isn't too close anyhow. There's a basketball court where you can shoot some hoops, or you can go on runs or hikes on the nearby trail to blow off steam. I got a weight room you can use. And there's a no frills swimming pool too. I see the chef you hired has taken over my kitchen already. My wife is real excited about that."

I shifted my weight. "Oh. We thought it was a good idea as they're a lot of us and we wanted to take care of that, plus Zack is vegetarian, which—"

"No, I wasn't being an asshole. Ella really is excited. So excited she's taking off for the weekend with her girlfriends."

"Oh. Cool." Zack grinned.

"So how about you all get settled this afternoon, and we can meet in here tonight so I can hear what you got so far. Or if you want to work alone first, that's fine by me."

"I think we'd like you to hear what we've got, right?" asked Myles.

"Yes," I said.

"Definitely," said Zack.

"All right then. See you in here at eight."

Earlier, when we'd arrived at the small airport in Rapid City with the private jet we'd chartered, the rental car and the van were waiting for us. Along with our instruments and assorted stuff, we'd brought our skateboards and mountain bikes. Wes had met us at the entrance to the ranch, having brought my Harley out from Meager in his pickup truck along with his own bike.

After settling in and having lunch thanks to Chef Andy, we were now getting ready to roll for a tour of the area. Adjusting their helmets, Zack and Myles were on their mountain bikes alongside me and Wes. Stewart had told them where to find the best trails.

"That is one hell of a view." Zack's gaze was glued to the endless rolling green and brown hills under a rich blue sky dotted with clouds.

This was raw beauty of a different, rugged sort from the infinite sapphire sea and crisp, clear skies I'd recently experienced in Greece with Violet. My chest filled with heat at the memory of her in that nude bathing suit stretching out on—

My phone buzzed. Ford. "Hey. What's up?"

"Did you all get there in one piece?"

"We did. We're all settled in, and we took a look at the studio, had lunch. Now we're about to check out the area on our bikes. Is something up?"

"Just wanted to check in."

I recognized that tone in his voice. Worried. Concerned but holding it in tight so I wouldn't be worried or concerned. "I'm glad you did. We're good."

"I think it was a good move to go out there, especially for Jude. I'm proud of you."

My back straightened. "Thanks, man. I talked to Jude this morning. He's psyched to come out. I think we gave him something unusual to look forward to. By the time he gets here, we'll have made some kind of sense out of what we came up with in L.A., and we'll be ready for him."

"I'm glad to hear you got something accomplished in L.A., because that was a hefty chunk of change we paid for studio time at The Shed that we didn't use."

"The time we did use was definitely not a waste. We came here with specific pieces to work with and developed ideas to explore."

"Good to hear. Of course, there's buzz about where you all took off."

"Don't say a word."

"I won't. I just got off the phone with Naomi and we discussed it."

"Good. We want to handle that when we're ready."

"Also, I took a look at Violet's work."

"And?"

"I like it. A lot. I'm going to call her once we get off the phone. You still want this to happen?"

"Hell yes."

"All right. We'll try her out."

"I'll let you get on that call then. Later, man." I clicked off and tucked my phone in my jacket.

"Everything cool with Ford?" Myles asked.

"Very cool. He just wanted to check in."

"Let's go. We're off. Catch you later," said Zack, and he and Myles sped off on their bikes.

Wes grinned at me as he revved his engine. "Let's do this."

I laughed and started my bike. The engine rumbled in my gut, vibrated in my veins. We'd be inside the sunset once we got back.

And I couldn't wait.

CHAPTER TWENTY-ONE

BECK

"I REALLY LIKE HER MELODY." Zack mimicked Isi's rhythm on the *touberléki* I'd given him, articulating quick rhythms with rolling strokes of his fingertips on the small goblet drum. He'd played with the dang drum for barely ten minutes, and he had it down already.

Stewart stopped the recording of Isi and my dad, his lips pressing together in a tight line. This was hard for him. He hadn't wanted to work with us. He was busy, tired. Then we flew out and Dad had him listen to the recording, and everything changed.

I told him I wanted to finish the song, he'd turned away from us both, muttering, "Motherfuckers." Dad had embraced him, and the two of them held onto each other, thumping each other's backs, talking in low tones. Then he'd grabbed me in a bear hug too.

And now here we were, playing the recording for Myles and Zack for the first time and prepping to work on it. I'd explained the history of the song to both of them.

"You got her lyrics down?" I asked.

Myles finished typing on his iPad. "Got 'em."

"I came up with a couple more verses we can work on."

"Great."

"This song is real special to me, and I wanted to ask you a favor." My chest tightened.

"Sure. What is it?"

"I'd like to sing lead on this song. I want it to be a gift for Violet."

Zack raised his head, eyes wide, lips parted, sticks in his fists.

Myles let out a deep, rumbling laugh, a hand on his chest. Hardly the response I thought I'd get.

"What's so funny?"

His lips twisted into that sly smirk of his. "This girl must be something."

"She is." My shoulders eased. "I know it's a big ask—"

He raised his hand. "You obviously feel strongly about it. I get it. The story behind this song is amazing, and I'm really glad you brought it to us to work on together."

"Yeah?"

"You should sing it."

"Thank you."

His attention went back to his tablet. "I was thinking we could work out a strong harmony right here"—he pointed to his screen—"where Isi's voice drops and creates that unexpected jab of dissonance. We could amp that up together."

"I like that. Let me work that section now without vocals first. From right here—" I hit my father's chords. And again. I hit the rhythm faster, a little rougher. "Zack, give me what you're feeling."

I kept going. I added a riff I'd worked on first thing this morning, Zack's beat following, enhancing, pushing. Would it all flow? *Hmm.*

Again, again.

I opened my eyes. They were all staring at me. Had I been the only one playing? "What is it?"

Stewart's face filled my vision. "That adjustment you made? You made the song a hell of a lot more wicked and absolutely right."

"Oh yeah," said Zack. "That was good."

"Let's work out the harmonies at these spots I highlighted," said Myles.

Three hours later we felt good about what we'd accomplished so far on Isi's song. Zack had come up with a more ominous layer for the beginning, then tied it up around the chorus and brought it back up at the finish. Myles and I worked on our vocals together. And he helped me make a better choice during one harmony. He took down the lyrics I'd come up with so far. There was still a way to go on this song, but it was an awesome beginning.

We broke for lunch and then worked on another song. Myles was on his acoustic guitar working on a melody line of his I'd helped him with in L.A. at The Shed, which was meant for another tune but we liked how it was working on this one.

"Can I take it?" I asked him, without looking up.

"Go for it."

I drove into his melody, opened up his chords, made them bigger, broader.

"Yeah, yeah..." murmured Myles. "Keep going, and I'll...." His fingers made circles in the air—his signal that he needed the melody again and again to get there, to where lyrics percolated and flowed, they were coming. He sang along, and we heard how they worked, if they worked, how they felt.

"Again on that last...." Again we started, and Myles made adjustments as we went, making notes, glancing at his notebook of lyric fragments and theme ideas. Scatting bullshit, bringing it back to a phrase and off again. Deciding on the lyrics that worked in particular sections, tweaking as he went.

Myles's rich voice filled the room, opening the song up to more. His voice was an instrument, and once it hit my chords, different colors filled my veins which urged me toward different chords as we left the verse and hit where the bridge should be.

Leaving the studio finally, we all stopped and sucked in the fresh night air. It was nighttime and we hadn't even noticed. We headed for the dining room to eat, the hum of cicadas all around us.

Later that night, alone in the living room, I got on my laptop and sent Isi's song to Dré in Nashville asking him for feedback. He emailed me back within ten minutes with five different samples. "Whatever you like, use it. Let me know."

I listened to them all. One loop hit me in the chest, entranced me. I picked up my guitar and played it. Played it over and over. It was open enough harmonically that I could write to it.

I played Isi's song from our session today that I'd recorded on my phone, and listened, and when that patch that I felt needed more hit, I played the loop of Dré's I'd worked on. I modified. Revised. Played again, and again.

I'd recorded what I'd come up with and emailed it to Dré.

He emailed back. "IT ROCKS!!!"

The next day, I played it for everyone. Stewart went to his old drum kit and hit the bass drum, providing a note of low definite pitch underneath Zack's snare. Zack picked it up.

Stewart returned to the board. "Keep going—let's go with it, see what happens. Then get this down."

And we got it down.

CHAPTER TWENTY-TWO

BECK

AFTER A WEEK ON THE RANCH, working out verses, bridges, expanding riffs into fully realized melodies, we had developed a good chunk of material.

Cleared by his doctor, Jude finally arrived in South Dakota. He scanned the wide expanse of land. The barn studio, the pen with horses. "This is one sweet set up."

"You like it?"

"What's that smell?"

Zack laughed. "It's trees. Pine, aspen. And musk de horse."

Jude snorted. "Really?"

"Really."

"I like it."

"You hungry?"

"No, not yet." He took in another deep breath, that smile still on his face. Although Jude was skinny, he ate like a wild man when he was hungry or excited. "I want to hear what you've got. I can't wait."

"Great. We need you on the song I told you about. Before Violet gets here tomorrow."

"Ah yes, we get to meet Miss Violet. His eyes flashed. "Show me the way, brother."

We played the tracks of the material we'd figured out. Jude

listened, head down, his bass in his grip as he sat on a metal stool, his one leg moving to the rhythms. Jude listened, his left hand sliding up and down his frets, his other hand tapping against his bass.

We got to Isi's song, and Stewart looped the track over and over while Jude skipped in and out of it, exploring, weaving a bass line here, slapping on his guitar for the opening of a verse.

He locked in to Zack's groove and found a consistent beat. Then, in true Jude form, skipped out....and slid back in at a totally unexpected moment.

"Whoa," whispered Myles next to me.

"Hmm," I agreed.

Jude rubbed a hand down his mouth. "Can we play it together now so I can…you know. It'll feel different when we're on it together."

"Let's do it." I settled back in my seat.

We worked on that one song until well after midnight. Jude came up with a darker line under my bridge, and with his bass in the mix, Zack's drum groove created momentum and more drama. The harmony Myles and I had worked on elevated a moment even more. With Jude's tones simmering through, we got layered sonic effects. He'd just shifted the whole damn energy of the song.

We stopped, each of us letting the final notes sink in. Zack bit his lip as he wiped his forehead with the side of his arm, nodding slowly to himself, letting out a breath. Myles's eyes were closed as he swayed to the tune in his head.

"Let's get this one down now, huh?" said Stewart.

We recorded this new version.

THE NEXT DAY, Violet arrived. My heart beat faster in my chest at the sight of her getting out of her vintage Cougar, dressed in black skinny jeans and an oversized black V-neck T-shirt, and on her feet, a pair of thick-soled and very colorful Vans. She shot me a smile. A shot of adrenaline flaring with spicy sweet surged inside me.

"Hey, you." As my fingers curled around the thick handle of her suitcase, I grinned. Same suitcase she'd taken to Greece. She hoisted her messenger bag and backpack on her shoulders. Her face was flushed, her darkly lined eyes bright.

"Good to see you, baby." I cradled one side of her beautiful face with my hand and planted a kiss on her cheek.

She slid a hand around my middle, holding me close. "Good to see you too."

I closed my eyes and breathed her in, fresh air, a botanical shampoo, and cedar. I breathed this moment in. Violet, here, us together at work. "We're working in the studio. You want to unpack first or…"

Her eyes widened. "I'd love to listen in a corner. Just listen, maybe shoot—is that okay?"

I laughed. "Of course it is. That's why you're here."

"I want to get a feel for what you're working on and how you work."

"I get it." I slung an arm around her shoulders as I wheeled the suitcase. "Let's get your stuff in the house and then we can go on in." I led her to my room and put her suitcase against the dresser. She unloaded her bags and took out her camera, putting it over her shoulder as we walked to the studio.

Stewart stood outside, leaning against the wall, smoking a cigarette, his eyes on Violet. He tossed the cig, stamping it out, and stood up straight as we approached.

"Violet, this is Stewart Longhat."

Her shoulders drew up as she held out her hand to him. "Good to meet you, Stewart."

He took her hand, his lips pressed firmly together. He nodded slightly, studying her face. "Violet." He didn't release her hand, and she didn't pull it from his grip. His lips curved into a barely perceptible grin we'd yet to witness on this man. "Yes. I see her in you."

Her chin lifted, she smiled. "Thank you."

We walked through the short hallway into the studio, and Violet stopped abruptly in front of one of the framed concert posters lining the walls. "Holy crap," she murmured. A poster from decades ago.

Black Hills
Rock Festival
— LIVE TONIGHT —
Isi & the Silver Tongues

"I've never seen one of these before," she breathed.

"Few have, hon. That's probably the only one left on the planet," Stewart said.

She touched the frame, her eyes scanning the colors, the logo, taking it in. She photographed it.

We entered the studio.

"Hey, there she is!" Jude came over and gave Violet a great big hug as if they were old friends being reunited, not introduced for the very first time. Violet laughed and hugged Jude right back.

Myles came forward, a grin on his lips. "Hello, hello at last, Violet."

And Zack. "Good to meet you, finally."

Violet beamed, grinning wide, murmuring her hellos. "Thanks for having me here. I mean it."

We all settled back into our spots and Violet sat down on the floor in a corner, her head against the wall, camera between her legs. We got back into it.

We fought our way through a section we just couldn't get right. Myles pulled on the sides of his face, grimacing, groaning. Frustration. We pushed ahead.

'You get stuck in a rut, yes it's tedious, so try the opposite, run in

the opposite direction and see what happens,' a music teacher had told me in high school. Every time I tried that strategy, I learned something new. Heard something different that sparked my attention.

My ear picked up on a slight tempo change in Zack's beat. Had he read my mind? I chased it, and he caught my gaze, lifting his chin. The two of us kept going, charging up the same hill. We found a rough alignment. We veered, found another and circled back again. Myles's voice weaved in between us, rode us.

I reworked the bridge in my mind, I could hear it, but my fingers hadn't found it yet. I kept my head down, my attention to the flow, in the notes. I changed up the third chord. *Yes.* Jude let out a sound, something in between a grunt and a murmur as the slide of his fingers had me picking up my tempo.

I tore through, again, again. *There.* Something. I wanted more. More. Again. Again. The air in the room changed. I kept on it, and again. The energy around me shifted, lightened. Heat chugged through my veins as I kept on, following the thread, listening to Myles's hitting the lyrics. He tried another combination. A prickle raced over the back of my neck.

Zack had stopped, Jude. Myles.

Stewart's voice cut through. "Beck. Beck! Stop a sec."

I raised my head. They stared at me. I blinked, focused. In her dark corner, Violet bit her lip, her whole body at attention, her camera in her right hand.

"That bridge, and the second one…that was good, man," breathed Jude. His fingers kept moving on his bass. "Real good."

"Grab your acoustic guitar," said Stewart. "And play both of those bridges back to back." I unstrapped the Fender from my body, put it in its stand, and grabbed my acoustic, my body adjusting to its weight. Stewart dipped his head, two fingers in the air.

I played them both. Again. Again. Again.

Zack entered, a low simmer, holding steady. Stewart called out my chord changes, keeping us on the tightrope. Jude came in with eighth notes, a cushion, an alternate energy that threatened, poked and jabbed. Myles's voice saturated it all with fresh, rich color, and my heart swelled.

Keeping up with our pace, Myles improvised lyrics as we went, his eyes darting to his open notebook. He was feeling what fit the space, the melody, the mood. His body moved in time with my rhythm. I grinned as I listened to his lyrics. He never hesitated to try new things, never held back.

He sang about the feelings we were all having. The doubt, the discord, disunity. Anger. The way he hit a word, dragged it out in opposition, sent a ripple of heat through my insides. Dramatic but authentic.

"This right here—again," I said loudly. We stopped and started it again.

At the end of the chorus Myles did something unexpected, and my gaze darted to him. The slight flourish in his voice right there at the finish of this section gave it a haunting feel. Specific and just enough, not overdone, not messy. Myles had the experience to be able to control it.

The energy picked up in the room. Everyone was reacting to the subtle dissonance. *More, I want more of that.*

Jude's bass went up to F sharp. That lifted the whole damn thing. I added feedback to my chords and the sound got bigger. We hit the bridge, which was currently a no man's land. Jude slid up the octave, giving us a cool build. Myles's hands were in the air like he was touching the notes around us, curling his voice around what he came up with.

"Keep going...hold it..." Myles's voice broke over us.

Again.

"Let's get what we have down now," said Stewart. "Beck, stay on the acoustic. We're going to jack it up all the way on the amp and see how that dirties up the whole damn thing."

Jude muttered, "The dirtier the better."

"Yeah..." I stretched out my back, taking in a breath. "Myles, hang onto that "da, da, da dum da" over the final notes." He did those flourishes so well. On someone else it would come off pretentious, but not from Myles. His voice was a powerful instrument.

The hairs on the back of my neck stood on end. Myles blew out a loud breath, his long, curly hair fisted in his hands, Jude moved to the beat in his head, his thumb thwacking his guitar. Zack arched his back, grinning, winking at me. Violet was sprawled on the floor like some sort of secret agent commando in the field, her camera trained upwards at Jude, shooting silently.

Stewart's steady voice boomed, "Let's do this."

CHAPTER TWENTY-THREE

VIOLET

THE WORLD JERKED UNDERNEATH ME. I was falling.

My hands gripped the bedding, my eyes flew open, the bed was moving.

"There. Perfect." Beck's deep voice boomed from somewhere over me.

My muscles relaxed. "What's going on?"

"I'm going to fuck you like a crazy, wild man, and I don't want the bed banging into the wall and waking everybody up."

Turning over, I laughed. "My good boy." My mouth dried as he quickly stripped off all his clothes. "You finished the song?"

"We finished the song. Now, I need you."

"Why don't we get on the floor?" I threw down the heavy quilt on the carpet along with the pillows.

"Shit, why didn't I think of that?"

"You're tired and jazzed up."

"I'm possessed."

"I loved watching all of you work together. I can't explain it, it was fascinating. The little things you guys could hear that actually made a huge difference to a song, how it feels, how it moves. I couldn't hear, I tried, I..."

He was naked and stroking his cock, and my brain stuttered. A detonation went off in my chest, zinged through my veins. That glorious cock would be inside me any moment now, that body would be mine. I could taste his skin even now. Yes, I would lick every firm plain, every etched muscle.

An ache spiraled inside me, not just lust—no, need. Anticipation. I'd missed him, truly missed him and how it was between us.

I'd missed us.

I clambered down onto the bedding on the floor on my knees. "Beck," my voice was a rough whisper, my breathing rougher.

He stood over me, my own Colossus. His incredible cock stood at attention for me.

I slid my hand around his hard, velvety length and stroked. He yanked my tank top over my chest, my breasts exposed to him, a small grunt escaping his lips as he cupped each one roughly. My body twisted under his heavy gaze, my entire body thrumming, at his mercy. He brought his hard shaft to my lips. "I want to watch you take my cock, Violet. Want to see me in your mouth." His thumb tugged roughly at my lips.

On a groan, I took him between my lips, one hand at his balls, the other on his ass. I sucked firmly up and down, and he groaned, his face crumpling with sensation, with emotion.

On a low hiss, he pulled out of my mouth and brought his wet cock between my breasts. I held them together as he slid his wet thickness between my tits, against my flesh.

His pelvis thrust. "Your gorgeous tits are all mine, all mine." He grunted, his cock jerked, his cum splattered on my lips, my breasts. I swiped it all over me. His eyelids fluttered closed. "Oh damn, baby."

His thumb, salty and wet, sunk inside my mouth and I sucked on it, my hips twisting. His forehead wrinkled as he watched me, and he licked his own lips. His free hand kneaded a wet breast, stroking, tugging roughly on the nipple. "Hmm." He got down on his knees and his mouth went from one nipple to the other, until a stiff peak formed under his attentive tugging, his nipping.

He eased me down on the floor and slid down my torso, hands around my thighs. "I'm going to eat you out now—"

I groaned.

He chuckled. "You can't yell, baby. We're not alone, and the walls are super thin in this old house."

I smashed my face into a pillow.

"Ah fuck..." His voice was low, husky as he blew air over my wet pussy. His face sank between my legs, his lips aggressive, demanding. His wicked tongue swirled rhythmically around my nub over and over and over, never touching it. "I just want to dive into you."

I cried out softly, my hips rising to meet his eager mouth. "Dive, Beck. Dive in."

The firm ridge of his nose stroked my clit back and forth, back and forth, and I gasped at the distinct, focused pressure, my breathing more and more shallow as the pleasure intensified with every stroke, every swipe of wet tongue. In the thick darkness, the intensity of his attention, the anticipation of his cock filling me, had my body twisting, flesh tingling. I wanted all of Beck now, now, now.

Rough whispers against my skin, callused fingers digging into my flesh, as a tight wave furled around us. He hoisted one of my legs over his shoulder, fingers sweeping down my thigh to between my ass cheeks as his lips suckled my clit. I was in a thick daze, a riot of colors swarming through me. My lungs constricted as the flat of his tongue pressed against the very core of me.

I curled my fingers in his hair.

The pleasure flared quickly, harshly, and I exploded, swallowing my scream. It burned in the pit of my chest, my heel pounding into his back, the other jammed onto the bedding on the floor.

On a groan two of his fingers slid inside me and churned. "I missed your pussy so fucking much, Violet." He flipped me over, spread my thighs apart. My fingers curled into the tangle of sheet and quilt as he licked up my ass. "Every inch of you. Every inch is all mine."

Holy hell.

Groaning into the quilt, I jerked in his hold, helpless in the demanding grip of his mouth and tongue. His fingers slid through my wet, toying with my pussy. Taking it. Making it his. Yes, his.

My body trembled, every inch of me a live wire. "I'm c-coming again…" Wet surged between my legs. I spiraled. Beck's moans and sucking sounds had me falling.

Soaring.

On a heavy sigh, he laid down next to me, his head on his hand, his other fingers lingering, swirling around my pulsing core, stroking gently down my damp thigh. He took my mouth, and my senses surged at the flavors of me on his wet lips, of me in his mouth. I dug my hands in his hair, bringing his face closer. "I want your cock inside me. I want to feel you take me where you want to take me."

"When you talk to me like that, baby, I'm your fucking slave." He rose over me, our gazes locking in the shadows, and he rocked inside me. One impossibly long, thick slide. My breath cut.

"Goddamn," he hissed.

The sensation of fulness, impossible fulness. "Oh, Beck…"

He pulled out slowly, drawing us both out, back in, out and in, pulsing, thrusting, driving, now faster, his grip on me painful, perfect.

There was no more control. There was only a freefall into Beck's vortex. There was no more me, or him. There was only *us* expanding, growing, bursting. I clung to him. I held him. My fingers clawed his hair as my jaw clenched. If I couldn't yell and makes noises I'd keep my eyes on him, the two of us in fuck sync, making this happen for each other.

We exploded.
We exploded and held on tight.

CHAPTER TWENTY-FOUR

VIOLET

A TICKLE, a zing. A nip on my earlobe. Warm, wet tongue on my neck.

Beck's tongue.

I nestled deeper against his naked body.

Hello morning wood. More like a morning missile.

I wiggled closer against him. He nestled his cock between my ass cheeks, and I let out a sigh. Tipping my hips up, a dark chuckle reverberated against my neck and he rocked inside me.

"Oh damn, damn," he groaned in my ear, his one hand played chords between my legs. So attentive. Beck clasped me so tightly it hurt, and I liked it. I suckled on his forearm, muffling my grunts as he pounded inside me.

I was in his grip as he used me for his pleasure, as he gave to me. He pulled out on a low moan, his cock spewing cum on my ass.

"Hold on, baby, don't move." I couldn't lift an eyelid. He returned with a T-shirt in his hand and wiped me clean.

My hair damp, sticking to my face, I reached up and brushed his lips with my fingers. He bent over and kissed me.

"I'm going to take a shower. I'd ask you to join me, but it's too damn small in there."

We both laughed, and I fluffed his very messy hair. "It's the thought that counts."

His phone beeped, and he picked it up from the nightstand as I climbed on the mattress with a pillow and pulled the quilt over me. "Naomi's setting up interviews for when the first single gets released." He typed out a reply, and put his phone back down, planted a kiss on my shoulder, and left for the bathroom.

His phone beeped again. My eyes blinked open from the fluffy pillow my face was buried in.

Another beep. I raised up from the bed and saw her name. Mae. And a photo.

A photo of Mae and another woman.

Both naked.

Both of them touching tongues, looking at the camera. Naked. My pulse jammed in my throat. A homemade porny boudoir shot.

I sat up and read the text.

"Come & get it! I missssssss u!"

Come and get it?

I miss you?

The door flew open. I blinked. Beck stood before me with a towel around his middle, his skin shimmering with water. "What is it?"

"Why don't *you* tell me what it is?" I tossed his phone at the edge of the bed.

He approached, and scooped up his phone. "Shit." His brow furrowed as he swiped.

I'd always known that I was the outsider to Beck's glittery rock and roll world. That was his way of life. And, of course, he was comfortable there. Like Mae was. I pulled the sheet around me. "Has she been sexting you all along? Showing you what you've been missing out on?"

"This is the first text I've gotten from her since the big blow off."

"Guess she wants you back, boy toy."

"Newsflash: She wants to play with both of us."

"What?"

"She's into open relationships, polyamory." He ripped the towel off his body and rubbed his wet hair with it. "We weren't monogamous in the classic sense of the word." His Adam's apple bobbed in his throat. "When I saw her recently at that party in L.A., she said she wanted to meet you."

My eyes widened, my spine straightened. "So we could all get down, the three of us?"

"Or you and her or you with a partner of hers."

"Is that what we're doing here? Are you sleeping with other people? Are you—"

He held my gaze. "No, baby. There's only you."

"But isn't that what you're into? An open-to-all-the-possibilities-and-all-the-people way of life?"

"Which is why I thought that polyamory was a cool choice for me. When she and I could spend time together, she cleared her schedule of anybody else, so I never experienced her getting busy with other people and we didn't discuss them. She tried, but I never wanted to, so she dropped it. Anyhow, I was never around long enough to see it or hear about it, and I put it out of my head. At the time, I thought it ticked all the boxes for me, especially with all my traveling. It wasn't difficult or disappointing for either of us.

"But when she broke it off with me, it was a real knife to the artery. It made me look in the mirror, and I was surprised by what I saw. I didn't like it. Hollow, tired, disconnected. Hungry for something. Didn't know what. And I had nowhere to land. No one to trust. I didn't realize how much I craved that. With you, I found all that and more. So much more."

My lungs burned. "She still wants you."

"I don't want her. I don't want anybody else. I want you.

There's only you, Violet." His gaze hardened. "And how about you? Is there only me or are you…" He swallowed hard. He couldn't say the words. "I guess we should have had this conversation before we had unprotected sex—"

"There's only you."

His chest expanded on a deep inhale, his eyes softening. "We're together. I need to hear you say it, baby."

I grinned. "Capital fucking T, baby."

"Violet."

"We're together."

A noise escaped his throat, and a smirk slashed his lips as he brought his attention to his phone, tapping and typing. He gave me his phone, and I read his text back to Mae.

"Not interested. Not at all. I'm in a committed monogamous relationship and very happy."

I bit my lip. This was for real. We were for real.

Me and Beck Lanier.

CHAPTER TWENTY-FIVE

VIOLET

I STEPPED down the stairs carefully. None of the guys were awake yet, and almost every floorboard in this house creaked. A clatter of pans and shuffling from the kitchen, the warm, caramely, roasted aroma of the coffee brewing filled the entire house, and my lips pushed up into a smile.

But first, I wanted to catch the early colors of the sun. I'd been here three days already and today I finally wanted to capture this landscape drenched in the fleeting drama of sunrise.

Out the door, I took pics of the ranch house against the virgin sky. The loping hills in the distance seemed taller than they actually were. Whoops and pummeling horses hooves filled my ears. The corral was busy and I stalked toward it.

Wearing a red bandana on his head, Stewart leaned against the gate watching five small children ride the horses. Riding bareback. An elderly man wearing a worn out baseball cap was in the center of the corral with Stewart's wife, Ella, coaching the boys on riding.

I joined Stewart. "Good morning."

"Hey."

The boys were very young, and not one looked anxious or afraid. They were excited, in a groove. Born to ride.

The elderly man eyed the children as their horses sped

around the corral. He gave them a directive I couldn't understand, and they pushed the horses faster and faster. The glee on their faces and the glee in their hearts was palpable.

"Could I take pictures of them, Stewart? I'll give you the photos so you can give them to their parents."

"Sure, go ahead. That'd be great."

They raced around the track, their little bodies taut, muscles flexed, holding on, flying, their focus completely on moving forward, forward, into the air.

I raised my camera. "They are something else."

"They sure are."

As the sun rose higher in the sky, growing stronger, hotter, the colors and shadows swiftly changed, transforming everything around us. I shot, Stewart silent at my side. Only the horses' hooves pounding the dirt, their snorts, the children's exclamations filled the air.

"Hey, good morning, party people." Jude came up next to us.

Stewart took in Jude's tank and shorts, his running shoes. "Went for a run?"

"Yep. Went up that trail Ella told me about. It was a bitch and a half, but I plan on smacking her down tomorrow." He wiped at his sweaty face with the side of his arm. "Is this a lesson? They sure don't look like they need any lessons." A noise escaped his lips. "No saddles?"

"Nope," said Stewart. "That's Ella's dad, Tom. He coaches the relay team, brings the little ones out here to get some basics down. They're always riding on the reservation, but here we can take our time and give them more attention. For them, coming here is a real treat. Some of these kids don't have dads, you know? Any time off the rez is swell. And that time being with horses..."

"The best," I said. "Growing up, riding was something we all did on my granddaddy's ranch. Now, I'm not riding as often as I used to, and I miss it. Had a chance to ride with my grandpa a couple weeks ago—"

"And?" Stewart's dark eyes glinted in the sun.

I grinned. "It was the best."

"Never been on a horse before," said Jude. "Maybe one day. Maybe not."

"I can teach you how to ride, and you can teach me how to skateboard, how's that?" I said.

"You're on."

"Good job, Stan. Way to go!" Ella clapped. The little boy smiled, his chest puffing out, his back straight.

"Look at that now, look at that," Stewart's voice was warm and rolling. A proud father. I took photos nonstop of all the boys. Their uncertainty, their satisfaction, their joy. Sunlight filtered through dust, dirt, heat. Determined boy, tense boy, grinning boy, horse alert.

Little Stan leaned forward and stroked his horse's neck and mane, talking to the animal. The horse nodded his great head. The two of them were one. My heart swelled, thudding in my chest, and I shot.

"When I was growing up on the rez, I always got told that horses can feel your feelings," Stewart wiped at his brow.

"It's true," I said.

"Sure is. Every time I was going through something shitty, which was a hell of a lot of the time, my horse, Hermit, would be kind to me. No other way to describe it. He understood, he knew I was feeling down. Still to this day, the worries go away the minute I go into the barn."

I slowly lowered my camera, blinking past the water gathering in my eyes at the memories of me, Jessa, and Five on our horses, just the three of us. We loved our animals and took good care of them.

Five's horse was the wildest of them all but he'd taken to Five right away, and my brother hadn't ever been afraid of him. Talking to his horse, Five's voice would be soft and kind and sincere, and after, Five would be calm, so calm. A kind of balance had been struck within him and between him and his horse. I always admired that in them. Did Five ever realize it? Had he been grateful for it?

Riding was the one thing that helped me after the fire. The one thing I craved because I could forget. Not feel.

I could be free.

"—And that's how it is with these kids," Stewart continued. "I want that for them. Riding is part of our history. It's in our genes back to the time when the Lakota roamed free on this land as hunters and warriors." He let out a dark chuckle. "My ancestors were the only ones able to steal horses from the U.S. Cavalry back in the day."

"Nice, I like that," said Jude.

"I feel real lucky to have had the success Cruel Fate had and be able to have all this now. It's a tiny patch but it's something."

"It certainly is," I said.

"Having horses to wake up to every day, is everything to me. Horses understand you. They heal you. They're my piece of good in this world." Stewart's lips curled. "I suppose everybody has their own piece of good. This is mine."

Jude closed his eyes and took in a deep breath. Was he holding onto this moment? Did this bring up emotions for him? I brought him into focus and shot.

"Are these boys training to be in an Indian relay?" I asked.

"That's right." Stewart grinned at me. He was pleased I knew, and proud of the boys.

"I've never been. I've heard about them, of course, but I'd love to see one. I bet it's way more exciting than usual horses races, right?"

"Much better."

"What's Indian relay?" asked Jude.

"It's intense horse racing," said Stewart. "Real high stakes competition."

My fingers smoothed down my camera strap. "Don't the riders jump on their horses for the relay—as the horses are moving?"

"Seriously?" said Jude. "And they ride bareback?"

"That's right," I replied.

"I always said if they'd show Indian relay on television, people would see what a damn bore all those fancy Derbies are compared to this," Stewart said.

We laughed, but Stewart's face sobered quickly. "We just lost two boys, barely twenty-four-years old the two of 'em. Relay champions, the type that don't come along very often." He let out a rough breath, his one hand gripping the top of the fence. "One to jail, one to suicide."

"Oh man," murmured Jude.

"Even though relay racing was their escape, it wasn't enough. When they were competing, those boys were on top of the world. Proud, on fire. Unstoppable. But then the competitions finish and they'd come back home and get swallowed up by the nothing. Marooned in nothing."

Jude and I shared a quick glance. Life on a reservation was infamously difficult in ways Jude and I would never know or truly comprehend.

"I know it's not the same thing," said Jude. "But for me, this past year when we were on on the road, every night we were riding that high of performing. The applause, the fans screaming for us, and we're doing what we love to do the most. You're flying, living on that adrenaline. On that energy."

"Yep, I remember that." Stewart sniffed in air. "Then all of a sudden it's over, and you get back home and it feels like you've been pushed off a rollercoaster from the top."

"Yeah. You feel cut off, bruised, out of sync…"

"No purpose," said Stewart.

"Dangerous place to be." Jude rested both arms on the top of the fence as the boys rocketed by on their horses. "But, of course, we've got money to play with, to entertain ourselves. What do these kids got?"

Crushing poverty in stark isolation.

Stewart's lips twisted. "A kid on the rez can't just take a walk and go to a convenience store and get a pack of gum and a soda. You want fast food? A pizza? You got to drive eighteen miles plus for it. Then winter comes along—"

"It's brutal," I said.

"I don't know how you all do it out here," said Jude. "Double digits below zero, the snow, the wind—"

"We do it." Squatting down I positioned myself to get a shot from the ground of the horses and boys shooting overhead.

Jude closed his eyes again, his face tilted, lips parted. He was listening. I aimed my camera at him. He took out his phone, tapped on it, and closed his eyes again. He was recording the thundering of the horses.

"You like it, huh?" Stewart said.

Jude tucked his phone away. "That's real pounding, booming. With an interesting thud under it. Powerful stuff."

Ella and her father ended the boys' session with one final gallop around the arena. I got her in frame. She studied each boy, her tanned face beaming pride and satisfaction without an obvious grin or smile. She touched her father's arm, and he nodded.

Stewart's hands went to his waist. "We've been trying to raise money to build an indoor arena, so the kids can ride in the winter. Can you imagine if that ever happens?"

Jude grinned. "Yes, yes, I can."

CHAPTER TWENTY-SIX

BECK

WE WERE WORKING on a song that Myles had written. I'd given him the lyrics I'd struggled with in Meager, and the lyrics that Violet had added in my notebook.

Violet was on the floor next to him, her eyes closed, listening.

You don't lie
You play
You make noise
In your plastic box
Where everything's pretty
Oh so pretty
Who are you
Spinning, spinning
Are you winning?
Pose and jangle
Damn good angle
No relief
You're a thief
Who's to blame for the bitter?
The bitter
Fake news
How many views?

Who are you?
I don't know, do you?
Spinning, spinning
Are you winning?
Nothing but bitter
Bitter
You think you have all the power
So much sour
Leaving behind your trail of bitter, bitter
Why am I paying for your sin?
No way I can win
Bitter
Bitter
Oh so bitter

The song was our ode to Lisa—to all the Lisas. Violet shot me a look, and I nodded at her. She'd recognized the final verse. Turning, she aimed her lens up at Myles, shooting him at all sorts of angles as he got deeper into the meaning of the song.

We recorded our final version—for now. Violet tapped on her phone, jotting down thoughts in her Notes app. She'd told me last night she didn't want to forget specific feelings and imagery that were going through her head as she listened. It would help her later in editing the images and creating a collection.

"I need a break." Jude peeled off the strap of his bass. "Need some board time." He let out an exhale, his hands rubbing over his head.

"Sure, man. Let's do it."

We took a break, all of us on our skateboards, swooshing around on the old driveway of the ranch where Stewart had a number of ramps and steps set up. It was pretty damn awesome. Violet shot us swirling and twisting on our boards, as a late lunch was set up for us on the back patio.

"This looks so good," Jude crowed. The table was chock full of salads—cabbage and carrot, mixed greens and roasted red peppers, a vegetarian black bean chili, and huge buffalo burgers dripping with melted gruyere and cheddar and sautéed onions. We attacked.

"Babe, soda or iced tea?" Beck asked me from the drinks table.

"Iced tea, please." I settled in my chair.

"So, Violet, are you going to show us what you've got on us so far or you don't like to share?" Myles passed Jude the green salad.

"I'd love to show you. Let me grab my laptop." Violet got up from the table and went into the living room, where she had her laptop. Back at the table, she opened it up, tapped on her keyboard, and turned it around to face us. Myles scrolled.

Loads of shots of us in motion. Melancholic shots of each of us working in the small studio, cables running everywhere, me and Jude in a serious conversation. Myles singing his heart out in the booth alone. Stewart on the drums, adding extra percussion to a song, his sticks a blur. All of it high in contrast, dark, almost black and white. Me and Jude laughing outside while he drank from a bottle of juice, my head on his shoulder. The two of us doing handstands together.

"For me these shots are personal," said Violet. "Meaning they show your relationships. Your chemistry together at play and at work. The photography on your first album was very high portraiture in that incredible corrosive black and white, which is Janus's trademark. Elegant and austere at the same time. And your music on that album is very tightly—um—"

"Produced," said Zack.

"Yes, that's it."

Zack pushed his empty dish out of the way, leaning forward on the table. "You've been listening all week, Violet. I'd like to hear how this new material sounds to you. Be honest. Whatever it is. I know you get that it's still cooking, still raw."

"Yeah, let's hear it." Myles's eyes narrowed.

Violet's eyebrows shot up her forehead. She was being put on the spot. "Um, guys, I'm no musician…"

"We don't want a musician's analysis," said Zack. "We want your feels and impressions. It's moved you somehow as you've been working, right?"

"It definitely has, how could it not?" She bit her lip, her fingertips stroking the table. "Compared to your first album, there's a less serious tone to it. You still have your serious edge, the subject matter is often serious, but instead of that…earnestness, there's more bite, more irony with a dash of fuck it. It's more playful, but in a dark way. Does that make sense?'

"Yeah, keep going." Jude chomped on his burger, his gaze riveted on Violet, like everyone else's.

"Overall, the sound feels more industrial but still melodic." She took in a breath, taking us all in.

We waited for more. Wanted more.

"It's...messier." She swallowed hard, sliding back against her chair. "That's what I've been feeling."

"Messier, darker, edgy is real good," said Zack. "Earnest, overproduced is real bad. Thus, I am very happy."

"Me too, awesome." Jude grabbed his soda and drank.

Myles caught my gaze and smiled as he leaned back against his chair. "Thanks, Violet. Sorry to put you on the spot, but all that was good to hear."

Her cheeks had gone rosy, and I took her hand in mine and kissed it. I don't think I'd ever witnessed Violet blushing. My chest swelled as my cock hardened in my jeans.

She squeezed my hand. "Guys, I wanted to make a suggestion for a shoot—if you're up for it. It would mean time away from the studio for a day."

"A shoot?" Myles wiped at his mouth with a napkin. "You mean something more formal than we've been doing so far?"

"I wouldn't say formal necessarily, but definitely focused, yeah."

"What are you thinking?" Zack refilled his water glass.

"Here in Sturgis there are some tourists, but it's not super crazy yet like it will be soon for the bike festival. We could do something in town quickly so there won't be much fan panic."

Myles munched on a sweet potato fry. "Wow, to be a tourist, wander around a town. Say whaaaat?"

"Right?" I laughed. "We were in Paris for two days, and I saw nothing but the inside of the theater, the inside of a luxury minivan, and our hotel rooms."

We all laughed.

Violet folded her hands on the table. "I know I was hired to document your studio time, but since we're here, why not play and see what happens?"

"Play how, little girl?" Jude wiped his fingers on a napkin.

"Hey, hey." I kicked him under the table.

Violet let out a soft laugh. "That word play keeps coming up for me. I thought we could take some shots to play in that unexpected new world you have going on now, especially now that you're exploring it, that's it's fresh for you still. We could use clothing, accessories to bring that out, that left of center, that bit of unexpected."

"You going to dress us up like Vegas showgirls hitchhiking down the highway with bikers going past? Is that what you're after?" Zack laughed.

"No, but damn, imagine that, huh?" Violet laughed. "I was thinking that in this spirit of the more subversive and decadent for Freefall, we put that in contrast with this wild, stark landscape of the Black Hills. I think it could be very intriguing."

"Subversive. I like that," I said.

She swirled the ice at the bottom of her ice tea glass, took it in her mouth, and crunched it. "And I don't mean go big production like full costumes, but a couple items on each of you that would bring out your own subversive playful. Those few swerves off center that will make the viewer go whoa what the fuck is going on here, and whatever it is, I want to be a part of it. That's where it's at for me."

Jude grinned as he swiped a thick french fry in ketchup.

"I like it," Zack said. "Why not?"

"I imagine you only brought everyday casual clothes here, right?"

"Yeah." Everyone nodded.

"Shucks, I left my rhinestone cowboy hat at home." Myles laughed. "I didn't think there was a disco out here."

"You in rhinestones? Perfect." She grinned.

"Violet, you could contact my mom," I said. "I think I told you, when she lived in L.A. she used to be a stylist on music videos and shoots. Being as she's in the fashion biz here, and vintage clothes are her thing, if you told her what you were thinking of, she would know where to find those things and pull them for us and help you out if you want her to. Because it's going to take forever to get people in L.A. to—"

"Yes! That's a great idea." Violet's eyes widened. I recognized that look. The wheels weren't just turning. They were attached to a high speed locomotive burning all the coal, click-clacking on a sleek track.

She tucked her hair behind her ears. "I'll get your sizes and measurements for Lenore, and we could see what she comes up with. Are you guys good with that?"

"Go for it."

"Great, thank you. To get this chance to do something like this with you and for you is a huge honor and I'm really grateful, you guys. I'm really excited."

"We have a design team for the promo and the album cover, the singles. All the packaging. If we can give them a variety to choose from and work with, that's a huge win in my book," said Myles. "Anyhow, we're the ones who need to like it the most."

"I'll call Lenore now, and see what her timeframe would be." She was beaming. She loved being in the thick of an idea, making it grow, making it come to life.

She picked up her phone from the table, gave me a kiss on the lips and took off.

"You're a lucky shit." Myles stretched his back. "She's terrific, man."

"She is."

"Jude, you up to play so I can rip your ass?" Jude and Myles both had to have a PlayStation wherever they went.

"Keep dreaming, asshole." Jude got up from his chair. "Let's go."

"I'm gonna take a nap." Zack stretched out. "Then I'm going to work on that opening for "Bitter." It needs something else. I'm going to use the Greek drum, see what happens. That fucking thing is addictive."

"I'm glad you like it." I got up from the table. "I'll meet you in there later."

"Okay."

Violet was on the phone by the swimming pool, her fingers rubbing her forehead as she talked a blue streak, the look on her face serious. She knew what she wanted. She was focused, excited. Sparks fired in my veins as she listened to whatever my mom was telling her. She laughed, her face animated, full of life.

Tapping on her screen, her gaze caught on mine. I lifted my chin at her, and she grinned right back and jogged over to me. "Lenore is so excited. We had a really good discussion, and now I have to get everyone's measurements so she can take off later today and start."

"Terrific. You gonna measure me first, baby?" I brushed her lips with mine. "Do it with your mouth for precision."

"Are you lengthening, Mr. Lanier? So many more inches. Will it still fit down my throat?"

I let out a groan. "Let's find out," I said against her smiling lips.

My heartbeat was on a different rhythm with Violet, a different cadence, a quicker pulse. A dizzying pace.

Laughing, we charged up the stairs to our room.

Yeah, totally different rhythm.

CHAPTER TWENTY-SEVEN

VIOLET

LENORE'S LAUGHTER RANG OUT, rich and deep as she and Stewart hugged each other.

"Dude, your mom just keeps getting hotter every time I see her."

"Shut the fuck up, Myles," Beck said.

"She is super hot," I agreed.

It was nine in the morning and Lenore had just arrived at the ranch three days after we'd talked. The moment she'd gotten out of her car, Stewart had grabbed her in a bear hug. He introduced Lenore to his wife, Ella.

A small smile swept over Beck's lips. "Last time my mom and Stewart saw each other I was maybe five years old."

"Fuck, that only makes her even hotter for me right now," said Myles. "Stop!"

I shoved a heavy box into Myles's broad chest, and he grunted. "Inside. Pretty please."

Jude grinned, grabbing two huge shopping bags from the back of Lenore's car, where there were a zillion other bags filled with clothes and accessories. Pirate treasure, all of it.

We brought all the bags into the living room. "We'll call you in to try stuff once we go through it all. Now scram." I pointed to the front door.

Lenore and Ella came in and soon the three of us had unpacked everything and laid each item out on every available surface in the room along with the groupings of shoes and boots the guys had brought themselves.

"This is insane, Lenore," I murmured. "I'm so excited."

"Such a crazy variety. I love it," said Ella.

"I love it too. I figured I'd bring you A to Z within the parameters of the ideas you gave me. There are a few extreme items that you might be thinking WTF woman, but no need for panic." She pointed to a boa scarf (WIN!), several baroque face masks, a pile of necklaces and bracelets and rings. "I had an instinct about them, and extreme items like these often inspire something else that you haven't considered before once things get going. Plus, I need to see how these particular pieces fit on each guy, as per color, texture, and the proportion. That way, we'll be able to see what works with each one's personality and body type and how they work together, because we don't want to go overboard without intention, but we do want to make a statement. And in order for the shoot to work smoothly for you, we need to know from now what works on each guy."

"I agree. Plus we need to see how it all works together."

"Exactly."

"What might be tragic on Jude, let's say, will be orgasmic on Myles." Ella laughed.

"So true," Lenore said. "And again, Violet, don't worry, I know this is a ton of stuff, but that's how I work. I need a lot of variety to choose from, improvise with, and then—"

"Lenore, honestly, I completely trust you and I'm beyond excited to be working with you on this."

She reached out and grabbed me, and we hugged. "Honey, me too. It's been so long since I've done this kind of work, and I've missed it. Thank you so much for asking me. Especially on a project with my boy and his band. I'm having a full circle feels moment." She put a hand to her brightly tattooed chest.

The guys were skateboarding and playing basketball just

outside the window, and Lenore studied them. "Okay, let me give you my first draft outline just from knowing them and seeing them in motion today."

"Go for it. Here's my list of location ideas for you."

"Great." She scanned the list we'd already discussed over the phone and began pulling pieces, assembling, making piles, all the while her gaze going to the men outside. More piles.

"Okay."

Ella and I came up beside her in front of separated mounds of clothing.

"This is for Myles, this one for Jude, Beck, and this for Zack."

"Who do you want to fit first, Lenore?" asked Ella.

"Get Myles since he's our frontman and the big personality and the bod. We'll start with him."

Ella went outside and brought in Myles as I set up my camera on a tripod to take test shots and simply see through the viewfinder how everything looked and felt.

For over two hours Lenore had each guy strip down and put on as she tugged, studied, smoothed, assessed. We conferred. Myles actually blushed as he took off his baggy shorts while Lenore waited, her features in stern business mode.

She dressed each guy individually, Ella assisting. Lenore chose a couple of different pieces for each, then we bought the guys back in all together and studied them as a group wearing different combinations. Lenore switched out jackets, belts, shirts, hats.

"Don't worry, I know it's a lot now, but I'm paring it all down, okay, Zack? Then I want you to tell me how you're feeling in it because I need to you feel amazing because that will translate." She smoothed down the shoulders of his jacket.

I grinned from behind my camera. Lenore had noticed Zack's lips twisting, his weight shifting, jaw tightening. He was uncomfortable.

"Okay, cool." Zack let out a short breath as she adjusted a chain around his neck. "I dig it. The chain makes a difference."

"Doesn't it?" Lenore smiled at him.

Ella took photos of the guys using Lenore's phone to document the final choices. I took shots, and Lenore and I studied them on my laptop. She'd switch out a scarf or a necklace or a shirt or a pair of shoes.

"What do you think?" Lenore crossed her arms as we both took in the guys dressed in the final grouping.

"I want to swallow them all," I whispered. *Oh damn!* "Uh…I mean…"

She chuckled, and the guys narrowed their eyes at us. "I know exactly what you mean, Violet."

"Are we done here?" said Beck, his voice curt.

"Yes, we are." I wiped the grin off my face. "Thank you for your patience. We'll meet out front in thirty minutes, okay?"

I PATTED dark purple lipstick on Zack's lips as we stood on a corner off the main road of Sturgis. "That feel weird?"

"It's all right."

"A bit of this and we're done." I brushed my bronzer powder on his cheeks, contouring his amazing cheekbones. "There."

"You got more hair gel?"

"Yep." I grabbed the tube from the tote bag at my feet, flipped open the cap, and squeezed gel in his open palm. He touched up the spikes in his hair that stuck in front of the brim of his fedora.

Lenore adjusted the ruffles of the vintage tuxedo shirt she had dressed Myles in. The shirt was open, showing his bare, long torso that women screamed for and penned blog posts about, with a large skull medallion hanging from a silver chain. He extended his arm for her as she tugged on the ruffles at the end of his sleeves, fluffing them out over his hands. With his fingertips, he smoothed the edge of his eyes which were lined in black kohl. He looked damn fine, in fact.

Beck smoothed down his vintage three-quarter length dark blue coat with aged brass buttons up the sides and along the lapels, something out of an eighteenth century pirate world. Jude wore a top hat with a feather in the front of it along with a long suede vest over a worn out V-neck T-shirt, his sculpted arms showing.

"Hold on—" Lenore inspected him from chest to toe. "One thing—" She took her shearing scissors from her tool belt and sliced at the V of his T-shirt, pulling, ripping, making the tee more eroded. "Oh yeah, much better," she murmured as she arranged the beads hanging from the chain around his neck. "We are beautiful. Let's do this."

"Aye aye, captain." Jude touched the rim of his hat.

With my camera trained on them, Myles up front, the four of them strode up the main road of Sturgis which was filled with parked bikes of every color, size, make imaginable.

Stopping, admiring bikes, a girl in a bikini and cowboy boots handed Myles a leaflet advertising a bar, and he shot her a suggestive look, his hand holding the paper as if it were an important hand-written missive while he trod the fashion runway in his mind, his curly longish hair in his face, his round sunglasses a bit low on his nose, his tongue swiping at his lip.

He was so damn hot. Perfection. And he was into this.

My stomach tightened, my brain razor sharp and clear. I took into account the warm glare of the sun, getting them all in frame or at the edge of the frame, focusing on two of them or one as they moved, watched for people taking them in, others ignoring them.

I anticipated the unexpected.

Jude did a two step as he walked to the rhythm of a Guns and Roses song that blared from the open doors of a bar, slinging an arm around a serious faced Beck. A smile tipped up Beck's lips. I shot their boots and high tops as they ambled down the sidewalk, Zack looking into a storefront like he couldn't get in and really wanted to. An outsider, a potential invader, a man from another time.

Myles led us into a restaurant, the long bar empty except for a couple of older bikers. He hiked himself up on a stool next to them.

Yes, Lord. Yesssss.

Ella quickly asked the bartender if it was okay for us to shoot. The bartender did a double take. She'd recognized Myles right away. "Hell yes," she exclaimed.

Myles ordered a whiskey, and from the end of the bar, I shot him drinking, licking his lips in the amber light glowing over him from the lighting fixture above.

Jude lit Beck a cigarette, the lighter's flame was extra large, eerily lighting up Beck's face. I shot and returned to Myles.

"Myles, turn three quarters toward me…" He did so and I kept snapping. Beck came up next to him, and Myles passed him his glass. With his hand on Myles's shoulder, Beck drank, looking positively decadent and worn out. Waiting to be picked up. Jaded with a slip of innocence.

I licked my lips as I shot them. That wash of radiant adrenaline that came over me when all the pieces fit, when the visuals and the feels melded, surged through me and I drew on it, my life-giving well. An energy source that fed me, that I gave to in return. Here in this zone I was open to receiving, to seeing and capturing through the filter of what I felt and what I knew was possible to feel, to see. What I wanted others to see and feel.

At the end of the bar, I got closeups of Zack, the neo punk rocker, talking to two bulky, muscly tatted older bikers with very long beards. A study in two eras of fringe society.

A number of people had gathered in the painted windows of the bar, pointing and taking pics with their phones. I shot them. The barbarians at the gate. Ardent admirers wanting to touch.

"Let's go," I said loudly.

"There a back way out, hon?" Lenore asked the bartender,

who was thanking Myles with a kiss on the cheek for his autograph on her arm, her hands planted on the bar, ass in the air.

Architecture.

Click.

Her eyes widened, her grin deepened. "Yes, ma'm. Right this way—" She hopped down and we followed her.

Once outside, we quickly got back to the truck and the car. "You guys were fucking amazing. Now let's get some exterior shots right before the sun starts to set."

We left Sturgis. Ella drove the car I was in. She was taking us to a meadow off the road that she'd suggested to me earlier. Fifteen minutes later we pulled over by a field filled with high grasses. Perfect.

"I'd love shots of you guys walking through here, and I'll take a few portrait shots too. Freestyle it."

I snapped shots of them stretching out as they took in the infinite rolling hills, the buttes in the distance, wide open sky above them. They tracked through the grasses, and I put the four of them together.

Lenore threw the bright blue boa around Beck's neck. He let out a small groan. He didn't like it? I grinned to myself. Lenore grabbed an eye pencil from her front pocket and worked on Beck's eyes. She fluffed out his hair and moved out of frame.

My breath caught. My heart stopped.

He looked dead on at me. The smudge of dark blue eyeliner made his eyes pop, and gave him a decadent, wanton look. Vulnerability soaked in raw sex.

My Beck.

"Right there," I whispered.

I got closer. He tilted his chin ever so slightly, an eyebrow popped up, his lips parted, the tip of his tongue peeked out and swiped the edge of his mouth, and a flush of heat rippled through my insides. I shot. I shot. Beck mouthed words. I read his lips.

"Lover girl."

My grip on my camera tightened. Light and shadow played over his features, and that need to capture, preserve, overwhelmed me. I soared in it. I breathed him in with my camera, with my soul.

A slow, sly grin tipped up his lips, and my heart drummed in my chest. His lips moved again. *"My Violet."*

Myles and Jude cavorted behind him. Were they doing an eighteenth century line dance? Several buffalo appeared in the distance, ambling slowly through the grasses, and I pulled back, getting them in the shot too. Beck raised his face to the sky, eyes closed. His long throat revealed itself, offering shadow and contour and simple beauty.

I shot, shot, shot.

Jude took off running in circles, his arms flying out. A little boy pretending to be an airplane. He circled Beck, and I stepped back to get them both in a wide frame. For all their playful motion, their faces remained serious.

Lenore had taken the jacket off of Myles, and Myles, shirt wide open, slim trousers and a long silky scarf around his corded neck, strode through the long grasses, his sunglasses low on his nose. He looked perfectly comfortable in the rural setting.

I got close-ups of his ringed hands, heavy boots in the earth. He and Zack talking. Laughing, Myles leaning his head on Zack's shoulder as Zack wiped down what was left of his purple lipstick from the edge of his mouth, down the side of his face. Ghastly, comical. Riveting. Myles stuck out his tongue.

"A couple last ones now, you guys. This is fantastic." I grouped them together, Lenore darting in and adjusting. She put a small gold face mask on Jude and he posed like a pretentious model—they all did, goofing around.

"Give me what you got right now. That's all I want."

Their chins lifted slightly, relaxed smiles, fluid postures. The orange red glow of the sun seeped through the sky, turning pink, a dash of amethyst, of light blue. A breeze kicked up, and Myles's hair tossed in his eyes. He shook it back a little, his tongue dragging along his lower lip. Beck put his arm on Myles's shoulder. His chin lifted, eyes gleaming.

Everything I'd wanted to see, everything I'd wanted this to day to be, it had been and more.

So much more.

CHAPTER TWENTY-EIGHT

BECK

WE'D GOTTEN BACK to the ranch, and in the shadows of near night, Violet took final shots of us in front of Stewart's rusted antique pickup truck that years ago he'd shoved in his front yard like a huge sculpture that had dropped from the sky. We looked like we were in some punked-out acid tripping version of the Grapes of Wrath.

Mom had gone straight home, and we'd had a great dinner. Everyone wanted to see Violet's shots, but she insisted on going through them first and editing, which she planned on doing first thing in the morning. After dinner, all the guys were in front of the TV playing video games, and me and Violet went up to our room.

She attacked me.

She pulled my T-shirt off, unbuckled my jeans, and I let out a laugh. "I'm sensing urgency. What's gotten into you, baby?"

"Post work adrenaline." She threw the quilt and the pillows on the floor like we did every time. "I had a great time today. I loved everything about it. Everything. Working with the band, with Lenore, especially photographing you. I liked that a lot. The camera just eats you up.

"Working with the light outside, the weather, the unpredictability of Sturgis. I loved it. The working on the fly, capturing everything I could. And all of you gave me so much to work with. So much. It was such a thrill, so gratifying, and I'm feeling all kinds of lucky right now. All kinds of blessed. My own shoot, my own, with Freefall. Even if you all and Ford don't like them or don't want to use them in any way, I won't care—"

"Of course you'd care."

"I'd be disappointed, but the important thing is that I did the work and I liked what I saw today, I liked what I got, and I did it the way I wanted, and that's what matters."

"Yes." I dug my hands in her hair and brought her face to mine. "That's what matters." I kissed her. She wrapped her arms around me tightly, and our tongues lashed together. "Don't forget what that feels like. Don't."

"I won't."

I lost her mouth. She pushed me, ripping off her shirt and her leggings.

My dick throbbed at the sight of her body in the lingerie I'd bought her in Greece. I palmed a breast, another hand sliding down the curve of a smooth hip. "How high are you, baby?"

"Very."

"You like how it feels?" My fingers slid between her ass cheeks.

"Hmm," she was breathless.

I moved in close to her mouth, but didn't kiss her. I spoke against her lips. "Take off the panty, but keep that fucking sexy bra on, Miss Hildebrand." I shoved her back from me, and biting her lip, she slid the panty down those amazing legs, yanked it off, and tossed it at me. On a smirk, I caught it, still warm, kind of damp from her luscious body. I stroked my cock with it.

"How you spoil me." She let out a soft laugh. "Get on the floor, lover boy."

Dropping the panty, I got on the floor. She straddled me, taking my cock in hand and easing my rock hard length inside her. Her chin lifted, she took in a breath. "You really spoil me."

She rocked over me and I thrust, her fingertips digging into my chest like tiny pincers. "Every. Damn. Time."

I let out a low laugh as the sting rushed over my flesh. Her gorgeous tits, encased in that tight nude colored demi-cup bra that was impossibly sheer, swayed with her movement. The fabric silky under the palm of my hand. "I like you high on adrenaline, baby."

I unclipped the front snap of the bra. Her breasts tumbled free, and I cupped them, nuzzled them, softly slapped at them. She let out a cry, her eyes closing as she ground down on me, small moans escaping her lips.

Those lips.

I slid my thumb in her mouth, and on a moan she sucked. My breath cut, my heart ached. "Babe, need you to look at me." Her beautiful big lit from within eyes found mine and I dove there, held her there, in my heart, inside me deep. My pulse was wired, my body hummed. We were aligned. Connected.

And I wanted more. More. Was that even possible?

I knew a way.

CHAPTER TWENTY-NINE

VIOLET

A SMILE FLICKERED over Beck's face as I rocked my pelvis against his, tightening myself around his fantastic cock.

His lips moved against mine, "Breathe with me." My forehead slid against his, and my breathing became, slower, deeper, matching his. Heat built at the base of my spine and traveled up, up, up. His lips brushed my damp skin, and I breathed him in. Every cell in my body lit up with the energy we created together. A force of need and want.

My gaze met his. Blue fire, gleaming, solemn, alert. His hold on me tightened. Freeing, I trusted him. Daunting, so truthful. I couldn't look away. Communion.

Why does everything have to be fast? He'd told me that first night together in Meager. He was so right.

The sweat on his skin became mine. I rocked my hips slowly, he ground against me slowly. Our groans, the scent of us, raw and crude, sensual and sublime, filled my senses. He reached between us and touched me, and I gasped at the intensity of the contact, my fingers digging into his neck. He had lit the fire, he stoked the flames.

His tongue licked at my neck and I shivered, his teeth grazed my ear. I was open, vulnerable to the elements; the storm was Beck.

I moved faster, and he took his hand away, his hips slowing, grip tightening. He pulled out of me, and my eyes blinked at the loss.

"We're going to build this. Bring you to the edge and pull back."

"Are you going Tantric on me?"

"Yes." He licked my jaw.

"Oh my fuck."

"That's right, this is our fuck. I want this to last, to be powerful…" His fingers dug deeply into my ass cheeks.

I let out a gasp at the shooting sting blending into my pleasure like watercolor paint diluting in liquid. A new color. I brought my focus back to his breaths. He reached between us and squeezed the gorged tip of his cock, a grunt escaping his lips, his brows furrowing. I kissed him, distracting him, both of us moaning. He slid his cock in my wet, not inside me, and I slid with him.

Silk. Indescribable. Velvet. All my senses sang. My pulse careened into hyperspace. There was no way out, only higher, only toward more. My lungs tightened. Suddenly, that pressure, that silky friction was gone. He'd pulled away once more with a hand at my breast and stroked, his tongue toying with mine, trailing down, his teeth nipping at my throat. I focused on his breaths once again, and the chain tightened between us.

Every move he made was intentional, to please, to give, to take away, to slow down, to enhance. He could feel my responses, he listened intently to my breaths, my moans, sensing my trembling body.

It was exquisite.

A mind body soul fuck.

My body yearned for his, I was all his.

He brought a nipple to his mouth, his teeth grazing my incredibly sensitive flesh. Another slick finger slid between my ass cheeks and delved lower and deeper. My hips raised, circled, giving him access.

My hand wrapped around his cock and stroked, pumped, drawing groans, his head knocking back. "Baby, that's it. You get right to the core of me, fuck…yes…oh yeah…" His eyes were heavy, gleaming. Expectant.

With a grunt, he pushed me back on the floor, my legs still wrapped around him. He raised up, and gripping my thighs, slammed his cock inside me.

"Yes!" My back arched, my breasts bouncing with his every deep, quick thrust. I was open to everything he gave me. I was his, all his.

"Oh fuck…" His fingers pressed against my clit.

My entire being blazed. I came, and came, and came. His body stiffened, an animal-like growl rumbled from him as he came.

We both collapsed into the mess of bedding on the floor. Beck's hand slid over my face, the scent of my musk teasing me as he pulled my hair back, lips brushed at the skin of my neck, throat.

We clasped each other. One beast, one heap of sweaty, satisfied flesh. Human, vulnerable.

Together.

CHAPTER THIRTY

BECK

ALL OF US were perched around Violet's laptop on the dining room table.

Zack's forehead creased as he took in the final photograph from our set out in the field. "To be honest, I wasn't sure how it would come off. But I really like them all. A lot. Which makes me happy because I had a lot of fun doing it."

Violet's back was stick straight in the dining room chair as we gave her our feedback on her presentation of the photos she'd taken of us after having spent almost two days editing them.

"Thanks, Zack. I had a lot of fun doing this too. It was a dream come true, especially after being in the studio with you guys. It wasn't just a cold shoot from an external idea."

"Truth," said Myles his attention on a photo of him and the bartender at Sturgis. "It's over the top, but not bombastic. Over the top in an edgy way that is very much more of us."

"I'd love to see what the art design people would come up with using these for an album," said Zack.

"I would too," I said.

Her gleaming eyes met mine. She was beside herself, bursting.

"Sure, the imagery is unusual for us. But that's what makes it captivating and powerful."

"I think it flows along with the new material really well," said Jude. "And punches it up."

"Thank you for giving me the chance to work with you. It's been the best experience ever. "I've learned so much about a musician's process, what it takes to work together to create a cohesive whole. It's been amazing, and I'll never forget it." She went to her laptop.

Myles threw his arms around her and they hugged. "It's been a good time, Violet."

She was going home tonight. Leaving us. Leaving me. Again. My jaw clenched.

Myles grabbed a fresh bottle of beer. "We'll tell Ford we like your shots and want to use them for the album, the promo, whatever it is."

"You guys don't have to..." Violet said.

"We want to use them." Myles drank. "They're spot on."

Jude squeezed Violet. "We like them hard." The two of them laughed together as he rocked her in his arms.

"Real hard," said Zack. "Dudes, I'm heading back into the studio to work out a couple things with Stewart. Hang on—Violet, you're leaving now, right?"

"Yes."

Zack hugged her. "It was great to meet you, loved working with you, and I'll be seeing you in L.A. real soon, right?"

"Uhm, yeah." Violet nodded, lips parting. She'd been caught off guard.

"Bye, babe. See you soon." She and Jude hugged. "Zack, I'll be there in a few, I'm going to take a quick shower first." Jude headed up the stairs.

"I'm going to call my parents, check in with them. Be there in ten." Myles took Violet in a big bear hug. "I really liked working with you, Violet. Thanks for the makeup tips too."

She laughed out loud. "Any time."

"Look forward to hanging in L.A." He went through the patio doors to the backyard.

I took her hand in mine. "Congratulations, Miss Hildebrand. How's it feel?"

She let out a deep breath. "What exactly? So much…"

"First and foremost, to have given your client what they didn't realize they wanted."

Her lips widened into a smile and she lunged at me. I caught her, hitching her legs around me. "I'm so proud of you."

"You really like it?"

"Violet—"

"Beck, I need to know. Your opinion matters to me."

I sat her down on the table and leveled my gaze with hers. "Your photos took me to a new place in Freefall world. We teased and intrigued. You enshrouded us in some kind of mystery, and yet through it all you revealed. What I just saw was alluring and seductive but like Myles said, still rough at heart, still rough around the edges."

And that's how I feel about you, baby. I planted a kiss on her cheek.

"Thank you," she whispered.

"You did all the work, thank you."

"We were all a great team, including of course Ella and your mom. Amazing chemistry all around."

"It was amazing. I loved working with you in your world."

"Me too." On a grin she hopped down from the table and turned to her laptop, closing it down. She gathered her battery and cable.

I took the laptop and together we climbed the stairs to our room, my heart getting heavier with each step. "I can't believe you're leaving already."

"I know, I can't either. But I have this family dinner tonight at the ranch and then the auction in a couple of days. And I need to go over all the Freefall pics, edit, and send them to Ford. I almost can't believe I just said that."

I went up behind her and planted a kiss along that curve of bare skin between shoulder and neck that I knew made her shiver. "Believe it." I wrapped my arms around her waist. "We made it happen."

She met my gaze in the reflection of the mirror, and that vibration between us shimmered. "We did."

I squeezed her hips. "I'm going to miss you."

She turned around and slid her hands around my neck. "I'm going to miss you too."

A tide rose inside me, pushing against my chest, my lips. I had to say it. I had to tell her. I'd only said it once before at the airport in New York when I'd felt like she was being torn out of my arms forever. Things were completely different now. I needed to scoop up this moment and claim it. I couldn't let it get away.

"Violet, you and I have had so many goodbyes. Goodbyes with question marks at the end of each of them. This is me answering those questions. I love you, Violet. I'm full on crazy in love with you."

Her head lifted, her body tightened as if my words, my emotions, were forces. They were. "Beck..."

"Baby, this is our moment. I can feel it. Can't you? It's—"

Her eyes widened, her lips parted. "It's so good. So good." She swallowed hard. Was she in shock?

"Babe?" My hands cradled her face. "Talk to me. Are you freaking out?"

"I feel like...when we skydived, right before we...I couldn't breathe. I couldn't believe I was about to throw myself out of a plane."

I let out a laugh. "But you did it, and it was fantastic."

"It was."

"What did I tell you after?"

"That we'd dive in tandem." A small smile brightened her face as my forehead slid to hers. "That's what this feels like right now. In the sky. Breathless."

We hugged. Hugged tight.

"Beck, you're so confident in us. But it's brand new territory for me. I've always purposely chosen the wrong men and purposely gotten out. But this with you is not any of that. It's beautiful and wild and rough, and a little bit scary."

"Like the Dakota Territory?"

"Exactly." She swept my hair back from my face.

No, she hadn't said I love you back, but she would, I knew she would. She hadn't gotten mad, or put things in reverse like all those other times. This was progress.

"So when can you come out to L.A.?"

"Um, not sure. There's the auction coming up."

"Right."

"Then there's the Founding Festival. You should come out for that."

"I'd like to."

"Good."

"Good."

We stared at each other, the air tingling around us.

Her brow furrowed. "Why don't you come with me?"

"Where?"

"To dinner tonight. Meet everyone. The immediate family, that is. They all know who you are, but they haven't met you yet. With me."

"Sounds official. You're up for that?"

She smirked. "I am. Are you?"

Good sign. "I am. Let's do it."

"Good." She zipped up her suitcase.

"Good." I blew out a breath, running a hand through my hair. "Well then, I better take a shower and get some clean clothes on. I'm meeting the Hildebrands of Meager, South Dakota."

CHAPTER THIRTY-ONE

BECK

"I REALLY LIKE YOUR COUGAR. A badass car for my badass woman."

Grinning, Violet expertly guided her car around the twist in the road leading out of Sturgis toward Meager.

"I love this car," she said. "For years, I saved my own money for when I found the right car. And when I found her, I spent it all. Best move. She's perfection. I want to take her to the One-Eyed Jacks soon to get some custom detailing. I kept putting that on the back burner, but no more."

"Get it done. They do amazing work. Finger had them detail my bike. So this is your first car?"

"No." Her chin lifted, lips twisted, her focus remaining on the road. "That was another car."

I sensed a story in the suddenly darker tone of her voice. "What other car?"

"After the fire, my parents gave me my brother's car. A beautiful vintage Trans Am that my dad had spent a lot of money refurbishing for him just the way he wanted. A real hot rod."

"Sounds amazing."

"It was. That car was an experience to ride in, to drive." She let out a short, bitter laugh as she hit the clutch and shifted gears. "I rode the fuck out of it."

"I'll bet." My stomach tightened. "What happened to it?"

"After I got it, I waited for Five's birthday to come up, about ten months later, and I pretended it had been stolen, but actually I'd sold it to a chop shop in North Dakota with Wes's help."

"You did?"

"I got good money for it, which I donated anonymously to a charity for autistic kids the One-Eyed Jacks were sponsoring that month." She took in a shallow breath.

"Why did you do it?"

"When he first got that car, I'd touched the hood, so glossy, so sparkly, so perfect, and he immediately warned me, 'Don't you dare, Violet. Don't even breathe on my car.'"

"So when you were given his car…"

"It was supposed to be a great privilege, that gift. But for me it was an opportunity. That's how I grieved for my brother. I did the things he always told me not to do."

I swallowed hard. "I'm guessing there were other things?"

"Oh yeah."

"You want to tell me?"

"Do you want to hear?"

"I can take it, baby. Whatever it is." Had she ever told anyone?

"One day Five's best friend, Derek, had driven me home from school and Five was pissed off. He stood there in our driveway, yanked me out of the car, yelling at me, cursing. Called me a slut and a bunch of other crap." She let out a bitter laugh. "I'd barely french-kissed at that point! He went on a jag telling all his friends to stay away from me. I didn't even like any of them. At the time I had a crush on a really nice guy in my math class.

"But after the fire, I dropped the really nice guy and fooled around with Five's friends, one by one. In that damned Trans Am too. I saved Derek, the best friend, for last. I chose him to have sex with for the first time.

"The jerk thought I was in love with him. They all thought I was so sad and broken. Poor Violet." Her voice was tinted with a sneer, and my back stiffened at the sound. "Idiots, all of them. They all thought they were kings, just like my brother did. All of them arrogant and petty and small. Out to conquer, twist your arm, take what they could get out of you. Have it their way or no way at all."

Her fingers tightened around the wheel. This was something other than grief and survivor guilt. Bitterness and anger. Simmering volcanic anger. Was this why she'd always skittered away from relationships? Real boyfriends?

"Baby…"

"I shouldn't have said all that, I'm sorry. Here we are off to a family dinner and I'm telling you all this crap…terrific."

I put a hand on her thigh. "I'm listening to your truth."

"Jesus, Beck. You always do," she breathed. "That night when you and I talked at Pete's, I was there with Derek and the guys and their girlfriends."

"Oh yeah?" My scalp prickled. I'd never even considered that she'd been there with a guy that night. The guy who'd had her first. A guy she'd never even liked.

"After your performance, I took off from our table. I didn't know where I was going but I knew that I had to get away from them, I couldn't breathe. I ended up in the back and bumped into you.

"When you and I talked, I realized what a horrible carousel I'd locked myself on at the expense of me, and I wanted to get off. I had to. You helped me see that clearly, Beck. And that stellar kiss sealed the deal." She let out a soft chuckle.

"You'd told me you were there with friends. Did you go back to them after we'd said goodbye?"

"No. I didn't. You left, and I took off through the emergency exit door and never had anything to do with Derek or the rest of them ever again. I was done."

Her words hung in the air between us, and I breathed them in and my heart started again.

"The next day I applied for that photography workshop and I

got in. After that, I focused on my photography. On developing my work and a career path that I really wanted. Every chance I got I went to shows and concerts and shot. I lived for it. For the live music, the wild energy, the outrageous everything. Trying to capture what I saw, what I heard and felt. There I could let go. It was my escape and my moving forward. And you, you were the spark for all of it. You turned everything right side up for me."

My pulse pounded at her revelation, my hand squeezing her thigh again. "But you're still angry, still grieving."

She took a sharp turn and a large arched sign that read "Hildebrand Ranch" loomed over us. The car raced up the hill under the sign. "I'm not grieving."

"Grieving for losing a way of life, losing the family you once had. The way you all looked at the world and your place in it. It's no longer innocent, is it?"

"It stopped being innocent for me a long time ago, before the fire."

"I think that you're still in that house with Five, flames and smoke all around you."

"Every damn day," she bit out as we drove up to a large home part original ranch house, part newly built modern log cabin. Sprawling. Impressive.

She shut down the engine, and I took her hand in mine. "Violet, please listen to me."

She blinked, meeting my gaze at last, eyes shuttered.

"Baby, you chose to go into that burning house and you got your sister out alive. You are fucking brave."

"I wasn't brave enough."

I wasn't sure what she meant by that, but she was wrong.

"You are one of the bravest people I've ever met." I squeezed her hand. "But you've got to get out of that burning house, Violet. Get out."

CHAPTER THIRTY-TWO

BECK

THE HILDEBRAND RANCH house was an impressive two story stone and wood wonder set on a hill in the center of an endless stretch of soft hills filled with gold and green grasses. We climbed the steps to the wrap around porch and I turned, taking in a deep breath of the fresh air. "Is this all yours, as far as the eye can see?"

"Pretty much."

"This house is beautiful."

"When my grandma and grandpa got married, they lived here, and it was kind of a mess back then. Grandma Holly took on the house improvements on her own, and finally the rest of the family gave in and renovated. She could convince people of anything." Violet let out a soft laugh. "Her little project took on a life of its own for a long while, but it was a job well done." She came up alongside me and we both took in the landscape.

"It's all so damned…magnificent," I murmured. "No other word."

"It is, isn't it?"

We headed inside through a large screen door. Muffled voices and clinking glasses filled the air.

A tall man with worn leather cowboy boots grinned at us. "I thought I heard you on the porch."

"Hey, Uncle Mad," Violet greeted him with a hug. "This is Beck."

"Welcome. Good to meet you." A firm handshake. He had Violet's eyes.

"Uncle Maddox is my dad's brother. He runs the ranch with Grandpa. Is Dad here?"

"Yep, he's already on his second whiskey."

"Oh."

"Your grandpa told me your mom is coming too. What can I get you to drink?"

"An iced tea would be great."

"What can I get you, Beck?"

"I'll have the same."

"Well hello." A blonde girl with a shy smile stood before us.

"And this is my sister, Jessa." Violet hugged her sister.

"Good to meet you, Jessa. I've heard so much about you," I said.

"Good to meet you too. I love your music, by the way." Jessa's face streaked with pink.

"Thank you."

"What can I get you to drink, Jessa?" asked Maddox.

"I'll have a glass of white wine." Jessa leaned into her sister. "Could I talk to you a sec?"

"Sure. Be right back." Violet touched my arm, and walked off with Jessa.

"Why don't you come with me to the bar," Maddox gestured, and I followed him to the far corner of the vast living room area. My attention was riveted by a massive fireplace made of big stones which reached all the way up to the pitched wood-beamed ceiling.

"Two iced teas." Maddox put two bottles of iced tea on the bartop along with two glasses filled with ice, and I poured out the teas. "And one white wine." He placed a stem glass on the counter and took out an already opened bottle of wine and poured.

As I drank my tea, my gaze went to the wall next to me which was covered in family photos. Decades worth of Hildebrands.

"Is there a photo of Violet here?"

"Sure is." He re-corked the wine bottle and set it down. "You see that black and white one on the far left—tall, skinny lady wearing a funny hat with five kids all lined up?"

I found the photograph, must have been from the forties. "Got it."

He opened a whiskey bottle and poured liquor into a tumbler. "On their left, is a photo of Violet and her brother and sister. I think Violet's no more than ten years old there."

Something in my chest twisted. A photo of the three of them, on the porch of this house, only Violet and Five weren't paying attention to whomever was taking the photo. They were focused on each other. They were laughing, laughing hard at a joke only they understood, making faces at each other, leaning into one another. Holding hands fiercely. On the same wavelength.

While Jessa, shorter and much younger, stood on her own on the other side of Violet in a pretty dress, her hands clasped together, posing politely, primly, perfectly, a "Say Cheese" smile on her face. She was following directions. Not Violet and Five. They were in their own world, having too good of a time together.

In their own world.

Maddox came up next to me, letting out a rough sigh. "My mom could never get those two to stand still. Only Jessa. This was the only kind of picture she could ever get of them. Violet and Five were thick as thieves from day one. Always had their own jokes, own way of talking to each other."

My mouth dried. "Seems that way."

"Little Jessa never had a chance, but she didn't mind much. She wasn't the rough and tumble type like Violet and Five. Those two? Like twins. Inseparable and very loud." He took a long swallow of his whiskey. "They'd take their horses and go off together never to be heard from again. I lost count of the times me and their dad would have to go after them." He chuckled to himself.

"It's a great picture."

"Best one."

"I didn't realize they were so close."

The lines of his face suddenly dulled, his body stiffening. "They were until…well, until they weren't." He cleared his throat.

"Teenagers." I lightened my voice on purpose. "What a strange breed, huh?"

"Right?" He turned away from the wall of photographs. Memories too beautiful. Memories too painful.

CHAPTER THIRTY-THREE

VIOLET

"DO you know what this dinner is about?" Jessa said, her voice low, trying not to be overheard.

"It's *about* something?"

"I got that feeling when Grandpa called me."

"I figured it's because we haven't had a family dinner in a long time at the ranch since Grandma died. She used to insist first Sunday of every month…"

"But it's not the first Sunday of the month, and Grandpa called Mom and invited her. She told him she didn't think it was a good idea, but he insisted. Then he called her a second time to make sure she was coming. You see where I'm going with this?"

"Ohhhh."

"Exactly. But an intervention under the guise of a family dinner is something Grandma Holly was good at. They were successful almost a hundred per cent of the time."

"I don't think any of the little feuds and spats she solved with dinners entailed adultery, did they?"

"I don't think so, but we were kids back then, what did we know? Anyhow, that's cool that you brought Beck."

"Maybe I shouldn't have. I didn't think that this dinner would have an agenda."

"Since Beck is here, maybe Grandpa won't bring up anything."

"When General Hildebrand is determined, nothing gets in his way."

She let out a breath. "Oh, so true. He always finds a way."

Beck brought Jessa her glass of wine and me my iced tea. "Ladies, here you go."

"Thank you. Could use a shot of vodka, but I'll take it."

Beck gestured back at the bar. "You want me to—"

"No, no. I'm kidding."

"I don't think you're kidding," said Jessa sipping her wine.

"Did something happen?" Beck asked.

"No. Not yet at least. Let me introduce you to my grandfather." We moved to where Grandad spoke with Dad by the fireplace.

"Ah. This must be Beck," Grandpa held out his hand and Beck took it. A firm handshake.

"Good to meet you, sir."

"Beck is in town for a few more days, and I thought I'd bring him to dinner so you could meet him."

"Ah, you're certainly special then, son. I don't think we've ever met any of—"

"Grandad, there's never been anyone special before. Ever."

Grandad slapped a hand on Beck's shoulder. "Welcome to the Great H, son."

"Thank you. It's good to be here."

"Dad, this is Beck."

He set down his glass on the mantle and offered Beck his hand. "Hello."

"Mr. Hildebrand." They shook hands.

Female voices rose up behind us. Mom had arrived and was handing over a cake box to Lacey, the ranch housekeeper. I brought Beck over to her as Uncle Mad handed her a glass of red wine.

"Lifesaver. Thanks, Mad." She took a quick sip.

"Thought so." Uncle Mad joined Dad and Grandpa.

"Hi, honey. Good to see you, you're back." Mom kissed me on the cheek and let out a small gasp. "Beck—this is a wonderful surprise." Mom shot me The Eye, which meant: *wow-good-for-you-fantastic-what's going on here?*

"Thanks, Erica. Good to see you too."

"Lenore was just telling me and Tania how fantastic the photo shoot went with all of you. Sounds wild. I can't wait to see the shots."

"They're amazing. Violet showed them to us today. They're really good."

"I have no doubt. My baby is talented."

Another setting was placed on the long oak table for Beck, and we all sat down to eat in the formal dining room.

Grandpa insisted that Mom and Dad sit next to each other, and Jessa flared her eyes at me, her lips pressed into a tight line. Uncle Mad shook his head as he took his seat.

Dad uncorked a wine bottle and Lacey brought out the final platter of food. A big mixed greens salad, grilled rib eye steaks, and scalloped potatoes au gratin, Grandma Holly's favorite.

Uh oh. Grandpa had rolled out the big guns.

From across the table, Jessa moved her lips silently at me: *"Told you."* I rolled my eyes in reply.

"Wine?" Uncle Maddox held the bottle next to me.

"Fill 'er up."

I scooped a spoonful of the creamy potatoes onto Beck's plate. "I hope you like the potatoes. They're my Grandma Holly's famous recipe. Only made on special occasions around here." I shot Grandpa a look, and he raised his glass of wine at me.

"I love scalloped potatoes," murmured Beck taking his dish.

"I'd like to make a toast," said Grandpa. "Here's to family gathering around the table and eating together."

Oh, he was dipping his toe in the water. When would his axe fall though?

"To family," everyone said. I sipped the dry Cabernet and it immediately soothed my limbs, filling me with cozy warmth.

"Hope you like your steak medium rare, Beck. Can't overcook a good piece of beef," said Uncle Maddox.

Beck sliced at his steak. "I agree. It's perfect."

"So you're not one of them vegan vegetarians?" asked Grandpa.

"No, I'm not."

"Glad to hear it."

Mom smiled at me, shaking her head slightly, and I smiled back.

Uncle Maddox told us a story about a runaway calf that gave him a headache today. Grandpa asked Beck if he'd ever ridden a horse before. Beck and I told everyone about the kids from Pine Ridge that Stewart and Ella were helping train for the relays.

"Violet took amazing photographs of the kids riding."

"I can't wait to see," said Uncle Mad.

"Me too," said Grandpa. "Those relays are something else."

"You've been, Grandpa?"

"A couple times, when I was in high school. I'd heard about them and cut school to go." He winked at me.

"You did not."

"I did, and it was so worth it."

"I'll show you the pictures after dinner," I said.

The table was cleared and coffee served. Lacey brought in the cake from the Meager Grand on Grandma Holly's delicate pink glass cake stand.

"I brought you the apple crumble cake, Dad," said Mom.

"Wonderful, sweetheart, thank you. I've been looking forward to that beauty all day."

"It's his favorite," I whispered to Beck.

"I'll go get the knife." Mom got up from the table.

"I'll get it," said Dad.

"I got it."

"You two sit down, Lacey will be right back." Sure enough,

Lacey returned with a pint of vanilla ice cream and a serving spoon and cake knife.

"Lace, you go on, we'll take care of the dessert," Grandpa said.

"Oh, okay." She put the knife down on the table and zipped out of the dining room. Mom cut slices of the cake and Jessa scooped ice cream onto each dish, passing them around to us.

I passed a dish to Beck, and took one for myself. I dug in.

"There's something I'd like to say," Grandpa's voice filled the room.

I put my full spoon down.

My father stiffened in his chair, and Mom took in a breath as she put the knife down.

Grandpa clasped his hands together on the table. "I think it was a mistake that we stopped our Sunday dinners together, and I'd like us to do that again. Next month on the first Sunday, we'll have the cousins over too. But tonight I wanted to see all your faces around my table. I know it's been a…trying time, but I'm hoping that you, Marshall and Erica, can find your way back to each other. If there's one thing I know it's that I miss my Holly and I'd do anything to have her back."

"Dad, please stop," my mother said, her voice clear and strong.

"Erica, honey, I imagine this has been so very difficult for you. But you two have been together for so many years, since high school, you got two beautiful girls, and it'd be a shame to—"

"Dad. Please." My father's sharp voice cut him off and Grandpa scowled. "Erica and I agreed to come here tonight because we have something to tell you. To tell all of you." My father blew out a huff of air and glanced at Mom, who nodded. My stomach tightened, my pulse bonged.

"Today we signed a stipulation agreement at our lawyer's. In sixty days we'll be divorced."

My breath cut. Muscles seized. I blinked.

"What?" Jessa said. "Oh my gosh."

Beck's hand closed over my leg under the table, but his firm, warm grip didn't stop the icy chill building in my veins.

"Aw now, don't you think you're rushing this?" Grandpa said. "It all just happened, let it settle a little. Take your time, you've just—You think your mother and I didn't have our problems? Sure we did. Every marriage does. But—"

"Dad." Uncle Maddox raised his voice gently, a hand brushing down his mouth.

My father winced. "We're not rushing. We discussed it and we agree that this is for the best, for both of us." He swallowed hard. "We wanted to tell the girls first but since you'd insisted on all of us getting together tonight, we thought it was a good idea to share the news with you all together as a family."

My sister's face grew pale, her lips parted, she spoke, but I couldn't hear what she was saying. Suddenly I could no longer hear what anyone was saying. Only buzzing, buzzing in my head.

As a family, he said. *This is for the best.* But Dad looked miserable, angry. Mom steely.

The vanilla ice cream melted on top of my untouched apple crumb cake masterpiece. My mother reached out a hand to Jessa, who took it. Jessa's eyes filled with water but she choked the emotion down.

Choked it down.

Strangled it.

Thatta girl. That's how it's done.

A cold shudder shook my insides. I had brought Beck here tonight as a sign of faith to him and to me that we were now together, that he was important to me, a part of my life. And I'd actually wanted to share that with my family. It was a triumph for me. A family dinner here at the ranch was where we'd always shared good news with each other.

But tonight, instead of our family gathering for simple reasons, for simple joys, we were breaking apart.

You win, Five.

My mom had every right to choose her own path in the face of dad's betrayal, but hearing the words *we'll be divorced* was a shock. The little girl inside me was curling up into a ball.

Never in a million years did I ever think that my parents' first love would dissipate, even after the fire. Their relationship had been dented and bruised, yes, but never did I think all these years after our family tragedy would we finally break like an egg rolling off a countertop to the floor. *Crack…splat.* Goop everywhere, no way to fix it, patch it up. None. Dump it in the trash.

It rose within me, that bitter slosh. Five's sneering laugh. I let it loose.

"Violet?" Beck's low voice echoed next to me, and my body flinched as his hand squeezed my knee. But even his touch, our connection, couldn't bring me to my senses.

"Why are you laughing?" Dad's brow furrowed. "Is this funny to you?"

"No, it's not funny. You're missing the greatest irony here, Dad."

"And what would that be?" He dared me, his jaw tightening.

"That your son isn't at this table to enjoy the show."

"Violet!" Grandpa bit out.

"I'm telling the truth, somebody has to. We're still breathing in the smoke and ashes he left behind. That's what this is. If he were here at this table, he'd be laughing at all of us. He's the reason we're at this point right here and now."

"Honey, don't talk like that," Mom said.

"We need to talk about it. We never really have. Am I the only that remembers? Because I remember it all. Why don't we take turns telling a tale of Marshall the Fifth. Anyone? No? I'll start. That fire brought us here to this signing of stipulations. He did that, and he didn't care, as long as he got what he wanted. That night he wanted to show all of us that he could still do whatever he wanted.

"That night he was so mad at Dad for taking away his car

keys, mad at Mom for not sticking up for him, mad at me for playing prison warden. Mad at Jessa for…just being there."

"Violet—" Beck's face was serious. "I can't imagine how traumatic the fire was for you and your family, but—"

"Nobody can. Nobody." My breath got shallow.

You've got to get out of that burning house, Violet. Get out.

"I think it's time I finally told everyone the truth, because I can't take this anymore. I can't take watching it rip us up anymore. It's been ripping at me ever since."

"Honey, what are you talking about?" Mom's eyes widened, her face paled.

"Violet, we know the truth," said Dad.

"You don't know mine."

CHAPTER THIRTY-FOUR

VIOLET

MY BOOTS SANK into the soft grassy earth as I charged up the hill in the dark. Next to me, Beck held a jumbo flashlight, and behind me were Uncle Maddox, Dad, Mom, Jessa, and Grandpa holding a big electric lantern.

I kept going, kept pushing my wobbly legs to move forward, forward, up to the knoll to the family cemetery. I'd insisted we all come up here.

The high, curved, iron gate seemed almost gothic in the evening darkness. My fingers felt for the latch, flipped it, the iron squawking at me as I pushed the old gate open.

I walked past my great, great, grandparents and their seven sons and their families, my great grandparents and their son who'd died in Vietnam.

My Grandma Holly.

"Gran, I promise I'll be back with flowers, because you deserve all the flowers. But tonight belongs to Five."

I charged to the left and trained the flashlight on where I knew it was. His massive tombstone. I dug my heels in the ground. Beck's flashlight shone over the granite.

Marshall Hildebrand V

- Beloved grandson, son & brother -

- Taken too soon -

Yes, taken too soon.

By me.

I wiped at the sweat on my upper lip. *Hello, Five. Except for these yearly anniversaries, where I'm forced to come here, I haven't visited you once in all these years that you've been gone. I've been avoiding you, but you know that, don't you? You've been coming to me in my sleep instead.*

Mom's bundle of irises and roses from weeks ago lay ruined and mushed in the grass, and my heart grew heavier. There was no lump lodged in my throat that I had to swallow past to speak. I was very clear on it all.

Dad's lips twisted. "Let's go back to the house, come on. It's chilly and muddy up here."

Oh, it's been chilly and muddy inside me for so long now. "No, I want him to hear." I pointed at Five's grave. "I want him to know that I came clean. That I told you. Because he's been after me all these years."

"How much wine did you have?"

"Marshall!"

"I'm stone cold sober," I said.

"Go on, Violet," said Beck. "Go on."

"Violet, the only thing that matters is that you and Jessa are alive," said Grandpa.

"Is it? Is it really? Every time Dad looks at me and Jess, he thinks, why only them? Why didn't Five survive too?"

"You don't know what I think," said Dad.

"You're right I don't, because we never talk about it."

"Whatever you have to tell me about that night—"

"He was still alive." My voice sliced through the dark.

Dad froze. Mom's lips parted. Jessa grabbed onto Uncle Mad.

"What are you saying, Violet?" Mom said. "What are you saying?"

"While Wes and Bo got Jessa outside, I stayed behind to find Five."

"But you'd said that the fire was overwhelming, that you couldn't see—"

"I lied."

"Violet..." Jessa whispered.

"I saw him. He was sprawled on the kitchen floor. Conscious, struggling for air, his face bloody, his hair, his skin ..." I sucked in air at the gruesome memory. "He was making these awful howling noises, I could hear them through the flames. I can still hear all those noises at night."

Beck's hand went to my middle. An anchor.

I swallowed hard. "He saw me. He reached out a hand toward me and tried to say something...was it my name? Was it help me? I don't know. I started moving toward him, to grab him, to get him out of that kitchen. But I stopped myself. I stopped myself from helping him because I was angry at him.

"I knew this was his fault. I knew he'd done this to himself, to us, and I was so angry. He knew, and he panicked. He cried out to me, louder, but I didn't go to him. I'd made my choice. I didn't move."

Mom's hands flew to her mouth.

"I heard Wes shouting out my name, and I tried to call out to him, but suddenly the smoke was thicker and breathing got harder. I stumbled and bumped into a table and I fell, stupid popcorn around me on the floor. Wes grabbed my arm and pulled me up, and I didn't stop him. I didn't say, *no wait, we have to save Five, he's right over there!*

"And I didn't feel bad. I felt nothing for him. I wanted him to suffer. He deserved to suffer. I got out of that burning house, and I left my brother behind. Left him to die a horrible death all alone."

Cold, thick muck pushed through my veins and churned deep inside me, a tsunami of mud and debris. "I did that. I did that to him." My words hung in the silence. Everything a blur.

"Violet, listen to me." Dad grabbed me by the arms, shook me. "That kitchen was the oldest part of that house. That ceiling was the first section to collapse. If you had tried to get to him, you would have been killed too."

Mom stood next to Dad. "We would have lost you too."

Dad squeezed my arms. "You did nothing wrong."

"That's just it—I did nothing for him. And at the funeral while my grandparents cried, when my mother had to be taken away, I stayed. I stood right here in front of his coffin with you and Grandpa and Uncle Mad like a good Hildebrand while we put Marshall the Fifth in the ground, on our land."

"Yes, yes, you did."

"And the whole time I held it all in. All the hate for myself, for him, for all of it. Was I as mean and cruel as he'd become? I was afraid that you'd find out what I'd done and …" My voice shook.

Dad's grip on my arms became tighter. "You did everything right, Violet. You saved your sister, and I'm so proud of you. I never said that to you back then or since, and that was wrong. I should have. What you did took so much courage. We could have lost you both, both my baby girls, I could have lost you both." Dad let out a ragged breath. "I'm your father, and I should have protected you better, even if it was from your own brother, but I didn't. That night he did a terrible, cruel thing, and I can never forgive him for it."

"Cruel? Are we still talking about him lighting up in the kitchen?"

"Tell her. She should know," Mom said.

"Your Great Uncle Ryan was Sheriff back then, and he didn't let it get out," said Dad.

"I know. We pretended it was a gas leak so the town wouldn't—"

"There was more."

"More than freebase cocaine in the kitchen and lighting the whole damn house on fire?"

"That night he'd gotten the two of you sodas."

"Yeah. He was very eager for me and Jessa to watch a DVD in the living room. I'd gotten the popcorn ready while Jessa set up the movie, and suddenly he brought us two glasses filled with orange soda."

Beck let out a noise, shifted his weight.

"Jess and I started watching the movie, and he said he had to go call someone first. But I knew what he was going to do."

"Did you drink your soda?" asked Dad.

I shook my head. "I didn't get a chance because Wes and everybody showed up, and I was excited to see them."

"So excited, you knocked over the popcorn bowl, and it spilled everywhere," said Jessa.

"I ran outside and left you alone with the movie, and the popcorn mess, and the sodas, and him freebasing in the kitchen."

"We had Jessa's blood tested at the hospital," said Mom. "Because the paramedic told the doctors in the ER it seemed like she was under the influence, not just smoke inhalation. I was so upset. I told them Jessa was so young, she wasn't a drug user, it had to be a mistake."

"But it wasn't a mistake," Dad said.

My flesh crawled. "What are you saying?"

"I drank all of my soda," said Jess. "And then I drank some of yours too."

"Jessa tested positive for Rohypnol. The doctor explained what it was," said Mom.

"The date rape drug."

"I was horrified. furious. Your mother was..." His voice trailed off and he sniffed in air, his hand landing on her shoulder.

My mother was destroyed.

"He'd roofied us that night?" My body swayed and Beck's steely arm wrapped around me. "That's just fucking rock bottom."

Jessa cried out in the darkness. Uncle Mad took her in his arms.

Nausea rose up my throat. Numbness crept through my veins; a cold, familiar thing. "Had he invited his friends over that night, and me and Jessa were supposed to be the party favors?"

"Jesus Christ," Beck muttered.

"I don't know, baby. I don't know," Dad said. "And that question drags a knife through my heart every goddamn day. We'll never know. Maybe he just wanted the two of you out of his hair while he got high. But he had those drugs, which means he must have intended to use them or had used them before on girls…and that makes me sick to this day. How could he have done such a despicable thing to his own sisters?"

"Marshall…" Mom grabbed his arm.

"I knew our house was burning years before it caught on fire. I knew he had a drug problem that only exacerbated his other issues, but I wanted to believe it wasn't so bad. I assumed it was a phase. That he was entertaining himself like we've all done—a teenage boy figuring things out, testing his boundaries.

"But it was so much more complicated than that. I should have pulled him out of school and put him in a program. I should've taken him to another doctor for a better diagnosis, other medications that could have made a difference, that could have helped him. But I didn't.

"He put himself in danger, my girls in danger, with purpose. He broke your mother's heart over and over, and after the fire, he finally broke mine.

"I should have never left you and Jessa alone with him. I put you in danger, Violet. I did that. And I thank God every day that your friends showed up, that you were outside on the street with them. Otherwise, you would have drank that soda, and you and Jessa would both be dead, or if there had been no fire, God knows…"

Beck's hand went to my back, and I leaned into him once more.

Dad cleared his throat. "After, I felt that if I admitted to you how proud I was of you, how relieved and happy I was that you and Jessa had survived, that meant that I was okay with the fact that my son was dead. And you know why?"

"Why?" I whispered.

"Because a piece of me was relieved he was gone. God forgive me, I was relieved, and that broke my heart all over again."

He pulled me in his embrace. "Ever since, you've done your best to take care of all of us, and we let you. You don't have to do that, honey. You don't. Forgive me."

I buried my face in my father's chest, and he held onto me. Dad's arms took in Jessa, tightening around us both.

"It's time to leave here now." Grandpa's deep voice boomed over us, his lantern shaking as he moved. "Let the dead bury the dead, the Lord said."

I wiped at my face with my hands. "So he did." I hugged Mom.

"Let's go home." Grandpa's voice was firm and solemn. Mom went over to him and slid her arm through his, and they slowly headed down the path. Dad and Jessa and Uncle Mad followed.

Beck held out his hand to me, and I took it. "Your sword, the vicious truth." He brought our hands to his chest, his heart thumping underneath my palm. "Your brother broke your heart, didn't he?"

"He was my best friend and then all of a sudden, that changed. He broke my heart for years and then he set it all on fire."

He kissed my hand. "No one will ever break your heart again."

We left the Hildebrand dead to their final resting place and made our way down the hill together.

CHAPTER THIRTY-FIVE

VIOLET

I PASSED my customer her Kenyan roast drip. "There you go, Candy."

"Thanks, Violet."

I turned to the espresso machine and prepared the next order.

Mom, Gigi, Jessa, and I had stayed up late last night, talking, revisiting the past, and letting it go, together. I'd even called Dad to say one last good-night. I'd wanted to hear his voice. Before going to sleep I'd texted Beck, who was spending the night at his mom's, letting him know that I was okay, better than okay. That his supporting me through everything meant the world to me.

This morning Mom and I got to the Grand bright and early. She had fired Aaron so I was on my own making coffees today, but I was good with it. I was interviewing two new candidates for the barista post tomorrow, and I was looking forward to hiring someone new. Now that Jessa was back at H&H with Dad full-time, I didn't have to be at the office regularly any longer. Perfect timing.

I had a lot on my plate now. All my favorite foods, in fact.

I was consumed with editing all the photographs I'd taken of the band so I could send the best to Ford. As I was working on those, an idea for another project began brewing inside me and I couldn't wait to get started on it.

I would now cut out a solid chunk of time every day to work on that idea. To work on my work. Every day. A grin swept my lips as I capped the cup of herbal tea and the cappuccino.

"Hey, Violet."

Lenore stood at the counter in all her blue-haired, tattooed splendor.

"Hi, Lenore, good morning." I tucked the drinks into the cardboard holder and passed them to the waiting customer. "There you go, Mr. Andrews. Thank you."

"Extra cinnamon, right, Violet?"

"As always." I winked at him. Mr. Andrews liked me to sprinkle the cinnamon on his cappuccino.

Lenore moved along the counter opposite me. "Thank you so much for sending me the photographs this morning. I looked at them with Beck before Wes picked him up. They're fantastic. You brought out a whole different edge in the guys."

"I'm so glad you think so too. I hope their manager likes that different edge and wants to use them."

"He's a fool if he doesn't see it."

"Whatever he thinks, it was the best experience, and I couldn't have done it without you. I can't thank you enough for everything you did and at the last minute, too. On top of it being so much fun, I learned a lot from you, and I'm very grateful."

"I had a blast. It was great to get back in there. Any time you need me, for anything, call me."

"I will."

"Photographs? From that photo shoot you told me about? I need to see." Tania whipped off her sunglasses and stood before us, dark eyes flashing, her keys in hand. "Ever since I heard about this, I've been dying to see."

Lenore took out her phone and showed Tania. "Right here."

Tania swiped through the photos I'd sent Lenore. "Fuck, these are so strong. And so very hot. There's a documentary feel along with the editorial sexy glam vibe. Love the tones, Violet."

My pulse did a double time. Tania's opinion mattered to me.

She owned an antiques store/art gallery in town. She had a good eye. She was a trained professional.

"There are a lot more, but I'm not done editing them yet."

"When can I see the rest of them?" Tania asked. "And, of course, anything else you might have."

"You want to see my work?"

She cocked an eyebrow as she handed Lenore back her phone. "I would like very much to see your work. Consider this an official request."

"Yesssss." Grinning, Lenore tucked her phone in her black satin backpack.

"Tomorrow morning at the Rusted Heart? Ten o'clock?"

My heart fluttered in my chest. "Okay. Yes, ten it is." I licked my lips. "In the meantime what can I make you both? My treat."

"Oh, thank you," said Lenore. "A velvet iced hazelnut with coconut milk would be great."

"That sounds good. Me too," said Tania.

"You got it." I prepared the iced coffees in the blender.

"You've never had one, Tan?" asked Lenore.

"No. I don't do pseudo-dairy. It's against my religion."

Lenore let out a laugh. "You'll love this."

I brought them their coffees. Tania grabbed two straws from the dispenser at the sidebar. "This looks fantastic." She sipped.

"Hey there, Miss Barista."

That deep voice slicked with mockery had us all turning. Ladd stood at the counter, his arms crossed. He wanted attention. He wanted servicing.

"Excuse me, ladies." I moved down the counter to Ladd. "Can I help you?"

"Still working here, I see? Not off with the superstar boy toy?" His gaze flicked over Lenore. Sipping her coffee, she cooly took in Ladd, one perfectly groomed eyebrow arching. Tania's one hand went to her waist.

"What would you like?" I asked.

"I'd like a lot of things, sweetheart."

"Place an order, sweetheart, or get the hell out."

He grinned. A brittle grin. "Two extra large velvet iced lattes. One with half and half, the other with soy milk and two pumps of vanilla."

I let out a laugh. Two pumps of vanilla and soy was Sissy's favorite. "Coming right up, Sissy's boy toy." My gaze darted outside where Ladd's car was double parked. Sissy, her long hair down and wearing oversized sunglasses, checked herself out in the visor mirror in the front passenger seat. He should have been at the office, but instead, he was having his good time with his good time girl. I got to making their coffees.

He leaned on the counter. "The auction is in two days. Are you going to be there or will you be too busy making espressos?"

"Of course, I'll be there. I wouldn't miss it."

"Good. It's going to be a big day." A smirk etched his lips as he swiped his debit card for Shelby at the register.

"It sure is." I slid the coffees in the cup holder toward him. "What's the plan with Whisperwind? You going to flip it as soon as you finish renovating?"

"Flip it?" He grabbed straws and napkins. "What are you talking about?"

"The house that you bought, Whisperwind?"

"Oh, that." He licked his lips as he grabbed the coffee cup holder. "I never bought that shithole. If I had, I would've torched it. Insurance is probably worth more than…"

An ice cold cocktail of sour relief and searing shock swished through my gut. "You didn't buy it?"

His jaw hardened. "I tried, but I got outbid while I was out of town."

"When you were in Mexico with Sissy, you mean?"

"That's right. Hell, I saved myself a lot of cash and a lot of headaches, you being on the top of that list."

"Hope you and Sissy enjoy your day."

"Oh, we will." Picking up the coffees, he flashed me that

macho asshole *fuck yeah* smirk as if he were being lauded in the boys locker room for having hooked up with the hottest chick in school.

He cruised out of the Grand, and something ticked in the back of my mind as he slid his sunglasses back on. He was relaxed and very pleased with himself, and came by to show that off to me.

"He's a class D dick," Lenore's voice cut through my reverie.

"He really is."

"A person shows you what they're made of, you have to believe them," murmured Tania.

"He certainly has, and I do." I leaned against the counter.

"Just checking," said Tania.

Outside the Grand, Ladd handed Sissy the coffees through the front passenger window and got in his car.

"Ladd is a lesson learned," I said.

"Exactly that," said Lenore. "Never let selfish little boys like him ever get the best of you. My grandmother used to say the old phrase, 'Don't throw your pearls before swine.' I never quite understood that as a girl, but the older I got, I certainly did."

"Right?" said Tania.

I crossed my arms. "You know who drove all these man lessons home to me?"

Lenore grinned. "I think I'm going to like your answer."

"You are. It was Beck. Beck did. And not with big words and grand gestures. But by being who he is. He listens, he has empathy. He's generous and supportive in ways that I find astounding." My face heated, and I bit my lip at my verbal rush. "He's only ever wanted the best for me."

It was true. While Ladd showed me his arrogant assholery over and over again, Beck had shown me his goodness in the best possible ways over and over. I'd never had that in a man before. Maybe because I'd never allowed myself to be with someone I really liked. Someone I really wanted.

But I'd never wanted anyone the way I wanted Beck. And

crashing into him at Pete's and then at the Tingle had changed everything.

Lenore put several bills in the tip jar. "I heard about the engagement, of course, and Beck explained it. Then I heard talk around Meager about you and Ladd being engaged, and Beck explained that too."

"Oh, Lenore—"

"One request—when you and Beck do figure it out, please let me and your mom know, because we're dying to plan an engagement party here. Or not. Up to the two of you."

"You're so bad." Tania laughed.

Lenore touched my arm. "I'm teasing. You know that, right? Your mom and I are enjoying this though. Teasing aside, I know my son, and he wouldn't have created the engagement thing to be a jerk or to trap you or—"

"He did it to protect me from that dick." I gestured out the window where Ladd was still trying to pull his car into Clay Street traffic. My pulse ticked up. It felt good to say that out loud. It felt good to say the truth.

"I'll drink to that!" Tania raised her iced coffee at me and Lenore.

"Hello, sister friends." Alicia, Wes's mom, catwalked over to us in her impossibly tight skinny jeans and high-heeled sandals.

"Hey, Alicia, what can I get you today?"

"Today's my cheat day, and I'm dying for an iced caramel macchiato. With whipped cream."

"Coming right up." I got to work on her coffee. Behind me the three ladies chatted at the counter.

"I just saw that fiancé of hers…" Alicia's voice carried, her whispers were always very loud. "He had Sissy in his car, what the fuck? For a while there, my son was seeing her, but looks like she's got her hooks into someone more suitable for her than Wes."

"She leveled way down, that's for sure," quipped Tania.

"Trust me," said Alicia. "She thinks she's leveled up."

"One caramel macchiato on the house." I slid the coffee to Alicia.

"Oh thanks, sweetie." She shoved a five dollar bill in the tip jar. "That's all I've been hearing about everywhere I go today—" Alicia poked a straw through her drink. "The market, the bank, the post office…who's Violet engaged to? I say, keep them guessing—the men included." Sipping her coffee, she leaned over the counter closer to me. "Now it seems one down, one left. Remember hon, if that shoe doesn't fit either, big deal, because you know that Wes is the best choice anyhow." She let out a high-pitched laugh.

I blinked, my pulse jammed in my neck. "Excuse me?"

"I've been waiting years and years for the two of you to finally get it together. Here's your chance."

"Are you kidding me? That's my son you're referring to as a shoe," Lenore interjected, my insides coiling at her tone. Pure steel. Sleek and sharp and cold.

Alicia's head tilted, her eyebrows shooting up at the sudden interruption. The entire Meager Grand sucked in air. Everyone knew Alicia, the once upon a time biker president's wife, was a woman not to be crossed. And everyone knew that only Lenore would do it and be victorious.

"Oh, come on, Lenore, you know what I meant." Alicia flipped her platinum blond hair from her face.

"Violet, Alicia's got a point there—" cut in Candy from the sugar bar getting her second round of packets as usual. "You and Wes are so cute together. Always have been." She turned to the café. "Don't y'all think so?" Her voice carried through the entire space.

"I do, yes!" my grandmother's friend, Sue Anne piped up.

"Um…" I shifted my weight.

"See? There you go." Alicia sipped on her drink shooting Lenore a pointed look.

"Oh geez." Tania let out a groan.

The crowd got loud. A debate over my fiancés vs. Wes roiled through the Grand.

"At the end of the day, it's a woman's choice," Alicia declared. "But hey, our girl has it going on—way to go, babe."

"Oh, leave Violet alone. She's quite capable of making up her own mind," steamed Frank Hollister as he paid Shelby for his daily slice of pound cake and a Columbian drip at the register. He strode to a table with his tray of goodies. "I came in here to have my coffee and cake in peace and what do I get? A squawkfest."

"Wait—did I miss something?" A voice rose from the back. "Does that make three contenders now or still only the two fiancés?"

Lord, help me. "Alicia!"

She spun around to face me, eyes wide at my tone. Next to her, Tania and Lenore stood stock still. "Wes and I have only ever been friends. Ever."

Gasps rushed around the Grand. Alicia's eyes narrowed. "Oh, come on. There's never been any…"

"Never. Ask him yourself."

"Are you done now?" Lenore eyed Alicia.

"This is quite a pickle, isn't it?" Mr. Andrews's voice piped up. "I saw the paper, and my granddaughter showed me that Instagram. Who's it going to be—bachelor number one or bachelor number two?"

"Ah, remember that show?" Sue Anne said, and a gentle roll of laughter rippled through the Grand. "I do miss that show."

"Are you talking about *The Bachelor*?" piped up a young girl sitting at a small table with her laptop open. "I'm so sick of that show…"

"No, dear, that's different," said Candy. "Way before your time."

"This is kind of like *Days of Our Lives*," another voice exclaimed. "Remember when…"

"What the heck is going on out here?" Mom's voice came up behind me. Silence.

Candy cleared her throat. "Nothing, dear. We were just wondering who Violet's real fiancé is."

I took in all the expectant gazes hanging on mine. "Certainly not Ladd Jeffries," I pronounced loudly for all to hear. "And no, not Wes. You got that?"

"Oohs" and "aahs" and murmurings rippled through the Grand as the customers shuffled their chairs and chatted loudly.

Lenore and Tania and Alicia grinned at me. I let out a breath and grinned too.

CHAPTER THIRTY-SIX

VIOLET

"ANSWER YOUR PHONE, Jessa, come on. Pick up."

No answer. Again. Where the hell was she? *Fine. Plan B it is.*

Since Ladd admitted to me that he wasn't the one who bought Whisperwind, I was prickled by an irritated sense of necessity to find out who had bought it. Needed to know. Had to know. Couldn't sit still for the not knowing. It had been barely two hours since I'd found out, and here I was on my lunch break, on the hunt.

I entered the Bank of Meager.

There he was, Mr. Sanders, chatting with Mrs. Jackson, who was holding her little Yorkshire terrier sporting a very large pink velvet bow. That doggy had a different bow for each day. I waited as their conversation wound down. Mrs. Jackson noticed me and a smile widened over her face. "Hi there, Violet. How you doing, honey?"

"I'm good, Mrs. Jackson." I stroked the dog behind the ears. "Aww. Sadie's bow today is the cutest thing ever."

"I made it myself."

"Did you? My."

"Keeping nimble."

"Good for you."

"Dear—I wanted to wish you congratulations on your engagement, but then I heard that—"

"Between us girls, Mrs. J—it's my way of keeping nimble."

She pursed her lips and nodded, shaking a finger at me. "You were always a smart one. Always. You keep them on their toes, honey. Good for you." Mrs. Jackson moved past me.

Cliff Sanders began to turn away, and I darted to his side. "Hi there, Mr. Sanders."

I'd known Cliff Sanders, the Meager bank manager and my father's friend, since I was a little girl.

"Violet."

"Do you have a moment? I have a quick question."

"Sure, go ahead, dear."

"Could we talk in private?"

"Oh. All right. Follow me."

We went into his office, and he sat behind his desk. "What's this about?"

I took a seat, my boots drilling into the dense carpeting. "I know the Putnams sold Whisperwind."

He pressed his lips together for a quick moment. "Yes, they did."

"Could you tell me who the buyer is?"

"Violet—"

"Mr. Sanders."

He clasped his hands together on his desk. "I realize that house once belonged to your family, and this must be difficult for you…"

"I would like to know who bought it. That's all. A name."

"You could go to the County Clerk's office and make a request to see—"

"I could, but right now, I'm feeling the need for immediate gratification. Well?"

"The sale was not conducted through this bank, so I'm unable to comment."

"Be that as it may, other than my father, your wife is the only broker in town, and even though word on the street is that they didn't use a realtor, both of you are very close friends with the Putnams. I thought Mrs. S might have handled it for them on the QT."

"She did not."

"Oh. Mrs. Sanders must have been disappointed."

"She was."

"They'd declined Dad's offer the year before. Back then they'd been considering leaving South Dakota, but wouldn't commit to it."

"Well, they were ready now."

"Were they? I can't imagine they pulled up and ran in the middle of the night without a word to you and Mrs. Sanders."

He slanted his head at me. "Violet, it would be unethical of me to comment on a private conversation that—"

"Cliff, Cliff, Cliff—" I crossed my legs, easing back in my chair as his head jerked at my using his first name. "I saw you at the Tingle that night with my father and Ladd, all you boys enjoying yourselves. Nothing like cocktails with a splash of titty after a hard day's work, eh?"

His fingers squeezed over his pen, his knuckles white. "Honestly."

"Did you make it up to a VIP room? I hear the most extraordinary things go on up there. I'm friends with several of the dancers. They come into the Grand all the time."

His face stiffened, his thin body rigid in his high-backed executive chair.

I kept going. "Do I need to mention what I witnessed to Mrs. Sanders?" Juliet Sanders was not only a real estate broker, but the church choir director. "I'm sure she would be devastated if she knew what her hubby was up to while she was attending choir practice or Bible study, hmm?"

He leaned forward, his small eyes narrowing at me. "They told us they had been approached by someone privately."

"I know Ladd made them a direct offer."

"He did, and they almost sold to him, but they weren't able to contact him when they'd come to the decision. He never answered their calls or their email."

"So he told me. Shame." Poor Ladd missing out on his deal because he was in a cloud of tequila fucking Sissy in Mexico still tickled me pink.

"And it just so happened that around that time someone else came in and made a much more generous offer, which they accepted right away. It would have been foolish not to. They said the buyer wished to remain anonymous and they only spoke with a lawyer." He clicked on the pen top. "They were very excited about this sale, not only because it was so generous and done sight unseen—"

"The buyer never even came to see the house?"

"No. It all went through very quickly. Cash deal. No mortgage application to process and approve. Can't say no to that."

"No, that's a very sweet deal. But it didn't happen through this bank?"

"Out of state."

"Which state?"

"Violet."

"Come on…"

"California. Which was perfect as they moved to—"

"San Diego."

California.

Cash.

Cash in California.

"Is that all?" He shuffled folders around his desk, his attention on a stack of documents. "I have a bank to run."

Yes, yes, I knocked you down a peg, but don't worry, you're still the powerful peen of privilege around here.

I forced my lips into a sharp smile. "That's all." I stood up and moved to the door.

"Violet Hildebrand, not a word about this conversation to anyone. If I hear—"

"Not a word, Cliff. Not one word."

"You are your father's daughter."

"You bet I am."

I charged down the street to H&H. Jessa was at her desk. "Where have you been? I've been calling you."

"Sorry, I just saw." She held up her phone that was plugged into her charger. "I got a last minute appointment to get my hair highlighted at Danielle's, and I didn't realize my battery died."

"What's the name of the lawyer handling Whisperwind?"

"Why?"

"Ladd didn't buy it. I want to know who did."

"Allen Daniels."

I leaned over her and tapped on her keyboard. "Move a sec." She got up from her computer, and I sat in her seat and waited for Google to do its job.

A listing.

Allen Daniels, attorney, Los Angeles, CA, partner at Winston & Manuel.

I kept clicking. Clicked on Images. Photos of Mr. Daniels with a television actress at a fundraiser. Golfing with another lawyer. I glanced at the headline. *Golfing with good friend Mack Yates, top music industry lawyer.*

I clicked on Mack Yates.

Mack Yates, Esq. - Yates & Carmack, Los Angeles, CA

Gossip bites about Mack with a singer girlfriend at an art gallery opening. Attending the Grammys with her.

Click

Click

An article from two years ago on a gossip site: "*Out for sushi in Beverly Hills…*" The thumbnail photo of three men eating and talking. I recognized the younger man.

My heartbeat picked up speed. *Click.*

"Father and son rock and rollers, Eric and Beck Lanier share a laugh over dinner with their lawyer, Mack Yates."

My lungs constricted. Gravity dragged down on my every cell.

I clicked. Photos of Eric and Mack shaking hands. A teenage Beck and Mack hugging.

Another photo of Eric and his wife with Yates and a very young actress at the Fire & Ice Ball.

"Violet what is it? What did you find?" Jessa peered at the computer screen, her lips parting. "Oh…oh boy….I had no idea."

I grabbed my phone and hit his name.

Beck answered right away. "Violet? Hey—"

"Why did you do it? Why?"

"Babe, what are you talking about? What's wrong?"

"You bought Whisperwind. How could you not tell me?"

"Violet—"

"I told you what it meant to me, I shared all that with you, and then you go and buy it without telling me?"

"It wasn't like that."

"And to top it all off, you hire my sister to renovate it? I don't understand."

"I was going to tell you, but there was never a perfect moment. And I wanted it to be perfect. Let me explain. Plea—"

I hit End Call and shut off my phone.

CHAPTER THIRTY-SEVEN

BECK

MY BIKE ROARED onto Clay Street, and I brought it to a stop in front of the Meager Grand.

The minute Violet had hung up on me, I'd texted Jessa and asked her where Violet was and she'd told me that she'd gone back to work at the Grand. I'd gotten on my bike and came down here.

Ripping off my helmet, I left it on the saddle, and headed into the coffee house.

"Violet, bachelor number one is here!" someone called out.

People turned in their seats and stared at me as I made my way to the front. She swiveled behind the counter, face red, two cups of coffee in her hands. Violet put the cups down. "What are you doing here?"

"Please come with me."

"I'm…I'm working…"

"We need to talk."

"Uh oh…when you hear that, forget it," said a girl wearing purple lipstick from behind her open laptop, arms crossed, shooting me a glare.

"It's a good thing, I promise," I said to her.

"Sure." She shrugged. "We'll see, won't we?"

I turned back to Violet. "Violet? Please. I'm leaving for L.A. tomorrow, and I need to explain."

A collective gasp.

"Ohhh, the plot thickens..." quipped purple lipstick girl, shaking her head.

"It's not what you think," I said to her.

"You're leaving tomorrow?" Violet said.

"We got everything done with Stewart. And we got real lucky and got studio time in L.A. at the last minute. We need to take it."

Violet took off her apron and headed out the front door. I caught up with her on the sidewalk, gesturing to my bike. "Get on."

She did a double take. All the customers in the Grand were crowded around the great front window, staring at us. An elderly man gave me a thumbs up.

"Oh Lord." She grabbed the helmet from the bike. I got on and she climbed on after me, her hands low on my hips. "Where are we going?"

Leaning back against her, I used her line from that night: "Do you always need to know?"

A noise escaped her throat and she adjusted herself on the saddle. I hit the throttle. "Now wave goodbye to your fans." She waved to all the customers at the window and they waved back.

I took off, tearing down Clay Street, and with her body pressing firmly around mine, I took us out of Meager and headed to the one place we both needed to be for me to lay it all out for her. To share my dream with her.

I remembered the basics of how to get there, but once I turned off the main road towards Spearfish, I slowed down. "Violet, where exactly?"

Her hands tightened around my middle as she sat up straighter. "At that broken tree, then to the right."

I did as she said and finally parked. There it was, the hidden pathway to our waterfall.

We got off the bike and she took off the helmet, her beautiful hair falling around her shoulders. "Why are we here?"

I took the helmet from her. "You said one day I needed to come back here to see the waterfall in the daylight. But I wanted to see it with you for the first time. And right now, it feels like the only place to be."

I took her hand and we headed down the grassy path.

The insistent pounding rush of the waterfall got louder and louder. She hiked down easily to where there was a small natural platform of glistening, slippery slabs of stone. I cleared through the brush and tree branches on the rocky path, and my feet froze. The waterfall and the high cliff from which it cascaded filled my vision. A thick stream of waters falling, falling, falling from a high mossy cliff down to this small lagoon below. Majestic, grand, and harsh. A secret, wild sanctuary.

Yes, this was the perfect place.

Her chest heaved with breaths as she took in the water, tilting back her face skyward.

"This is incredible, you were right," I said. "I was raised here in South Dakota but being here again, with you, has made it so much more special to me. I didn't realize how much I missed it, how much it's a part of me." I took her hand in mine.

"Tell me."

"When you took that selfie with the house and sent it to me, I realized how Whisperwind was a true home for you, and you knew what that meant. I saw it in your face. I heard that passion in your voice when you described it to me, told me its history. I could feel your desire to preserve it, to make it beautiful again. The woman I saw in that photo fit there. Belonged there.

"There I was, looking at overpriced trendy houses to buy because I had to make an investment, had to move out of my dad's and get my own place. I'd seen three by the time we talked. One more forgettable than the other. And you know what I felt? Nothing. They were nothing more than potential investments, temporary dwellings, not a home.

"I was overwhelmed with wanting to help you make your dream come true. And I could. My money could make that difference. Whisperwind was the better investment. And it was going to make a hell of a surprise gift."

"This is no ordinary surprise gift, Beck. Like the ring you gave me or the clothes. The little windmill, the scarves. You spent a lot of money, and—"

"It was a wild impulse that caught me off guard and wouldn't let go. I went with it."

"Very wild and very expensive impulse."

"The tour was real good to us. Very, very good. Plus, I have a trust fund I just came into. When I got back to L.A., I could've bought a fancy new car, more clothes, more boots, a few guitars I've had my eye on. But I didn't care about all that, sure maybe because I've always had it. This was…different and I knew it. It felt right, and I don't regret it one bit." I breathed in deeply, the damp air, so fresh, so clean. "I followed my gut and took the leap."

"You hired my sister too."

"I wanted to keep the family house in the family, and I thought you'd like that, to work on it together. I wanted everything perfect for you, down to the last crown moulding. Maybe that was overdoing it." I shrugged, my stomach churning, my mouth dry. "What I wanted was to invest in you and me, and that's what I did."

"How did you do it?"

"Just before we left for Greece I asked Wes about the house, the owners. Then I got my lawyer on it, and we made a healthy offer to be sure to get it. Turned out there was already an offer on the table, and I panicked. I raised my bid by a hell of a lot. And get this—the Putnams weren't able to contact the other prospective buyer. And then when they heard I didn't need a mortgage, and that I was banking out of California, where they were moving and already had an account, that tilted the scale in my favor and they accepted. I was so relieved, so excited. I'd won. I won it for you."

She laughed softly.

"What's so funny?"

"Do you know who the other prospective buyer was?"

"No, who?"

"It was Ladd."

My jaw tightened. "Ladd? Was he trying to buy it to seduce you back?"

Her laugh turned bitter. "God no. He threatened to buy it and rip it down so I'd do what he wanted."

"Which was to get engaged, right?"

"And get married. To stop his mom and my dad from fooling around anymore and to get more of Powder Ridge in his pocket."

"When did he lay that on you?"

"Our last night in Athens when he called me."

"You didn't tell me that."

"No, I didn't."

"I knew he'd try something. I knew it. And were you planning on going through with it when you got back?"

"I was going to handle it somehow—"

My heart knocked against my ribs. "Somehow? You mean all that time on the flight home you were thinking about—"

"No! I considered it for a millisecond when I was on the phone with him, but I knew there was no way. No fucking way. Not after Greece, not after you and me." The waterfall swallowed her last words, her burning gaze hanging on mine. "In the meantime, in order to force my hand, Ladd went ahead and put an announcement in the local paper that he and I had gotten engaged."

"But the fangirls from JFK had already spilled about our engagement."

"Right. And just like you said would happen, by the time I got home, social media had spread the word that you and I had gotten engaged in Athens, preempting Ladd's newspaper move. He was furious."

"Fucker." I wiped the spray from my face. "Celebrity did me a solid for a change, and cruel fate dealt me a damn good hand." The waterfall crashed around us. "Baby, Fate's been playing me nothing but good hands since that night we came here. Nothing but good."

"Oh Beck..."

"I wanted to tell you about buying the house our last night in Athens, but everything exploded with Tag's post on Instagram and whatever else. We were both getting a zillion messages and phone calls—"

"Like Ladd."

"And you were getting upset. Then you said you weren't interested in doing a long distance thing, in trying to be together. So, yeah, I didn't think it was the right time to surprise you with the news that I'd bought your dream house. But the thing is, since then, my dream became holding onto you and making that house our home."

On a cry, she threw her arms around me, her face in my neck. "I have no words to express what I'm feeling right now. You are...one of the finest humans I've ever known."

My chest swelled and I whispered in her ear, "And I'm all yours."

My skin heated under the penetrating gleam of her eyes, stung under the cold stinging spray of water.

Her hands slid under my jacket, my T-shirt, pressing into my back, their warmth steadying me. "And I'm all yours."

We kissed, there before the waterfall, our pledges carrying through its roar, settling in our thundering hearts.

CHAPTER THIRTY-EIGHT

VIOLET

THE LITTLE BRASS bells tinkled as I made my way through the front door of the Rusted Heart, Tania's antique store and art gallery in Meager. A dazzling shop filled with all sorts of antiques that were once rough and tumble pieces of farm machinery, odd pieces of handmade and hand painted furniture, old railroad lanterns, rose-colored period glassware. I placed the tall cup and napkins on the reception desk counter.

She'd become very busy and very popular in the few years since she'd opened her business. Interior designers from all over sought out Tania's eye for the unusual and interesting, the traditional, lost and forgotten, the stellar. Along with the antiques she bought and sold, she also had a small exhibition space where she showed new artists' paintings and sculpture.

I let out an exhale, but it did nothing to ease the knots in my belly. I was nervous as if I were applying for the job of a lifetime. I kind of was. This was next level for me. And although this was Tania, one of my mother's oldest friends, she was an art professional, and this would be a professional level discussion.

Tania came out of the back room. "Hey, honey, right on time." She hugged me.

"A little gift from the Grand. I thought you might enjoy it

with all this heat this morning." I handed her the iced ginger raspberry lemonade.

"Oooooo! Thank you." She took the cup and slurped deeply on the homemade lemonade. "What a great flavor."

"Just a tinge of sweet raspberry."

"Hits the spot. Thank you."

"My pleasure."

"Did you bring me more goodies?"

"I did." I raised up my portfolio case. "I've never showed my work to anyone—like this, I mean." My face heated. "It means a lot to me to get your feedback, Tania."

"I'm honored, Violet." She led me to the exhibition area of her shop where there stood a round table with a sculpture of a woman on it. She moved the statue, and letting go of the breath I'd been holding, I placed my case on the table and unzipped it.

"I've been putting together a collection of photographs, actually several collections…" I began arranging the prints on the table, on the floor. I filled the area with my pics.

Tania murmured to herself, her gaze darting everywhere. She focused on one grouping. I tried to look at the photos with fresh eyes, like Tania was.

Hildebrand cowboys of the past alongside the Hildebrand cowboys of today. Clay Street past and present. Bikers I'd captured at Bike Night, and Gigi's snaps of the One-Eyed Jacks of the past.

"Oh my God. Where did you get this photo?" She pointed to a shot of Isi's boyfriend from the late 70s on a vintage Indian motorcycle cruising through Meager with his brothers. "This is Wreck. He's so young here."

"My grandmother took that one. When Gigi was a young mother, she'd work at Dillon's General Store whenever her uncle needed help. If a bike club would drive through Meager, which was pretty often, she'd run outside and snap photos of them on her Kodak X15. Back then the One-Eyed Jacks had just come to town. Of course, she didn't know when she took this shot that years later, this guy would turn out to be the love of her cousin's life."

"Oh man…wait…I knew this…but it didn't click until now. Wreck's love was Georgia's cousin."

"Yes, Isi. Isi Dillon."

"Lock and Grace are going to flip out when they see this." She fingered the edge of the photo. "You know that Wreck was Lock's half brother?"

"My grandmother's mentioned it."

"When Grace and I were younger than you, she'd met her first husband, a One-Eyed Jack."

"He got killed, right?"

"Right. So sometimes I'd go to a club party or hang out with them at Pete's or Dead Ringers, and I met Wreck."

"What was he like?"

"Like the rest of them, rough and gruff around the edges, but he was older than most of them at the time. Didn't have anything to prove, didn't give a damn. The quiet gentleman. When I first opened my shop a few years ago, I got to go through all of Wreck's belongings and sort them out. He'd collected a heck of a lot of odds and ends on his travels—random antiques, bike parts. A lot of it I re-sold, a lot of it Lock and Grace kept. Going through his stuff, I felt like I got to know him in a different way. Made me wish I had gotten to know him better back then, but somehow I felt very connected to him. Funny, huh?"

"Believe me, I get it."

She gestured at my photos. "I can tell."

"Speaking of Wreck and Isi, I have these photos of Isi performing at a biker party in the late 70s, probably about the same time of that early photo of Wreck." I gestured at a section of photos on the left side of the table.

"Holy shit. Georgia took these too?"

"No. Finger got those for me. An old lady in his club had taken them at their summer festivals back in the day."

"Violet…these are gold…" Tania's expression grew serious as she went over the photos. "So what are you thinking of with these vintage shots?"

"I like to collage photos, combining and contrasting past and present. So I have plans to combine these old shots with the contemporary ones I've taken around town. A slice of Meager history and people's dreams and adventures over the years. Have they changed?"

Tania went to the next grouping of shots, studying the photos. "This is the Hildebrand ranch, right?"

"Yes. The vintage ones are from my grandfather's family albums, which inspired my shots over here."

"When Grace and I and your mom were in high school, parties at the Hildebrand Ranch were the biggest and the best. We used to look forward to them every year. Your dad and his cousins threw a crazy one our senior year."

"They've told me about those."

"They were epic." Her gaze settled on another set of photos of Hildebrand cowboys galloping on the ranch next to my shots of the Lakota boys riding bareback at Stewart's ranch. "I love these."

She turned back to me. "So from one addict to another, tell me about your obsession with the past. Why is it so powerful for you?"

"There's a thrilling energy for me between what no longer is and what we have now. An emotional tension between the two that I find magnetic and compelling. Wistful sadness about the past, a longing to know the secrets of that past. Do the "old days" offer a simplicity, a purity that we've lost today? Or is that simplicity and purity just an idea that we project onto that past?"

"Ah, yes." She picked up a photo of an old cowboy riding through an unpaved debris ridden Clay Street from the 1880s.

"And that tension helps us to connect to joy and positivity about what we have now, an appreciation for how far we've come as a community, as a family. Honoring that past has always been important to me. For me, past and present aren't divided. Both offer the other inspiration and connection and meaning. And energy. I really do believe that."

"I do, too."

I shifted my weight as Tania went back to the pics on the table, to the ones spread out on the floor. "Your work is an essay in bittersweet."

"I suppose so."

"You like it there."

Our gazes locked, and heat filled my chest. "I do."

"Me too," she said. "I love bringing the past to the present. Learning from it. Savoring it. When I find a piece, it can be the most mundane object from the past, but for me it's a tactile satisfying experience. It's a hum that I can hear, a rush that I can feel. There's nothing like it."

"Nothing like it." My heartbeat raced. I loved discussing these ideas, and I loved Tania making me articulate what I was going after. I loved that we shared this passion.

She crossed her arms and cleared her throat. "Here's the thing…"

I held my breath.

"As you of course know, Meager is having its Founding Festival celebration in a couple of weeks. Here at the Rusted Heart I'll be showing antique pieces that I've acquired in our area. I got a lot a few months ago from the owners of the Frick Ranch, in fact."

"Did you?"

"I've been saving them for the festival."

"Perfect."

"So the opportunity to show photographs of Meager past and present would be phenomenal. Talk about context. Furthermore, to have you, a Hildebrand and a Dillon, both families being original families of Meager, show your work at the Rusted Heart, which is the site of the old Dillon General Store, would make it incredibly mind-blowingly special."

"But you must have other plans to show something else—"

"I do. I did, but it can wait. This, right here, is what I wanted and didn't have."

My heart stopped at her words. At Beck's words echoing in my heart. *"Give them what they didn't know they needed."*

"Have you ever shown any of these before?" Tania's voice cut through the buzzing in my head.

"No, I've never shown these. I've only shown my rock photography publicly, meaning on my website or my Instagram, or I've sold the pics to the bands who wanted them for their promo materials. But these collages have always been just for me. These are my personal soul babies." I swallowed hard. My heart thudded in my chest.

"I understand. Would you want to show your soul babies in an exhibit here for the Founder's Festival?"

"To sell or just to show?"

"Completely up to you."

"That would be a huge honor, Tania. And an amazing opportunity."

She squeezed my arm. "Wonderful. What else do you need to do here to put together a show?"

"It's all organized, and I've started the process, but there's still a lot of editing."

"Could you have everything ready in a week?"

"A week?"

"By then I want to have narrowed down our final choices. We'll need to mount them or frame them, etc."

"Etcetera?"

Her eyes flashed at me. "Plenty of etcetera. Welcome to the world of exhibiting and selling art."

Something shuddered through me, around me. All those daydreams, visions, hopes, plans I'd had in my head from day one for one day....were coming true.

Hard wind. Loud roar.

"I'll get it done."

"Terrific! I have the perfect way to seal our deal. Be right back —" She went to the back room and brought out her oversized leather tote bag and fished through it. She brought out a lipstick and handed it to me.

Weird. "What's this?" It was old, slightly heavy, the plastic seemed worn.

"No ordinary lipstick. This was a little something I found in Wreck's stuff. Turn it over."

I turned it over. The letter "I" was scratched on its bottom and a chill razored over my flesh.

"Open it."

I pulled the cap and twisted open the wand. "Whoa!" Instead of a lipstick, a small knife poked up from the tube.

"This belonged to your cousin Isi. The story is that the night she and Wreck first met, they got into a fight and she used this on him. She nicked him."

"She cut a biker?"

"Wreck ended up taking it away from her, and by the end of the night, they were together."

"Now that's my kind of love story."

Tani let out a laugh. "Lock said that this was the only thing of hers that Wreck had kept. In the top drawer of his dresser, so he could see it every day, touch it."

My chin quivered, and I bit down on my lip.

"Lock let me keep it, which was a good thing, because it came in handy when I had to make a badass move one day not too much later."

"Oh?"

"We'll leave that story for another time—it's one for tequila, not lemonade."

"Looking forward to it."

"You should have the lipstick knife. It's a family heirloom. That I was given the opportunity to find it and save it, meant a lot to me."

"You touched the past," I breathed.

"Yes. And now being able to pass this down to you is very satisfying and moving to me." She wiped at her eyes. "I hope it will inspire you too, Violet, like it did me in many ways. With that in my hand, I stood up for myself when I needed to the most."

I hugged her. "Tania, thank you. Thank you."

"I have to go over to Grace's house and pick up flyers and postcards for the festival. Why don't you come with me? She has something you need to see."

"What is it?"

"I'll keep it for a surprise. After everything I've seen just now, you definitely need to see this."

CHAPTER THIRTY-NINE

VIOLET

WE ARRIVED at Grace and Lock's house which, once upon a time, had been Wreck's cabin at the edge of the woods. After his death, Lock returned from military service, joined the Jacks, and worked on renovating it. Once he and Grace married and had their son, the renovation had gone into full gear and was now complete. They'd enlarged it, and completely updated it. It was now a real home for a family. Comfortable and understated. Except for the collection of vintage Harleys and Indians out front.

"Hey babe." Tania gave Grace a quick kiss on the cheek as we climbed the steps to her front porch.

"Good to see you, Violet."

"You too, Grace."

"So glad you guys came over. I need some girl time badly. Thunder's had a summer cold and hasn't been able to go to day camp for two days now and he's been so whiney. He finally went down for a nap. Perfect timing. I made us iced tea. We can sit here on the porch."

Tania and I sat down on a sofa covered in colorful quilted cushions with the Lakota Star design while Grace poured us iced tea from a blue glass pitcher. "I picked up the festival flyers and the postcards from the printer first thing this morning." The boxes are next to you, Tania—they came out great." Grace sat down in an armchair next to Tania.

Tania dug out a pack of the postcards and handed me a few. "These look terrific."

"Very nice," I said.

"I have news," said Tania. "There's a change of plan for my exhibit. I'm going to show Violet's photographs. They're fantastic, Grace. Perfect for opening night of the festival. I can't wait for you to see them."

"Are these the photos that you took of the band? Lenore was over the moon about how they turned out."

"No, not those," I said.

"These photos are all about Meager past and present." Tania drank her iced tea.

"Ooo. Sounds perfect. Congratulations, Violet. That's terrific news."

"Thanks, Grace." I gulped the cool drink.

Grace moved a dish with familiar cookies toward us. "I can't live without your mother's divine ginger lemon cookies, Violet. I picked up a fresh stash this morning."

"They're my favorites too." Tania chewed on a cookie. "Grace, I brought Violet with me because after seeing her photographs today I feel she needs to read Wreck's letter. If that's okay?"

Wreck's letter?

"Absolutely. I'll go get it." Grace left the table and returned holding an old wood box carved with intricate notches, and placed it on the table.

I sat up straighter. "Is that a jewelry box?"

"It's actually a cigar box carved in the Tramp Art style from the Great Depression. Tania found it in Wreck's stuff. We keep the letter in here."

Obviously this letter was extremely special to Grace and Lock, but what did it have to do with me?

Grace opened the box and took out an envelope as I wiped

my hands on a napkin. She handed it to me. Wrinkled at the corners, the paper was thick and smooth in my hand.

"When Dillon's General Store was being cleaned out and renovated to make the three new stores," Tania said, "I'd rented one of the spaces right away for my gallery and helped clean out the stuff that was still there. I found this envelope hidden in an old tin canister."

"It's a letter that Wreck had written to his lover," said Grace. "We didn't know at the time she was your cousin, Isi. We don't know why it was there in a canister, and we're not even sure that Isi got to read it, because it may have been written around the time that she got killed. Wreck never really spoke about it, so not even Lock knows details."

"Oh." My heart plummeted below ground.

"After seeing your work today with your passion for connections between past and present, and of course knowing that you and Isi are related, I felt strongly that you should read it."

"Go on, Violet. Open it," said Grace.

I took in a tiny breath as I carefully extracted three pages from the envelope. A man's rigid handwriting in blue ink was steeped across the paper.

My Is,

Yes, you are mine, baby, you're me, part of me. I know that you and me together adds up to way the hell more than me apart from you. My center of balance is different now. It's at a new angle, a new measurement on the map of me. With you I'm more me than I've ever been.

You are the only one for me, baby. The only one, ever. And those aren't just some words in a sappy love letter, that's the motherfucking truth.

I know we won't be seeing each other again for at least a month. Like always I'll be counting the days, the weeks. Or I won't be counting to pretend I can hack it. I close my eyes at night, and I can hear your voice, feel your soft hair on me.

It's funny, but I like writing these letters to you. I like getting yours even more. Your letters are a story I can wrap myself in. Have I told you that before? I think I have. When I get my hands on your envelope, my heart soars and hurts at the same time. All I can think about is getting somewhere on my own to open it and read it and read it again and again so I can hear your voice in your words.

When I was in Vietnam, I'd see the other guys get mail from wives and girlfriends, and they'd either open their envelopes slowly and carefully or rip at them. Reading them over and over and over again, swallowing the words whole, rubbing the paper between their fingers, then folding them up and tucking them in a pocket over their chests. Knowing they were there did something for them. I never knew what that was really about, but now I get it. I get it because that's how I feel now. Reverent, grateful, blessed. And holding the fuck on.

Reading yours, writing these, it's my lifeline. Makes me feel, yeah, everything will be all right. It'll all be over soon enough. It will.

And when it is, we're going on a vacation together. Just you and me. I want to see you on a beach, your hair flying in the breeze, your skin golden brown in the sun. We'll drink margaritas, you'll wear pretty dresses, and we'll watch the sun rise and set over the Pacific.

Having to leave you at that motel, I felt low but full to bursting all at the same damn time. How do you explain that? It's loving you and you loving me, isn't it? That love has its own pulse that connects us, and nobody and nothing can stop it.

Every time we make love, it's a promise. A promise that builds and keeps building, keeps growing, bonding us, keeping us tight. It's also the only place and the only time where everything makes sense. That's our place, a place that no one can threaten. That place where your mustangs run and my eagles fly.

I got this smile plastered on my face as I write this at a truck stop diner having breakfast. It's only been a handful of hours since I kissed you, felt your body tremble against mine and mine tremble in yours. Missing you cuts, but that ache is searching for you, and you know what? I'd rather feel all that crazy than feel nothing. It's the nothing that's the true hell, and I never realized it until you.

I don't know if we'll laugh about all this when we're old and gray. I know I won't. But we'll know we can survive anything.

I'm going to say it again—don't take chances, lay low. Do not let your guard down, ever.

Send me the lyrics of your new song when you finish it. You got a gift, baby. Never stop.

I love you.

Signed,

Me, your man.

My lungs squeezed together. A crackle of electricity jolted my heart. I heard his voice—his yearning, his ache, and his deep, deep joy. My throat thick, vision blurry. "Could I scan this letter? I have an app on my phone."

"Of course," said Grace. She and Tania exchanged glances.

With a napkin, I passed over the tablecloth, making sure it was clean and dry, placed the letter on top of it, and took the photos with the scanning app. I folded the letter gently and slid it back into the envelope and placed it in its keepsake box.

"We need a shot of whiskey." Grace broke the heavy silence and darted from the porch, quickly returning with a bottle and three small glasses, which Tania filled for us.

I knocked back my shot. "Thank you."

"Mommy! Who's here?" Footsteps padded behind me. Grace and Lock's son, Thunder stood in the doorway, his long black hair mussed from sleep, face puffy, a tiny stuffed buffalo in his grip.

"Hey you!" I said. Whenever Thunder and Jill's children came to the Grand, they got free cupcakes from me.

His velvety dark eyes blinked at me. "Violet, you're here?"

"I'm here, boo. Gimme a hug, I need your hug." He threw his arms around me and I hugged him, kissing his cheek, taking in his warmth, his scent of little boy sweat and fresh laundry. "Hmm. Thank you."

He bit his lip. "Can I have a cookie?" He glanced at his mom. "Please."

"Can we have a cookie, Mommy?" I asked Grace.

"Yes, we can."

I gave Thunder a cookie, and he took a big bite and chomped with great satisfaction. I wiped his hair from his rosy cheeks, the crumbs from the corner of his mouth. This boy was Wreck's nephew.

"I need to find my grandmother." I rose from the table. "Grace, Tania, thank you so much for sharing the letter with me. I'm going to show it to Gigi."

"Yes, show it to her." Grace hugged me.

"Tania, thank you for everything."

"You're very welcome, honey." Tania blew me a kiss. "I'll call you tomorrow."

"Bye, Thunder." I waved at him and he waved back as I headed down the porch steps.

I got in my car, gulped in air, and called Gigi. "I need to see you. Where are you?"

"I'm at Sue Anne's."

I let out a laugh. Her friend Sue Anne lived down the road from Whisperwind. "Perfect."

"Honey, are you okay?"

"Could you meet me at Whisperwind in five minutes?"

CHAPTER FORTY

VIOLET

BANGING and booming noises of ripping out the old and worn filled the air. From the second floor, a landslide of debris tumbled through a funnel down a slide, crashing into a huge trash bin below.

Gigi waited for me at the fence. I showed her the lipstick knife. "Tania gave it to me. She told me about Isi and Wreck's first date."

"Oh my goodness, never thought I'd see this again. Her brother Leo had given that to her, so she could protect herself against men." Gigi laughed loudly.

"And there's this. It's a letter he wrote to her." I handed her my phone and told her what Tania and Grace had told me.

She read the letter, slapped my phone to her chest, and burst into tears. "He'd sent her away from Meager to protect her. Helped her and her band get gigs through his connections to keep her on the road. Leo was a wanted man and on the run—wanted by a local drug dealer, other bikers, the police. It was a mess.

"Wreck would go out to her whenever he could, wherever she was. They didn't have FaceTime back then, and cell phones were just beginning. Not like you all have today. She was using pay phones and...." Her voice drifted. She looked away and wiped at her eyes.

I put an arm around her. "Must have been so hard. She was finally in a band, singing professionally, had a good man—all under shitty circumstances."

"They were being watched, they had to be careful. We all did. Wreck set up this system where he'd have one of the men from his club drop off a letter at the store by putting it in one of the canisters I had set up on a shelf in the back by the bathroom. A Jack would come in every once in a while and drop off a letter in one of those canisters for me to send to her. And if Isi had sent me a letter for Wreck, I'd have it ready in a canister so the biker could pick it up and get it to him."

"Holy crap, Georgia Dillon Drake, young wife and mother, outlaw go-between. Did your brother, the town sheriff, know?"

"Ryan was aware, and he looked the other way."

"You Dillons..."

Her gaze went back to the letter. "They didn't have much time together, and yet, they made the most of it, were grateful for what they had. They were hoping for so much more. Even so, they had it all, Violet, more than most. Even if it was only for a little while." She handed me back my phone. "Maybe you can't see that because you're so young, but, truly, there is no time to waste."

"No, there isn't." Hadn't Tag said the same to me in Greece? The rebel who kept moving, kept challenging himself in new lands with new experiences because he had one life to live to the fullest. *"Time to stop wondering. Time to start feeling,"* he'd said.

She gestured at the house. "Isi wanted to hang onto her family house and the store, and she worked hard to keep it all together, but it was impossible. But at the same time, she wanted to be free of those burdens to pursue her dreams her way. She finally got that chance, but ..."

"But." I put my arm through Gigi's. "I also have some really good news for you today."

"Give it to me."

"Beck is the one who bought Whisperwind."

She hopped up in her tracks. "He did WHAT?"

"He bought it for me, for us," spilled from me. "It's crazy, isn't it?"

"That's the most amazing, wonderful thing I've ever heard!" She hugged me.

Both our phones beeped with messages. "It's Jessa," said Gigi.

I took out my phone. "Me too. She wants to show us something she found here at the house." I called Jessa. "Hey, what's up? Gigi and I are actually out front."

"Violet! Gigi!" Phone in hand, Jessa waved from the front yard of the house, as several construction workers moved in and out of it. "I can't believe you're here! Come in."

Gigi and I walked through the open fence and met Jessa in the front yard. "What did you find, honey?"

Her face was streaked with red. She was excited. "This morning they ripped up the old linoleum flooring in the entryway. It must have been put down at least fifty years ago. We found something—come see."

We followed Jessa inside.

The house was empty, cavernous, huge, light filling it through all the dusty old windows. The banister along the grand staircase had been removed. Old wallpaper was being peeled off the walls, old paint scraped away.

We stepped into the foyer, the original wood flooring stunning. A parquet border spoke of another era.

"Wow, this is gorgeous and it was under here the whole time..."

Jessa pointed to the center of the foyer floor. "Over here."

In the center the wood was laid out to form a sun ray design and in the middle of that sun was a word burned into the wood, engraved with fire.

Whisperwind

Chills raced over my flesh, my heart leaping at the sight of the house's name branded into the floor. Something steadying, rooted me right here.

"Jeremiah had to have put it there," said Gigi. "By all accounts he had a flair for the dramatic."

"Obviously. He built this baby." Jessa let out a soft laugh. "His personal touch of ownership forever, for us."

I squatted down, my fingers brushing over the blackened letters. "It's real, isn't it? The stories. It's real, not some family tall tale or legend. It's real."

"It's real. He made it their very own special haven away from the maddening crowd of Meager," said Gigi. "And he made it here to stay."

"Come look at the rest of the house, now that's it empty and cleaned out," said Jessa. "I love it like this."

That particular zest in her voice had me smiling. I knew in her mind's eye, Jessa was visualizing all the possibilities for improving the flow of the building, how to accent and punctuate it's glories to make it the best it could be. Transformation was her talent, her passion.

I rose and followed Jessa and my grandmother into the living room area, our footsteps echoing through the house. "It's so big."

"It was never this bright in here," said Gigi. "Not that I remember."

"And yet this location is full of light," said Jessa. "With the architect we're discussing the possibility of knocking down one wall over here to bring in even more light. Maybe adding a wall of windows on that section"—she pointed to an exterior wall—"then later, white paint will help with that."

Tired majesty. Worn and frayed. But waiting. Waiting patiently and full of expectation, full of possibility. A tingling swirl surged in my chest and through my limbs, tickling me. Dust floated in the radiating light like enchanted particles. I stood riveted in the center of the house, imagining what it could be. "Magic."

"Yes," murmured Jessa.

"I always loved this fireplace." Gigi stroked the edge of the ornate wood carved mantel. "It was a touch of old world elegance to me."

"It's a real centerpiece. It deserves more attention once we blow out the space. "

"Have you found any major problems in the house so far?" Gigi asked Jessa.

"The bones of the house, the foundation are solid which is a huge relief. The roof has issues, but I expected that. Plumbing, of course, is a top priority, there was mold in one of the bedrooms so we're ripping that apart and dealing with it. Updating the heating and cooling system. And although the Putnams had updated the electrical, we're going to update it again for wiring for a smart house and WiFi. There's a lot of work ahead of us. But so far, so good."

Outside, in the distance, men were digging and measuring. "What's going on out there?" I asked.

"A soundproof state of the art recording studio." She grinned. "With an adjoining photography studio and gym."

My pulse jumped. "Recording and photography studios?"

"Yes. And on the other side of the property, a Mediterranean style swimming pool area with an outdoor kitchen and bath, a fire pit and ..."

"Mediterranean style?" I let out a breath.

"That's what I was told. So I'm researching mosaics and Greek island design as we speak." Her eyes flashed at me. "Somehow I need to make it work with the South Dakota of the house." She let out a laugh. "For God's sake, Violet, did Beck find you? Did you talk? Did he explain? What happened? Tell me, I'm dying here."

My heart thudded in my chest, so loud, so insistent. "He found me. He always finds me. He explained, and I'm so overwhelmed right now in the most amazing way."

Jessa hugged me. "I'm so glad. Together we're going to make this house come alive again like we always planned. Like you always wanted. The way you want."

I closed my eyes and clung to my sister, taking in a deep inhale, the same way I used to when I was a little girl and we'd visit the property. Just before we'd get back in the car, I'd take in a deep breath of the special, sweet, vanilla-like fragrance of the ponderosa pine trees that surrounded the property to preserve the memory, the feelings.

Now I smelled dust, old wood, mustiness, a dry earthiness, and it was fantastic. A breeze came through the open front door, bringing with it that hint of sweet vanilla, and I let out a laugh.

"So you know"—Jessa released me—"no expense is being spared to get everything done thoroughly, and all of it top of the line quality with attention to detail."

I burst into tears.

"Violet!" Four arms wrapped around me, two bodies embraced me.

"When I came here after finding out it was sold and I saw that fence"—I hiccuped—"I felt cut out. Blocked. But the fence has been protecting all this wonderfulness. All this beautiful magic."

Gigi's hand rubbed my back. "I never ever thought I'd see this happen. This is beyond anything I could have ever imagined. You are blessed, dear girl." Gigi kissed my cheek and wandered around to the old formal dining room, through to the kitchen, her voice echoing through the empty spaces. "That young man…that special young man…"

"Beck is committed to making it a real home," said Jessa. He's been protecting your dream all along, Violet."

Something warm and delicious and utterly euphoric spun inside me, a multicolored tornado over the plains, making me lightheaded, dizzy. Giddy. "More than that, Jessa. More than that. All this time, he's been protecting my heart."

I CALLED Beck but he wasn't answering. I had to talk to him. I had to talk to him right now. I had to tell him how amazing Whisperwind looked and felt. I had to tell him...how amazing he was. How grateful I was to have him in my life.

They were leaving South Dakota today. Was he busy packing? Were they loading the cars? He'd promised he'd call me first. I knew he would. Was he planning on calling me from the plane?

A stone dropped inside me, dragging me down with it. *No. No. No.*

I called Lenore and asked her if she knew where Beck was.

"They're leaving for L.A."

"Right, but he's not answering his phone and I—"

"Violet, they're at the airport."

"What?"

"The pilot had to push up the schedule." Lenore said. "They take off within two hours."

"I need to see him before he leaves, I need to—"

"If you want to get there in time, Finger will take you."

"Could he?"

"Where are you?"

Within three point five minutes, Finger roared up the street to Whisperwind on his massive Harley taking my breath away with the thunderous rumble of his engine. I steeled myself as he handed me a helmet. "Let's go."

Somehow I managed to get the helmet on and secured, and climbed on the back of his bike. We blasted off, the extreme vibrations of the metal monster drilling through me.

Behind us, I could've sworn I heard Gigi's hooting laughter.

CHAPTER FORTY-ONE

VIOLET

I COULD BARELY BREATHE. Barely think.

The fierce wind pummeled us, and I kept my head down against Finger's broad leather-covered back, and held on for dear fucking life.

We had to make it there before they left. I had to.

I. Had. To.

Suddenly Finger tore into the airport, making turns and finally bringing his bike to a smooth stop. I gulped in air as I dismounted. Post G-force took over my body as I grappled with the helmet.

He unsnapped it, taking it from me. "Run, woman. I'll be right here."

I only nodded and put whatever I had into running into the private plane area. I found an airport employee and spit out my request. She pointed in the direction I needed to go.

Please be there. Please be there. Please be there was my mantra as I ran toward the area she'd indicated. Through the panes of glass to the tarmac were Myles and Zack climbing the small staircase onto the small plane.

Their skateboards, mountain bikes, musical instruments, packed boxes, suitcases were being loaded into the cargo hold.

From behind the piles of cargo, Jude and Beck appeared and began to climb the stairs. I grabbed hold of the door handle.

"Miss, I'm sorry you can't go out there!" A security guard blocked my path.

"Please, I know them—" I pointed out the window.

"Yeah, yeah. You and a million other girls. You think I'm dumb? I know who they are and why you're here."

"No, no, I know Beck Lanier!"

He smirked at me. "If you know him, why don't you call him on your phone?"

"Of course!" I took out my phone and hit Beck's name. He was at the top of the stairs to the plane. He glanced at the phone in his hand and stopped. He stopped. My heart stopped.

"Violet?"

"Beck! Beck! Thank God! I'm here at the airport. I can see you." I waved madly, maniacally, like I was a fangirl at The Beatles's Shea Stadium concert. He turned in my direction, his eyes narrowing, and a grin swept across his beautiful face. He spotted me. His hand shot up and he waved at me.

"See that? See? I know him." I hopped up and down. The security guard only grunted as Beck charged down the stairs toward me. The guard opened the door and Beck grabbed me, lifting me, twirling me around outside on the tarmac.

I sucked in his scent of leather and clean soap and a hint of wood. Relief and joy. He let me down, releasing me. "You're here."

"I had to come see you, to say goodbye, but more than that —" My heart pounded fiercely in my chest and I gulped past it.

"More than that? What? What is it?"

"I love you, Beck. I-I love you." The emotion I'd never allowed myself to feel before surged and streamed forth and with it I soared off that cliff into the sky. The blue blue sky in his eyes. "I love you, Beck. I was just at the house and…I love that you bought Whisperwind for us."

His lips parted, his chest heaved slightly.

"You're the best thing that's ever, ever, ever happened to me. From day one in that dark hallway at Pete's. And you keep on showing me that over and over again. From the very beginning, you made me feel big, big emotions that I'd never felt before, never let myself feel. You had me looking the truth in the face, and taking big risks. You're—"

He kissed me, and I groaned, melting under his assault, melting into his strong, firm body. We clung to each other.

"We're together, you and me," I breathed against his lips, my hands cradling his face, fingers in his wild hair. "Together, capital fucking T. And I wanted you to hear it before you left South Dakota."

"I know it. I've always known it." He hugged me, his face sinking into my neck, noises escaping his throat.

I held him close, my face against his warm chest. My wind charm that he wore pressed against my cheek. "You were right at JFK when you said this is our time and we need to grab onto it and not let go. Not for anything."

"Not for anything."

I cradled his face. "Thank you for taking care of the house, for taking such good care of me."

"Just kiss me. Kiss me, dammit. And tell me again, say it again. I need to hear you—"

"I fucking love you." My hands cuffed his neck, and his eyes flared. I crushed my lips to his, our tongues eager, our bodies fused. Us, together. Together.

"Lanier, you coming up for air?" Beck and I moved apart on a soft laugh, and I blinked up at the plane. "Hey, Violet!" Jude and Zack and Myles all stood at the open doorway of the plane, grinning. I waved at them.

"Had to come say goodbye, you guys! Bon voyage!'

"Later, Violet!"

"Bye!"

Beck's hand caressed my jaw. "Come with me to L.A. I miss you already. I have one day before we go back into the studio to set the final tracks. We'll stay at the best hotel and just make love and eat—"

My knees wobbled. "I'd love to—"

"Yeah?"

"But I can't."

"Why?" His voice pleaded.

"Because of this." I whipped out the postcard advertising Founder's Festival. "I'm exhibiting my photographs of Meager at the gallery in town for the festival. The opening of the exhibit is the first night."

He studied the card. "This is fantastic, baby. This is the best!"

"It is, it really is. I would so love to jump on that plane with you and hole up in a fancy hotel, but there's so much to do, I—"

He planted a kiss on my lips. "You do what you need to do. And we're coming to the opening."

"You will?"

"You bet. We'll be there."

"I-I need you there."

He shoved the card in his back pocket, his eyes never leaving mine. "I love you, Violet." He took my hand in his and kissed it.

I let out a soft giggle on a reflex. Delight. Awkward shyness. Relief. Thrill. The world was shiny, sparkly, and new, spinning fast. Wild emotion spiraled inside me, between us, our joined hands my giddy life force.

"Go get on that plane now."

"I'll be back."

"I know."

He released me and ran. My breath hitched as he darted up the stairs of the small plane and blew me a kiss at the top. He was gone. A male flight attendant emerged and, along with an airport staff member, brought up the steps. The door was closed, sealed.

I smiled and waved at the plane like a goof. The guys' faces filled the small windows and they waved back at me. I blew Beck a last kiss.

Not a last kiss.

One of so many, many more.

CHAPTER FORTY-TWO

BECK

WE SETTLED into our cushioned seats on the plane. Peter, our flight attendant, took our drink orders as the pilot prepared for take off. My gaze lingered out the window, taking in the flat stretches of green, gentle mountains in the distance, all that blue sky. My heart was here. Here.

Bye South Dakota, I'll be back real soon.

Myles stretched out his long legs in the seat next to me as Peter served our drinks. "I feel really good about everything we accomplished here."

"Me too, man. This whole thing worked out so well from us not having bullshit distractions to working with Stewart, pulling in Dré. All of it."

And Violet telling me she was in love with me. I smoothed a hand down my chest, my flesh still warm with the excitement of her surprise appearance at the airport.

Myles drank his apple juice. "Now all that's left is to master what we've got. And Violet's photos are fucking phenomenal."

I cracked open the bottle of vitamin water. "I'm looking forward to making everything work together."

"Seat belts on, please, everybody." Peter moved through the cabin.

I put on my seat belt, and from my back pocket I pulled out the postcard Violet had given me. Meager's Founding Festival. A street fair, art exhibition, food and crafts, performances…

"What's this?" Myles picked up the card and read. "Cool."

"You know how I've been against making a music video for every single of ours?"

"Impossible to forget, dude. Some of our best arguments have been on that topic."

"I was thinking with "Sugar" being our first single from this album, I'd like to do a special video."

"Like what?"

The airplane pulled out of the gate and turned onto the runway.

"How about a live concert where we debut the song at the Meager Founding Festival. And there we raise money and awareness for the indoor horse ring for the kids at Pine Ridge."

"Those kids should have that."

"It means everything to Stewart and Ella. Sure, we could all donate a huge chunk of change for it. I know I will."

"Me too. Definitely."

"But by doing a live show that we film and later drop on YouTube—just a clip of that song for now—we publicize the cause and ask for donations on an international scale, and that's priceless. On our YouTube we set up a link for information and donations."

"We did agree to donate the proceeds of Isi's song to a local charity, right?" Myles grinned. "It's perfect."

"It is. Jude had mentioned the idea to me after he and Violet saw the kids riding one morning."

"I think it's a great idea. I'm down for it."

My head sank back in my seat. "Something is still missing in that song for me."

Myles finished his juice. "Come on. It's good."

I let out a breath. "But my gut is telling me the song could be better."

"Well, your gut has never steered us wrong, so work it out before we get back into the studio in L.A." He laughed, stretching out his legs.

The plane taxied on the runway, gaining speed. Battling gravity and nature, our small plane rose, tilted. All of us peered out the windows for one last look at the Black Hills. Something tugged inside my chest. *I'll be back soon. I'll be back for my Violet.*

The golden green farmland below us was cut by a winding road perfect for a motorcycle. I let out a long sigh.

Myles peered out the window with me. "You gonna hook us up to perform at this Founding Festival at the last minute?"

"I'm going to find out. I'll message my mom, she's on the committee."

"Tell her I say hi."

"Shut up, Myles." I took out my phone and tapped it out of airplane mode.

My phone pinged with an email. Georgia Drake. I jerked up in my seat. Why would Violet's grandmother be emailing me? Had something happened? She would've called. I clicked, my pulse doubling in time.

Dear Beck:

Your father kindly gave me your email address so I could send you this attached letter. This is a love letter that Wreck, Isi's boyfriend, had written to her. It was given to Violet today by a friend here in town and she showed it to me. I am convinced that Wreck wrote this letter after that Valentine's night he and Isi had together on the road, after which she and your father worked on her new song inspired by that night. The song on the tape that you played for me.

I know it's true. I can feel it.

I don't think Isi ever got a chance to read this letter of Wreck's. He alludes to their one night together on the road and says: "don't forget to send me the lyrics of your new song when you finish." He never got to hear her new song.

Maybe this is too late, maybe you've finished the song already and don't need this, but I feel strongly that you should read this letter to give you a fuller perspective of the feelings between them at that very precise moment from which the song was born.

Bring them together, Beck.

This may sound woo-woo to you, but I think you get it.

I truly believe both the song and the letter were meant to come to light and be united in your and Violet's time. In your hands as artists.

In your hearts as lovers.

This letter hit Violet hard in the best way, and for that I'm grateful.

Don't let anything slide, Beck. Embrace it all, the good and the bad. I've told Violet the same.

Also, I want you to know that I'm thrilled that you are the one who bought Whisperwind. Violet and I were at the house today. The vision you have for this house is remarkable.

You are an exceptional young man. And I truly believe that you and Violet are a blessing for each other.

Sincerely,

Georgia

I CLICKED on the attached document and read the passionate, intimate words from the tough Vietnam vet biker outlaw to his woman. To his Isi.

A shudder went through me and burned in my center. My hands gripped my phone tighter as I read the letter again. And again, my heart thudding in my chest. Slumping against my seat, I closed my eyes, the steady drone of the plane's engines vibrating through me. Violet's seductive smile rose before me, her touch flared over my flesh, her hand in mine warm, secure.

"I love you, Beck."

I rewound the lyrics we'd put down, the notes, the chords, Isi's melody.

I listened.

Wreck's burning gratitude, Isi's playful joy, my ache for Violet.

"I love you, Beck."

Isi's melody.

I listened.

Imagined. Played.

Wreck's words came back up: *"Every time we make love it's a promise."*

Violet coming on my cock, eyes gleaming, drowning in mine. Her satisfied sighs filling my ear, the two of us tangled in one another.

Her sighs and moans filled my ears. Her soft hand slid in mine, the grip of her fingers at my waist deepened as we took off on my Harley.

I listened.

Her damp breath against my bare chest at dawn on the island. Her body pressing against mine at the waterfall, eyes gleaming, bright.

Yes.

My eyes blinked open, and I grabbed my notebook from my open backpack under my seat and wrote. "Myles?"

"Yeah?"

"Get out your iPad."

South Dakota down below us for only moments more, Myles and I tweaked Isi's song.

After, when my brain had settled, but the buzz in my veins remained, I emailed Georgia.

Georgia—

I can't thank you enough for sharing this beautiful letter with me. Your timing was perfect. Yes, the song needed it.

And I needed it too.

I have an idea that I'd like to run by you. My mother had told me that you are in charge of the Meager Founding Festival. I'm on my way to L.A. right now, and I'll call you when I get there, so we can discuss it.

Again, thank you for trusting me with Isi's song and Wreck's letter.

Violet found me at the airport before we left. I love her with everything I've got and everything I am, and I always will.

- Beck

CHAPTER FORTY-THREE

VIOLET

"I COME BEARING GIFTS." I placed the full coffee holder and the large paper bag from the Grand on Jessa's desk at Hildebrand & Hildebrand.

"Oooo!" Jessa grabbed her bran muffin from the bag and took a bite. "How I missed Mom's apple bran muffin with this cream cheese filling."

"Even in France and Vienna? With all those croissants and pastry delicacies?"

"Yep," she garbled through the food in her mouth. "Hmm… thank you." She sipped on her ginormous iced latte.

I took out the blueberry corn muffin for Dad and placed it on his desk along with his hot coffee.

"Thanks, honey." He glanced up at me as he read a document.

"You're welcome. Do you need me to check on anything before we go to the auction?"

"We're all set." His face beamed. "We'll be leaving in an hour."

I glanced at Ladd's desk. No Ladd. "Where's Mr. Jeffries?"

Jessa's gaze darted up at me from her computer screen. "He hasn't come in yet."

"He'll be meeting us there." Dad sipped on his coffee. "He texted me earlier."

"Hmm." I put a straw in my iced latte.

Dad's phone rang, and he answered, stretching out in his leather office chair. "Hi, Cliff."

His face turned stony, his shoulders stiffened. "I don't understand." He sat up, the chair jerking forward. His clipped voice had me and Jessa both putting down our coffees. He shot up from his desk. "You mean it's been postponed…"

My mouth dried. Something was wrong.

Dad paced the length of the office. "Is it Jenny Frick? She got all emotional and she—" He pursed his lips, his eyes widening at whatever Cliff was telling him. A hand went to his forehead as he stared out the big window onto Clay Street. "Are you kidding me? Are you fucking kidding me?" His voice exploded. "Who the hell does that? Who could possibly—no!"

Cliff's loud voice on the line was excited, rapid. Jessa rose from her desk.

"Who is it? Who?" Dad's chest heaved, his eyes as fierce as a blustering bull's. "How do you not know? Find out, dammit!" He pitched his phone across the room, the crash splintering the air, his phone smashing into pieces against Ladd's computer.

"Dad! What the hell is going on?"

He turned slowly, body stiff, skin pale, jaw set, breath ragged. "The auction's been canceled."

My heart stopped. "What? Why? How?"

"Someone strolled into the bank this morning and bought the Frick."

"Bought the Frick?" I sputtered. "You mean the whole damn—"

"The whole damn ranch. Every parcel, every acre. All of it."

"Oh my God." Jessa's hand flew to her mouth.

"That's crazy," I said. "The auction is in three hours. The land has been—"

"The land is gone, Violet! Gone! One buyer, one, walked into the bank and bought the whole damn thing."

"And Cliff doesn't know who?"

"He wouldn't tell me." Dad hands flattened on his desk, his head hung low, his breathing rough.

"But...but we checked!" My whole body vibrated with adrenaline. "No one's been sniffing around, asking questions. Nobody!"

"Someone swooped in just before the clock struck midnight and took it all." His fist smashed down on his desk rattling every thing on it. The coffee spilled. "Took it all!"

My gaze landed on Ladd's unoccupied desk. "What about Ladd and Armand Castillo? Uncle Mad saw them on the property. Castillo certainly has the money and a network of companies and investors. Why else would Ladd have given Armand the grand tour of Meager? He was mighty relaxed and pleased with himself when we saw them at the Grand, and he sure didn't give a damn that we'd seen them together. He enjoyed it."

Dad's face was pale. "Both of them played it very cool."

"I saw him the other day, and he was going on and on about how much he was looking forward to the auction." I grit my teeth.

Dad only stared out the window.

"I told you, Dad, between you and Anna and me and Beck, we only made him—"

"He could have been planning this all along, from the very beginning and played us both for fools."

My thudding pulse echoed in the hollow pit of my insides.

Dad let out a dark laugh. "That section close to I-90, that's what sold Armand right there. Can you imagine the shopping malls and industrial parks he has planned? Now we can look forward to a golf course three times the size of our original design, five restaurants, a huge hotel, vacation condos, a cineplex, a heliport. The Black Hills are going to go to hell in that goddamn commercial playground for the nouveau riche hand basket."

Jessa touched his shoulder. "You've been working against that all these years, to save all this—"

Dad barely heard her, he barreled on. "Maybe in a few days we'll be hearing the roar of bulldozers on the Frick as they plow up the sod settlement and the old dairy barn and the coach house—" His breath cut, his face tightened, he clutched his arm. "That entitled over-privileged prick. How could I have trusted him? He's nothing like his father!"

"Dad…"

"I brought him in on this," his voice seethed. "I brought him here to work with us to create something of lasting worth. He seemed to want that too. And I thought it was so great that the two of you…" He stiffened like a puppet whose strings were being yanked. A hand shot to his chest, his fingers clutching his dress shirt. A button popped, he grunted.

"Dad!" Jessa shrieked.

On a choking breath, his body jerked left, collapsing onto his desk, dropping to the floor like a collection of bricks obeying gravity.

A scream filled my ears as I ran to my father.

My scream.

CHAPTER FORTY-FOUR

VIOLET

"MOM, go on in, you see Dad first," Jessa said.

She squeezed Jessa's hand. "You girls go." She'd come to the hospital right away. The three of us clutching each other as we'd waited for the doctor, for Dad to be transferred to a room.

"Are you sure?" I asked.

"Go on." She chewed on her lip.

Jessa and I went into the hospital room. Dad was hooked up to several beeping machines, lights flashing, monitoring his pulse, his life. He looked better than he had when Jess and I had scrambled to his side and called 9-1-1. A bit more color in his cheeks. My pulsed thudded at the sight of him vulnerable, mowed down.

"Daddy." Jess ran to his side and planted a kiss on his cheek.

I took his large hand in mine and sat on the other side of the bed. His eyes blinked open.

"You look so much better," said Jess. "The doctor said it was a mild heart attack. That you just need some rest and no stress."

His weary gaze drifted to me. "Violet…" He took in a breath. "Have you heard from Ladd? Has he contacted you…to gloat yet?"

"No actually, he hasn't," I replied. "I've been expecting him to, but nada so far. Unless this is his strategy—wanting us to stew in it and then play the big man? I don't know and—"

"Will you two stop? Who cares?" Jessa's voice shook. "We could've lost you, Daddy. We can't lose you."

"You won't lose me, honey." He took her hand in his, threading their fingers together. "The news was such a shock. We were so close. I really wanted that property."

"We know you did," said Jessa. "We all did. For Five. Because—"

"No, no, you're wrong. I wanted it for us."

I lifted my gaze to his.

"Yes, that one piece of land by the powder houses was always special to us. The three of you would ride out on your horses up there, and your mom and I would come after you. We'd have picnics..."

"And we'd make big plans to build castles on that ridge one day. One day..."

"Yes. But this project wasn't about Five for me. It was about us. That even after our losses, we could still accomplish good things together as a family like Hildebrands have always done."

My chest caved in, my mouth slackened. I'd always assumed that what drove Dad on this project was the loss of his son. That hurt, that anger, his desperation was what drove him to build something arrogantly grand on the still smoldering ashes of his regrets in an effort to blot them out.

By making Five's childhood dream a reality, he would be building a monument to his son to somehow make up for Five's terrible mistakes and his own.

"Oh, Dad," Jessa whispered, lying down next to him.

My fingers curled in the sheet at his side. How I'd resented him, resented Five, this project. Even though I'd always believed in Powder Ridge, I'd felt obligated to it. Bound to it. Stifled by it like a stiff shirt collar around my neck, chafing, binding.

But I was wrong. Powder Ridge was about creating something positive, good, important from the rubble. Not broken dreams and horrible sorrows and wretched guilt. Not denial. But us moving forward together.

My breath stalled, but my thoughts, feelings, were all a chaotic cacophonous jumble. Dizziness swelled through me.

"Violet? Honey, are you okay?" His hand reached for me, and I took it. "You're pale. Jessa—water."

"I'm good." My voice came out small. She handed me a fresh bottle of water, and I drank. The tension in my muscles eased, and Jessa swept my hair of my neck. I capped the bottle. "I've never heard you say that before, Dad. That Powder Ridge is about us."

"I haven't said a lot of things that needed to be said."

"Right now you need to take it easy, please." Jessa adjusted his pillows. "We'll find another way, we will. Right now it's spilled whiskey."

I let out a small laugh, and Dad's lips curled into a weak grin. Great Grandpa Hildebrand always used to say that. *"Who cares about damned milk? It's spilled whiskey that makes me cry!"*

"Let's face it," she continued. "We were naive and arrogant to think that the land we wanted would definitely be ours, that no one would get in our way."

Dad grimaced as he shifted his head on the pillows. "I need to know if it's Ladd and Castillo. I need to know."

"I want to know too."

Jessa only shook her head as she refilled Dad's cup with water.

I squeezed his hand and his gaze met mine. I mouthed, "I'll find out."

CHAPTER FORTY-FIVE

BECK

I TEXTED VIOLET.

She told me about the auction being cancelled, about her dad's heart attack.

"I'm coming to see you."

"It's okay, really. Every single Hildebrand in the county is here at the hospital. Tell me how the new album's going?"

"Almost done. We're really happy with everything. I spoke with Stewart today and he & Ella flipped out over the photos you sent of the kids riding. They're epic. You told their story with this reverence & excitement. "

"Thank you! SO great to hear they love them."

"How's work on the exhibition going?"

"Really well. I'm pouring every free moment into it. I'm enjoying it so much."

"I'm proud of you!"

"TY! - got to go, my grandpa just got here."

"Ok - I LOVE YOU"

I LOVE YOU!! XXX

A grin overtook my lips at her words, her triple X. I missed kissing her. Holding her. Touching her. Sliding back in my chair, I put on my sunglasses again, the harsh glare off the swimming pool annoying.

Violet was now most definitely in full caretaker mode. But she needed taking care of, too.

"What's up?" Myles chewed on the last of the sushi he'd brought over for lunch.

"Her dad had a heart attack. They're at the hospital now."

"Shit. How's he doing?" asked Jude.

"She says he's okay. It was mild."

"Good to hear, but still shitty."

Myles tossed his phone on the table in between all the empty takeout containers. "Man, there's so much speculation about where we are, what's going on."

"A few days back in L.A. and we've managed to remain under the radar so far," I said.

"They're worried about us." Jude popped the last of the edamame in his mouth.

Zack cracked open another bottle of water. "Should we ask Naomi to issue a statement saying we're back and finishing up our new album. Won't-be-long-now kind of crap? Invite a journalist from some magazine to interview us?" He made a face. "Come up with some kind of *captivating content,* like Naomi says?" his voice pitched derisively. "I know—take a pic of our lunch leftovers and post it."

Myles groaned. "Fuck no."

"What is it you do control?" Dad came out onto the patio,

drinking a steamy hot cup of something. He was into organic green tea all of a sudden.

"Our music," I replied.

"Our relationships with each other." Myles glanced at me.

"Hell yes to both." Dad took a seat a the table. "So here's an idea: instead of all that posing and suggesting and Blah, blah, fucking blah, show them the genuine Freefall in the music. And what the hell, surprise them while you're at it."

"Something directly from us," I said. "Not packaged shit, but something that's immediate and genuine."

"And maybe not our normal shit." Jude wiped his hands on a napkin. "Mind fuck 'em."

"We could go live on Instagram," said Myles.

"Answering fan questions? Interviewing each other? All relaxed?" said Zack

"No. Dad's right. We go back to the music. We've distracted them with all the talk and the drama lately. How about we perform unplugged?"

"The new songs?" asked Myles.

I leaned forward on the table. "No. Like Jude said—not our normal shit. We could do covers of favorites, unusual picks that aren't typical us. Classic rock, current pop. One or two songs per live session, quick bites purely for the fun of it. Not scheduled either."

Dad grinned at me, raising his mug. The idea perked around the table.

Myles's eyes narrowed at me. "I got an idea to shake things up—how about I play guitar and you sing."

"Whoa!" Jude let out a sharp laugh.

Zack clapped his hands together.

My mind raced back to that night at Pete's with Violet when she told me how much she loved me singing and how she'd wished I'd do it again.

"I like it." I high-fived Myles. "How about every time, we

give them different combinations of us—solos, us playing different instruments. One of us on piano."

"I could play the Greek drum," said Zack.

"And every time they're waiting, wondering, who's it going to be?" said Jude. "What are they going to sing? How're they going to do it?"

"You're not making me sing solo," said Zack. "And I haven't played piano since I was thirteen."

"Start practicing," Myles said.

I let out a laugh. "You can sing harmony for me and Myles, and play anything you fucking want. Dance in the background. Tap out a beat on my guitar."

"That I can do," laughed Zack.

Myles grabbed his phone. "Let's pick out some tunes, set a schedule for ourselves."

"We should do a Bruno Mars," said Zack. "Maybe Harry Styles…"

"Only if you sing Watermelon Sugar High." Jude stuck out his tongue.

"Me? No way, man. That would be a desecration."

We came up with a list of songs and started making decisions. And through the outlining and the laughs, one thought propelled me forward: *I'm going to serenade you, Violet. We can't be together right now, so I'm going to serenade you, baby, and make you smile.*

I TOLD Naomi and Ford our idea, and they were excited about it. "Freefall Serenades" we were calling them. We'd chosen our songs, worked out the arrangements.

The first one was right now.

"You ready?"

"Let's do this."

Myles had set up his phone and lighting at the small studio

in his house. He leaned over and hit buttons. "I think I'm freaking nervous." He let out a laugh.

I blew out a breath. "I think I am too."

I knew why I was nervous. Because I wanted Violet to see this. To hear it. I was doing this for her. To make her smile in her hard times.

Myles's foot tapped. We were live.

He started strumming, gently shaking his head to the rhythm he created on his guitar. I moved to his chords, smiling at the screen as the number of people tuning in to our live multiplied and multiplied.

And blew up.

Myles grinned at the screen. "Hey, hey, everybody, thanks for joining us today. We got something special for you."

CHAPTER FORTY-SIX

VIOLET

I CAPPED the two extra large iced mochas and turned the cups around to see the names. We'd been so busy this afternoon that I'd been brewing and crafting non-stop along with our new barista. "Tania! Jill! Coffee is ready!"

Tania glided over to the counter. "Hooray."

"Sorry, I didn't realize you were here."

"You're busy. That's okay." She took a sip of hers. "So good."

"Ladies coffee hour today, right?"

"Yep." She gestured at the large table with the settee and armchairs, where Mom and Grace and Lenore were already sitting and drinking and nibbling. "We're just waiting for Jill. I ordered for her. How's your dad doing? Erica was telling us that you and Jessa have been staying with him."

"He's much better, thank you. He has to learn to take it slow for now, and eat cleaner. He's always been active, which is good, but he's an original meat and potatoes guy. He's handling it, though. All hail, the power of the greens and fruit smoothie."

She laughed. "Well, if anyone can handle a challenge, it's Marshall Hildebrand. I'm glad he's doing well." Even though Tania didn't care for my dad, I knew that her father had died of a sudden heart attack.

"Thanks, Tania. And don't worry, I've been getting my work done for the show. I'll be ready."

"Oh, I'm not worried, babe."

"Violet!" Shelby was at my side, holding her massive cell phone out at me. "Sorry to interrupt, but Freefall is doing a live on Instagram."

"A live what? An interview?" I wiped my hands on my towel. I hadn't talked to Beck for a couple of days now. We were both on crazy schedules at the moment. We'd been texting a lot, but hadn't really spoken.

"Are they making some kind of announcement?" Tania had gotten her phone out too.

I glanced over at Lenore. She and my mom and all the ladies were talking excitedly and tapping on their phones.

"We shall see," Shelby murmured.

Jude was at an electric piano, and Zack held the small Greek drum. Beck sat on a high stool, a microphone set up in front of him, and Myles held an acoustic guitar in front of a mic. They were in a studio somewhere. Why wasn't Beck holding his guitar?

My pulse kicked up. This was Beck Lanier of Freefall, rock star, celebrity. But now I knew every line of that face, every flicker of his grin, every twist of those lips. I knew how those long, lean, muscled arms felt around me. And I also knew the vibration of his voice against my skin. I'd lived them all, reveled in them.

Beck grinned into the camera, and my knees weakened, an ache growing in my chest. "Hey, everybody, me and Myles and Zack and Jude haven't been on here in a long while since the tour finished, and we've missed you. So we thought we'd hop on and fool around with a few tunes and have a good time."

Jude hit the keys of the piano. "Hopefully we can brighten up your day."

"Let's see if you recognize this one…" Myles played the

opening notes on his guitar, Zack providing a beat to the melody. Beck looked straight into the camera and sang.

Beck. Sang.

His gorgeous voice drilled straight into my soul, making my heart squeeze to a stop. Myles joined him for a quick, gorgeous harmony. Holy hell, they were switching roles.

"This is Justin Bieber's 'Somebody.'" Shelby squeaked. "This is crazy. I love it."

Beck lifted his head as he sang a long note, and my jaw dropped. I leaned into the phone, my hands steadying me on the counter. A new tattoo was visible on his throat. Wind, wind blew across his throat.

"That's a new tattoo, isn't it?" Shelby whispered.

"Yep." My voice barely registered.

The comments scrolled fast and furious down the screen.

- *OMG FIRE!*

- *Justin who???*

- *OMGAAA BECK IS SINGING! His VOICE!! Y'all! Kill me now!*

- *Look at Myles- he put his hair up! SO HOT!*

- *WE LOVE YOU, Jude!*

- *Beck has a new tattoo! DYING! What does it mean??*

- *Kisses from Singapore!!! When are you coming here???*

"Violet, are you watching?" someone called out.

I glanced up. All our customers were swaying at their tables watching Freefall's IG live on their phones, their tablets, laptops, huge grins on their faces. My mom and all the ladies were jamming. A hand in the air, Lenore winked at me.

Myles danced and swiveled holding his guitar as Zack's fingers pounded and rolled on the small drum. Jude went to town on the piano. He played so well. Who knew?

Beck's voice rose through the Meager Grand singing about joy to have found his loved one, his commitment, his…all the while staring straight into the camera. His genuine enjoyment at singing this song was palpable. His genuine *everything*.

This song was a super catchy, uplifting, danceable pop tune about needing your lover, about no longer being alone, and believing in magic.

I believe!

I believed in Beck's magic. His singing was effortless, colored with sincerity, feeling, good times. And in a vibrant contrast, Myles's harmony provided an earthy, rough sexiness to Beck's easy velvet. Freefall jammed on an unlikely for Freefall song, a song to which they gave their own rough and high-watt twist.

Their energy was infectious, mesmerizing. I was rooted to the spot with Shelby as Beck licked the screen with his snarling lips and bedroom eyes as he sang about being in the throes of love. About being devoted. My insides swooshed with molten heat as I took in my lover's new wind tattoo up the side of his neck.

Jude, Zack, Myles, Beck were all in having-the-time-of-my-life-with-my-bros mode and they swept us along with them. Myles picked up the vocals for a verse as Beck grinned at Zack and then dove into the next verse, its tone pleading, joyful. Zack came up behind Myles, the two of them shimmied with the quick rhythm, Jude bopping his head in that way only he did. The song wound down and Myles's hand flew off the guitar. They burst into laughter.

"Dude, you got pipes on you," Myles said on a rich laugh as he and Beck slapped at each other's palms in the air.

Laughter filled the Grand. Comments filled the screen. Red, red love filled my heart.

Beck faced the camera. "We hope you liked that. I liked it. Did you like it Jude?"

"I really, really, really, really fucking liked it," Jude hooted. "Sorry, was that bad? Are we going to get chopped now?"

"It's cool...." Myles's eyes narrowed as he focused on the screen reading the rush of comments. Fans from Malaysia, France, The Netherlands, the UK, Japan. Flame and heart emojis flew.

- More please, more!

- OMG, Beck's voice is EVERYTHING! SING FOR ME, BECK!"

- MYLES, u are a GOD!!

- Becccccckkkkkkk we love u!"

- I can't...! I'm dead, DEAD!!!! I NEED MORE!

- JUDE RULES!

- Play me with those fingers, Zack!

A grin slashed Myles's face. "You guys are amazing. I'm living for these comments. Thank you so much! We got another...."

Beck had grabbed a guitar that had been on a stand next to him and strummed chords as everyone shifted into readiness. Jude pulled up a stool and grabbed a guitar and sat next to Beck. Myles leaned into the microphone, his large eyes staring into the camera, and sang.

"My favorite—Backstreet Boys!" someone shouted in the Grand.

Gasps and hoots went up in the coffeehouse for "Tell Me Why."

"No way, I love this song!" Tania said.

Myles's thoughtful vocals were stunning. They'd brought the song to an intense ballad all the way through. Heat rushed through my chest at the sound of Beck's smooth, clear tenor hitting the perfect harmonies for Myles, the intricate way he and Jude played their guitars to each other—Jude sitting still as he played was a revelation never before seen. Zack next to them on the small Greek drum.

Beck wore an unbuttoned shirt, my Alessio wind pendant necklace hanging against his beautiful bare chest, sending a hum through my middle. Myles's rich, deep vocals pleaded and declared. Beck maintained a steady rhythm while Jude's chords became complex and dramatic. Zack's primal beat was haunting. They lifted the song to a whole other level.

They finished and dove straight into another. I recognized the chords immediately. Bruce Hornsby's "Mandolin Rain," with Myles and Zack sharing the vocals on this one.

My heart twisted. "Damn, that's gorgeous."

Everyone in the Grand was riveted to their screens.

The song came to a finish, and Myles and Beck dipped their heads at each other. Both in agreement, both pleased.

Beck flicked his hair from his face, a finger stroking down his new tat. His tongue lashed out at his lower lip, and warm goo simmered in my veins.

My dirty, good boy is calling to me. Beck adjusted his guitar in his hold. "We hope you enjoyed this session. We're calling this our Serenade Series. With a capital fucking S, baby." He grinned at the camera, and a flaming arrow blew into my chest, my clit pounding.

"We're together you and me, capital fucking T, baby."

The guys crowded around their phone to read the comments. "We have the best fans!" said Zack.

"Our serenades will be saved in our highlights here on IG," said Myles. "Have a great rest of your day, and stay tuned 'cause we're going to have some new music news for you real soon."

Jude ran his fingers over his guitar strings. "We're impulsive, so this could happen again at any time."

"Any time…" added Zack on a drum roll.

"And always, always find a way to live your wild every day," said Beck.

"LIVE SESSION HAS CONCLUDED" said Shelby's screen.

"Holy shit," I breathed. Currents of electricity spiked though me.

"Holy shit is right." Shelby clicked off her phone. "That was amazing."

"That was incredible."

She leaned into me. "That was for you, you know that, right?"

"It was, wasn't it?" We both giggled.

"He's so hot for you! He sang for you, Violet. And I'm sure that tattoo is all about you, too."

"Yes, it's about me." My limbs were still gooey, my insides bubbled.

"I knew it! I knew it! YES!" She raised her hands in the air. A triumph. It was a triumph, me and Beck.

The Backstreet Boys were right. No matter the distance, Beck was my one desire.

"Can I get a coffee around here? Why is everyone in a daze?"

Shelby straightened up. "Right here, Mr. Fieldston." She darted to the register. "What can I get you?"

A grin swept over my mouth. He had serenaded me. I would serenade him right back.

Grabbing my phone from under the counter, I went out to the seating area of the coffeehouse. "Everybody! Could I have a minute?"

They turned around, expectant gazes filled my vision from every table.

"I'd like to take a picture of all of us and post it on the Grand's Instagram account, saying how much we loved Freefall's live, show our support for Beck and the guys. What do you say?"

"Let's do it!" Chairs scraped and shuffled as everyone stood up and bunched together in the center of the room.

"Hold up your phones and tablets, so we show we were all watching. Lenore, get over here." With a wide grin she darted next to me, and I put an arm around her waist, and she slid hers around mine, holding me close. Tania, Grace, and Mom joined us up front.

"Oh my gahhh, what's going on?" Jill flew threw the front door with her daughter Becca, her toddler, Nic, and Grace's son, Thunder.

"Get over here now!" hooted Tania. Jill scooted in next to Tania, as Grace grabbed onto the kids' hands.

"Mr. Fieldston, you're going to have to take this, we're just too many people for a selfie," I said. "Shelby, get in here."

A beaming Shelby darted over and took my phone, gave it to

Mr. Fieldston, who only twisted his lips. Shelby nudged in next to me.

"Scooch in closer now." Mr. Fieldston shook his head at us. Everyone followed his hand gestures. "That's it, that's it." He looked through the camera.

"You got us all in there, Mr. F?" I asked.

"Young lady, you're not the only one who knows how to take a picture in this town, and with a real camera, I might add."

"Duly noted." I let out a laugh. "Here we go, people."

"On three, everyone." Mr. Fieldston brought the phone to his face. "1-2-3—"

"Cheese!"

Perfect.

I posted it to our IG:

All of us at @TheMeagerGrand had a blast listening to
@Freefall_TheBand's live "Serenade" just now.
*AMAZING with a capital f**king A, baby!*
Congrats to Beck, Jude, Myles, & Zack from all of us here in Meager,
SD. We can't wait for the next one!
Hugs & Kisses from the Black Hills xxx

#Freefall #FreefallLive #FreefallSerenades #BestMusic
#musicofinstagram #RockAndRollForever #BlackHills #SoDak
#TheMeagerGrand #CoffeeLover #MusicLover

CHAPTER FORTY-SEVEN

VIOLET

"I STILL CAN'T GET over that Dad ate broccoli last night. He's always refused to eat it before." Jessa tapped on her computer, bringing up her design software.

"Try cauliflower tonight. That will be the real test." I checked the clock on the wall. Ten minutes to three. We had an appointment with a lawyer who'd called out of the blue yesterday about property in the area, and I promised Jessa I'd be here with her to help her handle it.

"Oh yes, cauliflower. You're so cruel." She laughed. "I'm going to roast it in the oven with olive oil and sea salt, so much better than boiled."

"You're so merciful. But yeah, that does sound good."

"He's too quiet. That worries me."

"He has a lot to come to terms with right now."

"Grandma Holly always used to say bad things happen in threes. I keep thinking—first the auction, then Dad...now what?"

"That's superstitious non—"

The front door pushed open and in strode Ladd.

"You were saying?" Jessa crossed her arms.

"Well, well, well, and there he is at long last." I moved toward him, stopping him from further entry. "Did you come for your shit? Because I have it ready for you right here." I shoved the box on the floor toward him with my foot.

He glanced down at it and raised his head, giving me a withering stare. "I'm here for more than a box of stuff. I came for an explanation."

"An explanation? Of what? My father's heart attack?"

"Oh yeah, I heard."

"And that's all you have to say?"

"Tell me what the hell is going on?"

"Shouldn't I be asking you that question? How long have you been planning this?"

"Me?"

"Unbelievable. You brought Armand in. Very impressive. Did you plan this all from the beginning?"

"I brought Armand in, yes, but only after you and Daddy couldn't keep your panties on. That's when I knew that the two of you were all about yourselves. My father always said Hildebrands don't partner with anybody, and he was right. I wasn't ever going to get guarantees for the long term on this project. You both just wanted my cash between your legs."

"Are you kidding me? Everything between you and us on this project was above board and in writing."

"Right. I was always going to be the outsider, so I brought Armand in to buy up the pieces I wanted for the mine and for my golf club, and he—"

"He wanted that piece by 1-90, didn't he?"

"That's right. That's how I got him excited by the whole idea. Otherwise, it would've been a hard sell."

"Well, congratulations, you got what you wanted," said Jessa.

"Now get the hell out," I added.

"Are you two on crack? We didn't buy it, and I want to know who did," Ladd spit out.

My pulse squashed to a halt. "Armand isn't the buyer?"

"No. He wasn't interested in the whole fucking ranch. That's just crazy. When I found out the auction was cancelled, I got so pissed off. I was looking forward to us outbidding you. I couldn't wait to see the look on your face. I wanted the satisfaction of you and Marshall knowing I'd outmaneuvered you."

"You are such a small, petty man," I muttered.

"And you're a fucking bitch."

"Hey!" Jessa's voice flared.

"Who is it, Violet? Did you set this up to get rid of me?" Ladd's jaw tensed.

"My dad had a heart attack because of this, fool. We thought for sure it was you and Armand. I don't know who it is, and I'd really love to find out. "

The door opened. "Miss Hildebrand?"

"Yes?" Both Jessa and I answered.

"I'm Ted Shales, we spoke on the phone. We have an appointment."

I glanced at the antique brass clock on the brick face wall. Three o'clock on the dot.

"Yes, of course, Mr. Shales. I'm Violet Hildebrand." I shook his hand firmly. "This is my sister, Jessa Hildebrand." Jessa shook his hand, and gestured at a chair, and he sat.

I cleared my throat. "We have an appointment, Ladd. You need to leave."

"I want answers. Your father knows everything that's ticking away in these Black Hills. Everything. Marshall's full of shit if he's telling you he doesn't know."

I leaned into him. "Don't you dare even say my father's name. Now get the hell out of here and never come back."

"You'd said your client would be coming as well, Mr. Shales?" Jessa's bright voice rose behind me as Ladd and I continued our stare down.

"I'm right here," a deep voice boomed from the entrance to the office. My body flinched. I knew that voice.

Behind me, Jessa gasped loudly, sharply, and I turned.

"Holy crap!" we both said.

Walker strode into Hildebrand & Hildebrand.

Walker, who I'd met in Greece. The big handsome hulk of muscle and tattoos was now a figure of a different sort of power. My breath cut. Gone were the tank tops and Bermuda shorts and pricey sneakers.

Walker was stunning in a dark blue cut to perfection suit, a bright white dress shirt open at the neck, revealing the tattoos that swirled over his tanned-in-Greece chest. "Hello, Violet. Good to see you." His gaze went to my sister, lingered, grew heavy. "Jessamyn." He uttered her full name with precision.

What. The. Fuck.

I glanced at my sister. Jessa's lips parted, she shifted her weight, red streaking her face.

"You know Walker?" I asked her.

"How do you know him?" she shot back.

"We met in Greece."

"You did?" Her eyes widened.

"What the hell is going on?" Ladd glared at Walker.

"Is this some kind of joke, Montana boy?"

Walker licked his lips, his gaze lasering over Jessa. "You didn't tell your sister about me?"

The rough tenderness in his tone made the hairs on the back of my neck stand on end. *Jessa, Jessa, Jessa.* "Oh, you're kidding me, right?"

Jessa took in a deep breath.

My gaze shot to Walker. Back to Jessa. "Holy crap," I muttered again. "Mr. Shales, Walker here is your client from out of state, who wanted to discuss a commercial property in the area?"

"Yes, ma'am."

"I'm here because I recently bought a property in this area, and I wanted to discuss it with Mr. Hildebrand," said Walker. There was a teasing quality to his tone, his bulky shoulders raised. He was amused.

"What kind of property?" Jessa asked as if she were treading a tight rope for the first time.

He chuckled as he leaned in close to her. "A really, really big one."

Jessa's face reddened, she was scalded.

My heart ticked in my chest. A time bomb. "Did you buy the Frick Ranch?"

"Yes, I did." Walker rubbed his hands together. "And it's all thanks to you, flower girl."

CHAPTER FORTY-EIGHT

VIOLET

"ARE YOU FUCKING KIDDING ME?" My insides shook.

"No, I'm not," Walker said. "Jess and I met. And then ..."

My sister turned beet red.

"And then?" I pressed.

"I couldn't get her out of my mind. But then"—he pointed a finger at me—"I met you."

"Oh God…" Jess groaned.

"You're unbelievable, Violet!" said Ladd.

"For the love of God, everyone, I was with Beck."

"That's right, she was. And she made quite an impression on me." Walker's cold gaze fell on Ladd. He was enjoying this. He was enjoying Ladd steaming and sputtering and burning like a kettle of water on high heat abandoned on the stove.

"Did I? Ah, that's right—" I turned to my sister. "You used my name with him, didn't you?" Jessa turned three different shades of maroon, her teeth dragging across her bottom lip.

"Yes, she did," Walker said. "So when you and I met at that club in Mykonos, and you told me your name, I was shocked. How could I possibly meet two Violets from the States within a couple of weeks of each other as I was traveling across Europe? No. Fucking. Way. And when you told me about living here and about your dad's business, my curiosity was peaked."

"Peaked, huh?"

"When I got back to my hotel, I looked up you on Google, and epic pictures of the Great H Ranch came up. So many generations, so many family photos. Quite a dynasty. Imagine my surprise when I saw a photo with my Violet standing next to Mykonos Violet." He took in a breath, standing before my sister. "The Hildebrand sisters. Violet and Jessamyn."

The way he said Jess's full name had me blushing.

He continued. "I dug a little deeper and found articles on your dad's plans for Powder Ridge. Terrific idea. Fantastic once in a lifetime property."

My head swirled, and I ground my heels into the floor. "It sure was until you—"

"It was a perfect opportunity for me."

"How's that?"

"I told you how I wasn't interested in what my father and brothers are doing."

"And what's that exactly? Are they con artists? Grifters?"

Mr. Shales sat up straighter. "Miss Hildebrand, the Edwards family is one of the biggest landowners in the state of Montana."

"Are they?" My cold gaze remained on Walker.

"Yes, they are," Ladd said. "Fracking, isn't it?"

"It was," Mr. Shales continued. "They sold their successful fracking parts company for three billion dollars to a private firm from Singapore, and they began investing in land, and currently own over ten ranches in Montana."

"Oh my God." Jess's hand shot out to the desk at her side.

I crossed my arms. "Jessa, you didn't know that your hot fitness professional is a billionaire landowner?"

"I only knew his first name," she bit out.

A rich chuckle escaped Walker's lips. "She insisted we keep it that way. It was kinda hot. I went with it."

"Jesus."

"Stop, it. Both of you!" said Jessa.

"Busy day at my office?" Dad strode through the door.

"Dad, what are you doing here? You're supposed to be resting at home," said Jessa.

"I was bored, and I thought I'd drop in." His gaze snagged on Ladd. "Looks like I have perfect timing."

"Marshall Hildebrand?" Walker approached Dad.

Dad's forehead creased. "Walker Edwards?"

"You know who he is?" Jessa said.

"Of course I know who he is. It's my job to know. You should know too."

"Mr. Hildebrand, I happened to meet your daughters in Europe, which led me to reading about your plans for Powder Ridge and the Frick Ranch. I found it fascinating, and I put Ted here on the job of purchasing."

"That was quite decisive of you." I came up alongside Dad.

"That's the way I roll, Violet. My gut never steers me wrong. All in."

Dad said nothing, only stood there, taking in the spectacle that was Walker Edwards. My eyes shut, my chest burned. This was my fault.

"We've been waiting for years for that land to become available," said Jessa. "It was only a matter of time. The ranch was parceled up for auction, and we were counting on that auction for specific pieces of that property for my grandfather's cattle ranch, as well as for Powder Ridge."

"Now it's mine, Jessamyn." Their gazes locked, the silence ear-splitting.

"So you just walked into the bank and bought the whole damn Frick?" Ladd sputtered.

"Who is this guy?" Walker gestured at Ladd with his thumb.

"A former business associate on Powder Ridge," replied Dad.

Walker eyed Ladd. "I needed to take the bank out of the equation. I took the bank out. Stopped everything."

Our collective stunned silence. Except for Ladd, who sounded like a balloon losing air.

"Well done," said Dad.

Mr. Shales cleared his throat. "Both the bank and Mrs. Frick were quite pleased."

"I'll just bet. A financial wet dream come true," I said. "But I can promise you, Mr. Edwards, that local landowners like us won't be happy about this."

"I didn't expect you to be. I'm the foreign invader, right? The exploiter who'll ravage the area of its riches and its women?"

Jessa's hands fisted at her sides.

My chin tipped up. "Something like that."

"So what's the plan?" Ladd interjected. "An airport for the hotel and casino with daily charters from all over the country? A great big shopping mall with a rollercoaster? A year round Christmas village?"

"Is that what you wanted to do?" Walker shot back, his sculpted chin raised.

Ladd only pressed his lips together into a thin line.

"I do know that it has to make me money," said Walker.

"Of course, such an investment," said Dad.

Jessa's shoulders fell. She was overwhelmed.

"Mr. Edwards, you couldn't find any more land and history to snap up in Montana? Nothing left up there after your daddy got through with it, huh?"

"Violet." Dad shot me a look.

Walker only laughed. "It's all right, Mr. Hildebrand. I enjoy Violet's sass."

Jess let out a tight noise.

Ladd's chest expanded. "You screwed this guy too, didn't you, Violet? And he followed your tang all the way here?"

"Whoa." Walker's eyes flashed.

Ladd moved toward me, letting out a hiss of air. "You are one busy little whore."

"Don't you dare talk to my daughter that way!"

Walker rose up. "Sir, if you're not going to—"

"I got this." Dad pounced on Ladd and his arm flew. *Crack* and a *grunt* filled the room. Jessa gasped. *Thud.* Ladd was sprawled on the floor, moaning, blood spouting from his nose. "Appreciate the offer." Dad flexed out his right fist.

"Dad!" Jessa cried out.

"Nice," said Walker.

Ladd grunted, groaned, struggled to sit up, his face reddening. "I'm going to sue you all for—"

Fwap. Walker kicked Ladd in his middle, and he crumpled once again. "Shut the fuck up already."

Amen.

"We should go, Mr. Edwards." Mr. Shales stood up, smoothing his fingers down his tie. "We'll make another appointment." Mr. Shales held the door open for Walker.

"Mr. Hildebrand, I look forward to speaking with you very soon." Walker held out his hand to Dad, and Dad took it. "I'm staying in town, so I'm around." Walker's gaze went to Jessa. "If you need anything, don't hesitate to contact me. Good to see you again, ladies." Walker stopped next to Ladd. "Let's get you out of here, huh?" He yanked up Ladd by the arm and pushed him out the front door, his bulky frame moving with ease.

Ladd stumbled on the sidewalk. Mr. Shales murmured his goodbye and followed them. The door clipped shut behind them as the oxygen sucked out of the room.

"Tell me that didn't just happen." Jessa's strained voice was just above a whisper.

"It happened."

"You both met Walker Edwards in Europe and neither of you knew who he was? Unbelievable." Dad shook his head.

Jess headed to the kitchen area in the back of the office.

"Beck and I met him in Mykonos. He was traveling alone. We spoke a couple of times. He was very nice. I told him a little bit about working for you, and he told me a little bit about his dad and brothers and how he was going to have to join their business once he got back to Montana, and he wasn't happy about it. Neither of us offered the other any details. For Pete's sake, I'd guessed he was a cowboy or a bartender, and he only laughed at me. Jessa assumed he was a fitness trainer."

"And yet he was impressed with both of you and did some digging."

"Dad…"

"It's funny the way things work out, don't you think?" He let out a sigh, rubbing his hand. "The land may not be ours, but Walker Edwards saved the Frick from Ladd and Castillo. And not only that, he saved the whole damned Frick, and that's something I wish I could've done. Quite impressive."

"It is, isn't it?"

Jessa brought an ice pack for Dad's hand. "You shouldn't have punched Ladd. You're not supposed to be exerting yourself."

"Of course I should have done it. That piece of shit insulted my daughter."

I grinned. "What will Walker want to discuss with you, you think?"

"You made a good point earlier. He's an outsider who did something dramatic. Things will be difficult for him here."

"He might need someone to point out the mine fields."

Dad shifted the ice pack over his hand. "Whatever it is, I look forward to hearing it." His phone rang, and he answered it.

Jessa took my arm and led me away from Dad. "I can't believe you met him in Greece."

"I can't believe he's the one you—"

"He is."

"Wow." My sister, always so controlled about everything. Always choosing the nice, bland boys. *Good for you.* "All shaken up in your lady parts now, Jessa?"

"Violet…"

"He's stuck on you, that's for sure. In Greece he'd told me how he'd met one memorable girl. And that he wanted to find something for himself. Something he really wanted." I gazed at her pointedly. "He found it all right. An all in one."

"This is crazy."

"This is very real," I said. "You know who he reminds me of?"

"Who?"

"He's a real life Fortinbras."

"The conquering soldier prince in "Hamlet"?"

"Yep. Hamlet's always getting uptight and emotional, freaking out over every little thing."

Jessa let out a sigh. "But Fortinbras knows what he wants, and he just does it."

"Oh, Jessa, he *takes* it. Bam. There goes Poland. Bam, he closes in on Denmark."

"The usurper of kingdoms." Jessa's voice was cold and sharp as she moved to her desk, her lips taut as she rolled up a drawing of hers into a tight cylinder. "Bam, there goes Powder Ridge."

"You look a little pale. Are you feeling okay? Do you want to talk about it?"

"Leave me alone!"

"Bam, there goes Jessamyn."

CHAPTER FORTY-NINE

VIOLET

"SHE LOOKS BEAUTIFUL!"

"Yes, she does." Lock's fingers stroked the side of my freshly painted Cougar, the glossiest black ever. "And I have good news for you. That metallic purple paint you wanted for her finally came in."

"Terrific." We both studied my car which stood in the painting area at Eagle Wings Repair & Design at the One-Eyed Jacks property. I was finally doing up my car my way.

"Along with that cranberry color." His usually serious face broke into a deep grin, lighting up his features.

"I'm so excited."

"So I'll need another couple days for the stripes and the other detailing we talked about, and she'll be done. Back in your hands."

"That's what she's been missing, her muscle car stripes. There's no rush, Lock. I don't rush the art process."

Lock laughed, his long black hair moving across his massive shoulders with the movement. "I appreciate that, Violet. We'll call you and let you know when you can pick her up. She's a beautiful car in great condition. Good for you for grabbing her when you did. I would've snapped her up myself if I'd seen her."

"My dad knows a guy who knows a guy…"

"Oh yeah?" He laughed, a hand brushing down his sculpted face. "I'll bet."

"If you need something in particular, let me know."

"I will. Thanks."

My phone buzzed. It was Ford, Freefall's manager. My stomach tightened. "I have to take this. Thanks again, Lock. She looks terrific."

"I'm glad you like it."

I walked out of the building and into the courtyard and answered. "Hello?"

"Violet? It's Ford in L.A."

My pulse pounded. "Hi, Ford, how are you?"

"Doing great. I love your pictures. They're astounding."

"I'm so happy you think so."

"I've listened to the band's new tracks the past couple of days and these shots are spot on. Spot on."

I'd delivered.

"That's so good to hear."

"I'd like to pitch a few of them to this online music magazine in connection with Freefall's upcoming single releasing. So if you're good with that idea, I can send you a contract. The rest will go to the Art Department to come up with album and release artwork."

The rush of delirium inside me knew no bounds, my feet riveted to the ground, my eyes closed. YES. "Really? I mean, thank you!"

"You came through, Violet. This is a solid collection. It's different, and I like it."

A runaway locomotive roared out of my heart, and I was the one feeding coal to the engine.

"Violet, you still there?" His chuckle filled the line.

"I'm here." I cleared my throat. "I'd love to work with you on this."

"Terrific. My assistant will email you shortly. And I'll be in touch once I know more."

"Great. Thank you, Ford." I tucked my phone back in my messenger bag and let out a breath.

This was happening. The dream. The better than my dream. I'd photographed a band working on their music, documented their process, captured their vibe, and those images had been deemed worthy of their album cover. My lungs squeezed painfully. I'd made it to the top of my personal Mt. Everest.

"Violet?"

I blinked. "Mom?"

"Hey. What are you doing here?"

"I was checking out my car. She's getting a new paint job."

She shifted her weight. "Oh, that's right. How's it look?"

"Really good. And you?"

Both her hands latched onto her handbag. "And me, what?"

"What are you doing here?"

"My car..."

"Is it okay? Did something happen?"

"It's fine. I mean, it needed a tune-up."

"But you always bring your car to Delaney's in town."

"Your father always insisted on Delaney's, to keep that ball greased. I always wanted to come to Eagle Wings, so today, I came to Eagle Wings."

"Ah. Good for you."

"Very good." She grinned, letting out a short breath. "Great service."

"Certainly is. Did you just get here or..."

"I was just leaving. Do you need a ride?"

"No, I have Gigi's car."

"Ah. Okay."

"See you at the Grand this afternoon?"

"Actually, I'm going shopping in Rapid with Grace and Jill." She swept her hair behind her ears.

"Didn't you all just go shopping the other day?"

"We did. But this is for something…else." A grin perked over her lips. "For Jill."

"Oh. Have fun."

She kissed my cheek. "See you, honey."

"Bye, Mom." My teeth scraped my lip as she darted off. There was something different in the way she moved today. Fluid, with ease. I took out my camera and captured her lightweight steps over the courtyard of the Club. The sun shining over her dark blonde hair that she had loose down her back, not tied up in a pony tail as it usually was.

Lightweight, swift. Confident. A twenty-something with all of life's possibilities before her. A thirty-something who knew she was on the right path. Had I ever seen my mother like this before? Not in a long time.

I put my camera away, got out my sunglasses from my bag and as I turned to head to Gigi's car, I looked over my shoulder on a whim. Mom stood there in front of her car talking with a tall man. I couldn't tell who it was. He was built, and wearing an Eagle Wings hoodie with "STAFF" printed on the bottom of the shop's logo, and a baseball cap like all the guys who worked here.

She laughed, and he nodded and said something more, and she laughed again. He was flirting with my mother. And she was flirting right back. That lightness in her expression was there again, that fluidity as she spoke.

Something twinged in my chest.

Mom wasn't fragile, wasn't breaking, tipping over. Not now, not like before. She was enjoying herself, and, dare I say it, moving on with her life. I didn't know how much "moving on" had been going on, but she seemed open, at ease.

She didn't need me holding her hand like I had years ago to hold on, to hang onto the way things used to be. To hold her pieces together. Now she was flowing, in the moment, not stuck in the past or in a dark tunnel of sorrow and hurt. She was working her way out of disappointment and loss.

Lately we'd all been so busy and hadn't had a moment to really talk, only checking in with each other, quickly catching up. Gigi was up to her ears with heading the Festival, Mom too with assisting her and working the Grand. And every free moment I had, I'd been working on my photographs.

She wasn't confiding in me about all this just yet, and that was okay, I knew she would eventually. She had her friends for all this, and that was good. She'd told me she didn't want me in the middle, in between her and Dad. My mother was always thoughtful and fair and just to a fault and always a straight shooter, and a very kind one.

Change. I could take it. We middle children could handle all kinds of shit.

As Mom got into her car, the guy closed the door for her. She waved at him and drove off, and he raised his hand in good-bye, lingering there as she sped off the Jacks property. There was something sweet about it.

The intense scream of a motorcycle filled the air and yanked me out of my haze. Turning, I followed the sound to the small race track on the other side of the Eagle Wings shop. A man with longish blond hair zipped around the track on a massive bike in super high gear. I grinned. It was Butler, Tania's husband, the Vice President of the MC.

He rode as if he were in a motocross race on a Ducati. Only he was all alone on a shiny chrome and glossy red Harley-Davidson. A couple other Jacks watched him closely, probably looking for issues in the bike's performance. I recognized Boner, Jill's husband, his long dark hair and goatee clearly visible. He shouted something at Butler, who raised his hand as he shot by.

That familiar tight swirl of feeling sparked through me. That knowing. That need. I took out my camera and captured the dynamic lines of man and form and rush and geometry and light and shadow. The acrid smell of burning rubber and exhaust filled my nostrils.

Butler hooted loudly as he roared by me, the Jacks on the

edge of the track cheered and clapped. A chill razored around my neck, goosebumps raced over my skin.

Butler's long-sleeved yellow shirt was a bright blur of gold, his bike a roar of metal as he zoomed past again. My breath cut in the change in air pressure, my hair flying in the wind. My muscles stilled, and all of me focused on the juggernaut of freedom that was man and machine. Chrome and glare and heat.

Everything else fell away. There was only this.

My breathing deepened, my body steadied, my finger pressed.

This.

CHAPTER FIFTY

VIOLET

I READ IT AGAIN, the stencil on the wall of the Rusted Heart Antiques & Art Gallery.

"The Soul of Meager, South Dakota"
A Celebration of Our Town Through the Years
- Photography by Violet Hildebrand -

Underneath stood a framed, very large, black and white photograph of two of my great grandfathers's cowboys galloping after cattle in another century overlaid with One-Eyed Jacks speeding on motorcycles up Clay Street in the seventies. The cowboys and the bikers charging toward the same point in the distance.

Tonight Clay Street had been closed to traffic and was jam-packed with people enjoying the street fair on the opening night of the Founding Festival. People spilled in and out of the shops and restaurants, musicians played on the small stage set up in the center of Clay. Special decorative lights had been strung overhead, giving the street a cozy festive feel.

"Thank you for coming tonight, everybody!" Tania's voice cut through the big loft-like space, and my stomach tightened and flopped over all at once. Opening night jitters. "So great to see everyone here to kick off the opening night festivities of our Founding Festival. I would like to introduce our artist to say a few words about her work. I'm very pleased to give you our very own Violet Hildebrand."

The applause echoed through the Rusted Heart, and my skin heated. So many faces beamed at me. Faces I've known all my life. My mouth dried, my heart knocking against my chest as I stood next to Tania.

"Hi, everyone."

"Violet! Wooooot!" Wes's voice blared from somewhere in the back, and I let out a laugh. Cleared my throat.

"I want to thank you all for being here tonight to celebrate Meager, and I want to thank Tania and the Rusted Heart for making this possible." We all applauded for Tania, and she brought her hands together at her chest and bowed her head at me.

I shifted my weight. "I was born and raised here in Meager. As a young girl I came across my families' collections of old photographs, and they lit up my imagination like nothing else. I wanted to dive right into them, into those pastures alongside those cowboys from the 1920s. But I couldn't.

"But what I realized I could do was preserve those moments all around me that I found so special like those photographers had done. So I set about to try to do that. To capture what this land means to me, my family, our community every day. And combining what I see and feel now with what I see and feel in those documents of Meager's past lives."

My gaze snagged on Mom and Dad and Jessa standing with Grandpa and Uncle Maddox, with Gigi and her brother, Uncle Ryan. Listening, hanging on my every word, beaming.

"I'm offering them to you so that we can all connect to our past here. I think we need to do that to see a clearer present and a better future.

"I hope these collages that jostle time and place and people spark an ache, both difficult and moving, a yearning inside you the way they do me." I licked my lips and took a quick breath.

There he is. Beck's face filled my vision and my galloping heartbeat eased. Jude, Myles, and Zack stood next to him. They'd come.

"I also wanted to say that the proceeds from this exhibition are going to the Saddle Up Fund, which is raising money for a winter horse corral at Pine Ridge Reservation so that the young boys and girls can ride all year round and train for the Indian relays. It's a very important cause to our region, and I thank you for your support.

"Back in the day, they may have named this town for its sparse and paltry pickings, but you know what? The gold rush is done with, the droughts come and the droughts go as did the carpetbaggers, the cavalries, and all the economic depressions, but we're here. We're here thriving.

"We, as well as all those who came before us, the good and the dubious made Meager prosper and endure through fierce determination, faith, and the God-given talents we were blessed with. All of us together, red, white, black, yellow, brown. All of us. Thank you. Thank you, everyone."

My vision blurred as my pulse blasted through me. Applause thundered in the Rusted Heart.

I took in all their faces. Mom, Dad, Gigi, Grandpa, Jessa, Uncle Mad, my cousins, Sara, friends from school, Shelby, Wes and Alicia and her man, Ronny, the guys from his tattoo shop. Lock and Grace, Jill and Boner, Butler and Tania, and a number of One-Eyed Jacks, applauding. And Walker, he was here too, standing with Beck.

My Beck. I smiled, and his own smile widened, holding mine.

A BLONDE WOMAN dressed in leather and studs and high heeled boots shook her head, murmuring to herself. Finger's VP, Drac, had his arm around her as they and Boner and Jill took in the huge poster-sized photo I'd created of Isi singing at the biker festival, hair wild with her movement onstage, overlaid with Wreck speeding through Meager, he and his bike zooming from her torso.

"Krystal?" I came up in front of her. She blinked, stiffening as she wiped at her eyes.

Drac's huge dark eyes widened. "Babe, this is Violet."

"Violet!" She lunged at me, and we embraced tightly. "This is so epic. I can't even—"

"Your photos helped me make these epic. I can't thank you enough for sharing these spectacular shots with me. It means so much to my family to see these early pics of Isi performing. Thank you forever."

"My pleasure, hon. She was fucking amazing onstage." Her gaze went back to the grouping of vintage biker pics. "It's great to see those times blown up big 'cause this is how it felt. Big, and so damn loud."

"Those were good times," Drac murmured, a sly grin slashing his face.

Krystal gestured at the descriptive tag on the wall by the photo. "And you gave me photo credit, too."

"Of course I did."

"There you are." Lenore and Finger came up next to us. Lenore and I hugged. "You look hot."

"I don't know what I would have done without you styling me tonight." I hadn't even thought about what I was going to wear until Lenore, Jill, and Tania had cornered me one day at the Rusted Heart, where Tania and I were organizing and setting up. The ladies had asked me, and I'd had no response. Lenore immediately declared, "I've got this."

"Perfection on you." Lenore smoothed the silk fabric on my hip of the long silk dress with a purplish indigo color scheme, and slits on both sides. She'd found it for me at a secondhand luxury online shop owned by a stylist friend of hers in L.A. I paired it with high espadrilles that had leather and metal accents, and wore earrings and a long pendant necklace that Jill, Tania's partner at the Rusted Heart, had made me. Jill had made sure her pieces coordinated with Beck's dolphin necklace and his ring that I always wore.

Finger slung an arm around his wife's waist. "Congratulations, Violet."

"Finger if it wasn't for you, a lot of amazing things wouldn't have happened for me. Thank you for being there in so many ways. I mean it." I wanted to hug him, but I didn't feel it was something I should attempt.

He lifted his chin at me and offered a small grin as he stroked Lenore's back. "I'm glad. I really am."

"Look who I brought!" Zoë came over, holding Eric Lanier's hand, alongside Beck. "Beck's daddy came."

"Hey, Eric," Lenore said. "What a great surprise. Good to see you."

"Good to see you, too."

"Eric, this is my husband, Finger."

"Ah, yes. Good to meet you. Finally." He let out a short chuckle.

Finger only lifted his chin and stretched out his maimed, scarred hand. Eric swallowed hard, and they shook.

"These pictures are so big!" said Zoë loudly, breaking the sudden grip of tension. Finger let out a laugh at his daughter's declaration. We all laughed.

"I made them all super big for the show," I said.

Her cheeks were rosy. "I love your photos, Violet."

"Thank you, Zoë. That means a lot to me."

Beck gave me a hug and a quick kiss. "Congratulations, baby. Mind blowing."

"Thank you. This is all completely mind blowing. I'm so glad you're here."

"Wouldn't miss it for the world." Slinging an arm around my shoulder, Beck kissed my cheek.

"Boom, boom, boom." Zoë giggled.

"What's that, honey?" Lenore asked.

"Beck knows," she said.

"That's right, Zo." Beck winked at her. "Boom."

She adjusted her pink glasses on her nose. "I'm going to look around some more."

"I'll come with you." Eric went off with Zoë, bumping into Jill's kids and Thunder, who scurried around the room giggling.

"There go the kids again," Jill groaned.

Boner darted after them, "Hey now, we said no more running!"

Beck pressed into my side. "How you holding up, my starlet?"

"This is all a little surreal." I squeezed his hand. "You know the feeling well."

"I do, I do." He brushed my cheeks with his warm lips. A small, delicate touch, a strong possessive rush of heat. Intimacy. Excited voices came up behind us and we turned around.

In front of the black and white photos of the racing relay kids at Stewart's ranch, Stewart hugged Lock, Grace's husband. Grace's face was streaked with emotion, her hand on her husband's back as he and Stewart spoke, their hands gripping each other's arms.

"Grace told me that Lock, who was Wreck's half-brother, grew up on Pine Ridge," said Lenore. "And Stewart helped Isi and Wreck find him on the reservation, and that's how Wreck brought him back to Meager to live with him."

"Holy shit, really?" Beck murmured. "There you go, baby. Your art making connections, bringing people together."

Over his shoulder, I spotted Dad and Grandpa in front of the grouping of photos of Hildebrand cowboys and Meager bikers past and present.

"Go on, starlit goddess of the night. Mingle, do your thing," Beck said. "And let me admire your glitter."

"Lord, the things you say. Be right back."

I went to my father and grandfather. "Dad?"

He faced me, his lips parted, his eyes full of water. "Violet. This is…." His hand gestured at the photograph on the wall. Dad as a teenager, riding over the open prairie on the edge of the Great H, chasing two wild horses, his hat whipping in the air, his hands fisted in his reins. Pure bold purpose.

Overlaid was a photo of a thirteen year old Five on his horse chasing after Grandpa, who was up ahead of him. All three Marshall Hildebrands in full forward charge on their beautiful horses.

"I made it for you, Dad." I slid an arm through his and pressed against his side.

He planted a kiss on the top of my had. "Best present ever."

Grandpa stood up close to the photo, inspecting every detail. His lips pressed together. "You are a very talented young lady, granddaughter. I always thought so, as did your Grandma Holly. I wish she could be here to see this."

"Thank you, Grandpa. I wish she could be here, too. She used to go over all the Hildebrand photo albums with me, even let me sneak a few pictures home."

"Did she?" He grinned.

"I never imagined that one day I'd be sharing these pieces on this scale along with my very own. But it feels good to share. Especially with you all. By sharing it, I feel like I'm hold onto it in a better way."

Dad squeezed me tight. "Proud of you."

My heart swelled. "Thanks, Dad."

I caught Beck's glance and I waved him over. "Dad, Grandpa, you remember Beck?"

Dad's chest expanded with a deep breath. "Good to see you again." They shook hands.

"Thank you, Mr. Hildebrand. You too." Beck extended his hand to Grandpa. "Sir." They shook.

Grandpa's eyes narrowed. "So you're the fake fiancé or the

real fiancé or there's no fiancé?" Grandpa shot me a look. "Don't think I don't try to keep up, young lady."

I laughed. "Beck is the real everything."

I FOUND Walker in front of a small framed photograph of a Lakota warrior that Tania had on permanent display in her store. "Walker, thank you for coming. I didn't cut you for an art lover. Are you here to look good with the locals?"

He laughed. "I like art, Violet, and antiques, very much. I like a lot of different things. Rachel, here, likes art too." He gestured to the tall, glamorous bottle blonde who stood at his side in a perfectly fitting dress and very high heels.

I stretched out my hand to her. "Good to meet you, Rachel." She smiled at me as we shook.

"Rachel is one of my lawyers. She's visiting from Montana."

"Ah."

"My firm has an art collection at our offices," Rachel said. "I like your work."

"Thank you."

"Are you represented by anyone?" she asked.

"By me, right now."

"Uh-huh."

Walker grinned at me. "Tania is the owner of this gallery. Right?"

"Yes, that's right. She's over there, tall, dark hair, red dress."

"I think I'll go talk with her." Rachel drifted off toward Tania.

Walker leaned into me. "Is Jessa around?"

"She was." My gaze darted to Rachel, who had stopped to in front of a collage of Meager Grand customers of the present along with Drake's Coffee Shop customers in the 60s. "Maybe she skedaddled after seeing you with Ms. Rachel."

His lips twitched. "Maybe."

"Hey, Violet."

I turned around. "Lars? Oh my gosh, what are you doing here?"

"Beck told me and Tag about your show, and I had to come. I had a couple of jobs in L.A., so I hopped over here with Beck and the band. I told them not to tell you. I wanted to surprise you."

I hugged him. "You being here means so much to me."

"Your images are so strong. They hit you right in the nuts. Tag was sorry he couldn't make it, but he's still out in the Pacific. He sends you his best—and this." He handed me a 5 x 7 envelope. I opened it.

A photograph of me and Beck at the edge of the infinity pool at Tag's villa in Mykonos, the unique blue of the Aegean Sea stretched out around us and twinkling in the sun's light as we embraced and kissed. We were one.

My breath cut. "It's beautiful."

"He took it. He wanted you to have it. There's a note on the back."

I flipped it over.

"V - I'm sorry for the shove, but I'm not. I saw the signs in you from a mile away, because once I was the same way, pulling back, one foot in, one foot out. And I lost.
I created chaos, and you and Beck both had to swim to the surface or perish. The best of you made it. Never forget that feeling. Love in the light and love on the edge always. - T

"Thank you, Lars." I cleared my throat as I tucked the photograph back in the envelope. "Can I get you something to drink? Beer, wine?"

"No, Violet, you go on. Enjoy your party. I'll see you after, outside."

"The band playing tonight is really good. They're local."

"Oh yeah?"

We parted, and I moved through the crowd and found Lock and Grace holding their little son's hand before a photograph of the old Dillon go-kart factory track back in the late 1950s. I'd collaged young, determined boys riding go-karts on that track with Butler and Boner testing sleek, massive motorcycles on what was now the Jacks' club track. The thrilling rush of speed and the intensity of the men's and the boys' focus was shared.

"I want to ride that!" Thunder pointed at the go-karts.

"Hey, guys." I ruffled a hand through Thunder's long, dark hair. He grinned up at me.

"Violet, these pics are so great to see." Lock's voice was husky. "They really hit home."

"I want to thank you both for sharing Wreck's letter with me. I feel like we're family now."

"We are." Lock's big hand rested on my shoulder, his dark, velvet gaze held mine, and my heart thudded in my chest. "We are."

"So you know Stewart?"

"I knew who he was when I was a kid on the rez. We haven't seen each other since. He just told me that Isi had asked him to find me for Wreck." He pressed his lips together, sniffed in air, his gaze going to his black boots. "He found me, saved my life."

"Some people might say that all this was a crazy coincidence, but it's not."

His dark gaze leveled with mine. "Oh, I don't believe in coincidences."

My pulse skipped at the severity in his voice. A severity born of conviction. A conviction born of experience.

"Neither do I." I shifted my weight. "I want you and Grace to know that I made a copy of the photo of Wreck and Isi for you. I thought you'd—"

Lock let out a noise, lifting his son in his arms. "Thank you."

"Violet, would you consider one day photographing Lock with Thunder on his bike and then doing your magic with that photo of Wreck? The bike is a vintage Indian that Wreck had given him, that they re-built together, and it would be a perfect, perfect piece for us to have in our home."

"I would love to do that, Grace."

"Thank you."

Butler and Tania came up to us. "Violet, your photo of me is insane." Earlier I'd given Tania a gift of my appreciation. A framed photograph of her old man speeding tightly around a bend on the club track, the bike at a dangerous angle, dust flaring up in his wake, the afternoon glare of the sun hitting his chrome, streaking through his longish blond hair, his sculpted face drawn, focused, yet with a sly grin slicing over his features.

"I couldn't resist taking those shots when I was up at the Club a couple weeks ago."

"It's everything. My man loving the danger." Tania grinned, and Butler only let out a dark laugh.

"Ah, Scarlet." He pulled her close and planted a kiss on her lips. Scarlet was his nickname for his wife.

"Sweetheart, Violet captured that zest you have for speed on a bike…It's a part of you, and it takes my breath away. To have it forever on a photo…the best."

I FOUND BECK AGAIN, and slid my arm inside his. "Hey, you."

"Well, hello, Miss Hildebrand." His voice rumbled deep, and I giggled at the ticklish heat it had inspired inside me.

We strolled around the Rusted Heart, admiring Tania's intriguing collection of antique farm tools, railroad accessories, vintage dinnerware from the Frick Ranch, a number of old handmade music boxes. We ended up once again in front of the picture of Isi and Wreck.

Beck slid an arm around my shoulder, holding me close. His eyes narrowed, lips parted.

"What is it? Say it."

"These two, this pic…two rebel souls, one beating heart."

"Hell yes," I breathed.

"My couple goals, right there."

I kissed him. "I love you." I took in his scent, the smooth cotton of his dress shirt under my hands, the thrum of his beating heart. My wild pulse.

"Baby, you hear that?" he said against my lips.

"Hmm?"

He whispered in my ear, "It's your roar."

I hugged him.

"Sorry guys—" Jude popped up next to us. "Beck, uh, I need you."

"Oh yeah?" Beck's hold on me loosened.

My glance went from Jude to Beck to Jude again. "What's up?"

"Uh, Eric and Myles wanted your opinion on something." Jude's lips twisted.

"I think the concert is about to start…"

"Right. I'll catch up with you outside, sweetheart." Beck kissed my cheek and took off with Jude.

Jessa came up to me. "Let's go outside. We don't want to miss Gigi's speech before the concert."

"Walker was asking about you. I suppose you succeeded in avoiding him so far this evening?"

"Avoiding him? Please."

"By the way, Blonde Barbie is one of his lawyers if you were wondering."

"No, I wasn't wondering."

"Hey, cousins!"

"Tara! Oh my gosh, you came!" I hugged my cousin.

"I had to. This is huge, and I'm so excited for you."

"Let's go, you guys, come on…"

Tara slid her arm through mine as we followed Jessa outside for the official kick off of the weekend festivities.

Little did I know what was about to really kick off.

CHAPTER FIFTY-ONE

BECK

MY HEARTBEAT THRUMMED in the cool darkness, my hands resting loosely on my Strat. Jude's gaze was glued to the massive black sky above us filled with thousands of stars. "Epic," he murmured.

Myles bumped me with his hip. "I'm so ready, man. So pumped for this." We high-fived each other.

"Me too, Myles. Down deep."

He flung an arm around me, yanking me close. "Love you, Beck."

I thumped him on his back. "Love you, too."

"I wanna love huddle, assholes." Jude wiggled his body between us, and Myles and I both laid sloppy kisses on his cheeks. "Yassss." We turned and faced Zack seated at his platform. He raised his hands with his sticks in the air and pointed them at us. "Let's do this!"

I patted my chest over my heart and checked my watch. Any second now.

"Ladies and gentleman," Gigi's clear microphone voice rang out down below us. "Welcome to Meager's Founding Festival Weekend!"

She thanked all her committee members, the mayor.

Applause. Applause. She mentioned the other activities going on tomorrow and the next day. More cheering.

"And tonight we have a huge surprise for you to kick off this celebration in honor of our town!" Georgia's voice flared over the speakers. "We're very excited to bring you a son of the Black Hills and his rock band. Please welcome Freefall debuting their new single—a world premiere—right here in Meager just for us tonight! This is being filmed to be shown to the world!"

The whole town cheered and screamed loudly, and Jude put his head on my shoulder.

Cell phones lit up below us, lighter flames dotting the dark crowded street below with sparks of light.

Stars above, flames below. My kind of gig. My kind of life.

"Coming from the roof of the Rusted Heart—it's Freefall!"

Zack's drum exploded along with the lights set up along the edge of the roof.

Yells and shouts rose. "On the roof! Look—they're on the roof!"

I drove into our last top ten hit and so many voices rose up, singing along with Myles as he pranced and raced along the roof, leading them with his vocals and his energy. Everyone bopped and jumped, hooting as the song came to an end.

"Hey, hey, Meager!" Myles's voice boomed over the speakers.

"Hey! Hey!" the crowd shouted back.

"We're so excited to be here tonight to celebrate one hundred and forty years of Meager with you!" The crowd cheered. "We've spent a good chunk of time recently in the Black Hills working on our new album. It's become a very special place to us, and we want to give back. So we're dropping our first new single tonight, a single that will benefit a cause that is real, real important to us and to the Black Hills.

"We're raising money for Saddle Up—an organization that wants to build an indoor horse arena for the kids on the Pine Ridge Reservation. I know we can do that together, right?"

"Yes! Yes!" the crowd shouted back.

"Yeah! There is a booth set up for donations so you can show Saddle Up the love."

Myles lifted his chin at me, and I went to my mic. "Tonight we're dropping our first single from our upcoming album and we wanted to do it here in Meager and on the roof of this building for a reason." The crowd went wild, phones were up in the air. I searched for Violet in the crowd below, my pulse jamming in my veins.

Georgia, Erica, Jessa, Tara. There she was, next to my dad. My Violet, my wind, my love, hands clasped tightly together. She was bracing.

"This song is real special to me because it was co-written in 1989 by my dad, Eric Lanier—who's here tonight—and a girl from Meager—Isi Dillon. Isi and my dad were in a band together in the eighties, The Silver Tongues."

"I remember the Tongues!" a man shouted out. "Yeah!" Clapping burst out, rippling through the crowd.

"I wanted to finish the song, and then Isi's cousin, Georgia Drake, who we all know and love"—cheers and whoops went out for Georgia, who raised her arms—"Georgia wanted us to finish it too and bring it to the world, and that's what we've done. Tonight this song is for Meager. We hope that Isi would have liked how we finished it and sung it herself."

Violet put a hand to her mouth, my dad said something to her.

I continued, "I'd like to dedicate this special song to Isi and her man, Wreck, who are here in spirit, and also to my own girl from Meager, who happens to be Isi's cousin—the love of my life, Violet Hildebrand."

Girls screeching and shouting spiked through the crowd. "Violet! Violet! WOOOHOO! YES! VIOLET! VIOLET!"

Jessa and Tara jumped up and down clapping, screaming. Wes and my dad whistled and clapped, laughing. All the ladies cheering, Mom and Finger and his friends whistling.

Down the block the massive sign glowed in the dark "Pete's Tavern." My head knocked back and I breathed in the stars.

This was it. This was the moment. And I'd grabbed it, made it happen.

Here on the roof of this old turn of the century building in a quirky, tiny town in the Black Hills of South Dakota. I'd claimed, I'd exclaimed, I'd declared.

Soul on fire, fingers on my strings, leaning into my mic, I grinned. "This is for you, baby."

The crowd went fucking wild. Violet's eyes were huge, her hand at her mouth, Wes whistling next her.

Strumming the opening chords, I stepped back from the microphone, and turning, lifted my chin at Zack. The snare drum exploded. I glanced at Jude, Myles, that moment they all waited for from me, that I'd done thousands of times, every time we hit a song onstage.

This is happening, hit it, let's rock it out all the fucking way.

Myles raised the tambourine in the air and shook. Zack kicked in a shimmying cymbal as I moved back to my mic.

My heartbeat steadied, every cell of my being on. I breathed in, sucked in, resonated with all the energy rising from Clay Street. All of it whipping around us on the roof under the stars, all of us together.

1-2-3-4

I leaned in to my mic.

WHERE AM I now
No one knows
So noisy, so loud
All that matters is
Being with you
Being with you
Even when I'm not

In the wind I feel
your lips against mine
Drill down
Drill deep
Mine to fill
Mine to keep
No matter where
You're my prayer
Nothing else matters
Only you and me
I can be strong
Won't be long
'Cause you give me all the rush
That red hot flush
Leaving me with sugar on my skin
Your sugar on my skin
I don't know
Which time zone
Only your flesh, my bone
Our heartbeat blown
Your words burn:
Forever
All mine
Wreck me
Adore me
I push
You pull
We howl
Your whisper like the wind
Sting on my skin
Sugar and sin
You flew down the road for my lips
You laid me bare
stung me with your kiss

A promise, our bliss
You left me with sugar
Sugar on my skin
I push
You pull
We sting
Sugar, sugar, sugar on my skin
Your sugar on my skin
You're a new road
On the map of me
Wilder than fire
our bright desire
Only gets higher
Brighter than the sun
We live this crazy
With you I'm more than I've ever been
Or hoped to be
'Cause you give me all the rush
That red hot flush
All over me
All over me
Your sugar on my skin
Sugar, sugar on my skin

Myles dove in on the last lines with me at my mic, our gazes locked. He grinned, his head rocking back, tambourine in the air. Jude let loose his final manic wizardry on his bass, Zack banged out the final notes. Adrenaline pounded through me, and I raised my guitar in the air.

Applause and cheers roared around us. The crowd was a living, wild surge of cheering, shouting, applauding. Of love, of the best, most positive energy.

A thick wave of emotion rolled through me, taking my breath

away. My limbs lightened, and I lowered my guitar, keeping it close.

Violet's hands were raised in the air, and I pointed at her. She blew me a thousand kisses, and I caught them with my hand, bringing my fist to my chest.

I leaned into my mic. "Let's rock and roll, Meager!"

CHAPTER FIFTY-TWO

VIOLET

AFTER FREEFALL FINISHED their incredible show, I ran back inside the Rusted Heart, tore up the back stairs to the roof. A team of One-Eyed Jacks bikers who'd volunteered as roadies tonight dismantled speakers, microphones, cables, handling instruments, packing them in crates with a couple of Freefall techs.

Lars was in deep conversation with Ford as he packed up his camera equipment. Ford left him and spoke with a tech.

"Hey, you." I went to Lars. "You were in on this the whole time?"

"Pretty cool, huh?" He laughed. "What'd you think?"

"I can't think. I loved it."

"It was awesome. I've got to edit this video ASAP so it can be uploaded to the band's YouTube channel as soon as possible. I might even start on the plane back to L.A. tonight."

"You're going back tonight?"

"We all are."

"Oh." My insides dropped like an elevator whose steel cables has been chopped. "Okay."

He planted a kiss on my cheek. "We'll talk."

"Definitely. Can't wait to see the video."

"Violet." Ford held out his hand, and I shook it. "Great to meet you in person. Congrats on your show."

"Thank you. And congrats. That's a hell of a first single."

"It sure is. They were on fire tonight. I haven't seen them play with this kind of energy in a while."

"It was something else. It was the best."

"The magazine spread comes out next week. You ready?"

"Ford, I've been ready all my life."

He laughed hard. "I've got to get going. We'll talk soon." He joined Lars in a hustle of bikers hauling packed crates and speakers and equipment.

I let out a breath and the crowd cleared. I blinked, a shiver racing through me. *There he is. My Beck.* A grin on his sexy mouth. I ran and hurled myself at him, and he swooped me up in his embrace.

"That was the most beautiful song I've ever heard."

He wiped my hair from my face. "I thought "Waterfall" was the most beautiful song you've ever heard."

I laughed. ""Sugar" is my new number one." I squashed my face in his firm chest. "Blew my heart and soul away. The whole story behind it? I have no words. All this time you were working on it? And Gigi knew?"

"Dad and I had come to Meager that time to give her the original tape and to ask her permission to work on the song." He ran his fingers through my hair. "You need to listen to it. I'll send you the digital file."

"She showed you Wreck's letter, didn't she? I recognized some of his sentences in the lyrics."

"She did, and it came at the right time. After I read it, Myles and I finished the song on the flight to L.A."

"And Freefall playing here on the roof…that was the wildest surprise ever. How the hell—"

"My mom had told me that Georgia was heading the Festival, so I called her when I got to L.A. and asked if she could fit us in, and told her about promoting the fundraiser for Stewart's kids. I told her I wanted to debut Isi's song tonight, and she made it happen. It all came together, baby." He took my hand in his, flexing his fingers, threading ours together. "At the end of the day, a lot of love was being shared by so many people with the same goals. People whose lives had been touched by those two. Powerful stuff."

I kissed his chest. "I think you are a special force of nature, and so much goodness whirls around you and you recognize it, see it, and somehow you're able to tune into it and make magnificent music out of it in many different ways, bringing all kinds of people together."

His arms went around me, pulling me close, fitting me perfectly against the hard length between his legs. "When I sense a good idea, I'm like a dog with a bone to make it happen. This song, for me, from the very beginning, from the moment my dad played me the tape, was all about you. I felt it in my veins, in my heart." He kissed me, his lips trembling against mine.

"I love you, Beck. I love you so much."

He let out a soft moan, his hands rubbing my ass. "I want to make love to you so bad, baby."

"Me too," I breathed against his lips.

"I like it when both of us have post-show adrenaline, huh?" He chuckled darkly, a finger at the side of my lips. My tongue lashed out at it, and he let out a hiss.

"Wait—you guys are leaving now, right? I thought you'd be spending the night, but—"

"Not me. I'm staying tonight."

"You are?" My soul flew, my fingers curling in his shirt.

"Tonight is all ours." He kissed me as he lifted me up, bringing us into a corner back by the doorway to the stairs. My back hit the brick wall. His cool hands went up my dress and I gasped as he found my panties, a hand slipping past the waist band, cupping my ass.

"Here?"

"I can't wait. Can't fucking wait…" His eyes glinted at me, his voice smoky. He nuzzled my throat.

Two One-Eyed Jacks carrying crates filled with cables, shot us smirks as they went through the door, clomping down the stairs.

Rip.

My insides clenched at the sound, at the torn panty pressing into my flesh as he yanked it off me.

I dug my heels into the floor and my hands flew to his belt buckle, I tugged, unclasped, pulled.

Cock. Beautiful cock.

I climbed on Beck as he steadied us both against the wall. He thrust inside me.

"Oh!" My head knocked back against the hard surface.

I forced my eyelids to stay open. I wanted to see the stars in the sky and the stars in Beck's eyes.

He thrust into me. *Yes. Yes.*

"I love you, baby. It's been so long, too damn long. I missed this, I missed you so fucking much."

He drowned our words with his groans, drowned our thoughts with his pounding us both into a blissful oblivion under the velvety night sky. The thickness of him seared my insides, his hips rocking against mine. All of me on fire, alive.

Together.

Together.

Together.

We exploded, clinging to each other in one sweaty, sticky glorious heap against the wall.

He pulled out of me on a groan. "Come on. Let's go. I want you to ride my face."

Laughing, I planted my wobbly legs on the floor and straightened my dress. "Where are we going? A hotel somewhere?"

"My mother's."

"Are you kidding? No way!"

He tucked in his cock, stroking the fabric of his jeans as he buttoned up. "Have you gone shy on me now, Violet?"

"Beck, I can't with Lenore and Finger down the hall. You're always saying how loud I get…"

"Babe, they won't even notice. They'll probably be at it all night themselves."

My mouth dropped open. He only laughed as he tightened his belt.

"Stop laughing at me." I shoved at his chest on a giggle.

He grabbed my arm and pulled me close. "I'm teasing you. Mom and Finger took off for his club in Nebraska with Drac and Krystal. They've got some wild party going on tonight. The house is all ours."

My shoulders dropped, and on a grin and a huff of air, I said, "So they'll probably be at it all night, but just not under the same roof as us."

"Exactly."

I shoved at his chest again. "Let's go."

Hand in hand we sped down the stairs to the Rusted Heart. We ran past Butler and Tania making out on the reception desk. "G'night!"

"Bye!"

Outside, Beck guided me through the last of the crowd at the street fair, the smell of corn dogs and caramel popcorn lingering in the air, around the corner to where his motorcycle was parked. My body curled against his, we zoomed to Lenore and Finger's house, the cold wind razoring over us.

At the front door, he fumbled with the keys as I kissed his cheek, the side of his mouth, a hand rubbing down over his erection, and he laughed softly. I slid my arms around his waist and a kind of melancholic euphoria spread through me like steam. "Last time we were here, like this, we were both very lonely people who didn't know any better than a quick fix, a bite, a grab."

The loud slide and jolt of the key in the lock had me lifting my gaze to his. "Very lonely," he whispered, a hand stroking the side of my face.

"I've always loved you, Beck. You were the whisper in my heart that always showed me the way and I listened and took heed. I love you, baby, and I always will."

He kissed me, gently and brought us through the doorway, kicking the door shut behind us.

CHAPTER FIFTY-THREE

@JUSTJANA

DID you watch the premiere of Freefall's new single which dropped on their YouTube channel only moments ago? The song is called SUGAR and we love it! Part romantic ballad, part hard driving rock and roll. All of it sexy hot!

It's EVERYTHING!!!

Lead guitarist Beck Lanier dedicated this song to "the love of my life," he said —shivers!— "Violet Hildebrand."

These two are together and hotter than ever!

Rumor has it that Hildebrand, a professional photographer, spent time with the band while they were working on their new album at a remote location in South Dakota, and that her photos are startling!

Freefall manager, Ford MacGregor stated in a recent press release that the band will be featured in an upcoming cover story in "Rock Times" with a photo essay by Ms. Hildebrand.

And there we were wondering if Freefall would make it back from the divisive final days of their previous tour.

Freefall is ON FIRE!

Go stream "Sugar" NOW!

<Click HERE for SUGAR on Freefall's YouTube channel>

<Click HERE to stream SUGAR on Spotify>
<Click HERE for photos of Beck and Violet>

FOLLOW our stories for all the latest updates and hot pics!
#CoupleGoals #AllTheSexxy #AllTheNews #couplenews #BeckAndViolet #ViBeck #Freefall #JustJana

CHAPTER
FIFTY-FOUR
BECK

THE NEXT AFTERNOON, after we finally sat upright, Violet made us coffee and toasted English muffins with butter and cinnamon sugar and we lounged on Mom's flowery patio out back. Ford messaged me that "Sugar" was being streamed at outrageous rates. And the video already had over 700,000 views.

The journalist from "Rock Times" who had interviewed us back in L.A. posted his review of "Sugar" online:

"A standout track, a moody, rich ballad with surprising turns and wild urgency. Lanier's vocals give the piece an unexpected complexity twisted with sensual decadence."

"Congratulations." Violet snuggled in my lap, and I held her. The fragrance of the rose bushes rustling in the rippling breeze, the scent of us on Violet's skin, the coffee and cinnamon lingering on my tongue.

"I have to go back to L.A. tonight. We're putting finishing touches on the next single, finalizing our schedule for the next year. Wherever this new album takes Freefall, I want to live it with you. I know you have your career taking off now, and I would love for that to include you on the tour with us, babe."

She hugged me. "That's what I want, too. Us together,

working together. The only thing on my calendar for the coming months is going to Italy to shoot Alessio's fragrance ad. We have a Zoom meeting next month to discuss all the ideas."

"Italy is beautiful."

"It would be more beautiful with you there so I could lick you."

I laughed. "I do have a fashion shoot in February for Roberto Santore in Milan. Not only did he design new boots for me, but he wants me in the campaign for his new menswear line."

"Oh—speaking of you and your fetish for boots, I have an idea."

"What's that?"

"Let's take a shower, get dressed—"

I groaned. "I don't want to leave the house. I just want to fuck you some more." His teeth nipped at my lower lip and tugged.

"As much as I concur with that idea, it'll be worth it. I promise."

My hand went between her bare thighs and slid down her pussy. Her breath got jagged, and her cunt slickened under my rough strokes. "Only if we come back here and I eat you one last time before I leave."

"Uh-huh…"

"On the dining room table."

She let out a low moan, her lips pressed together. "Well, if you insist—"

"I fucking do insist."

She grit her teeth. The pleasure was building inside her. Her back went rigid, her fingers dug into my skin. "Okay…."

I thrust two fingers inside her slick heat, and her eyes went wide, a muffling cry escaping her throat. Her walls tightening around my fingers, her hips rocking. My dick hardened at the sight.

A lawn mower exploded to life next door, and her hand dug in my shoulder. A dog barked, a bicycle bell rang.

My arm tightened around her waist holding her tight. "Ride my fingers, baby." My tongue darted across her lips. "Look at me." Her melted gaze found mine again. "Making you come is my fucking drug. Watching you come, can't get enough. Give it to me."

She moaned and ground her hips, her movements matching the thrust of my fingers. Her robe fell open and she rubbed her hard nipples against the dolphin charm necklace, her pace quickening.

"That's it, that's my hot Violet. So fucking beautiful. Your skin in the sun, your tits hard and bouncing, your cum dripping on my hand, so fucking beautiful."

Her head knocked back at my words, and she cried out, her body twisting in my embrace. I bit the underside of her breast, holding her tight, and as the pleasure rocked through her. Everything else faded, even the insistent drone of that fucking lawn mower.

THE STOREFRONT WAS TINY. The store inside? Huge. Nothing but floor to ceiling shelves crammed with every type of cowboy boot probably known to mankind.

"How can I help you today, Violet?" said a wiry older woman with thick glasses on her face. Her hair was a distinctive blue purple.

"Hey, Miss Eileen. I brought you a new customer."

Miss Eileen, wearing tight jeans and a bright red T-shirt that said, "Pepper's Boots - Meager, SD" scrunched her face as she gave me a thorough scan from head to toe. "You're Lenore's boy, aren't ya?"

"Yes, ma'am."

"Hmm. Liked your show last night. Real good."

"Thank you."

"He needs boots," Violet said.

Miss Eileen's gaze shot straight to my boots. Two thousand dollars of hand sewn custom fit Italian leather. "Those are mighty fine, but they aren't for around here."

"Exactly. My man needs some South Dakota. Whatcha got for us?" Violet asked.

"Size eleven and a half?"

"That's right." My eyes darted from one woman to the other.

"Hmm."

Thirty minutes later we exited the store with me wearing a pair of black leather western boots which were detailed with dark purple embroidered flowers up the sides. Violet had bought them for me.

"Go wow them in LA, baby." She swung the Pepper's Boots shopping bag which held my Italian footwear as we walked down Clay hand in hand.

"I will."

She planted a kiss on my lips, a slash of her insane tongue. "There's one more place I'd like us to go before we go back to the house."

We climbed on my Harley. "Where to?"

"The town cemetery."

ROCK HILLS CEMETERY sat on a rocky hill that seemed windier than the road we'd just ascended to get here.

As we entered, my gaze tracked the high iron gate with the cemetery's name spelled out in old-fashioned lettering over two arches. Violet held white roses from her grandmother's garden that we'd gathered on the way over here.

We found Isi's grave amongst a big section of Dillons where stone markers dated back to the late nineteenth century.

Isadora Dillon
Beloved daughter

We will always hear your voice

A sheaf of wheat was engraved under her name. Violet squatted down and laid half the white roses on the emerald green grass.

"Thank you for the song, Isi," I murmured. "Thank you for inspiring so many of us with your gifts and your spirit."

Violet plucked two dandelions growing by the tombstone, tossing them away. Her fingers grazed her cousin's name engraved in the thick slab of stone. "Love you, Isi," she said. "Thank you for always inspiring me to be bold and loud and to follow my dreams."

I held out my hand to Violet, and she took it and stood up. "Gigi said Wreck is just opposite, down seven…." We counted as we went and came to a stop.

Richard "WRECK" Tallin
Ride Hard & Ride Free Forever

I turned around to where Isi's grave was. "Wow, they're facing each other." Wreck's headstone was engraved with a motorcycle on one corner and a skull logo with a star in its eye on the other.

The tombstone next to Wreck's had the same bike and skull logo. "Jake "Dig" Quillen." I read his dates. "Damn, he was just a few years older than us."

Violet sniffed in air, adjusting her sunglasses.

A lot of the stones in this section were engraved with some version of *loyal brother* and *taken too soon*. "Is this the One-Eyed Jacks area?"

"It is. Wes's dad is in the back corner." Violet laid the rest of the white roses before Wreck's massive tombstone and placed a hand on the stone as she pressed her lips together. She came to me, sliding an arm around my waist.

I held her close, the pine-scented breeze ruffling our hair.

"Thank you for sharing your beautiful, passionate words with us, Wreck."

"I hope you and Isi are together in peace and in bliss because you deserve to be." Violet's voice trembled, and she leaned her head against my chest.

"Amen to that."

"Amen, indeed."

My heart expanded, full, aching, and joyous. A crescendo of perfect notes. "Speaking of bliss together—I realize maybe I shouldn't be saying this in a cemetery, not to mention without a diamond ring in my hand, but it feels totally right and I'm going with it—Violet, will you marry me?"

She laughed loud and hard, a rich ringing sound that made me laugh too.

"Is that a yes?"

"Yes! Yes! Yes!" She kissed me, held me, and together, in a tiny ages old cemetery in Meager, South Dakota atop a windy, rocky hill, we pledged ourselves to each other forever.

CHAPTER FIFTY-FIVE

VIOLET

WE STARTED PLANNING our wedding immediately. We had to, Freefall's schedule was full.

One month after our official engagement, all of us gathered at the Great H Ranch on the farthest pasture on the ridge overlooking the Frick lands under an arbor of purple, berry-colored, mandarin orange, and dark blue flowers.

Lenore designed and made my bridal outfit—a long, wide-sleeved white coat with silver embroidery over a backless halter dress with a plunging neckline. Autumnal bohemian chic with a semi-long train along with a brand new pair of black boots with purple flowers from Pepper's to match Beck's. As a wedding gift, Alessio sent me a breathtaking pair of drop earrings glittering with small diamonds and moonstones.

Lenore also styled Beck, who wore a black slim-fitted suit with an ivory Nehru collared shirt, open down his chest, with a vest over it, which was embroidered with purple and silver. Topping it off, he wore a beige prairie hat along with his Pepper boots. My sexy glam rock god.

My Beck.

Mom and her team created the three-tiered cake with a mocha bourbon filling and all the food. Three long tables were decorated with small candles and bouquets under magical white canopies. The music was provided by a country duo, Thorns & Roses, who were local folk music legends—a married couple who played Pete's all the time for many years and who had played at the Founding Festival.

The service began. Lars and Stone took photographs from different angles. Myles's voice rang out, clear, strong, a beautiful a-cappella song. The service had begun.

Any tension I had left in my body transformed into a flow of adrenaline. I was getting married to the man of my dreams, and I was blessed.

My three little cousins tossed flower petals in the air, which fluttered onto the ground. Beck's sister, Zoë, and Sara were my two bridesmaids, and Jessa, my maid of honor.

Thorns & Roses played two fiddles as my father and mother walked me down the aisle in the center of all those white chairs filled with our friends and family. My entire being was focused on Beck, who waited for me, eyes gleaming, jaw flexing, hands clasped. Wes, Jude, Zack, Myles stood at his side. His dad, Eric, stood in the front row next to an emotional Lenore, who held onto Finger's hand with both of hers.

We arrived at last. Beck shook my father's hand and kissed my mother's cheek. He held out his hand, and I took it in mine, our fingers threading together tightly. Warmly. Perfectly.

"You're so beautiful," he whispered in my ear.

"You're so gorgeous," I whispered right back, the two of us blushing. My heart swelled as we turned and faced the pastor together. The final notes of the two fiddles dissipated.

"Ladies and gentlemen, we are gathered here today to witness and celebrate the union of Beck and Violet Isadora."

The union.

I was getting married, something I thought I'd never do. My chin lifted. My heart was full, a confidence soared through my veins as I breathed in the hilltop air. This was a cementing of so much goodness, this was a new foundation, a new beginning. A new family.

Our family.

I swallowed hard, my gaze darting to our clasped hands. Wes had tattooed his ring finger with the letter V in an endless chain of Vs at the base, and my ring finger with an endless chain of Bs.

I focused on Pastor Robinson's words.

Understanding and forgiveness

Sacred union treated with reverence

Grow and evolve together

Together

Yes, together. Together always. Always evolving, always growing. Together.

My little seven year-old cousin Trudy came to my side along with Grace and Lock's son, Thunder, and with great ceremony Trudy opened the small antique jewelry box Thunder held in his small hands. Beck took a breathtaking platinum diamond eternity band from the box and slid it on my finger at the base of my amethyst ring.

I pledge my love.

I promise my faithfulness.

A seamless circle.

Forever.

From the jewelry box, I took the ring we'd chosen for Beck, its smooth, sleek weight in my fingers making the butterflies in my tummy awaken and flutter. A wide band of platinum with both our names engraved inside.

I pledge my love

I promise my faithfulness

A seamless circle

Forever

I was lost in the words of our vows, in the grip of our hands, in the blue green flow of his eyes, in the rapid movement of his chest, in the shuffle and flutter and whip of the breeze through the grasses.

This image now. I took a photograph with my soul, printed it on my heart. *I'll never forget, not ever.*

Beck's lips moved silently. *I love you, Violet.*

I love you, Beck, I squeezed his hand once more.

"By the power vested in me by the state of South Dakota, it is my great pleasure to pronounce you husband and wife."

Beck slammed into me, his hat flying off with his fierce movement and a sudden whip of wind, and we kissed.

We kissed, my husband and I.

We were one.

CHAPTER FIFTY-SIX

VIOLET

IMMEDIATELY AFTER OUR ten day honeymoon in Tahiti, Freefall had a rolling schedule of releases, video shoots, interviews, appearances, more Serenades on Instagram. We landed in L.A. ready to go and bought a small house to have as a base there.

"Bitter", the second single dropped and the reviews were fantastic—most especially by the music journalist who'd written the *Rock Times* piece who'd heard the entire album.

"Freefall plunges into the experience of adulthood and the quest for meaning in the sensual, the material, the emotional—all clashing on the battlefields of ambition, insecurity, and desire. Ostensibly decadent, often dark, it is a record of, and for, these times and shows a striking maturity and complexity.

The photographs taken by the talented Violet Hildebrand bring this to the fore in an unusual, moving exploration of gritty dissatisfaction, reckless seduction, and unapologetic swagger. These boys play and, watch out, they bite."

"My first review."

Beck kissed my cheek and took a screenshot of the article. "I think I'm going to have it printed out to poster size and frame it. Yep, that's what I'm going to do. Put it over your desk in your new studio."

"Jessa just messaged me. She said that it's going to be at least another eight to nine months to finish the renovations and the interiors. They're trying to get as much done as possible in between blizzards."

Beck laughed. "Ah, South Dakota."

I stretched out on the big lounger by our swimming pool. "I'm really enjoying the weather here in L.A. I've never experienced a summery late autumn before. It's a little weird, but I'll take it."

"Did you finish packing? We've got to leave real early tomorrow. I'm not looking forward to that."

"All done. Oh—on the plane I thought we could go over my Pinterest for the interior of the house. Jessa said she needs us to make specific decisions on paint colors, furniture, lighting, and architectural motifs so she can finalize her plans."

"Cool. Let's get cracking."

"I warn you, there's a ton of stuff on there. I've been hoarding ideas for Whisperwind since Pinterest first started up."

"Of course you have."

"But Jessa and I've been whittling it down, so it won't be too crazy."

He handed me a greens juice bottle and laid down next to me on the lounger. "It'll be so good to move in after the tour is over. I'm really psyched."

Draining the bottle, I took his hand. "Me too."

Freefall's North American tour would begin next month. We would be criss-crossing the nation for over eight months. My first real and very massive rock band tour to photograph, to experience, to live. This was my new surreal reality, and Beck and I were so excited.

Tomorrow we were on our way to Lisbon for the European Music Video Awards where Freefall would be playing "Sugar."

The entire album would drop while we were there and Naomi had set up several interviews with European journalists. Then Beck and I would pop over to Italy so I could shoot

Alessio's fragrance ad. Beck and Roberto Santore had managed to time their photo shoot for Roberto's new menswear line and new boots that same week.

I was hoping to be able to have to time to sit in on Beck's photo shoot, which was being done by a famous fashion photographer whose work had been splashed across the covers and pages of British and Italian Vogue the past few years. I'd been following him for a long time in print and online magazines. I was going to be the happiest fly on the studio wall that day.

"You ready for all this, aren't you? You're so psyched." Beck squinted at me, a smirky grin on his face.

"I drank that mucky green juice, didn't I?"

Laughing, he kissed me. "That's what tipped me off."

CHAPTER FIFTY-SEVEN

BECK

- FIVE MONTHS *LATER* -

"FIVE MINUTES, EVERYBODY!"

I'd done my vocal warm up. Closed my phone. Sipped some more lukewarm water. Checked my in-ear monitor for the hundredth time.

We were halfway into the tour and it had been going really well. Every performance had been full of energy, tight, and lots of damned fun, the audiences amazing.

"Here we go." Violet hugged me from behind, her camera swinging around her side, her ID tags pressing into my back.

"Here we go." I squeezed her tight and turned my head, we kissed, her palms pressing over my chest, over my pounding heart.

It was our pre-show ritual; the magic elixir to our adrenaline jammed insides. Rooting us to each other, keeping it real and true. Honoring each other's work, giving each other support and a fiery jolt of hell-yes-let's-do-this-baby.

"Catch me good, lover girl," I whispered in her ear.

"I will, lover boy," she whispered back. "You sing "Sugar" for me."

"Always."

Our fingers released, and with her blowing me a kiss and my wave goodbye, I took off with Zack, Jude, and Myles down the shadowy hallway of the arena with the team of security and arena staff.

Jude sang to himself as we finally hopped up the steps to the stage. In the dark, the audience pounded out their anticipation and eagerness with clapping, their feet stomping. Phones lit up like alien starlight in the vast dark universe that was the arena.

"Freefall! Freefall!"

The four us hugged and slapped each others' backs. "Let's do this!"

Zack took his place as I hopped up and down on my toes next to my pedalboard and mic. Jude on the other side, Myles taking his spot front and center at his mic stand, hands on his hips, legs spread, grounding himself into the stage, ready for blast off.

Our techs handed me and Jude our guitars, and I adjusted its weight against my body, a weight I knew so intimately, a weight I treasured, a sensation that had my pulse ticking up even higher as my hand slid up and down its neck.

I let out a breath as the laser lights began their dance over us and the crowd howled. Myles moved to the beat in his head, to the beat we were about to give him.

1-2-3-4

His voice roared out, Jude hit his bass notes, Zack simmered behind me and exploded.

"Bitter! Bitter!" the crowd chanted.

I hit that F7 chord and drove into the opening verse, giving Myles the thunder in his smoldering red sky.

Myles took off stage right, and as I played I moved toward the edge of center stage. The front liners screamed and jumped up and down.

There she is.

My Violet. Body still. Camera focused on Myles, shifting to

me. I knew her heart pounded like mine, I knew her lips were curving into a grin as she hit it.

Hit it hard.

Myles's voice leapt into the arena as he dove in next to me. He leaned in, sharing his mic with me, and we both sang the chorus together. The crowd sang along with us. The verses Violet had once written in my tossed off notebook.

Myles stalked off to Jude as I hit my guitar solo. Any fatigue I'd had earlier this afternoon was history as I grooved into the song we'd written together, drawing out the notes giving him even more to respond to.

Applause thundered around me as my hand flew up. Zack's throbbing drumbeat filling the space, I drove into the chords for the next verse, my foot hitting a pedal to work that shimmer sound effect I liked on this section.

We were on it.

Violet moved the camera from her face, her other hand in the air rocking to the music.

We finished off "Bitter," and the spotlight highlighted Jude, who kept playing as the audience howled, segueing us right into "Sugar" where he picked up his pace.

At my side, Myles shimmied and hit the tambourine. I hit my first chords, another spot shone on us. The crowd went berserk.

"Hey, hey Nashville!" Myles shouted.

"Hey, hey!" the crowd howled back.

My middle tightened as my feet planted on the floor in front of the mic stand. An electric charge coursed up my spine, through my limbs, right into my Strat. I wanted to swallow all the energy in here and give it back with the lyrics, give it back with the notes, with the rhythm, all of it woven with soul, with heart. With so much intention, so much love.

I love you, Violet.

I leaned into the mic and my voice filled the Bridgestone arena.

Twenty-four more songs to give.

Four more months to tour.
So much fucking wild to roar.

CHAPTER FIFTY-EIGHT

VIOLET

- 4 MONTHS *LATER* -

BECK LIFTED me up in his arms as I unlocked the front door, and I let out a yelp. "Seriously?"

"I'm a traditionalist at heart."

My arms wrapped around his neck, and I kissed his cheek. "Let's do this, Mr. Lanier."

He swung open the door, and we entered. A whirlwind went off in my heart at the sight of our Whisperwind. Clean lines mixed with the original ornate touches, a new archway leading to the back hall. A credenza with an antique mirror that Tania had restored, thick square baskets on either side. The staircase spindle had been revived and reattached. Everything gleaming, clean, fresh. And ours.

All the comfortable furniture in natural textures and soft colors that we'd chosen with Jessa. The vintage brass lighting Tania had found for us making bold, gleaming statements.

"Ah, wow. Look at this…" Beck put me down gently. "I love it."

At our feet, Jeremiah's Whisperwind brand had been cleaned

and polished, and around it, the original parquet flooring in a sun ray pattern restored to glossy splendor.

"Beautiful," I murmured, taking his hand.

Together, we entered the living space.

"Ah, Violet…" he murmured.

"Wow…"

The living room had been expanded with the loss of one wall and was now airy and filled with light. Contrasting textures in the variety of throw pillow accents, straw baskets, clay pots, green plants, and small potted trees added to that airy light. You could breathe in here, relax, unwind.

The original wood pocket doors had been stripped of their old, dark paint, now their beautiful wood grain was visible under a clear gloss. Antique Persian rugs that Tania had found for us, as well as a vintage leather sofa alongside a new made to order sectional, in the center completed the main living area.

Beck crossed the room to the baby grand piano in the library nook by the fireplace. And the fireplace was now paneled with gleaming zellige tile in a lapis lazuli blue, giving the room a mesmerizing splash of offbeat glam smack in its center.

His fingers touched the keys, and delicate notes filled the room. He let out a soft laugh as his hair caught the golden light filtering through the large windows. Yes, this house would be filled with light, filled with music. A much needed oasis for us, the most comfortable refuge. And a comfortable place for our family and friends.

Beck sat at the piano and played, beautiful notes filling the room, vigorous notes, declaring that we were here. My heart swelled. He would compose here, work out confusions, frustrations, create. Play for the family. *Our family*. For me.

He caught my gaze and smiled, relaxed, so happy.

The tour had finished on a high note. The new album had hit number one and stayed in the top five for weeks. Millions of streams and downloads and two popular music videos later—

one having been shot at the band's show in Nashville—Freefall was riding high.

Through the new great window in the living room, I spotted the two small adjoining buildings in the snow-filled property. Beck's recording studio with a gym and my photography studio kept each other company in the glistening white field.

"I can't wait to get into my new studio and spread out and work on everything." I had a zillion folders for each show and all the shots of the band I'd taken in between— prep times, down times, silly times.

I wandered into our kitchen, now a large room with two archways enabling the flow of traffic. A small butler's pantry in the rear had counter space for larger appliances and extra cabinets for storage.

The long and wide granite island dotted with six leather stools gleamed in the sunlight. A basket of goodies lay on the center. Bottles of wine and craft beer from our local winery, a bottle of bourbon from Nashville, and gourmet food treats in small packages. I opened the card.

Welcome home, Beck & Violet!
To dreams coming true, forever…
xx Jessa

I'd helped Jessa document our design choices and the transformation of the house on her Instagram and her blog, and the whole darn thing had blown up for her.

Yes, because they knew it was my and Beck's house, but that was only the surface glitter. People's response to Jessa's genuine warmth and excitement about the project and to her fresh design choices was insane. There was a simplicity to it all yet it was utterly sophisticated, each detail chosen with intent. My soft-spoken little sister was becoming a popular style influencer.

Beck came up behind me. "Home cooked meals, I can't wait."

"Me too. It feels like forever, huh? I don't know if I remember how to even make a grilled cheese anymore."

"We got time, don't worry."

"I'm glad my mom and Gigi and your mom will be coming over to cook for all of us tomorrow."

He laughed. "I can't wait to see everyone."

"Me too. Let's go upstairs. I'm dying to see how our bedroom turned out."

Together we raced up the grand staircase to the second floor where there were four bedrooms and two bathrooms, including our grand suite. We entered our room.

"Yessss!" The walls were painted with a washed out purple, curtains in dark mandarin orange, gold trim along the molding, an an Aegean blue on the ceiling. Gorgeous. Our kind of glam, our kind of sensual.

I squeezed his arm. "I wasn't sure about all these colors working together, but babe, it's fantastic. You did good."

"Our den of sin."

"Our sumptuous and luxurious den of sin." The bedding was a cavalcade of fine cotton, silk, and velvet - a comforter and a crazy variety of pillows, a cashmere throw. Comfy yet stimulating at the same time.

"We needed a wild contrast to all those low key natural vibes going on downstairs."

"Our colorful private getaway."

The walls of our bathroom were glossy turquoise and sapphire mosaic tile, a copper standalone tub, an oversized glass shower with a massive shower head, and a very long vanity with two sinks.

Adjoining was a dressing area for two with plenty of storage for our accessories, shoes, jewelry, and my makeup. Not to mention shelves especially made for our boot collection.

"I have a surprise for you." I took his hand and led him up the smaller staircase to the turret room.

As we climbed the steps, my heart hammered in my chest. I'd

given Jessa specific details on how to set everything up for this very moment. I knew it would be perfect.

I brushed his lips with mine. "Close your eyes, honey."

Grinning, Beck closed his eyes for me, and we stepped inside. The gasp that escaped me had him tilting his head. "Open."

He opened them. "Babe..."

Jessa had designed a built in banquette sofa lining the room under the windows. A black crystal chandelier hung from the high ceiling. A ceiling that was painted bright blue green like my husband's eyes and sparkled with a thousand crystal stars.

The around the room windows offered a breathtaking panoramic view of the Hills, the craggy granite sheathed in evergreens. The open sky.

The walls were painted in a deep turquoise blue. Sunlight filled the space with blue, blue joy. We were in the sky, in the sea, here together. A cozy, dreamy escape spot for us, to work in, to relax in.

One of Beck's acoustic guitars stood in its stand. Next to it stood Isi's guitar that Gigi had in storage for years and given to us as a wedding gift. On an antique wooden desk sat a laptop and a tablet ready to be filled with music. Thick pillows of all shapes and dimensions were scattered on the antique silk Persian rug on the floor.

On the walls hung my two favorite photos. One was of Beck performing that night at Pete's overlaid with the lyrics of his song and a photo of the actual waterfall, our waterfall. I'd made one for his mother and Finger too and, over the phone through her tears, she'd told me she'd hung it up in her living room.

Our version, however, overlaid on the cascade of water was a photo of me wearing my prairie hat holding my camera to my face, taking a photograph.

Because that innocent, unexpected night, Beck and I had not only crossed paths in a significant way, but our connection had created a bolt of electricity that had altered our voltage and the flow and charge of our currents forevermore.

Connecting us, fusing us. Inspiring each of us for more, for better.

I had to capture that so we would honor that moment and always remember.

The other framed photograph was the one I'd made for Tania's exhibition of Wreck riding and Isi singing. Our version had a few lines from Wreck's letter in his handwriting seeped over it. Lines that Beck had included in "Sugar."

These two photographs facing each other in this special to me room gave me the chills in the best possible way. Warm satisfaction seeped through my veins as if I were reading the end of an intensely emotional fairy tale.

On a small built in bookshelf, the Dillon's General Store snow globe had pride of place, along with the many, many souvenirs from the tour that I'd sent to Jessa to have ready in here, souvenirs from every city. And the other trinkets from our Nashville trip and, most especially, the little windmill from Mykonos.

My dollhouse, a tiny version of Whisperwind, stood erect on a special pedestal, cleaned and freshly painted.

Beck squeezed my hand. "And one day, our kids will be in here. It will be their playroom."

"Yes, it will." I squeezed his hand back. *One day. One day soon.*

I took in a deep dizzying breath. A family with Beck. Whisperwind filled with our children's laughter, their singing, their father teaching them to play music.

There would be laughter and shouting and crying, storytelling, intense conversations, chasing each other, hide and seek, arguing, hugging, cooking, scribbling, dreaming. Yes, yes, I wanted it all.

"I love you, Beck," I breathed.

Outside, the trees rustled, their great branches shaking. A slight whoosh of air prickled over my skin, a murmur whirred past my ears. I stilled. A sigh quivered through the room, wrapping around us, and my heart leapt to embrace it.

"Jesus." Beck let out a gasp, his grip on my arms tightening.

"Did you hear that? Did you … feel it? The windows are closed, but it was as if the wind was here, inside."

"The whisperwind."

"So it's true."

"My great uncle Ryan had said it could be a combination of the construction of the turret, the trees right outside, the location of the house on this particular hilly point on the property and its angle that could create this odd rush of sound that you can only hear up here when everything is working together." My eyes filled with water. "Beck...I've been hoping to experience that all my life, since I'd heard the stories when I was little."

"Oh, babe…" Beck stroked the side of my face.

"Such a delicate sound, a gentle feeling, but I felt it deep inside."

"It was powerful, and it will always be here for us, baby. And our kids."

I hugged him hard. "Yes, it will."

That night at the waterfall we'd shared raw whispers under the glitter of the stars.

Together, we'd roared on the plains of our desires.

Now, in this house, our house, a house born of such desires and great determination and bold love—both in its inception and its renewal—Beck and I were truly at home.

Here was the touch of so many souls. Here was the punctuation of our new beginning. A triumph.

I knew that nothing lasted forever, certainly not things, not buildings, not our frail time-measured bodies. But here, right now, in our glorious home, after the din and bluster of our battles and the noise of all our victories had receded, now that the ghosts and the wounds and the gaping holes haunted no more, this whisper that had always guided me, beat through me, that I shared with so many who had come before me, shimmered in my heart and soul and pulsed through both of us.

Oh, the whisper reigned.

THE END

AUTHOR'S NOTE

Please visit **Sage to Saddle at www.sagetosaddle.com** to support the building of an indoor riding arena on the Pine Ridge Indian Reservation. Visit their amazing Instagram at @sagetosaddle

---

Need more passion and adventure in Meager and beyond? Lose your heart to all the characters from this trilogy in their own books...

Wreck & Isi: The Dust and the Roar | The Fire and the Roar

Lenore & Finger: Fury

Grace & Lock: Lock & Key | Random & Rare | Lock & Key Christmas

Grace, Tania, Erica in high school: The Year of Everything

Jill & Boner: Iron & Bone

Tania & Butler: Blood & Rust

Turo & Adri, Alessio: Dagger in the Sea

BOOKS BY CAT PORTER

- Lock & Key MC Romance Series -

Lock & Key - Lock & Grace

Random & Rare - Dig | Lock & Grace

Iron & Bone - Boner & Jill

Blood & Rust - Butler & Tania

Fury - Finger & Lenore

Lock & Key Christmas - Lock & Grace

The Dust and the Roar - Wreck & Isi

The Fire and the Roar - more Wreck & Isi

The Year of Everything - everyone in High School

Lock & Key - The Series Boxed Set

Boxed Set of books 1-4

- The Wind & the Roar Duet -

Beck & Violet - Friends-to-Lovers Rockstar Romance

Whirlwind

Whisperwind

Dagger in the Sea - Turo & Adri

Mediterranean Romantic Suspense Adventure

- Unraveled Destiny Series -

Steamy Arranged Marriage Historical Romance

Wolfsgate

Ironvine

ABOUT THE AUTHOR

Cat Porter was born and raised in New York City, but also spent a few years in Texas and Europe along the way, which made her as wanderlusty as her parents. As an introverted, only child, she had very big, but very secret dreams for herself. She graduated from Vassar College, was a struggling actress, an art gallery girl, special events planner, freelance writer, restaurant hostess, and had all sorts of other crazy jobs all hours of the day and night to help make those dreams come true. She has two children's books traditionally published under her maiden name.

She now lives on a beach outside of Athens, Greece with her husband, three children, and three huge Cane Corsos, freaks out regularly, still daydreams way too much, and now truly doesn't give AF. She is addicted to reading, classic films, cafes on the beach, Greek islands, Instagram, Pearl Jam and U2, bourbon she brought home from Nashville and whiskey she brought home from Ireland, and reallllllly good coffee. Writing has always kept her somewhat sane, extremely happy, and a productive member of society.

for more more more

www.catporter.eu

For a FREE Beck & Violet bonus novella, join the CatList, and don't miss any Cat news, special offers, and exclusives!

Follow Cat on BookBub + Amazon

Join Cat Porter's Cat Callers Facebook group

See the inspiration images for Cat's novels on Cat's Pinterest

Email - catporter103@gmail.com

amazon.com/author/catporter
bookbub.com/authors/cat-porter
instagram.com/catporter.writer
facebook.com/catporterauthor
twitter.com/catporter103
pinterest.com/catporter103
tiktok.com/@catporter_writer

Made in the USA
Monee, IL
02 May 2025

16760414R00215